MW00667687

PARAGRAPHS

Mysteries
of the
Golden Booby

Bob Doerr

David Harry

Pat McGrath Avery

Joyce Faulkner

Copyright: 2014 Red Engine Press

All Rights Reserved. No part of this book may be reproduced or transmitted in any form or by any means, electronic or mechanical, including photocopying, recording, or by an information storage and retrieval system (except by a reviewer who may quote brief passages in a review to be printed in a magazine, newspaper or on the Internet) without permission in writing from the publisher.

DISCLAIMER

Everything in this book, except for the establishments listed and a few local folks, is fictitious. The words spoken by any of the locals is, of course, also fictional.

Library of Congress Control Number: 2013954516

ISBN: 978-1-937958-54-1

Red Engine Press

Bridgeville, PA

Original Oil Painting by Marne Law
Photography by Pat McGrath Avery
Cover design and layout by Joyce Faulkner

Printed in the United States.

This book is dedicated to the residents and visitors of South Padre Island. All four of us feel a special attraction to this island paradise, and we hope that sentiment is evident throughout this light-hearted mystery. We especially want to express our appreciation to Griff Mangan, Joni Montover, and Paragraphs bookstore — the inspiration behind our book. While this is a work of fiction, we won't go so far as to say that the real Golden Booby isn't still out there somewhere.

CONTENTS

Legends of the Golden Booby
Bob Doerr

The Professor
David Harry

Murder Can Be Golden
Pat McGrath Avery

Paragraphs
Joyce Faulkner

LEGENDS OF THE
GOLDEN BOOBY

Bob Doerr

~ Chapter ~
1

S am Wiesel sat on the balcony of the third story condominium and watched the sun rise over the Gulf of Mexico. He had always been an early morning person, and the sunrises here were spectacular.

They were one of the reasons he savored these seven days he spent each year on South Padre Island, Texas.

Two of the usual five fishermen who had been out every morning since he arrived four days earlier, had not appeared this morning.

"Well, even fishermen deserve a day off," he said to the large sea gull that had landed on the balcony rail about nine feet from him. "Oh, look, here she comes again."

As though the bird understood him, it followed Sam's gaze down to the beach where a young woman jogged past the fishermen. Two of the men turned and waved and she returned the wave. Sam thought it peculiar that he always saw her running to the north and never saw her return. She ran every day, and twice Sam had leaned out as far as he could over the rail in an attempt to see where she stopped running, but she ran too far, and the larger buildings further down the beach ultimately blocked his view.

He finished the cup of coffee and stood up to get more. The sea gull flew away when he stood. Sam wore only a bathrobe, and the sea breeze this spring morning felt cool against his bare legs. It gave no hint of the heat that would arrive in a few hours.

The aroma of the coffee wafted up to him as he poured the new cup. He experimented with mixing blends of coffee and believed this new batch was one of his best. Time to shave and get dressed he thought, and walked into the small bathroom.

"If I lived here, I'd definitely have to find a place with a bigger bathroom," he said to himself.

Maybe he should live here. After all, he did kind of dread going back home to Dallas and his third wife. Dallas wasn't that bad as far as cities went, and his third wife was at least an improvement over his second, but the idea of dumping them both and moving here to the island seemed appealing.

He thought about his chances with the lottery drawing later that day. If he could just hit that number once all his problems would be gone. He had heard that some people had hit the jackpot twice. Hardly fair. They ought to have a rule you can only win once. He felt good about today, didn't the Chinese think thirteen was a lucky number, and today was the thirteenth.

He finished shaving and studied his face in the mirror. His hair had turned to more salt than pepper this past year, but at least he still had it. He didn't think he was as plain looking as his second wife had accused him, but so what if he was. He leaned in close to the mirror to study a small blemish starting to develop on the end of his nose.

"Damn, that can't be a pimple —"

BAM! BAM! Two loud gun shots that sounded like they came from his living room froze Sam in place. Someone nearby screamed, and Sam dove into the dry bathtub and covered his head with his hands. He cowered in the tub while people shouted from the adjoining condos. Semi-silence took over again, and Sam heard the sounds of approaching sirens.

After two to three minutes enough courage returned, and Sam slowly climbed out of the bath tub. He peeked into the main living area but saw nothing. The shots had come from one of the neighboring condos.

He put on some clean shorts and put his ear against the door to see if he could hear anything.

His condo had no windows facing the street, so he couldn't be sure that the sirens he heard had foretold the arrival of the police. He considered leaving the apartment to discover what happened, but bravery had never been one of Sam's strong points. He stayed in the apartment and waited. A knock on the door ten minutes later finally rewarded his patience.

"Who is it?" Sam asked. His voice came out at a little higher pitch than he would have liked.

"The police, we simply want to talk to you. We're talking to all the residents."

Sam opened the door a crack and after verifying that the two individuals were dressed in police uniforms, he opened the door wide.

"Come in," he said.

The two walked in. Other than the fact that one was male and the other female, the two looked so much alike it almost spooked him. Both stood around five foot nine, just a hair shorter than his five ten, and both had red hair, green eyes that seemed too green, and freckles. Despite the differences in sex they had similar builds, and both had a tattoo of the American flag on their right forearm. Her hair was a little longer than her partner's, but not by much.

"I'm Officer Morris, and this is Officer Duron," the policewoman said.

"Here about the shooting?" Sam almost stammered out the question. He felt his armpits getting damp.

"Yes," Morris answered. "We just want to talk to you in case you might have heard or seen anything that might help us." She moved to the sliding glass doors that looked out at the Gulf and opened to the patio. "Nice view."

"Yes," Sam answered while following her.

"The shooting happened in the apartment next door. Did you know your neighbors?"

"No, I come down here every spring for a week to relax and unwind. I really don't know anyone here in the complex."

"Did you hear anything unusual this morning or last night?"

"You mean other than the gun shots?"

"Yes," she said with a smile.

"No, nothing at all." Sam suddenly realized that the male cop had disappeared. "Where did, oh."

The policeman emerged from the bedroom. "We wanted to make sure you were safe, Mr...?"

"Sam Wiesel, that's Wiesel with a strong i." He explained the pronunciation without even thinking. All through his school years, the other kids had harassed him by calling him Sammy the Weasel, or just Weasel.

"Have you had any conversation with your neighbors since you arrived?"

"No. Said hello once or twice but nothing more."

"And I'd be correct in saying that you have no idea why the two were shot and killed this morning?" she asked.

"Right," Sam answered. "Killed?"

"Yes."

"Oh my God."

"We don't believe there is a threat to anyone else in the building. It looks like the two men were very specific targets."

"How can you tell that?" Sam asked.

"We can, but we'd rather not elaborate. Some things you just know from experience," Officer Morris said.

"Why were they killed?" Sam asked.

"That's why we're asking everyone questions, Weasel," the male cop said. He sounded sarcastic.

"Wiesel." Sam had no doubt the guy said it that way on purpose. "And I'm sorry, but I don't know anything."

"Have you seen anyone strange in the complex lately?" the policewoman asked.

"Everyone here is a stranger."

"Have you seen anyone visiting your neighbors since you've been here?" she asked.

"No, no one."

"Okay, we'll leave you alone, Mr. Wiesel. If you can think of anything, please give us a call." She handed him her card.

"I will."

He followed them to the door and locked it after they left. "A murder next door," he mumbled to himself.

He debated walking the quarter mile to *Ted's*. He ate there every morning and enjoyed their pecan waffles, but now he didn't know if he should go outside. Despite what the police told him, the killers could still be out there somewhere. They might think he saw something. He decided to forego his morning ritual and stayed in the condo.

At noon, another decision had to be made. He had reserved a spot on a bay fishing trip. It was the only open spot left on any of the bayside boats for the rest of the week. He knew if he didn't go today he wouldn't only lose his money, but he wouldn't be able to fish during his entire vacation. The condo had remained quiet all day, but the killers could still be out there somewhere waiting.

Finally, moments before it would be too late for him to get to the boat before it sailed, the doorbell rang and rescued him from his dilemma.

Another policeman stood outside his door. "Hello," he said after he opened the door.

"Hey, Mr. Wiesel?" the young policeman asked while studying a clipboard that he held out in front of himself.

"Yes."

"I'm a member of the police forensic team. We're going to be working next door for the next several hours. We wanted to make sure if you heard some strange sounds that you knew it was just us."

Sam looked out the door and saw a couple of other policemen walking into the neighboring unit carrying briefcases or small hard shelled suitcases.

"We're just bringing our equipment in now."

"Oh, that won't bother me, I was just leaving. Is it okay if I walk through you all?"

"Of course, you're welcome to come and go as you please."

"Thanks," Sam said, and followed one of the other forensic specialists out to the street.

~ Chapter ~
2

S am arrived at the dock just as the shore crew was starting to untie a fishing boat with *Fish Tales* painted across its transom.

"Wait! Wait a minute, please!" he shouted. The two men on shore looked up at him. "I'm booked on this boat. Sorry I'm late."

"Actually, you're not late. You had another five seconds," the older man of the two spoke.

Sam saw one of the deck hands on the boat shove the ramp back across the three feet to the pier. He gave the old man on shore his ticket and walked onto the boat. Once he had moved a few feet away from the ramp, the engine kicked in and the boat started its move away from the dock.

Sam looked around and counted another eight men and one woman who were not part of the three-person crew. He guessed there could be someone inside the cabin, but the door was shut. All but one man and the woman stood against the boat's railing, taking in the scenery while the boat moved away from shore.

In addition to some benches, Sam saw four comfortable looking chairs positioned around a small round table at the rear of the boat. It did not appear that anyone had made an effort to claim any of them, so he took the one that faced forward. The bright sun had already jacked the temperature up a dozen or so degrees from the morning. He took the sunglasses out of their holder on his belt and put them on.

"Bright, isn't it?"

Sam looked up and saw a tall, fit-looking man.

"Sure is, and I think it's going to get hot," Sam replied.

"No doubt. Can I join you?"

"Sure." He smiled, which the tall man took as a friendly gesture, but Sam had noticed the tautness of the man's tee shirt across his chest and the well defined muscles in his arms. Sam figured few people would have the nerve to challenge the guy.

"My name's Clint, Clint Smith," he held out his hand.

Sam shook it. "I'm Sam Wiesel."

"Nice to meet you. You live here on the island?"

"No," Sam said. "I come down here each year for a vacation."

"Great place. It's home for me, but I'm gone a lot, so it's almost like a vacation when I can come back."

"Are these seats still open?"

Sam looked up to see another man, closer to his age than Smith, who he thought was about ten years his junior. This guy had some grey showing up in his hair, but still looked in pretty good shape. No match for Smith, he thought, but Sam acknowledged that this guy was in a lot better shape than he let himself get into the last few years.

"I think so," Smith said but looked at Sam for final approval.

"Of course," Sam said.

Something about these two guys joining his table made Sam feel good. Kind of like the popular guys at school coming to join him at a lunch table. A stupid thought, Sam told himself, but he couldn't avoid the feeling.

"I'm Clint," Smith said to the new guy.

"I'm Jim West," the new guy said, "nice to meet you."

"And I'm Sam Wiesel," he said and joined in with the hand shaking. The three sat down just as a crew member came by with a cooler of drinks.

"Anyone want a soda or beer? It'll be about fifteen minutes 'til we get to our fishing spot."

West asked for a beer, and the other two followed suit. Sam wasn't much of a beer drinker, but he wanted to be one of the guys.

"Can I join you all?"

Sam looked up and saw an older-looking man, possibly in his eighties, wearing bib overalls and a white tee shirt. He bent a little forward as though his back bothered him. His face had that leathery look, like he had spent way too much time in the sun. Sam thought one would almost have to look twice to see the thin, sparse white hair that did little to cover his scalp.

"All right with us," Clint said.

Sam realized that Clint had taken a few seconds to answer, and he wondered if Clint had waited to give him a chance to say something since he was the first to claim the table.

"Yes, please do."

When the old man sat down, he placed an Atlanta Braves baseball cap on his head.

"A Braves fan! I always liked the Braves, too," West said.

"Grew up liking them in Milwaukee," the old man said.

Sam didn't comment on the Braves. He had never paid much attention to sports.

"I'm Clint," the big guy said and reached out to shake the old man's hand.

"Buster," the old man replied, and Sam and West joined in the greetings.

Unlike the Gulf that bordered the other side of the island, the water in the bay was rarely choppy. The boat moved through the water like it was moving through a big lake.

"Sam," Buster said, "you almost didn't make it today. I saw you get out of your car and hustle toward the boat, but I thought they were going to leave without you."

"Got held up at my condo. A murder took place there this morning. I had to stick around for the police. You know, questions and all." Sam tried hard to sound relaxed and confident.

"I heard about the shooting," West said. "So the police think it was murder?"

"Yes, that's what they told me. Said they knew, but wouldn't elaborate to me. I guess they have ways to tell."

"Yeah, especially if they had their hands tied behind their backs and were shot in the head," Buster said and followed it with a short laugh.

"Is that what happened?" Sam asked. He silently cursed himself for letting that high pitch sneak back into his voice.

"Oh, I don't know," Buster said. "I've probably seen too many movies."

West didn't say anything but he figured the old man's comments may be closer to the mark than not.

"It's rare that we have a murder here on the Island," Clint said.

"True," Buster said. "I've been here for nearly twenty years and don't believe there have been twenty murders here in that time frame."

"Any idea what caused it?" West asked.

"No," Sam said. "None."

"You know in the old days life was a lot more dangerous here than it is now," Buster said.

"Why do you say that?" Clint asked.

"This place really didn't get civilized until the first half of the last century. I'm not saying that the people here were bad, I'm just saying a lot of wild and ruthless people passed through here since the days of Columbus."

"I guess that's the same for a lot of the southwest, and one of the reasons that they established the Texas Rangers," Clint said.

"But there is another aspect of the island that most of the rest of Texas didn't have." Buster paused, but no one interrupted him, "the ocean."

"True," Sam said becoming engrossed in the conversation.

"We know about a handful of the shipwrecks that happened around here, but explorers and pirates sailed these seas for a couple centuries without much accountability or record keeping. From here to Corpus Christi, you have a lot of island that some pirate could have called home."

"And we know that today's drug smugglers use ships to transport their contraband. Running a smaller boat off a larger ship up the coast fifty miles from the nearest person may still be possible in today's world," Clint said.

"Probably so," Buster said, "but today the cops and Coast Guard are pretty damn good. Up until about a hundred years ago, there were no cops or Coast Guard down here. Can you imagine what it was like back then? Say you were a Captain of a large ship and a large storm was coming in from the east. This island might have looked like a safe haven, or they could have been thrown up onto the island and destroyed."

"Sounds like you're a student of history," Jim said.

"Ahh, more of a hobby. I never did have much real education other than high school. Back then it wasn't all that important. Besides, the Korean War came up during my college years, and I chose the army over school. Man, that was a hard war."

"I was in the Air Force," Jim said.

"So you think there could be buried treasure somewhere around here?" Sam asked Buster. He didn't want the conversation to digress to guys talking about their military career. He had avoided the military much like he had stayed out of sports.

"I'm sure of it. Now, it may not be buried treasure in the sense of having some pirate finding a spot to hide his loot. It could be as simple as a ship being blown up on the island and destroyed. No one would survive for long here without provisions. Anything of value on the ship would have been buried in the sand."

"That's certainly possible," Clint joined in. "Visitors to the island centuries ago would have taken the wood and other things that they could use, but I doubt if they excavated the areas around the shipwrecks looking for anything at all."

"I imagine the few known shipwrecks off the coast were first spotted by someone, and then we learned more about them, rather than knowing about them first and then finding them," Jim said

"Exactly," Buster said.

Sam could see that the old man liked the fact that everyone had joined him in his conversation. Sam knew the conversation had gotten his interest, too. Hell, he thought to himself, he might have better chances finding a buried treasure than winning the lottery.

"Have you found anything?" Sam asked.

"Nothing of substance. The trouble is not in the theory, but in proving it. Without a map or some other specific documentation that can point someone in the right direction, where do you look?"

"Always a catch," Jim said with a smile. "More than one Spanish or French merchant ship sailing from New Orleans never showed up in Europe, and no one ever knew why. If a ship sailing south out of New Orleans, or for that matter north to New Orleans, ran into a hurricane coming out of the east, which is their normal route, trying to outrun it to safety might have brought them here."

"Exactly," Buster said with a grin. "One of the oldest legends is about a guy named John Singer. He was shipwrecked here and loved it so much he stayed. Story has it that in the 1800s he found millions in gold and jewels washed up onto shore from other shipwrecks. During the Civil War he buried his treasure on the island, but then when he returned to look for it he could never find it."

"I've seen people out on the beach with those metal detector things," Sam said. "Have they ever found anything?"

"I imagine so, or there wouldn't be an incentive for anyone to be doing it," Clint said.

"Besides, those people are mostly tourists, and they cover a very small portion of the beach right by the city. There are hundreds of miles of beach on these islands."

"Could someone fly over the island with those fancy radars they have these days and look through the sand?" Sam asked. His interest had kicked into high gear.

"I think those things can identify different layers in the earth from the density of each layer. I don't think they're fine tuned enough to locate a treasure chest," Jim said.

"A treasure chest, whoa, that would make my day!" Sam said.

"Doesn't even have to be a treasure chest. A small leather pouch full of precious gems, say diamonds and rubies, could be a very valuable discovery," Buster said.

"Buster, are there any legends about missing treasure in the area?" Jim asked.

"Oh sure, mentioned the one about Singer already. Allegedly Jean Lafitte, 'The Gentlemen Pirate,' may have buried some treasure here, too. But everyone knows about these guys. There is one that I've heard about that few others have, and that one has few believers."

"One's all you need," Clint added.

"But like you said, Buster, three hundred years ago if a ship crashed here there might not be any record of it, except that it went missing," Sam said.

"Oh, I do agree with that. A handful of ships could have crashed on these shores three to five hundred years ago, and there might be no specific record of any of them doing so."

"So what is this legend about?" Clint asked.

"It's an interesting one, and totally different from the rest. I picked up a book years ago at the *Paragraphs* bookstore here in South Padre," Buster said.

"I know the place," Clint said.

"The book was written by some lady professor up north, I think, but I may be wrong on that."

"Uh huh," Sam said without meaning to.

"Supposedly, nearly a thousand years ago when the Aztecs were building their empire throughout Mexico and Central America, they had a ruler who had this thing for birds. He had his craftsmen mold dozens of birds in gold or silver and cover them with precious gems."

"We're going to be at our fishing spot in a couple minutes," a crewman announced over a loudspeaker system.

"Go on with your story," Sam said.

"Well no one knows what happened to most of these bird statues. One or two are in Mexican museums, but one, the *Golden Booby*, is supposed to be here on the island somewhere."

"Booby?" Sam asked.

"The bird kind," Clint said.

"Yeah," Buster said with a grin. "Did you know that Al Capone visited the island at least once?"

"No," all three said in unison.

"Well he did. In Port Isabel, across the bay, there was a night club resort that brought a lot of high rollers and other dignitaries down here to this tip of Texas. President Harding came here too. The place was called the Port Isabel Yacht Club."

"Does Capone fit into the legend?"

"Yes. The *Golden Booby* belonged to a very wealthy Mexican family. They kept it secret from the government because they didn't want it taken from them and put in some museum. Over the couple centuries the family possessed it, the Booby bounced between the original Gomez family and its related Gonzalez wing of the family. Family members killed family members over it," Buster said.

"I guess it has a curse of its own," Jim said.

"Seems like it. Luckily they never melted it down. The legend has it that Capone's trip down here wasn't just for a vacation. He was supposed to meet up with a member of the Mexican family and receive the Booby."

"Why would they give the statue to him?" Jim asked.

"It was supposed to be in payment for something. Apparently, the Mexican family had itself been involved in a number of illegal activities both in Mexico and up here in the States. Something they were doing in the States ran afoul of Capone's empire. So rather than be run out of the US, which was a lucrative part of the family's business, and be challenged in Mexico by Capone, the family allegedly acquiesced. Capone sweetened the deal by offering half million in cash for the Booby."

"Wow, that's still a lot of money," Clint said.

"The statue is priceless. The historical value alone must be incredible. Even if you settled for the reward that Mexico would give you, you'd likely walk away with a hundred thousand or so."

"So did Al Capone get the *Golden Booby*?"

"No, it was all a double cross. The question is whether the statue ever made it to the island. What we do know is that the Chicago boys came more prepared than the Gomez family expected. Back then the island didn't have many residents. The two gangs came by boat from the mainland, met on shore a few miles north of where the center of the city is today, and a gun fight erupted."

"I've never heard that," Clint said.

"No reason why you should have. Neither family would advertise their activities. Most of the dead died on the shore line. The bodies would've been taken out to sea during the next high tide. What I've been able to piece together is that two members of the Mexican gang fled on foot with a couple of Capone's men chasing them down the dunes."

"I hate to run in the sand," Sam said.

"The captain of the small boat and Capone returned to Port Isabel where Capone took refuge at the Port Isabel Yacht Club, without the *Golden Booby*. The boat returned to the island to pick up the couple guys they left behind, but could find no sign of their men or the two Mexicans. They decided the four must have killed each other."

"Didn't they search for the statue?" Jim asked.

"Yes. I don't think Capone had many men left down here after the gun- fight, but those who were left returned to the island the next day. They didn't find anything. No bodies, no statue, nada."

"So, what happened?" Sam asked.

"If I knew that, I'd be a rich man," Buster said.

~ Chapter ~
3

"Time to fish," a crewman said. He had walked up to them as they were talking.

"How about if we have a small wager among the four of us?" Buster said.

"What do you mean?" Sam asked.

"We all commit five dollars, and the person who catches the largest fish of any variety wins."

"Winner takes all?" Clint asked.

"Sure," Jim said.

"Let's do it," Clint said.

Buster looked at Sam. "How about it?" he asked.

"I'm in," Sam said, still pleased to be included.

The four grabbed fishing rods and individual buckets of bait and took open positions along the side of the drifting boat. Jim and Clint found adjacent positions, but Sam and Buster ended up between others on the boat. The morning breeze had weakened to the point that Sam wished it would return to give them some relief from the hot sun.

Sam hadn't fished much in his life but had come to really enjoy these outings during his trips to South Padre. He thought he had the system down but still managed to hook his finger while putting on fresh bait about an hour into the excursion.

The only female participant happened to be on his left. She saw and heard the accident; Sam never could take pain quietly. In seconds, she had his wounded hand in hers and had it cleaned and bandaged. She also finished baiting his hook and tossed it into the bay.

"Thanks,' Sam said.

"No problem. It's usually my husband who sticks himself. I'm used to it," she said with a smile and returned to her position.

Sam watched as she picked up her rod and gave it a few gentle jerks. He saw that she had already caught three fish to his one. He also began to wonder if her comment about her husband was some form of an obscure insult. Did she mean "usually it's my husband who is stupid enough to stab himself with the hook?"

Just then, Sam felt a tug on his line. He tightened his grip on the fishing pole. He felt another minor tug followed seconds later by a powerful jerk. Sam's whole body tensed as the line became taut, and something down in the deep tried to wrench the rod out of his hands.

"Hang onto him. You've got a big one."

Sam took a quick glance behind him and saw one of the crewmen. "It certainly feels powerful," Sam said.

"I saw the rod bend," the crewman said. "It's definitely a good-sized fish. Keep the line tight and let him tire himself out a bit before you try to bring him in."

"Got a good one there, Sam?"

Sam glanced back and saw Buster had also walked up next to him. "Look at the bend in that pole," Buster said.

Sam felt the strain already. He wondered if he had the strength to reel in the fish. He also noticed that he felt exhilarated. He had never landed a big fish, and it had been a long time since he had been the center of attention. He held onto the rod determined not to let this one get away.

The woman next to him reeled in her line to prevent Sam's from tangling with it. The man to his right, whom he had not said more than a hello to, did the same.

"You can do it, Sam. Get that bad boy in," Jim said as he walked over to watch Sam.

Suddenly the reel screamed as line was forced out despite the resistance. Sam felt like he might be pulled overboard. The crewman put a hand on his shoulder and helped steady him.

"Need some help?" he asked Sam. "Not yet, but I might."

The line went slack.

"Think he snapped the line?" Sam asked the crewman.

"Nah, reel it in. It's probably just swimming back at us," Buster said.

Sam started reeling in the line. He felt only the resistance of the water and wondered if the fish had escaped. For a few seconds doubt gnawed on him, but a tug on the line followed by a steady pull told him the fish was still there. He kept reeling in the line.

The fish had some fight left in him. Just when Sam thought he had won the contest, the fish dove with all its strength. The rod bent like it would break. The reel again squealed as the fish forced the line out.

Once again, the crewman grabbed Sam to keep him stable on his feet.

Sweat got into his right eye, and Sam blinked. He realized he was sweating. Someone else must have seen his predicament, because someone ran a cold wet towel across his forehead and then placed it on the back of his neck.

The line went slack again.

"He's worn himself out," Buster said. "Reel him in."

Sam looked over at Buster and grinned. He saw that the Captain of the boat had a video camera in hand and had positioned himself at the stern to get a good angle of the fish being pulled out of the water — if Sam could do it.

The fish had put up a valiant battle, but it too was exhausted. It felt the steady, upward pull of the line and resigned itself to its fate. Although it didn't understand the loud, raucous noise that erupted when it arrived at the surface, it certainly heard it.

"Look at that fish!" shouted someone to Sam's right. "Don't let it get away!" another shouted from behind.

Sam believed everyone on the small boat had come to watch, but he couldn't take his eyes away from his prize. He expected one last fight, but it didn't come. The line brought the fish to the surface and a hand reached over and pulled the fish on board. It seemed like everyone was taking photos of the fish, but Sam could only sit down exhausted.

"It's a giant redfish. One of the biggest I've ever seen," the Captain said to Sam. "What do you want us to do with it?"

Sam looked at him for a second. "Can we throw him back in? Will he live?"

"Sure," the Captain said.

Something in the Captain's eyes made Sam believe he had said the right thing.

"First, though, let's get a picture of you with it."

Sam had to use two hands to hold the redfish up for the camera. It measured forty-two inches long. Seconds later a crewman eased the fish back into the bay. With the vocal encouragement of a number of people on board and minor applause, the large fish slowly swam away.

"You got some class, Sam," Clint said and put a hand on Sam's shoulder.

"Thanks. Seemed like the right thing to do," Sam said.

The Captain told everyone who hadn't reeled in their lines to do so. He said it was time to move to a different spot. Most people onboard realized that the Captain wanted to give the large fish a chance to recover before he bit into the next hook. There was no dissent.

The rest of the day Sam didn't get a nibble, but he didn't care. He felt like he was sitting on a cloud, content now to watch others have some fun. The breeze even picked up sending cool salt-scented air to counter the hot sun. Sam wondered if he had ever felt this good before.

Late that afternoon Sam got off the boat with the twenty dollars in his pocket. His fish doubled the size of the largest caught by the other three. He had said goodbye to the three and doubted he would see any of them again. They were nice guys and he had liked them all, but they would now head in their own individual directions. However, he had asked for and gotten Buster's phone number. The *Golden Booby* had fixed itself in Sam's mind.

~ Chapter ~
4

S am stopped at the *Padre Island Brewing Company* on Padre Boulevard to celebrate. He had only been there once before and that was two years earlier. He had met a woman on the beach and they had come here for dinner. He had told her he was divorced, but had not told her that he had remarried.

Nothing had come from that dinner, and looking back Sam realized that was a good thing. At the time, he remembered he had been bitter when she refused his offer to come to his condo for a night cap. She had made some excuse about a headache, but Sam had no doubt she simply hadn't been interested in spending the night with him.

He ordered pale ale to accompany his cheeseburger. A group sitting nearby laughed and talked loudly, something that would have normally gotten on his nerves, but tonight it didn't bother him. He smelled the odors from the kitchen and watched the hundreds of cars drive slowly by.

His cheeseburger arrived, and he ate it thinking not of the woman he had brought here but of the fish he had caught that day.

When he finally got back to his condo he didn't see any police vehicles or personnel. The adjacent condo had been sealed with police tape, and he surmised the forensic people had done their thing and left. Sam grabbed a Dr.

Pepper out of the refrigerator and went out to his balcony. It had gotten dark enough for him to see the lights from the ships and oil rigs out in the Gulf.

A few diehards still sat on towels in the sand, but for the most part everyone had left the beach for the day. Sam could hear the music from the handful of nearby bars. He realized that his own building seemed quieter than normal, and he wondered if any of the occupants had decided to leave. This morning, the thought of leaving did cross his mind, but now, after the day that he had, he felt pretty good about life.

He watched an hour of the Walking Dead on television and then part of an old movie before going to bed.

That night he didn't dream of the two people killed next door. He didn't dream of his long hard victory over the fish. Rather, his dreams took him to the sand dunes miles north of the city and to a wooden chest partially sticking out of the sand.

The next morning he again sat on his small balcony and sipped coffee as the sun rose in the east. All five fishermen were out there this morning. He waited for his jogger with more anticipation than he had before. A light mist seemed to float from the low clouds, and the air was a little foggy which limited his vision to a few hundred yards.

When she first appeared, she looked like an apparition, like something created for a scene in a movie. He thought he saw her, but then she was gone. Part of her reappeared and almost disappeared. The haze cleared around her, and Sam saw her clearly. She jogged northward, and this time all the men turned to pay their respects. In less than a minute, the fog had swallowed her again.

Sam remembered it had been different in his dream, the morning sunnier for one thing. The fishermen weren't there, either. He wondered why, but who could explain dreams. In his dream he had been standing alone on the beach thinking that he should try to do some early morning fishing from the shore. He sensed her rather than saw her at first.

He turned. There she was twenty yards away running right at him, her long blond hair pulled back by a band flowing loose behind her. He stepped back, and she ran by with a smile. Just as she passed him, she gave him a little nod of her head.

"She wants me to follow her," Sam said to himself. He took a few steps after her.

"I'm not a runner," he shouted, "slow down."

She turned and faced him but never stopped running away from him.

"Come on," she said. She turned away and kept running.

Sam ran, and ran, and ran. He remembered in his dream that he ran so far there were no longer any buildings around. She slowly got further away from him, but just when he was about to give up, she turned away from the shoreline and ran up a small dune fifty or so yards from the beach.

She stopped there and waved at him. She signaled to him like she had reached her destination and wanted him to join her. Sam waved back as she walked down the other side of the dune and disappeared. He slowed down to catch his breath. She would be there.

Sam smiled at himself on that balcony, while the mist started to soak into his hair and bathrobe. He remembered what he had thought in his dream as he approached the dune. She would be waiting for him and would want him like he wanted her.

"One track mind, you old fool," he said out loud.

His dream, however, had surprised him. When he followed her footprints over the dune, she wasn't there. Looking around he couldn't see her anywhere. Rather, a corner of a small wooden chest stuck out of the sand. Intrigued, he pulled the chest out the rest of the way and studied it. It was maybe eighteen inches long, twelve inches wide, and another twelve deep. He didn't see any writing on the chest or any spot that seemed to indicate where one would open it.

He did notice it had been sealed with nails and one of the nails had come loose. He pried the nail off with a small sharp stone. Enough of one corner lifted up that he could work it back and forth to pry out the next nail and so forth. Finally, he opened one side and pulled out an item wrapped in a leather cloth. He peeled off the cloth.

The thing astonished him. It seemed to glow in the sunlight. Different colors sparkled from it, and it suddenly felt heavier. The statue had to be solid gold and was adorned with dozens of gemstones that included diamonds, rubies, and emeralds. The bird itself looked a little odd, but the statue was breathtaking.

The discovery had shaken Sam out of his sleep. Yet, even while awake in bed, the vivid memory of the dream and specifically of the statue dominated his conscious mind. Some of the excitement remained with him on the balcony. He knew that the jogger didn't look like the woman in his dreams, and he certainly knew he couldn't run as far as he had imagined, but that wasn't what had piqued his fascination. It was his discovery of the *Golden Booby*, and that, he believed, could become a reality.

He had a couple days to do some research, and he could always stay an extra day or two. He would call Buster later in the morning and try to meet with him again. He wouldn't tell Buster about his dream. He would only say that he'd like to know a little more about the legend.

Sam left his condo a little earlier than normal to head to the café. He had a lot to do today. The mist had stopped, and the fog had already dissipated. The short walk invigorated him. Pleased to find his favorite table vacant, Sam ordered coffee and treated himself to two pecan waffles instead of his usual one.

The coffee seemed hotter than usual, and he held the cup close to his mouth blowing on it. Focused so much on the steam floating away from the rim of the cup, he never saw the teenager stumble next to him. He did, however, feel the crash of his body on the back of his chair.

"Dammit!" the teenager shouted from the ground next to his chair.

"Damn," Sam said, rising quickly to his feet and trying to brush the hot coffee off his lap.

"Oh, I'm sorry, sir," said a short slender woman. She had run up to them from the counter area.

Sam didn't know what to say. His stare alternated between his wet khaki shorts and the two people in front of him.

"Here, let me get this," a server appeared out of nowhere with a towel to clean off Sam's table top, chair, and the floor around his chair.

The woman knelt over the teenager and helped him to his feet. "Are you okay, Jay?" she asked the teenager softly.

Sam barely heard her.

The kid growled out a yes which Sam thought was impertinent, but the woman let it pass by. Sam guessed Jay was sixteen to seventeen years old. He looked unstable even after he got to his feet.

"Sorry, Mister," Jay said without any prompting from the woman, who by now Sam had correctly guessed was his mother. "I stumbled."

Sam wanted to say something sarcastic and might have if he hadn't noticed the woman leaning over and picking up a book and a cane. She handed the cane to Jay.

"The coffee will just blend in with the color of my shorts. Don't worry about it. My neighbors were murdered yesterday. I guess this is nothing." Sam had no idea why he said anything about the murder. It simply came out surprising him as much as Jay had.

"Really?" Jay asked.

"Actually, yes."

"I heard about that on the news," Jay said. "Remember, Mom?"

"Yes, of course I do. Here you go, sir," she offered Sam a handful of napkins.

Sam took them and started wiping the remaining coffee off his legs and blotting at the stains on his shorts. "Thanks."

"Did you witness the murders?" Jay asked.

"Luckily no," Sam said. "As far as I know the killers are still out there somewhere. I wouldn't want them to have any reason to be after me."

Jay didn't respond. Sam figured he was weighing the concern for safety versus the excitement of being a critical piece of the police's investigation.

"Come on, Jay. Let's find a table," his mother said.

"Okay," Jay said, "how about this one?" Jay plopped into a chair at the table adjacent to Sam.

"Do you mind?" the woman asked Sam.

"No, not at all." Sam noticed the wedding ring on the woman's finger. His glance at a woman's left hand had become almost second nature these days, but what caught his attention was not the ring but the book the hand held. Titled *Birds of Texas*, the book almost shouted out at him.

"Who's the bird fan?" he asked.

"Oh," the woman said looking down at the book, "I guess we both are." She passed the book to Jay as she sat down.

"Ever hear of the booby?" Sam asked.

"Sure," Jay answered.

Sam looked at the two of them knowing it was his turn to say something, but he had already stepped out of his comfort zone. He rarely said more than a hello to strangers, and anything more he might say would lead to the legend, or at least the little he knew about it. He wondered if they would think he might be a little crazy if he brought it up.

Fortunately, a server saved him for the moment by approaching their table and taking their order.

"Excuse me," she said to the server as he turned away.

"Yes?"

"Could you please bring him," she motioned to Sam, "another cup of coffee?"

"Of course," he said and walked away.

"Thanks," Sam said.

"What's your interest in the booby?" Jay asked.

There it was, Sam thought. He still didn't feel comfortable in opening up.

"I heard someone talking about the booby yesterday, and I didn't even know it was a bird. Seeing the book made me think of that conversation."

"What do you want to know about it? My son is quite the expert."

"I guess anything you might know. Is there a picture of it in your book?"

"I don't know," Jay said and started thumbing through the book. After a few seconds, he stopped looking for it and went to the index. "No, it's not in here, but I can tell you about it."

"Do you mind?" Sam asked Jay but also moved his eyes to the teenager's mother to offer her a chance to answer.

"Go ahead, Jay," she said.

"Well boobies are a species of sea-birds that spend their lives at sea hunting fish and are found on the east coast of Central and South America, and across the tropical islands of the South Pacific like the Galapagos islands. There are different species of booby such as the blue-footed booby. There are also red-footed boobies. They are all large birds, similar in size and appearance. The blue-footed booby is the most well known. The boobies are good flyers, and great divers, but appear to be clumsy. Due to their large size and the areas they inhabit,they have few natural predators. The main ones are owls and large birds of prey that steal the booby chicks, but the adult booby is far too big for another bird to eat. The human is the main predator of the adult booby, and occasionally the odd shark."

"Wow, that's pretty good. I'm impressed," Sam said.

"It's a hobby. I like birds, especially birds of prey. I could tell you loads more about hawks, but boobies are great hunters of fish. Since my accident, I've had a lot of time on my hands."

"Accident?" Sam asked before he could cut himself off. He knew it was none of his business.

"Motorcycle accident. Stupid, really stupid of me. I took my bike off-roading even though it's not designed for it. I wasn't even going that fast, but lost control and shattered my left leg. Luckily I had my helmet on."

"Part of growing up," his mother said, shaking her head. "We're just so happy nothing else happened to him. Spent his Christmas holidays in and out of the hospital and surgeries, but now we're just waiting for the healing process to do its thing."

"That's why I stumbled into your chair, sir. I'm not an expert with this cane yet. I turned and put too much weight on my bad leg. Tried to catch myself on your chair."

"That's okay. Do you get most of your info from that book?" Sam asked.

"Oh no, most of what I learn I get from the internet. I've been to the library a few times back home to look at their books, too. The library has some good books, but you can find out a lot more and quicker from the internet," Jay said.

"You might be able to," Sam said, "but some of us aren't that good with the computer."

"Don't you use a computer at your work? It's not that hard."

"Sure, Jay. That is your name, right?"

"Yes."

"I use a computer and can surf the net, but when I try to look up stuff I get too many choices that don't really have what I'm looking for. It's frustrating for me."

Jay simply smiled at Sam. A pity look, Sam thought.

"I agree with you ….." Jay's mother said drawing out "you" and pausing at the end.

"Sam, my name is Sam."

"I'm Jane and my son, as you said, is Jay. Do you live here in South Padre, Sam?"

"No, I'm just taking a week off."

"What do you do?" Jay asked.

"I work in an office, nothing exciting," Sam said.

"Jay's taking more than a week off," Jane said.

"Yeah, since the accident, I've been out of school. Set me back a year," Jay said.

"We tried to work something out, but it got too hard, and none of us needed the stress," Jane said.

"I used to teach school." Sam said. "I understand what you're going through, Jay. You'll see. It'll work out."

"What grade did you teach?" Jane asked.

"High school."

"Why'd you stop?" Jay asked.

"Now Jay, let's not be nosy!" Jane said.

"Oh, it's okay," Sam said. "I just got burned out."

"We had a teacher break down in tears last year," Jay said. "I felt sorry for her. Couple of creeps hassled her all the time."

"Jay's missed not being in school this year," Jane said. "I think that's why he's spent so much time researching things. He has to have a project. Right, son?"

"I just like to discover things. I'd love to be a scientist when I get older," Jay said.

"Got a current project?" Sam asked. The question came out by itself; like someone else possessed his mouth. He knew where the conversation was headed, and while his mind debated whether he should even mention it, the words kept coming.

"No."

"I had an interesting experience yesterday that's piqued my curiosity." Sam noticed a guarded look come over Jane's face but ignored it. "I know it's silly, but I keep thinking about it."

"What?" asked Jay.

"It was a story, maybe you could call it a legend, about a priceless statue of a bird made of solid gold and covered with diamonds. The person who told me the story believed it was buried somewhere here on the island."

"Wow! Here on the island?" Jay asked.

"Are you serious?" Jane asked.

"Yes. I know, it sounds silly, but this guy seemed very serious about it."

"He didn't want you to contribute money into his effort, did he?" Jane asked.

"No, no. He was telling us about the statue. He didn't ask any of us about any help or anything."

"Is that why you asked us about the booby?" Jay asked.

Now it was Sam's turn to smile. He nodded.

"Want me to try to find out about it?" Jay asked.

"Jay, you don't —"

"Mom, I'd just be looking it up on the computer."

"Well, I don't want to cause any trouble," Sam said.

"I guess it's no trouble," Jane said, "but I do think you need to tell Jay a little more about this statue."

"Okay, but it might take a few minutes."

"I need another cup of coffee anyway," she said.

The server came and poured some more coffee for Sam and Jane and took the plates away.

"The old man who told me the story seemed very level headed," Sam started. Over the next ten minutes he tried to recite the story as verbatim as possible. They both interrupted him with questions now and then. Jay took out a pen and jotted notes onto a napkin.

"So what do you want me to find out?" Jay asked when Sam had finished.

"Can you research the net and see if you can find any mention of this *Golden Booby*?"

"That should be easy," Jay said.

"You should be able to find anything that's out there about this statue in just a few hours, don't you think?" Jane asked Jay.

"May take a little more than that, but certainly by tonight I should be finished," Jay said.

"That would be fantastic," Sam said. "Could the three of us meet here tomorrow morning?"

"Of course," Jay said.

"I'm sure we could, say about eight?" Jane said.

"Can I have your phone number, so I can call you if I have any questions as I go along?" Jay asked.

Sam gave him his number.

"You know, Jay," Jane said. "This will give you the chance to practice your Spanish. You might find something on a Mexican museum or historical website."

"Don't worry if you can't find anything about it," Sam said despite the fact that he knew he'd be worrying about it.

"If it's out there, Jay will find it," Jane said.

"Mom, before we go I need to use the restroom," Jay said.

"Don't let me stop you," his mother said.

Jay got unsteadily to his feet and walked off.

"Nice boy you have there," Sam said.

"We're really lucky. The original prognosis was that he might never walk again."

"He's definitely proving that wrong."

"By summer, he should be just about back to normal."

"That's good," Sam said.

The server came up to their two tables and delivered their checks. "Let me get this," Sam said.

"I should buy yours, since we made you spill your coffee."

~ Chapter ~
5

By the time Sam started walking back to his condo, the sun had definitely taken charge of the sky. The early morning cloud cover had burned off, and even the sea breeze had dissipated.

A drop of sweat rolled into his left eye as he climbed the last few steps to his floor. His eye burned, so he rubbed it gently.

"It's not that bad, is it?" a woman's voice asked.

Sam looked up to see who spoke. The policewoman who had interviewed him the day before stood in the open doorway to the condo in which the murder had occurred. She had a red towel draped over a shoulder that covered her name tag.

"I'm not crying," Sam said, somewhat irritated that she should think that. "Sweat got into my eye."

"If you say so," she teased him. Sam didn't know what to say.

"Are you sure you didn't hear or see anything yesterday?" she asked.

"Like I said, I didn't see anything, and I only heard the two shots."

"We've learned that two men were seen leaving this complex shortly after the gunshots. One was carrying a briefcase or a satchel. Do you have any idea what may have been in the case?"

For some inexplicable reason Sam's mind raced to the *Golden Booby*, but that didn't make sense.

"What are you thinking of?"

Sam realized the look that had come over him when he thought of the *Golden Booby* must have been pretty obvious.

"Nothing. I was just thinking. I really have no idea."

"You know, most of your neighbors have left. Why are you still around?" she asked.

"I'm leaving in a couple of days."

"Well, I don't think they'll be back. We think they left the island immediately after the shooting. They're probably a hundred miles away sitting in some ranch house thinking they're safe."

"I would think they'd head to Mexico," Sam said.

"It's possible, but if they did leave here with a satchel full of money, drugs, or something else, it may not be that easy to get across the border."

"So you think it would be easier for them to hide out for a few days somewhere?" Sam asked.

"Naturally. There are thousands of small ranches down here and throughout the valley. A person could hide out in one of those forever," she said.

"I never thought of that."

"By the way, do you have any coffee at your place?" she asked.

"Yes," he answered a little put off by her forwardness. As she didn't say anything else, but simply stared at him, he acquiesced. "I'll make some."

"Thanks. I have to lock up. I'll be over in a minute."

Sam left the door to his condo slightly ajar and made some fresh coffee. He wondered what the police woman was up to. He also wished he could remember her name. She took longer than Sam expected which only heightened his anxiety.

"Okay if I come in?" she asked.

"Yes, the coffee's ready."

"Thanks, I need some. Sorry if I was a little pushy."

She took the cup from his hand and continued walking to the sliding glass door that faced the water. She no longer had the towel draped over her shoulder, but Sam didn't have a chance to get a good look at her name tag.

"Yes, you do have a good view," she said.

"It's the main thing that drew me to this condo. I rent it every year."

"Did you know the owner of this condo also owns the one next door?" she asked.

"No, no I didn't," Sam said.

"Have you had a chance to talk to him since you've been here?"

"No, I work through an agency on the main road. I think I may have talked to him a couple years ago. He was here fixing something when I arrived."

"So you think you talked to him?" she asked.

He thought he heard a little sarcasm in her voice.

"No, I'm sure I talked to someone, but after he left I wasn't sure if he said he was the owner, or that he was fixing the sink, yeah that's what it was, for the owner." Sam tilted his head forward a little to try to get a look at her name tag, but hit his head on the glass before he had the correct angle to see it.

She looked at him suspiciously, and her hand went instinctively to make sure her blouse was buttoned. He reddened when he realized what she must have thought.

"How's the coffee?" he asked.

"The coffee is very good."

"It's my own blend."

She smiled at him and took another sip. "Are you a scuba diver?" she asked.

"No, not much of a swimmer really."

"The diving's not the best around here unless you're exploring an old wreck. Got a few of them out there, too."

"Ever hear of any sunken treasures?" he asked.

"I wish. I did hear of someone finding some Spanish gold coins. Might just be a tall tale though, lots of those around. More stories than treasures, that's for sure."

"Think you'll catch the guys that committed the murders next door?" Sam felt like changing the subject again.

"At some point most of them do get caught. They do something else and make a mistake, or someone hears something months from now and squeals. Most of them get caught."

"I guess so."

"How come your wife isn't here with you?"

"It's good for us to get away from each other now and then. At least that's the idea."

"Whose idea?" she asked.

Sam tried not to show his irritation. He debated whether to tell her that this was none of her business. Cop or not, she had no right to pry into his private life.

"Are you married?" he asked her.

"Me? No, no time, married to my job as they say. Besides I'm too young. My Dad always said don't get married until you're thirty. You need to experience life before you tie yourself down. I've got a few more months."

Maybe that's where he went wrong, Sam thought to himself. He first got married when he was twenty-four. He remembered being so happy that he finally had a steady girlfriend that he had decided to marry her before she could leave him for someone else. Self confidence had never been his strong point. That marriage lasted a dozen years before it fell apart. Two years later he married a woman after a short courtship. The fact that she was an alcoholic had made him feel superior, and he erroneously thought he could have some control over her drinking. Three years later he divorced for the second time.

"I guess I better get back to the office," she said, jerking Sam back to the present.

"Oh, okay."

"Thanks for the coffee. It was really good."

"Thanks. Hope you catch the guys."

"We will," she said as she walked out the door. Sam never did get a good look at her name tag.

He took his coffee and went out on the porch. He remembered thinking about that third wedding while he stood there in the church waiting for his bride to appear. He recalled that he questioned his wisdom to get married that third time, but he knew at that point it was too late to back out. By the time of his third marriage, he had already reached the point where he didn't like his life. He hoped that getting married again might change everything.

Sam didn't blame himself for either of the divorces. He had lived under the perception for too long that the world never gave him a break, and he had become an expert in pointing blame at someone or something else. In fact, the sudden realization of this mindset startled him. Not that it was a new revelation, but he had disciplined himself long ago to stay away from any serious self analysis.

He decided to refocus his mind and pulled out his cell phone.

"Hello, Buster?" he said into the phone when he heard a voice answer.

"Yes, may I help you?"

"This is Sam, from the fishing trip yesterday."

"Oh yes, Sam the fisherman. I thought I might see something in the paper today about you and that giant fish."

"Hey, it wasn't that big. Besides the Captain said if it got into the paper it would be in Saturday's edition."

"Yeah, I guess that's right. That's when they do the fishing reports and updates. I'll be looking forward to it." Buster said.

"That's not why I called, Buster. I wonder if I could meet you for a few minutes, maybe buy you a hamburger somewhere in exchange for some additional information on the *Golden Booby*."

"The Booby? Ha! So it's gotten you intrigued, too?"

"Just a little, but we were interrupted in the middle of your story yesterday, and I thought of a few questions," Sam said.

"Today's no good for me. Wasn't going to eat lunch, because I've an appointment with my doctor."

"Is everything okay?"

"Sure," Buster said. "Just a physical, but I know they'll want to take blood."

"Oh."

"But I've a few minutes right now. What questions do you have?"

"I wondered how you learned about Al Capone's involvement with the statue."

"Didn't I tell you?"

"Not that I can remember."

"I heard it from a person who allegedly had connections in Capone's operation. I guess I can say who he was. He's been dead nearly fifteen years. He was my Uncle Mick."

"Was he down here?" Sam asked.

"Oh, no, and he only knew the thing as some fancy, expensive bird statue. He ran some numbers for Capone's operation, but he had access to a lot of the inside gossip. The story about the double cross and the shoot out followed Capone back to Chicago. Hard to keep it completely hushed up when so many of the guys didn't come back with him."

"So there's nothing documented about this?"

"I wouldn't think so," Buster said.

"How'd you know that the item was the statue of the *Golden Booby*?"

"Got that from talking to the former island historian. He said that he had friends who worked for a Mexican museum who were following their own leads concerning the whereabouts of the statue. He never heard about Capone's involvement and sort of discounted it, but what he heard actually supported my theory."

"What do you mean?" Sam asked.

"The guys from the museum told him that they had heard that a rich family in Mexico had kept the statue of a strange bird for centuries. The description of the statue being solid gold and adorned with valuable gemstones matched the Capone story."

"That's interesting."

"Well Sam, the icing on the cake for me was when he told me the statue may have disappeared some seventy years ago, about the same time one of the family's sons also disappeared. Rumor has it that he brought the statue up here, but as no one's found the statue, and no one ever learned what happened to the son, we really don't know."

"Do you think the current historian might know more about it now?" Sam asked.

"No. I talked to him nearly a year ago and he didn't know anything about it at all. Couldn't have him talk to the old historian, because he passed away a few years back."

"So you're at a dead end?"

"Temporarily stalled, I'd say."

"Not giving up though?" Sam asked.

"No way. I walk the beach a little each day looking for some sign. At my age, it gives me a purpose to keep on pressing."

"Good for you, Buster, good for you."

"Did I answer your questions okay?" Buster asked.

"Yes, you did. Thanks, Buster."

After getting off the phone, Sam could see why little would be known about the statue. Capone would not have wanted his involvement to be known, if it happened at all. The family secretly keeping the statue wouldn't want anyone to know it. Finding out about something that only a few people knew about, and wanted to keep it secret, wouldn't be easy. He wondered if Jay would have any luck at all with his research.

~ Chapter ~
6

S am rinsed his coffee cup out in the small kitchen sink and started thinking about lunch. Since he was not really hungry, he considered walking along the beach for a mile or so. He had never walked very far to the north. Better eat first, he decided. He didn't want to start getting hungry a long way from nowhere.

With his mind focused on a lunch that would include an order of cheese enchiladas, the noise that came out of the condo next door surprised him. He stopped dead in his tracks right outside the door that led into the murder scene. The noise sounded like a book or something falling onto the wooden floors. He noticed the door ajar a few inches.

It had to be the cops again. Sam inexplicably reached over and pushed the door open a few more inches. No way he was going to be stupid enough to say anything, at least until he knew it was the police, but he did stick his head in the room just a little.

Someone inside jerked the door open, and Sam froze. A man grabbed him and yanked him inside. A second man pressed a pistol to the side of Sam's head.

"Don't shoot him here. The cops are on the street."

"Okay. Let's go. We got what we came here for," the second man said.

"You're going to walk out of here with us. Don't make any sound or give anyone a sign, or we'll kill you on the spot," the first man said.

"I won't say a thing," Sam gasped.

"That's good. Play your hand right, and we'll drop you off before we cross the border." Sam nodded, too terrified to even consider the odds of being released at all.

The three of them moved out of the condo and down to the street. Sam didn't think either of the men was any bigger than he was, but that pistol looked huge. He could feel it pressed into his side as the two men had him squeezed in between them while they walked down the street. Sam felt dizzy and wondered if he could make it to the car without fainting.

"Right over there," the man holding the gun said, motioning to an old Dodge truck in the small beachside parking lot. The city planners had squeezed a number of these small lots in between buildings to provide more parking for the million-plus tourists that visit South Padre every year. A dark Mustang convertible was parked next to the pickup.

"Be quiet, or else," hissed the other man.

Sam didn't catch on right away, but then he saw two men coming into the parking lot from across the street. It appeared the five would intersect near the pickup unless one group or the other altered course. Sam didn't think the two who had him would yield for anyone. He felt the throbbing in his head increase. He wanted to shout something at the two men. The big one might... wait a second, he knew them.

Everything happened too fast for Sam. He remembered seeing the foot. He didn't see it coming, only the impact of the foot, inches away from his own head, into the face of the man with the gun. The man flew backwards and then down to the ground, unconscious.

Sam plopped to the ground in a sitting position. He hadn't meant to, it just happened. As he landed on his ass, he watched as the second of his two captors was thrown head first into the side of the Dodge truck. The man slid down the side of the truck and rolled back and forth on the ground. Clint Smith searched him and pulled a knife out of one of the man's pockets.

"You okay, Sam?"

Recognition set in and Sam saw Jim West holding the pistol that had been dropped.

"I think so, Jim. Thanks."

"Thank Clint, he did all the work."

"Thanks, Clint. You guys probably saved my life."

"Thank Jim," Clint said as he stood back up. "He recognized you and saw the gun. He had it all figured out and told me. My part was the easy part."

Sam looked back at the guy Clint had kicked in the face. Sam thought the guy might be dead. The other guy had moved to a sitting position. Sam noticed blood streaming lightly down his face.

"Let me help you up," Clint said, offering Sam a hand.

"Thanks," Sam accepted the help. He still didn't think he had the strength to stand, but his head had begun to clear, and he felt like his breathing was back to normal. "I think these are the two guys who committed the murder in my building."

"Thought they might be," Jim said, "but I thought you said you didn't see or hear anything."

"I didn't, but a few minutes ago when I left my condo for lunch, the door was open a few inches. I heard something and looked in. That's when they grabbed me. I guess because I saw them."

"You're lucky they didn't kill you right then and there," Clint said.

"I think that guy," Sam looked down at the still unconscious figure, "would have, but the other guy cautioned him about the noise."

"I would have just used this," Clint said holding up the knife.

Sam shuddered. "I guess I'm glad he wasn't you. Did one of you call the police?"

"Didn't need to," Jim said and pointed to the small crowd that had gathered where the parking lot gave way to a path that led to the beach. "My bet is one or more of those guys have already called them."

He had no sooner said that when the sound of sirens could be heard. "Where you learn how to do that?" Sam asked Clint.

"You mean fight?" Clint asked.

"Yes."

"I was the only boy in the family of five kids. Got tired of them always kicking my ass."

Sam smiled and knew Clint had to be joking, but he didn't press the issue. The first police vehicle pulled in with a sudden stop. He noticed that Jim had already lowered the pistol and held it flat in his hand.

Despite the calm at the scene, the two policemen who emerged from the vehicle took positions behind the open doors of the police car and aimed their weapons at Sam and his entourage.

"Hands up, palms facing me, and put the gun on the ground!"

Sam noticed Clint and Jim had already started moving in anticipation of the command. Sam hurriedly shot his arms skyward.

"We're the good guys!" he shouted, embarrassed that his voice had taken that high pitch again.

"Take it easy, Sam," Jim said calmly.

Once the pistol was on the ground, the two cops approached them. A second police vehicle pulled in next to the first. The two officers whom Sam had met jumped out of the car and joined the first two.

"Officer Morris," Sam said pleased that she had shown up, and surprised that her name had somehow come to him at this moment. "These are your two killers."

She looked at the two men on the ground.

"I thought you said you didn't know the killers," she said.

"I didn't. They came back. I heard a noise in the condo where those guys were killed. I was walking by when I heard it, and the door was open a little. I peeked in. I thought you were there. That's when they grabbed me. They would have killed me if it wasn't for them."

She glanced at Jim and Clint, her eyes lingering a little longer on Clint.

"Better cuff those two," she said to the other three policemen. Turning back to Sam, she leaned in and whispered, "Hoping it was me?"

Sam didn't know what to say. Was she flirting with him or pulling his leg? Too startled to feel flattered, he simply nodded his head and wondered why some women intimidated him.

An unmarked police vehicle showed up along with an ambulance. Morris walked over to greet the person getting out of the passenger seat of the car. The guy had a lot of stars on his shoulder boards.

"Probably the chief," Jim said.

Sam noticed he was the only one still holding his hands in the air. One of the policemen had taken Clint aside. He looked like he might know Clint. Sam lowered his arms and edged closer to Jim.

Officer Morris motioned with her hand for Sam to come over. "Yes," Sam said when he approached them.

"Sam, would you repeat to the Captain what you told me a minute ago about how you, umm, how you met these two guys?" she asked.

"Sure," Sam said. He recited the events starting with his departure from his condo and hearing the noise from the condo next door.

"So they said that they got what they came for, but they didn't say what it was?" the Captain asked.

"That's correct."

"Why do you think the two are the killers?" Officer Morris.

"Well, I don't know. They said they came back, so they've been there before, and because they were going to kill me just for seeing them."

Morris looked at the Captain.

"Between us, that makes sense, but we'll need to hold off any claims until we get a match with ballistics, a confession, or something that'll hold up in court."

"Good point, sir," Officer Morris said.

Sam also thought the Captain's remarks made sense, but he couldn't help but feel that Morris was so quick to agree with her boss, that she would have agreed with him if he said the two men were from Mars.

"Sam, you're handling this thing pretty well. Most civilians would have been pretty shook up over all this."

"I was a little nervous," Sam said. "My two friends saved me."

"That's Clint Smith over there, isn't it, Joan?" the Captain asked.

"Oh, yes, that's who it is. I knew I'd seen him before," she said. "I imagine those two never knew what hit them."

"I think they were a bit surprised," Sam said.

Two medical technicians rolled the still unconscious man to the ambulance on a stretcher. A single cop escorted the other suspect to the back seat of a police vehicle.

Sam, Jim, and Clint hitched a ride in another police vehicle to the police station where they spent the next two hours making official statements. Somehow, toward the end of their interviews either Jim or Clint brought up that Sam had landed a giant fish the day before.

Sam spent the last five minutes at the station trying to downplay what Jim and Clint had exaggerated into a record-breaking catch. Whereas only four police officers handled the interviews regarding the capture of the two suspects, the entire police force came in to listen to the fish tale.

When they left, Sam was a little disappointed that Clint and Jim had to rush off to meet some female doctor flying in from Massachusetts. Supposedly she had decided to bring a female friend at the last minute, and Clint wanted Jim to tag along for support. Jim didn't look all that excited about the idea but had agreed to help Clint out.

Sam decided to walk the mile back to his condo. He had missed lunch, and the restaurant was on the way. Besides, he had a lot on his mind. Could he be dreaming all this? Things like this didn't happen to Sam Wiesel. He was the kid no one picked to be on their team. The guy who went to one college reunion only to have no one remember him. The teacher who joined three coworkers at a teacher workshop, only to have them say he should have come to the crazy, crowded, happy hour the night before. He remembered being too embarrassed to say he had attended the event for over an hour.

For the past twenty-four hours he had not only been the center of attention, he had been somebody whom even he had to acknowledge had accomplished or survived a couple of significant ordeals. Perhaps more importantly, he felt accepted. It seemed like every cop in the building shook his hand before he left. Jim and Clint said they looked forward to seeing him again, in court if not before.

Sam thought about calling his wife. He hadn't talked to her since the day he arrived when he told her that he had made it safely to the island. He knew they had grown apart over the last few years, and while he rarely acknowledged it, he knew the fault was mostly his. It's hard to love someone else when you don't like your life, and you don't even like yourself.

When he ordered his enchiladas, he figured they'd be dinner rather than lunch, so he ordered a bottle of Sol beer to go along with the food. He enjoyed his ritual of having a beer with dinner down here on the island. Not that he couldn't have a beer when he wanted to at home, he just didn't.

His phone rang in his pocket. The sound surprised him. Other than an occasional call from his wife, he almost never received calls.

"Hello," he said.

"Mr. Sam?" a young man's voiced asked.

"Yes, that's me."

"This is Jay. I got a break on that project you asked me to work on. You know the statue of the booby."

"You did?"

"Yes. I wasn't finding much until I discovered a research paper published in Spanish in a small Mexican university magazine. It was in a special edition about missing Aztec relics. I'll translate it for you."

"That's great Jay, you're a genius!"

"And guess what?"

"I don't know," Sam said.

"I made contact with the author. She works for the same university now. So far I've only verified that she is the author of the article. But I've also asked her a bunch of questions in an email that I hope she'll answer. She implied that she would," Jay said.

"That's fantastic. Think you'll get a response by the morning?"

"I hope so. The questions I asked she should be able to answer off the top of her head."

"Is your Mom still fine with all this?"

"Oh yeah."

"Then I'll see you in the morning, Jay. Tell your Mom hello for me."

"I will. See you tomorrow."

"Well how about that!" Sam said to the server who arrived with his dinner.

"Pardon me?" asked the man.

"There may really be a *Golden Booby.*"

The waiter leaned in close when he placed the plate on the table. "The flesh ones are just fine with me."

"No, I mean the bird. The bird."

The waiter looked confused and a little embarrassed.

"I guess I thought the same thing the first time I heard about it, too, but I'm talking about a statue of a bird that's made of gold," Sam said.

"Oro?"

"Yes, oro. Gold."

"You have it?" the server asked.

"No. I wish. It would be worth millions, but no, I don't have it."

"Do you know where it is?"

"No. Right now I'm just happy to find out that it may exist," Sam said.

The server gave him an odd look and left.

"Probably thinks I'm a bit loony," Sam said to himself.

He ate the rest of the meal in silence thinking about the dream from the night before. It would be nice to discover a treasure. Nice? He laughed at himself. He thought it was remarkable when he won five dollars on a two-dollar lottery scratch off. Finding a buried treasure, that would fall more in the incredibly marvelous category.

~ Chapter ~
7

He heard the doorbell to the condo ring. At least he thought he did. He sat up in bed and listened. The bell rang again. Sam looked over at the radio clock next to the bed.

"Crap!" he shouted to himself. He had overslept. In fifteen minutes, he was supposed to be at breakfast.

The bell rang again.

He climbed out of bed and walked out to the door. He opened the door about six inches and peered out. To his surprise, a young woman stood there alone. She was about average height and build, but had a cute faced ringed with short, curly, brown hair. She wore a navy blue pants suit and carried a small briefcase that gave her a professional look.

"Mr. Wiesel?" she asked. "Yes, that's me."

"I'm sorry if I woke you, sir."

Sam didn't say anything. His first inclination was to make some kind of rude comment.

"Mr. Wiesel, I'm with the *South Padre Island News*. I'd like to interview you about the terrible incident that happened to you yesterday."

"Me?" he asked.

"Yes. It must have been terrifying," she said.

"I can't right now. I have to get to a meeting."

"How about later today? I can meet you at any time that's convenient to you."

Sam didn't know what to say. Something in the back of his mind said it might not be too smart to say anything to the press, but he had never been interviewed for a newspaper before. Besides, she seemed to only being her job, and she was cute. Funny how a woman's appearance always affected his thinking. He wondered if other men were affected by a pretty face.

"I guess you could come back around eleven."

"Okay, I'll see you at eleven. Thanks, sir." She turned and walked away.

Sam dressed quickly and left for his breakfast meeting. On the way he wondered why he hadn't asked for the reporter's name. He wished he had, because he thought it would have been prudent to call the paper to verify that she was an employee. What if she was with the two men who abducted him?

He arrived five minutes late. He saw Jay and his mother at the same table they had selected the day before. They appeared to be in good moods as both were laughing about something.

"Good morning, sorry I'm late," Sam said.

"You're fine," Jane said. "We haven't even ordered breakfast yet."

"Good morning," Jay said. "I got a lot of info for you."

"Why don't we all order breakfast first, then you can brief Mr. Wiesel."

"Makes sense to me, and while I know I'll say it again, Jay, I really appreciate your helping me out."

Jay and Jane ordered eggs and sausage, and Sam ordered a Pecan waffle.

"Remember, I'm buying breakfast for both of you, so order anything you want," Sam said.

"Oh, that's not really necessary. Jay had a good time doing it."

"I did, and I made a neat contact at a college down in Mexico. I told Mom I might go down there to college."

"No way," Jane said. "You get your undergraduate degree in the States. After that you can get another degree anywhere you like and you can afford."

"Makes good sense to me," Sam said.

"I think he's just interested in the contact he made down there," Jane said.

Jay grinned. "You saw her picture, too. Besides she's not that much older than me."

"Ha! She'd have you for breakfast."

Jay rolled his eyes and made an expression that Sam interpreted as "and that would be bad?"

"She's a member of the faculty there," Jay said.

Sam nodded. He remembered a professor at his college who he had a crush on for his entire senior year.

The breakfasts arrived, and the three started eating.

"Do you mind if I start telling you what I found out while we're still eating?" Jay asked.

"Go right ahead," Sam said and pulled a pen and small notepad out of his pocket.

"I had a real hard time getting anything at first. All my searches kept taking me back to that actual, living bird. A lot of people have done a lot of research on the booby. More than I would have ever guessed. Every time I thought I had something, it fizzled. Under a search for bird worshippers or Aztec gods who protected the birds, I got my first break."

"The Aztecs primarily occupied Mexico?" Sam asked.

"Their empire covered nearly a fourth of the western hemisphere at one time, but the heart of the empire was in Mexico. The interesting thing is that both the Incas and the Mayans had a similar fascination with birds, along with their own sets of gods."

"So is this statue an Aztec relic or what?" Sam asked.

"What Anna told me —"

"Anna is the woman in Mexico he's been chatting with on Facebook half the night," Jane said.

"Only until midnight, and besides, this is a topic that has fascinated her, too," Jay said.

"So what did Anna tell you?" Sam asked.

"That until someone finds the statue, and it can be studied, we won't know its exact origin."

"Why is that?"

"Well, she knows the Aztecs had the statue at one time, and like your friend told you, a Spanish governor general stole it from the descendents of the Aztecs. He kept it secret from the Spanish crown, and his descendents did the same. Of course, his descendents stayed in Mexico but didn't even tell the new governor general about it."

"Can't blame them," Sam said.

"Not if they wanted to keep it," Jane said.

"Well, then came the Mexican revolution and the statue was seized by a powerful Mexican family. That's where it has remained over the last couple centuries. That family was questioned by the Mexican government and denies ever seeing it. They claim that they heard stories of the "Golden Booby" from their grandparents, but that it allegedly disappeared some eighty years ago."

"Are the grandparents still alive?" Sam asked.

"Oh no, they died in the sixties."

"Probably the great grandparents of those alive today or maybe even the great, great grandparents," Jane said.

"So no one has seen it for years?" Sam asked.

"That's right, unless the current family members are lying. Anna doesn't think they are, but she did say the family has been lying to the authorities for years about it, so she wouldn't be surprised if they were still lying."

"What about the origin of the statue? You were going to say something about it earlier," Sam said.

"That's right. Anna said that the Aztecs may have stolen the statue themselves from an earlier empire. The empires of both the Incans and the Mayans overlapped each other as well as part of Aztec empire. In addition to raping and pillaging, they would usually steal anything valuable they could find."

"Jay, I think pillaging means stealing," Jane said.

"And the Aztecs were the last of the great Western civilizations," Sam added. "Did your friend Anna mention anything about the Capone connection?"

"No, but that fascinated her, and I think is what kept her chatting with me for so long. She wanted to know all about it. I hope you don't mind that I shared it with her."

"No problem at all."

"Good, because she said that sort of jived, that's her word, but I like it, with one of the stories that the family's grandparents told them." Jay paused for a second as he finished off a whole piece of bacon in one bite.

Sam saw Jane shake her head at Jay's table manners.

"Supposedly the brother of one of the grandparents disappeared in the thirties. No one knew where or what may have happened to him. Stories that they heard at the time suggested he was double crossed and killed during some business transaction."

"That could be with the Capone gang," Sam said.

"That's what she thinks, too, but she has never been able to develop any information that puts the booby in the US."

"Good work, Jay," Sam said.

"But that's not all. There's a curse that goes with the booby." "A curse?"

"Yes sir. The legend has it that as long as a person can maintain possession of the statue, then fortune will be theirs. However, loss of the statue brings death to the owner," Jay explained.

"Sounds a little far-fetched," Sam said.

"Well, it fits with the history of the booby. You know the Aztecs taking it from people they conquered and likely killed. The Spanish taking it from the Aztecs after conquering them. The Mexicans from the Spanish during the civil war, and now Capone."

"It also could explain why the families who had possession of it kept its existence secret," Jane added.

"That's right," Sam said. "On the bright side, if you can hang onto it until you die then your life might be a rich one. You did say having it brings you fortune."

"If you believe all that stuff," Jane said.

"Only one way to find out," Sam said, "find it and turn it in for the reward."

"You wouldn't want to melt it down and sell the gold and gemstones separately?" Jane asked.

"It would be tempting, and a couple of days ago I might have said yes," Sam said.

"I would contact Anna and split the reward with her," Jay said. "She said the Mexican government would pay a lot of money for its return."

"So you wouldn't melt it down either?" Sam asked Jay.

"No way. Anna said she would become a national hero if she found it and returned it to Mexico. She said she would collaborate with me on a book and share the royalties, too."

"Sounds like a very good idea," Sam said, and he was surprised at how much he meant it.

"That's about everything I can remember. I'm sorry I couldn't find out anything definite that puts the statue here on the island. Anna said that while the Capone connection was worth pursuing, she doubted that the brother would have brought the statue with him if he planned all along to double cross Capone."

"That's true. I imagine his death may have been just a good way to point those searching for the statue in a different direction," Sam said.

"Mom, can I run, I mean stumble, around the corner to the comic book place?" Jay asked.

"It's fine with me, but have you answered all the questions that Sam might have for you?"

"Is there anything else that you want to ask?" Jay asked.

"No. You did a great job, Jay. I'm honestly impressed."

"It was my pleasure. I enjoyed it. See you in a bit, Mom." Jay walked off with the aid of his cane.

"He seems to be doing pretty good with the cane," Sam said.

"He is."

"I wish my students had been as eager as he is to learn something new."

"Oh. He's not always this eager. You just found something that got his interest."

Sam realized that in his statement he had put himself back in the role of a teacher, something that he had walked away from a few years ago. He didn't think the move to a new profession had made him any happier. In fact, if he was honest to himself, it had likely only made things worse.

"Well, whether I did or didn't, he still impressed me with his ability to develop so much information in such a short period of time," Sam said.

"He's a good boy," Jane acknowledged. "I don't know if you want my opinion or not, but I think you should go back into teaching. You have a manner about you that I know made Jay more comfortable than he would have been with most strangers who wanted him to do something."

"I think teenagers these days are very comfortable looking up things on the internet."

"True," Jane said, "but there is something more there, believe me. You have a good manner with kids. At least with Jay you did, and I imagine that comes naturally with you."

They talked for another fifteen minutes before they went their separate ways. Sam drifted back to his condo. His discussion with Jane had germinated into an idea that he had not let himself consider in the past few years. The prospect of going back into teaching had him both nervous and intrigued.

When he quit teaching, he had blamed the education system, the students, and their parents. Deep down he knew he also accepted it as another one of his own failures in life. Perhaps, though, he had simply needed a break. Everyone got burned out once in a while. He knew that ninety-nine percent of the teachers he had ever known looked forward to summer vacation. They needed a time to regenerate. Maybe that was all that he had needed.

"I'm glad you're back," a female voice shouted at him from in front of his building.

He looked over and saw the perky, young reporter who had wanted to interview him earlier that day.

"Something has come up, and I was hoping could do the interview a little early," she said as he crossed the street to her.

"Oh, sure," he said. "Would you like to come up to my apartment?"

"Please, and I promise I won't take up much of your time."

"Would you like a cup of coffee or a coke?" he asked once they were inside.

"No, but thanks. I just need to get a few specifics from you. You know: the correct spelling of your name, your home address, what brings you to SPI?"

Sam rattled off the answers. However, he didn't say coming to South Padre was his attempt to escape his real life. Besides inviting questions he didn't want to address, he suddenly felt that was actually a stupid thing to say, or for himself to believe.

"I'm surprised you're willing to go outside today. I think, if I went through what you did yesterday, I'd be hiding in my house or fleeing the island altogether."

"That's a good point. I can't really explain why the incident hasn't affected me more than it has. You know, I was terrified when they took me out of the building and to their car. I had no doubt that they were going to kill me."

They talked for almost fifteen minutes before she said she had everything she needed.

Sam thought she had done a very thorough job at getting to all the facts and to his emotions throughout the entire event.

At the door she turned to him and asked, "Can I say to Clint Smith that you recommended I interview him, too?"

"Sure, uh ... I never got your name." Sam said.

"Bonnie." She answered as she left, and Sam wondered if getting the intro to Clint might have been her primary objective in the interview. After all, she didn't ask about Jim West. It seemed like a lot of women on the island were interested in Clint.

~ Chapter ~
8

The police had his home address and phone number and had told him he could leave the island whenever he wanted. He might have to come back and testify at some point, but they believed the trial might not occur for a year, and that the two men would likely try for a plea bargain agreement to avoid a trial altogether.

Sam thought about leaving right then and there. Feeling emotions that he had long thought were gone forever, he actually wanted to get into his car and drive home. He pulled his cell phone out of his pocket and started to dial his wife. He stopped short of completing the call and put the phone back into his pocket. He would wait until this evening to call his wife at the prearranged time they used to always call each other when they were separated. It was a habit he suddenly regretted having let lapse.

Instead of making the call, Sam went out to the beach to take a long stroll along the water's edge. He wanted to think things through and commit to whatever decision he made. Besides, this would give him another chance to stumble across the *Golden Booby*. Ha! Wouldn't that be something?

The *Golden Booby*, he thought. What an interesting legend, especially with all the mysteries that surrounded it. He wondered how much of what he heard was true. He also wondered if he went back to teaching and gave his students a semester, or even a year, to come up with more info on the statue and the legend, could they uncover something new.

He knew about Itzpapalotl, the Aztec Goddess of Fire and Birds, and he imagined if the Aztecs had stolen the statue from the descendents of the Mayans or Incans that those cultures likely had a similar god or goddess. He also remembered something about the Quetzalcoati bird and the Aztecs. Finally, how about the curse that implied both wealth with the statue's possession, but death with its loss? He had no doubt that as a group research project it would be a fun and educational activity for his students.

At ten o'clock he dialed his wife's cell.

"Hello," she answered, somewhat more softly than he anticipated.

"Hi, sugar," Sam said and immediately realized he hadn't called her that in a long, long time.

"You sound like you're in a good mood," she said.

"I guess I am. This has been an odd week for me, really odd." He thought she might say or ask something, but she didn't.

"It's hard to explain, honey, but in the last few days I've caught a near record-sized fish, been involved in a murder investigation, kidnapped at gun point, and have learned about a buried treasure."

"What? Did you say kidnapped? Are you okay? Buried treasure, really?" she asked in a fast sequence that gave him no chance to respond.

"Yes, it's called the *Golden Booby...*"

"Booby?"

"Yes. It's a statue of the bird," Sam explained.

"Did you find it?"

"No, no, and I don't really know if it even exists. It's just that this week has really had an impact on me. Maybe it was Jay more than anything else."

"Sam, were you really kidnapped? You're not making any sense."

"I know. I'll explain more when I get home, but the important thing is I want to tell you that I'm sorry for the way I've been for the past few," he paused for a moment as the significance of the next word that he was going to say hit his mind with the same surprise and pain that the fish hook had made with his finger earlier in the week, "years."

"Oh let's don't go into all that," she said. He thought she almost sounded defensive.

"No, I need to let you know that I'm sorry. I want to come home and try to be a different person for you than I've been. I also want to try to get my old teaching job back."

"What?" her voice so soft that he barely heard her.

They didn't talk much longer. He said he would explain it all in more detail when he got home early in the afternoon the next day.

Stella hung up the phone. A tear broke free from the rest of the moisture that had built up in her eyes and rolled down her cheek. He had sounded like he had meant it, but could he change? She wanted him to, and more than once had tried to talk to him about depression, a condition she was certain he had long suffered.

She looked out the window at the bright sign that advertised the hotel's presence and made up her mind. She would leave early in the morning and drive back to their home in Dallas. Her drive from Amarillo would be shorter than his. She'd get there, destroy the note she had left him about leaving and divorce, and unpack her things before he would get home. Perhaps one day she'd tell him that she had driven off that afternoon to never return, but not now, and not for a long while.

THE PROFESSOR

David Harry

~ Preface ~

Port Isabel/South Padre Island Press

Police, responding to a call from a *Sutherland's* employee, found the body of a partially decomposed man at approximately eleven PM last night. *Sutherland's* is located in a shopping strip directly across from where Route 48 intersects Route 100 in Port Isabel. The deceased, who was discovered lying face down under a dumpster, has not been identified. He is believed to be homeless. A police spokesperson said, "This incident is being listed as a homicide until we receive the coroner's report. Persons having knowledge of a missing person are encouraged to call the police."

~ Chapter ~
1

Belle Neuva found a parking spot almost directly in front of the Port Isabel police station. She dutifully applied her parking brake, slipped the shift lever into park, and reached for the ignition key. She sat back in her seat contemplating her next moves. On the one hand, her grandfather had gone missing and finding him was her top priority. On the other hand, from as far back as she could remember his advice had been to keep her distance from the police. "Get them in your business and you'll never get them out," he had counseled on more than one occasion.

Taking a deep breath to settle herself, she once again went over why she was here. Her grandfather didn't answer his phone. He also didn't answer when she knocked on the door of his mobile home. It was parked in what to her was a disgusting lot on the edge of town. The trailers on that lot might have been respectable at one time, but now they were mostly rusting shells slowly sinking into the sandy earth.

Her reluctance to seek police help was bolstered by the fact this wasn't the first time her grandfather had gone missing. But those disappearances had been accounted for because of his occupation. From as early as she could remember he would disappear for long periods at a time. Suddenly reappearing, he usually had a present for her — and a story to tell of exciting adventures. Was this disappearance just Granddaddy being Granddaddy?

What harm would it be to ask the police if they had seen him? At eighty-five any number of things could be wrong. The hospital claimed no knowledge of August Villanova, but she was not certain they would acknowledge his presence even if he was a patient.

Taking another deep breath, Belle stepped from the car and marched toward the one-story unimposing building. Inside, she paused, once again steeling herself for the ordeal certain to follow.

"Can I direct you?" The voice startled her. Belle looked up to find a woman sitting at a small table. "Are you looking for the police or the offices?" The woman's soft eyes were in counterpoint to her hardened face. Sensing Belle's confusion, she said, "Go that way for police," the woman said, motioning toward Belle's left. "The city offices are this way." The woman pointed in the opposite direction.

Without acknowledging the assistance, Belle turned to her left and walked slowly down the hallway, pausing before going through the doorway at the end. A uniformed woman police officer sat at a small table staring blankly at a computer screen. Without looking up, the officer said, "What's your problem?"

"I don't...know if...if this is the right place or not. And I don't have a problem."

"This is the police station. The clerk's offices are down the other hall. Make up your mind."

"Police is right, but I...I came to see if you have any information on my grandfather."

The officer looked up and studied Belle a moment. Then becoming interested she asked, "Is he missing?"

"I think so. But I don't actually know. He's done this before."

"Done what?"

"Not answering his phone. But usually it's because he lost it some place."

"Did you go to his house? Does he live here in Port Isabel?"

"No answer there either, I'm afraid."

"Age?"

"Eighty-five or so. I'm not exactly sure."

The officer typed something into a keyboard, studied the screen for a while, then said, "Nothing here. No open files. The one we did have was claimed. No one else that age has been reported missing — or found."

"What about the hospital?"

"Does he have dementia? Alzheimer's?"

"The last time I spoke with him he was fine."

"And when was that?"

Embarrassed by the question, Belle's cheeks grew hot. "About a month ago. Maybe a little less than that. But not much." Reacting to what she perceived as a disapproving glance, Belle added, " I usually call every week, but I...I've been busy. Traveling in Mexico."

"Take a seat over there. I'll take down his information and we'll file a missing person's report. He'll turn up. They always do." Boredom gone, the officer was now fully engaged.

As Belle answered the questions, a picture emerged of a man by the name of August Villanova, age 85, retired Texas Southernmost College professor of natural science living alone in the *Paradise Found* trailer lot. Villanova, according to his granddaughter, was a man who since his retirement in 1991 kept to himself. His wife had died seven years before the retirement and since that time Villanova kept mostly to himself.

"And your name is?"

"Annabelle Neuva. But I go by Belle."

"Birth date?"

"Two, three, eighty-three."

"Occupation?"

"Teacher."

"Oh, like grandfather, like granddaughter."

"Only I teach in Mexico. He taught in Brownsville."

"Relationship to the missing person?"

"As I told you. He's my grandfather." As the questions continued, all Belle could think of was fleeing the drab building. She had already given this woman more information than she had ever given anyone in her life. She was now convinced it had been a mistake coming here in the first place. The hole seemed to be getting deeper by the minute.

Finally, the officer looked away from her screen. "I'm sorry your grandfather is not responding to your calls. Possibly he's on a trip somewhere — or just out fishing. Lots of our retired folks go out for several days. Bring back more fish than they can possibly eat."

"He's not a fisherman. But he does love being on the water, that much I do know." The vision of her and her grandfather out on the water together flooded over her. He loved to sail, but never went out alone. Hopefully he didn't break his own rule and do something stupid.

"Before when I asked you if he had any distinguishing marks or tattoos, you hesitated. The more information you recall, the easier it will be to get a match in the database. Now-a-days the computers do all the work. But computers need data to match. You have anything more I can put in?"

"Do scars count?"

"What type of scars?"

"I think an arrow — or a spear — went through his right shoulder. When I was young he took me out in a kayak. His shirt got wet and I saw the scar. It was puffy and...and nasty looking. He said it didn't hurt him and he never complained about it. The only thing he would tell me was that he got hurt in Peru."

"Peru?"

"Are we done yet?" Belle was uncomfortable getting into this topic. Peru had nothing to do with his going missing — not this long after his retirement. She now had to get the door closed on this data gathering. Her grandfather had been right, give them an inch and...

"Just about," the officer replied. "I'll enter this report and it'll take a few minutes to process. We'll see if there are any hits." The officer returned her attention to the keyboard. A few moments later she announced, "Finished! It's now in the hands of the data gods." She swiveled toward Belle, but before she could say anything her computer pinged and paper began spilling out of the printer. "We have a match!"

"Where is he? Is he—"

"I'm sorry to have to be the one who tells you this, but a man matching his description was found over behind *Sutherland's* three days ago. Shows here his grandson made a positive identification. That's why it was not in our open files. According to the autopsy he was in his mid 80s and his right clavicle evidenced an old wound of the type you described."

Belle's stomach involuntarily tightened and a wave of nausea made her close her eyes. She wrapped her arms around herself, as if to keep herself from falling.

The officer came over to her. "Can I get you a drink of water?"

The question was met with silence.

"If you require the rest room, it is —"

Belle stumbled to her feet, put the palms of her hands on the desk, and in a tone she intended as menacing, but came out closer to a whimper, demanded, "Why didn't anyone call me? There's something wrong here. I'm his only grandchild, and I'm listed as his guardian."

"You say your name is Annabelle Neuva and you're the granddaughter of August Villanova? "

The sudden seriousness in the officer's eyes — a seriousness that signaled that her full attention was now focused on Belle — sent a chill down Bella's spine. "Of course he's my grandfather. I should know my own —"

"Indeed, Miss Neuva, there is something wrong. There appears to be an inconsistency in the data. The dental records, together with a positive physical identification from a close family member, matched a person by the name of Simpson Hugo.

"And just who is this *close family member*?"

The officer consulted the printout. "A Mr. Oscar Hugo. He's the grandson of the deceased."

"Then it's not my grandfather!" Visible relief flooded Belle. "I'm sorry I've wasted your time." She turned to leave.

"Not so fast young lady," the officer called. "The fingerprints of the deceased do, in fact, match the name of a man by the name of August Villanova."

~ CHAPTER ~
2

Belle was ushered into a small windowless room and told to wait. Wait for what, she didn't know. The desk and single chair suggested that the room might have been an office at one time, but there were no files or papers. A single used Styrofoam cup, a brown coffee stain along the rim, was the room's only artifact. It was strange how such an object imparted a past life on the room.

Finally, the door opened and a man wearing an ill-fitting faded blue-plaid sport jacket, rumpled grey slacks, and a tie hanging loosely around his neck came through the door. "Miss Neuva, thanks for waiting. I'm Detective Vega. I am truly sorry about your grandfather."

"I didn't know I had a choice. I mean about waiting."

Ignoring the sarcasm, and the implied rebuke, Vega continued, "I suppose you should know that while you were waiting I went ahead and put a hold on the cremation. It was scheduled at Buck Ashcraft's funeral home, over in Harlingen, for — actually your timing was perfect — right about now."

"Cremation! Grandpa didn't want to be cremated. He wanted a full military funeral. Honor guard and all."

"Let me understand this. Your grandfather is August Villanova. Is that what I am to understand?"

'Yes."

"And he lived here in town?"

"In the *Paradise Found* trailer lot. I told it all to the officer out there."

"Just verifying. Don't believe in working from bad information. Do you know a person by the name of Simpson Hugo?"

"No."

"Ever hear that name before? In any context?"

"No. Should I have?"

"That's what I'm trying to determine. Does the name Oscar Hugo mean anything to you?"

"No."

"Not a relative? Cousin, anything?"

"No."

"Well, he claims your grandfather, August Villanova, is his grandfather as well."

"He's lying! I'm the only grandchild!"

Vega allowed Bella's outburst to pass. "Mind taking me out to your grandfather's place. Have a look around?"

"You mean look around the trailer park?"

"I mean look around inside his place. See what we can find out about… your grandfather."

"No. I mean I do mind."

"I was hoping you'd be cooperative and do this the easy way."

"What would the hard way be?"

"I get a court order. It'll take a while. Meanwhile, we'll seal the trailer. You don't go inside until we're finished, however long it takes us."

"What about his things? Maybe he left instructions for his…funeral."

"Maybe he did. Maybe he didn't," Vega said, continuing his bluff. "Funeral will be long over by the time you're allowed inside."

"How do I know you won't take stuff that belongs to him?" Belle's mental inventory of her grandfather's small living quarters satisfied her that the police would find nothing of monetary value. But she was just stubborn enough to know that if the police were interested then she should also be interested.

"You don't. And we probably will, as you say, take stuff. Particularly if we find evidence of foul play."

The vision of her grandfather being killed in his own bed and then dragged to a filthy lot flashed into mind. "And what exactly does that mean?"

"It means if there is evidence of, shall we say, of someone assisting your grandfather to meet his maker, then we'll take it."

"I can't believe—"

"I'm not saying it happened that way. We just want to run everything to ground. Would you be kind enough to allow us to accompany you to the trailer? We can do this together. That way you'll see what we see."

Belle's response was more in the nature of a nod than anything that came out of her mouth.

After the police left, Belle stood in the doorway, not wanting to remain in the trailer and not wanting to leave. During the brief investigation her thoughts had dwelled on the Brownsville house, with its large yard and swimming pool, a crooked old tree weaving its way to heaven. She had often played in that tree. For one brief summer, she had held tea parties in the tree house her grandfather built for her. Hurricane Bret ended the parties and in hindsight now, marked the end of her childhood. Her parents were lost a few months later on a flight across Peru to join the Professor, as her father liked to call his father-in-law, on one of his many exploratory excavations.

The Professor blamed himself for the loss of her parents and did everything he could to make it up to Belle. She spent her high school years living in that wonderfully magnificent house — only the house didn't seem so wonderful after her parents were gone, even though the Professor reduced his travels and spent his evenings talking to her about his adventures in Peru. On special nights, he would also tell her of his travels in the South Pacific. He had great stories of research in the Galapagos Islands and as far west as the Vanuatu Islands.

In her eighteenth year, and just before high school graduation, cancer took her grandmother Clare. Everything changed at once. She went off to UT Dallas and her grandfather resumed his travels. Explorations, he called them. They would spend two weeks together each summer, but never doing explorations together. When she pressed, all he would say was, "I killed your parents doing that. I can't bear to have anything happen to you. Study hard in school and someday you'll make your own explorations."

Despite her protests that their deaths were not his fault, he would not relent — but as her education advanced, he would consult with her on projects and during the summers, she cataloged his findings. By the time she graduated with her bachelors degree in South American history, she was more than ready to pass any PhD exam.

Moving back home after college graduation proved to be a mistake. The house seemed empty. At first she believed the feeling came from the absence of her grandmother. But it was more than that. At first she was puzzled as to what had happened, but the puzzle was solved the next afternoon when she climbed out of the pool, dried herself off, and turned to drape the wet towel over the urn that had been beside the chaise for as long as she could remember. The urn was gone.

She looked around the pool area on the chance that it had been moved. All the artwork that had been in the yard was gone. She knew from her cataloging work that those pieces had all come from Peru — pre-Incan art at its very best.

Later in the day, the missing yard art gained significance when she realized that other art objects inside the house were missing as well. She dug through old pictures taken at a happier time trying to get a sense of what exactly was missing. It didn't take long for her to realize that almost all of the three-dimensional art pieces, both inside and out, were gone.

Do all old people do this, she wondered. One day living in a grand old house and the next in a trailer park. Extreme, but perhaps not unusual. People downsized their lives, and in the process squeezed out life's possessions. It's as if her grandfather had pushed his life aside — or left it behind. When she had asked him about the boxes of old photos that were in the garage when the Brownsville house was sold, he had been most definite. "I'm finished with them, my dear Belle. Finished. Give them away."

"Now who in the world would want your old pictures?"

"Then burn them for all that I care. You can't live backward. Someday you'll learn. Always move forward. Look ahead, not back."

"But your family, they're all here."

"Belle, my dear. You are my family now. Just come visit me, be with me as I grow old. That's all I ask. The rest, everyone I care about, are gone."

"But —"

"There are no buts, except for sitting on."

Belle turned to face back into the dimly lit trailer, tears making it hard to focus. Before locking the door, she reached for her phone and snapped a picture. Then a second. And a third. This is not the way she had envisioned it ending. Not with all she had done for him in Mexico and elsewhere. "Grandfather," she said, not caring who heard her, "it wasn't supposed to end this way. What have you done? What have you done?"

~ CHAPTER ~
3

It is normally a forty-minute drive from Port Isabel to Harlingen, but it took Belle slightly over an hour. She played and replayed her conversations with Detective Vega. Pieces were missing. Maybe pieces that were not important for police work, but they certainly were to her. Starting off with a lack of bank account info, tax records, or even a checkbook. Nothing was found in the trailer. "Who paid his bills?" Detective Vega had asked. "Someone must have been paying the trailer lot rental and the cable bill." He never asked her directly so Belle didn't volunteer that, in fact, she had been in charge of her grandfather's finances for several years. Nor did she volunteer anything else that she had been doing for him.

From what Belle understood from years of watching CSI, the police had found nothing of importance to lead them to suspect foul play at the trailer. No drawers were found half-opened, their contents spilled on the floor. Nothing was knocked over; no sofa was slit open; no blood-stained knife was lying on the floor; no gun lay smoldering in the corner. Most important, no traces of blood were visible anywhere. The police were finished — at least with this round — in less than a half-hour.

On the drive to Harlingen, Belle realized that she hadn't been told the cause of death. She recalled Vega saying something like, "...evidence of, shall we say, of someone assisting your grandfather to meet his maker." But those words meant nothing. Had he been shot? Or stabbed? Those forms of death were without ambiguity. So was suffocating, strangulation, burning, and poisoning. The harder she worked at listing possible causes of death, the slower she drove.

"Mr. Ashcraft please," Belle said to the man who greeted her as she came through the door of the funeral home. "I need to see Mr. Ashcraft. It's important."

"I'm Fernando de Cordoba, chief assistant. The others are not here at the moment. How may I help you?"

"My grandfather is here — and I want to see him."

"His name?"

"August Villanova."

"I am most sorry, we do not have—"

"Maybe you have a…a." Belle struggled to recall the name that had been used. "…a…Hugo. A Sampson Hugo?"

"Simpson Hugo. And you say you are his granddaughter? And your name is?"

"I'm Belle Neuva. August Villanova is my grandfather. I don't know who this Simpson Hugo is. There is some mistake."

"Please come back to Mr. Pitt's office, Miss…Miss Neuva. He's the manager, but as I said, he is out. We can use his office."

"If my grandfather is here, I want to see him, now."

"Please come with me." Before Belle could argue further, de Cordoba turned and marched down a hall lined on both sides with portraits of men who, Belle surmised, owned or had run the funeral home over its one-hundred-year history. She had to walk fast, almost to the point of running, to keep up with de Cordoba. He disappeared around a corner and by the time Belle caught up, he was sitting behind a massive wooden desk in an office the size of a small living room. The desk effectively set the director apart from grieving family members and served to shield him from irate customers.

"Please take a seat, Miss Neuva," he began, his voice tentative, as if he was uncertain of where this would lead. "I think it best if we started from the beginning."

"Beginning of what?" Belle cried. "When he was born or from when I was born?"

Doing his best to ignore the outburst, he said, "You say your grandfather's name is August Villanova. And I said —"

"His name is August Villanova! I'm not just saying it! It's a fact!"

"I'll be frank with you, Miss Neuva. The person we have here is named Simpson Hugo. I've personally verified his identity. In a moment I will take you downstairs and you can tell me if Mr. Hugo is the person you believe to be your grandfather. Normally, I wouldn't do this for a non-family member, but —"

"I am a family member!"

"Pardon me, but I believe you just informed me you are not related to Mr. Simpson Hugo. It is Mr. Hugo's family that is paramount in this situation. However, the Port Isabel police called earlier and they believe there is some confusion as to Mr. Hugo's identity."

"How did he die? The man you have. How did he die?"

"I don't have the official report. I doubt if it's even been released yet. But I've prepared enough bodies in my time to know cause of death."

"What was it?"

"I'd say a blow to the back of the head."

"Like someone hit him with a…a…board — or a hammer? Or he just fell and hit his head?"

"Most likely by falling. Could have been something else. But my money's on a fall."

That guess, or whatever it was, certainly coincided with what Vega had said. "Please allow me to see him and get this over with."

"If you will follow me. The mortuary is directly below us." De Cordoba came out from behind the desk and instead of giving Belle the courtesy of ushering her in front of him, or at least walking along beside her, he again marched several steps in front of her. Stopping at a wide door halfway down the hall, he poked buttons on a keypad and pushed the door inward. He held it open for her, seemingly impatient that it took her so long to catch up.

The door closed behind them and de Cordoba motioned for Belle to precede him to the elevator at the end of the hall. The man was silent as they walked, the perfect demeanor for a person who spent his life with dead people.

The elevator doors closed with an unexpected clang that caused the cage to rattle before starting its downward movement. A moment later the elevator lunged to a stop and the doors opened revealing a room that housed several tables. Cold air enveloped Belle and her arms involuntarily wrapped themselves around her body. The table furthest from the elevator, held a blue sheet draped over what Belle took for a body. de Cordoba walked briskly in that direction and without hesitation folded the top corner back to reveal the waxy face of a man whose expression would never again change. The mortician had done a wonderful job of manufacturing calmness as if his charge were simply sleeping, about to wake at any moment. Except, her grandfather was never calm, he was always in motion, excitement always present in his demeanor. This plastic expression was now forever burned in Belle's mind.

Tears welled up instantly and flowed down her face. de Cordoba produced a box of tissues. Without a word, he stepped back, his eyes down, his hands crossed below his stomach, as if admiring his handiwork. Only it was wrong. Her grandfather was always thinking, always working, relentless in the pursuit of…pursuit of what? She knew he was the head of the Earth Science department at the university. She knew he traveled to digs and excavations all over the South Pacific and in the coastal mountains of Peru. But only a part of what he did, what he found, what he brought home was ever imparted to her — and through her to the public.

Turning away, she said to de Cordoba. "You said you were certain of his identity. What makes you so certain?"

"Primarily, his dental records."

"From his dentist?"

"From his grandson. He brought the records with him."

"He just happened to be carrying dental records?"

"I must admit it's strange. But Mr. Hugo, the grandson, has been searching for his grandfather for a while and he thought the best way to prove identity was to use dental records. People don't typically alter their teeth even if they do alter their identity."

"And the records he brought match the man you have here?"

"The dental records of Simpson Hugo match exactly the teeth of the man you are viewing. I have no doubt."

"Do you have those records?"

"I do."

"I'd like a copy sent to his dentist in Dallas for verification. Name's Solomon. Dr. Gary Solomon. My grandfather said he was the best."

"When you are finished down here we can go up to the main office and tend to that matter."

Belle kissed her grandfather's forehead and followed de Cordoba into the elevator. Once back in the office, de Cordoba said, "How much of this do you wish to see. Some people —"

"Everything you have."

Without a word, de Cordoba retrieved a large file, pulled out two sheets of paper and slid them across the desk. The name *Simpson Hugo* was hand-printed in the upper right corner of the first page. The printing was faded, but clear — each letter perfectly formed, as if this paper was a penmanship test. *October 27, 1948* appeared on the next line directly below the name. *C. Male, born January 12, 1928* was written on the line below that. *Examined at the request of University of Pittsburgh* was on the fourth line, followed by the notation: *Football injury.*

Then followed the words: *Observation. Upper left lateral incisor and adjacent cuspid are broken, roots in place. Lower left bicuspid missing.*

Proposed course of action: Remove upper lateral Incisor and adjacent cuspid. Replace upper lateral incisor, adjacent cuspid with a bridge. Replace lower bicuspid with bridge.

Belle turned to the second sheet of paper. This one showed a preprinted chart of each tooth of a person identified only as Number 06275. There was a hand-written notation beside each tooth. The paper noted that the chart had been prepared by Fernando de Cordoba two days ago.

Belle's eyes went to the three teeth chronicled on the first page and matched them against the same teeth on de Cordoba's chart. A perfect match in that those teeth were noted as missing, replaced by a bridge. "Three teeth," Belle commented, grasping at the slimmest of hopes. "Could be a coincidence."

De Cordoba reached into the file and produced another sheet of paper. The heading was the same as the first sheet Belle had read, only this sheet had several other teeth listed. "Here is the full dental report Dr. Kriegstein generated. Hugo was 17 at the time, not much work done, but take a look at the notation for the top incisors."

Belle knew what she would find, but still the last vestige of hope lingered, forcing her to read Kriegstein's notes. Sure enough, the dentist had documented an excessive space between the top two center incisors. A space that Belle knew all too well. Grandfather Villanova had refused to have his teeth cosmetically adjusted. "Just to make absolutely certain," Belle said, "Please send your sheet to Dr. Solomon in Dallas."

Without comment, de Cordoba typed the information into his computer, jotted something on a notepad, then picked up the desk phone and dialed a number. Belle, lost in her desperate search of the full medical report for something that would prove de Cordoba wrong, didn't hear his conversation with the dentist office.

De Cordoba was now talking to her. "I emailed Solomon's office. They said the doctor would review the files and call you on your cell. They said it would be about an hour. You can wait in the sitting room or come back after he calls. I'll be here."

"Where can I find the guy who claims to be the grandson? Do you have his phone number or email?"

"Here's his cell. I wrote it down for you. Also his email. But I must have written his email wrong because I sent him two messages and they both came back undelivered. He doesn't answer his cell either."

"Where is he staying?"

"Checked out two hours ago, I'm afraid."

~ CHAPTER ~
4

Almost exactly an hour later, fifty-six minutes to be exact, Belle answered her cell phone. "I'm sorry about the Professor," Solomon said, "but I'm afraid we have a perfect match." Solomon paused, then said, "That is, except for the cracked lower right cuspid. That tooth was perfectly healthy when I last saw your grandfather. That was two-and-a-half months ago. Unfortunately, based on Mr. de Cordoba's report I must conclude the body he examined at the funeral home is indeed that of your grandfather. You have my condolences. He was a fine man. A really fine man. A generous man as well. He will be missed."

"What do you mean generous?"

"The educational funds he set up a year or so ago. At least ten kids have gone to college that I know because of him. And we have another twenty-five in the pipe line."

"I don't understand? I didn't know of —"

"He set up the Villanova fund for education. He asked me to sit on the selection committee."

"I didn't know anything about it. How much did he put into the fund? May I ask?"

"Seeing as you will become the new CEO now that he's gone there is no harm in telling you. Ten million."

Trying to hide her surprise and not doing a good job of it, Belle said, "Where did he get all that money?"

"The only thing he would say was that he sold some old trinkets."

"Trinkets?" Her mind again focused on the missing pieces from his home in Brownsville. She knew from her cataloging that what he had were reproductions, some would call them fakes. All of it combined couldn't be worth ten thousand dollars, let alone ten million.

"That's what he said. But I do believe he set up other funds. Well, at least one other. I received a call from the University of Pittsburgh. They were looking for someone by the name of Simpson Hugo. The person who called was vague about where he got my name, but my impression was that a guy by the name of Simpson Hugo had set up a similar fund at the University. In view of the dental records from Pittsburgh it appears that Simpson Hugo and the Professor were one and the same."

When Belle didn't answer, Solomon added, "It also appears your grandfather went to school in Pittsburgh and played football."

"They do seem to be one and the same." Belle was finally beginning to accept the reality of the situation.

"Teeth don't lie," the dentist said. "If Mr. de Cordoba gave us an accurate account of the teeth of the body he has there, then I'm confident the two are the same."

"Can teeth be rigged?"

"Anything can be staged. But I think not. If you want, I can come down in the morning and take impressions. I have his last impression and we can match them up. "

"Would you do that? I would appreciate that very much."

"That's the least I can do for you and for your grandfather. I suggest you call the University of Pittsburgh and see what they want with Mr. Hugo."

"Who should I call?"

"His name is Winston Demont the Third. He heads up the antiquities department."

"Antiquities? I thought you said he ran a fund or something."

"I said he got the name from someone running a fund, or so I thought that's what he said." Solomon paused. "I should have thought of this sooner but I didn't put one and one together before this, but on the one hand we have the head of the antiquities department calling and on the other your grandfather got the money by selling trinkets."

Belle, not waiting for the punch line said, "Trinkets equals antiquities. That's your thought, isn't it?"

"It is," Solomon admitted. "It most certainly is my thought."

"I think now it is important for you to come down and make certain Simpson Hugo and August Villanova are the same person. If not, my grandfather is missing and may be in grave trouble."

Solomon let the pun slide and instead said, "I'll be there first thing in the morning. Please tell the funeral director to expect me.

By noon the following day Belle knew for a certainty that Simpson Hugo and August Villanova were one and the same. Not only did the new teeth impressions match Solomon's old impressions of Villanova, but the birth record footprint of Simpson Hugo matched the heel print of the dead guy as well.

Belle, however, was troubled by the fact that she had been unable to reach her cousin, the man claiming to be the grandson of Hugo. But she did speak with Professor Winston Demont in Pittsburgh. "Call me Winnie," he had said. "Everybody does. Now who are you again?"

She explained who she was, but it was not until she could bring herself to claim Simpson Hugo as her grandfather that Demont finally understood

"So you know Hugo," the now energized voice said. "By any chance do you know where he is? I must speak with him on a matter of some urgency."

"I'm afraid that won't be possible, Professor Demont. My grandfather... passed away this week."

"Call me Winnie. Oh my life! My condolences to you, my dear. That is indeed a shame."

Belle couldn't be sure if it was a shame for her that he died, or a shame for him. It seemed to her he was thinking more of his own situation than hers. "Is there something I can help you with, Professor?" It didn't seem right to call the man Winnie.

After a lengthy pause, Demont replied, "This is perhaps the wrong time — and certainly the wrong modality — to be discussing business. May I ask where he is interred? I'd like to pay my respects."

"Actually, he hasn't been." Belle didn't want to get into the identity confusion any more than she already had. "Funeral will be tomorrow," she tossed out without much thought as to who might be attending. "We can do it late afternoon. He wanted a military funeral but the timing won't allow for that."

"And where will the ceremony be?"

Belle hadn't even considered a ceremony. "Funeral home called Buck Ashcraft in Harlingen, Texas."

"Texas?"

Are there any other Harlingen's, Belle thought. She responded, "Yes, Texas." Then to soften what she thought had been too harsh, she added, "The easiest way to get here is to take *Southwest Air*. One stop in Houston. Plane arrives before five. It's just a few miles from the airport. We'll wait for you."

"I'll be there. And if you would be so kind, I'd appreciate if you would set aside time with you afterward. About an hour will do nicely, I should think."

Belle doubted an hour would be enough to answer all the questions she herself had. "I'll be available."

She then called Detective Vega to be sure it was okay to proceed with the funeral now that she accepted that her grandfather and Simpson Hugo were actually the same person. He gave his blessing and then added, "And whose name will be on the grave marker, mind telling me?"

"There won't be a marker," Belle responded, not at all certain her grandfather would approve of what she was about to do. But frankly at this point she didn't approve of him living a double life. And she didn't at all appreciate finding out in this manner. "He's being cremated."

The funeral plans complete, Belle drove to her home on South Padre Island and dug out her old photos, the ones taken before all the art had vanished from the Brownsville house. She began listing the art and beside each item name she added a description. Two things became clear. The first was that the collection was constantly changing with pieces being added and pieces being removed. She confirmed this with the old pictures she had salvaged from the garage. The second thing that became clear was this was not an ordinary art collection. It was much larger than she had remembered — and certainly larger than she had catalogued. But there it was, scattered around his home as if the items had come from *Target*.

One of the pieces now resided in her own home. A bird with a huge wingspan sat in her kitchen, perched on a table by the side window. But the photos confirmed her memory that there had been a pair of these birds sitting on an old carved desk. The birds were facing in opposite directions seemingly standing guard over an even larger bird, perhaps of the same species, but resting with its wings folded in on itself. She knew that bird to be a replica of the famous — at least in her circles — *Golden Booby*. It seemed to weigh a ton and its wings had been encrusted with jewels. Costume jewelry she knew from the catalogue, but gorgeous nonetheless.

Considering the revelations of today and following up on research she herself was involved with in Mexico, she began to believe that the missing bird, the one that had been guarded over by the bird now in her kitchen, actually was the real *Golden Booby* — the now missing *Golden Booby*.

The phone rang before Belle could dwell further on the missing booby and what it would mean to her if she could only find it. The smooth, well-modulated voice of the funeral director greeted her. "Miss Neuva," de Cordoba began, "I'm calling to let you know that all is in order for tomorrow afternoon. Because there will be no interment, we can delay the service until six PM if the plane bringing your friend from Pittsburgh is late."

Belle refrained from explaining it wasn't her friend. She also refrained from explaining her feeling that Demont's visit was more to see her than it was to attend her grandfather's funeral. The image of the *Golden Booby*, the again lost *Golden Booby*, floated above her. When she tried to focus on what it meant the image was gone.

"Are you still there, Miss Neuva?"

"Yes, I'm here. Thank you for the information."

"Oh, I almost forgot the other reason I called. I did get in contact with Mr. Oscar Hugo, the grandson. It appears I wrote his email down wrong. He left his phone charger in Pittsburgh and his phone was off until he bought a new one. Anyway, he's still here in Harlingen and plans to be at the funeral."

"Could you please give me his phone number?"

"I see no reason why not. The two of you share the same grandfather. That makes you cousins, does it not?"

"Something along those lines," Belle replied, not pleased with the thought, but anxious to talk with Simpson Hugo's grandson, a man also from Pittsburgh.

~ CHAPTER ~
5

T he voice on the other end of the line was rough — smoker-rough — and older, at least forty or possibly forty-five, than what Belle had imagined her so-called cousin to be. "I'm Oscar Hugo," the caller announced. "I'm sitting out in front of your house. May I come in?"

Belle was uncomfortable, but she couldn't pinpoint the source of her concern. She knew she had to talk with Hugo, but hadn't yet made the call. She preferred somewhere in public, anywhere, but not her own home. There was very little crime on South Padre Island, but the fact remained that two men had been shot not long ago. The police had not explained that shooting, except to say they had arrested two suspects. The thought of allowing this guy, the person who had suddenly shown up to identify her grandfather's body, into her home sent shivers through her body. She had no way of knowing who he was, or even if the man on the phone was who he said he was.

"Tell you what," Belle finally managed, pushing her natural southern hospitality aside "on Padre Boulevard, about a mile from here, back toward the bridge, there's a place called *BadaBing Bagels*. On the right, set back in a small strip mall. I'll meet you there."

She expected a push back and was pleasantly surprised when Hugo responded, "I'll wait for you there. I'll be the guy wearing the 'South Padre Island is for Lovers' tee shirt. In bright yellow I might add."

"I won't be able to miss you then, will I?"

"You got it. See you there."

The line went dead and Belle heard a car pull away. Through the window she saw a white Kia. Fighting her instinct to flee, she took a deep breath and with an attitude of in-for-a-dime, in-for-a dollar, she went down to her garage.

"You must be Belle," a voice she recognized from the earlier phone call called from a corner table. The voice belonged to a man wearing a bright yellow tee. He stood as she approached. "I'm buying. What's your favorite?"

"Plain. And an orange juice as well," Belle answered. Her mind swirled and she had to work to keep from hyperventilating. The eyes of the man speaking to her were the eyes of her grandfather — kind, with an edge of defiance — intelligent, but playful — at once your best friend. It was as if time had gone backward forty years. Any doubt she harbored as to Oscar's authenticity was swept away in fond remembrances of her grandfather — his grandfather.

When he returned to the table, she said, "Hard as it is for me to accept, it does appear that August Villanova had a second life — and a second family. Care to tell me about it — what you know of him?"

"It took me a while to wrap my head around it all," Hugo responded, his smile mimicking her grandfather's. "But the way I see it, August Villanova is the one with the second life. He was born Simpson Hugo, just outside Pittsburgh."

"Okay, Belle said, fighting back the desire to argue, "so tell me how you see it."

"Simpson was in Altoona. He was a walk-on football player at a time when Pitt was rebuilding their football program. Actually, they were trying to become accepted into the Big Ten. But that's another story. The only team

Pitt beat in 1947 was Ohio State. Grandpa is credited with a game saving tackle. He hit the Ohio State player so hard that Grandpa shattered a few teeth. He may have knocked himself out, but he insisted on walking off under his own power. He collapsed on the bench and was transported to the hospital."

Belle, anxious to know where Hugo fit in, jumped ahead. "He must have married — I assume he married...your grandmother — shortly after graduation."

"Her name was Kathy — Kathleen O'Connell, a nice Catholic girl. My father, Harold, was born in 1950 and I was born in 1973. My mother's name was Lucy. Lucy Stone."

"So when—"

"Grandpa left about the time my father was born. He actually may have left before he even knew Grandma was pregnant. Dad would never say one way or the other. According to Dad, he hadn't known his father before he graduated from college. At graduation a man slipped him a note telling him that he was getting a trust fund for graduation. The trust was worth over a million dollars."

"A trust fund? Where did Grandfather get that kind of money? Wasn't that about the time he was just starting as a professor at Texas Southern College? I need to check the time frames."

"All he would tell my father was that it was a small payment for a kid growing up without a father."

"How did your grandmother manage? I mean your real grandmother. Did you say her name was Kathy? Did she work?"

"Kathy. I think my father gave her money from the fund, but I'm not certain. Now it's your turn. Tell me what you know about my grandpa — our grandpa."

"From as far back as I can remember we — Grandfather — lived nicely. When I was a little girl we had big picnics at his mansion. That's what all the kids in school called it — the Professor's Mansion. We had a large, even by Texas standards, swimming pool. He had several giant salt-water aquariums with all types of fish. The aquariums were set to mimic the South Pacific in temperature and salinity. He would go on long explorations and new fish would appear. The new fish would be put in what he called the acclimation environment. After they were acclimated they would be moved to one of the other tanks. Sometimes they would eat the fish that were already there." Belle paused to reflect on those years. "Grandfather saw me crying when a Tiger Barb ate a Yellow Assessor. That had been my favorite fish, all yellow with red along the tips of its fins. I loved to watch that fish swim upside down. I would spend hours with my nose pressed against the glass and the yellow fish would perform for me, swimming upside down and just hanging in the water. That's when the Tiger fish got it. Grandfather lifted me onto his lap as he often did when I needed… comforting. To this day I recall his exact words. 'Belle, my dear, the harsh truth about nature is the mighty swallow the weak. It's called survival of the fittest.' I protested that the Tiger Barb was twice the size of Goldie. That was the name I had given the yellow fish, Goldie. Grandfather replied, 'If you're not the biggest it's best if you get out of the way. The mighty swallow the weak. It's always been that way, always will. Remember that lesson and life will be easier for you.'"

"I wish I had known him growing up," Hugo said, then fell silent.

"You haven't touched your coffee," Belle said, trying to steer the conversation back to her grandfather and his early life. But she suspected that since her cousin hadn't known their grandfather as a child he wouldn't have much to add to what he had already said.

"I'm sorry. I was just thinking how lucky you are to have known him. Can we go back to your house. I'd love to see pictures of him when he was younger. What happened to…to the Mansion? I understand he was living in a trailer when he…he died."

"He sold the mansion a few years ago. He said he was tired of it all and wanted to downsize."

"That's extreme. From a mansion to a run-down dump of a trailer park. It looks as if he put himself in a witness-protection program."

"You were there?"

"Took a ride down there earlier today. Place is creepy. The inside looks barren — at least through the window."

"A few of his things, but not many, are there." She studied the man across the table, wanting to know more about him and at the same time uneasy by what she might give up in the process. Making up her mind, she glanced at the untouched coffee and said, "If you're finished, you can follow me back to the house."

Driving out of the lot, Belle studied the rear-view mirror to be sure her cousin was following. Indeed, a car did fall in behind her. The problem being that the car behind her was a dark color. Black, or possibly brown or blue. It certainly wasn't the white car that had pulled away from her house an hour ago.

~ CHAPTER ~
6

Her newly found cousin was somewhere behind her, but she couldn't see his car. A plan formed calling for her to race home, pull into the garage — and quickly close the door. Almost immediately that plan was discarded in favor of her making a quick turn into the *Blue Marlin*'s parking lot. She could run into the grocery store where she knew most of the clerks. Cousin Oscar would just have to fend for himself.

The Blue Marlin was coming up fast. She exceeded the 30 MPH speed limit, hoping to attract attention. The black car was still behind, but had dropped back several car lengths. There was no sign of the white car.

Ready, set…go! Belle twisted the wheel hard to the right, came over the small curb and headed for the front door almost hitting a woman pushing a shopping cart filled with several cases of beer. The black car swung in behind her and stopped. Belle twisted the wheel to the left — and for an agonizing moment her car teetered on the verge of tipping over. Oblivious, she flung open the driver's door and her feet hit the pavement running. Not looking back, she pushed open the grocery store door and ran inside.

No one was behind her. At least she didn't see anyone. She couldn't see the black car, but knew it was in the lot, not far from away. Instead of going to her right, which was the natural flow and where the empty shopping carts were stacked, she went left toward the cashier check-out lines.

Belle waved to one of the clerks, a girl barely out of high school, calling attention to herself. The girl threw her thumb in the air as if to signal it was all okay and at the same time cocked her head in puzzlement. Belle continued to the back of the store, trying to keep an eye on anyone coming through the door behind her.

Two women entered, followed by a teen-aged boy. Her back to the meat counter, Belle tried to focus on what she was going to do next while also trying to monitor the front door. Her thoughts were interrupted when Hugo came in, glanced around, and then walked calmly toward the shopping carts. He pulled one free, took a few steps, and loaded a case of water into the cart. He then paused, giving the appearance of trying to remember what item he was supposed to get next.

Watching him fumble in his pants pocket and pat his shirt several times apparently searching for his wife's shopping list that had gone missing, Belle had the distinct impression that Oscar was a man well practiced in deception. Whose side was her cousin on? Conflict raged within her as the minutes passed. Oscar moved down an aisle, adding items to his cart as he made his way to the back of the store. Was he searching for her? Or was he trying to provide cover for her? The question remained unresolved.

"Belle!" The sound of her name startled her. It was the store manager, a man she had known for years, standing beside her. "Oh, Carlos. You startled me."

"Is something wrong. You look...well, to be honest, you seem frightened."

"Someone followed me into the lot," she blurted. "I'm not sure if he's in the store."

"Should I call the police? " Carlos reached for his cell phone and began to dial.

Oscar turned the corner at that point and said, "Oh, there you are! I've been looking for you."

"Is this the man?" the manager asked, taking a step backward.

"No, he's...he's my...cousin. It's a long story," she hastened to add. "This is the first time, I mean few minutes ago we met for the first time." Belle knew the words were flowing together, sounding confused, anxious, but she was unable to slow down. "I never knew I even had a cousin. He's from Pittsburgh. He's not the person—"

Holding the phone in front of him, Carlos said, "You want me to call or not?"

"No. Please don't. He's not —"

Oscar broke in. "We're on the way to her house. I'll be with her. I didn't see anybody out there following her. She'll be fine."

Carlos looked at Belle and when she nodded, he said, "Well, call out if you need help or anything." He turned and walked around to the back of the meat counter, keeping his eye on her.

"How did you know someone was following me?" Belle demanded when Carlos was far enough away not to hear.

"I...I overheard you telling him. Come, let's go."

Reluctantly, Belle followed his lead, not knowing whether to trust Oscar or try to slip out the back way.

Sensing her reluctance, and guessing what she was thinking, Oscar said, "Listen, I'm on your side. Blood lines and all. I'll go in your car with you. Can't very well leave it parked out front as you left it. I'm surprised the police aren't here already." Oscar gently ushered his younger cousin out to the parking lot and then into her car.

A few minutes later she turned the corner to her street and there, parked across the street front of her house, was the black car. Its lights were off, but Belle could see a shadow sitting behind the wheel. The head — or what Belle assumed to be the head — moved to the side and a hand came up. Belle was certain the person in the car was using a cell phone.

She stopped midway down the block, not more than twenty yards from the car. The headlights came on and the car began moving toward her. She was concentrating so hard on trying to see who was driving that she nearly hit the guy who ran across the road from the direction of her house and jumped into the back seat. The car's wheels threw up pebbles as the car accelerated past her. At the intersection of the main road the black car, without slowing to check for traffic, turned left toward the causeway. Belle reached for her cell phone.

"Don't bother calling the police," Oscar said, "what will you tell them?"

"That someone ran out of my house and sped away."

"Did you see anyone come out of your house?"

"He came down my driveway."

"Even so, you don't know for certain anyone was in your house. Before you sort that out with the police they'll be long gone. Let's go in and see if anyone was even in there."

Belle studied her cousin for a long minute. What he said made sense. But yet…she was uncomfortable. Forcing an external calmness, she asked, "How can you remain so calm, Oscar? Because it's my house, not yours?"

"That, and the fact someone did my house a few weeks back. That's what brought me looking for Grandpa. They dropped a bird sculpture Grandpa gave me. Bent a feather tip. Nothing serious. They went through my desk and personal papers. The only thing I found missing was some notes on Peruvian art. Nothing important. But I did change my bank accounts to be on the safe side."

"I don't understand," Belle said, playing dumb even though she was intrigued by the mention of a bird sculpture. Her own activities in Mexico made her cautious.

"Neither do I actually. Neither do I. But, and my imagination is running wild here, I think someone is looking for something Grandpa had. Something important — or very valuable." Oscar fell silent a moment, then added, "I would say valuable."

"Grandfather sold everything of any value," Belle answered, not wanting to open the subject of the *Golden Booby*. "I'd say it was about three years ago, judging from the before and after photos I looked at."

"That was about when he set up the Arts Council at Pitt. Three years ago. Let's talk inside if you don't mind."

"I'm afraid to go in. Maybe someone's still —"

"I'm with you. That black car was tracking you and if they wanted to take you, they'd not have tipped their hand. They're after something of Grandpa's, not you."

"How do you know that for sure?"

"You just have to trust me on this. They went through my stuff and I'm positive it was Grandpa they were after, not me. "

Belle agreed, but only reluctantly. No one had remained in the house and the only thing out of place was the large bird. It was now facing away from the window as if it had just landed after a long flight. Belle always positioned the sculpture to appear as if it was about to take flight. Often she would sit across from it thinking of the places her grandfather had told her about and wondering what it would be like to have wings and be able to fly anywhere she wanted.

"That bird sculpture," Oscar exclaimed, "is identical to the one I have! That's the one I told you they dropped on the floor! It's the only thing Grandpa ever gave me. He told me it was valuable, to never part with it."

"That's exactly what he said to me!" Belle picked it up, remembering to use both hands because of its weight. "Is yours this heavy as well." She held the bird out to him.

Oscar set the bird back on its perch, but not before examining the nest of eggs at its base. "This is exactly the same as the one he gave me. At first I thought it was mine. But this one has all of its eggs."

"What do you mean it has all of its eggs? Of course it does."

A red tinge crept up Oscar's neck and across his jaw line. "I got to fooling with it one day. To tell the full truth, I was trying to figure out whether it was real gold or something else."

"Did you find out? I was wondering that same thing."

"It most certainly is. Solid gold, I might add. That's why it's so heavy. Anyway, I was fooling with the eggs and one felt loose. The one behind and under the leg. It unscrews. Let's see if yours comes off as well." Oscar twisted the egg but it refused to move.

"You'll break it! Stop!"

Oscar reached inside his shirt and pulled out a gold medallion shaped exactly like the egg. It was hanging on a gold pendant around his neck. He slipped the chain over his head and handed it to Belle. "This is what it looks like. I've been wearing mine ever since I unscrewed it. I'll bet yours is the same."

"There's writing on it," Belle said, "Did you have it inscribed?"

"It was there when I unscrewed it. Under a magnifying glass you can make out the letters P-O-R-T-L-A-N-D. I don't know what it means."

"Portland," Belle repeated, not knowing what to make of the inscription. "You think that's Portland, the city? Or something else?"

"At first, I thought it was the city. I know of only one Portland so I thought whatever he wants me to find is there. But the city is a big place. Then I got the idea that Grandpa would have given it to a school, a museum, or something of that nature. I spent over a month up there and came away empty. So now I don't know what Portland means."

"Is there anything else on the egg? Any letters or numbers?"

"If you have a magnifier you can see for yourself. I had it checked out by a jeweler friend. That's it. Portland. Nothing else."

"As it so happens, I had to buy one to see the details of some of the pieces in Grandfather's collection. I'll get it." Belle retrieved the viewer and studied the tiny egg from every possible angle. When she was satisfied, she handed it back to Oscar saying, "You're right. The letters are P-O-R-T-L-A-N-D. Nothing else."

"My friend was impressed with the detail and said he had never seen that alloy before. Gold is soft. This egg seems indestructible. He wanted to run some tests. I refused. Is it okay if I remove your egg?"

Belle nodded and Oscar picked again up the bird and again twisted the egg. "Do you have pliers?" he asked when he was still unsuccessful. "And a cloth?"

"Promise not to break it."

"Can't promise. But it shouldn't break. Mine didn't. But I suppose the salt air could have corroded the screw."

Belle went out to the garage and was back in a moment. Oscar wedged the bird under his left arm, wrapped the cloth around the claws, and carefully twisted the egg.

"Run it under hot water," Belle suggested when the egg didn't budge. "My grandmother taught me that trick years ago. Usually works."

"Gold's a good conductor of heat. I don't know if—"

"Don't over think it. Just try."

Oscar followed Belle to the kitchen, waited for the water to get hot, then said, "Here goes." He held the base of the huge bird under the tap for a full minute before twisting with the pliers.

"Do it again. This time tap it lightly with the pliers," Belle instructed when the egg hadn't so much as wobbled.

"It moved," Oscar announced. "A fraction. But I could feel it." He then reapplied the hot water and again tapped the egg. "Moved some more."

"Go slow. We're in no hurry."

It took ten minutes before the egg was finally free of the bird and resting in Belle's hand. She held the magnifying glass over it. "I can see the scratch marks you made with the pliers. Some of the scratches are over the top of the letters. W-I-N-D-S. Then one or two—I think two—letters are scratched so I can't read them. Then there's an R and an H and a T."

"This makes no sense," Oscar said after examining the egg himself with the magnifier. "WINDS and RHT."

"It made sense to someone."

"No, I mean the scratch marks. I didn't scratch it. At least not that deep. Someone else tried to get this loose."

"I suppose that could have happened even before Grandfather got it."

"Not if my theory is correct that Grandpa was trying to send us a message. Perhaps he was trying to give us the location of something. My thought is those letters will lead us to the *Golden Booby*."

"I don't recall seeing the birds being uncrated from Peru. I would have remembered them. They just showed up one day on his desk. All that other stuff came in crates. They would arrive shortly after he came back from his explorations and he and I would unpack them together. I was always so excited when that happened. Sometimes they were just bones. Bones imbedded in rock really. Grandfather said they were rare bones baked into mud. I never cared about the bones, but I loved the primitive tools and the writings scratched into rock. Best of all I loved the faces and the furniture. That's what he put in the house; the faces and the furniture mostly. Some tools. Oh, and all the early pottery. I have pictures of the artwork he collected. I scanned it all. Then all of a sudden the art disappeared from the house. All of it except..."

Deciding to tell him about the bird, Belle continued, "...except for a giant booby sitting between this bird and yours. These birds, big as they are, seemed small in comparison to the booby. I tried to pick it up one time and couldn't. Grandfather said the booby alone weighed over sixty pounds."

"Sixty pounds is how many ounces?" Oscar said, pulling out his cell phone. "Let's see. Sixteen ounces per pound times sixty pounds. That's 960 ounces." He entered more numbers into the phone and turned it to face her.

"Is that in millions?" Belle asked, hardly believing the value. She had never thought about the artwork in terms of money. To her, it had always been important for what it was, not for what it was worth.

"Almost a million and a half. And that's just its value melted down. The actual value of the real artifact is multiples of that amount. If it was made in the South Pacific, and if it's the real *Golden Booby*, then it could be worth in excess of a hundred million."

"Look it up," Belle said, already knowing the answer and also knowing there was nothing to find on the Internet, except the articles she had published under her Mexican name. The legend of the *Golden Booby* had been swept clean — transformed — she had seen to that. "Peruvian gold birds is where I would start," she suggested, trying to appear helpful.

"We can start there, but these birds, the ones you and I have, are not from Peru. They were crafted in the South Pacific. Let's use your computer, this screen is too small for anything serious. Besides, I've done the computer research on the booby and there's not much out there. Maybe I'll have better luck with your help."

Something in his tone caught her attention. Boredom? Fake boredom, that's what it was. He was more interested in the bird than he let on. And he already knew there was nothing much out there. More importantly, he knew the real *Golden Booby* was from the South Pacific and not Peru. "So, exactly what did your research find?" she asked, renewing her quest of finding out just exactly who this "cousin" really was.

"It's a long and rather complicated story."

Belle settled back on the sofa. "I've no appointments. Take as much time as you need."

"Let me work backward if you will. About a month ago there was a murder not far from here. Actually, two men were shot in a condo overlooking the Gulf. They were looking for a particular book in a condo un —"

"Killed for a book?"

"It was a code book. The *Golden Booby*, it seems, is the missing treasure in any number of fantasies going around. You know, a ship is wrecked and gold coins are washed ashore type of stories. Usually, the tale has a pirate burying his treasure somewhere along the Gulf coast and it somehow gets lost. Over the years, just enough coins and valuables have been found — or claimed to have been found — along this coast to fuel interest in treasure hunts."

"I take it you're skeptical?"

"Mostly. But there's one story that has more merit than meets the eye. That's the story about a missing *Golden Booby*. But the stories making the rounds have it wrong. The most popular, and one that has legs, is the one where Al Capone comes down here to Port Isabel to pick up the *Golden Booby*. But it's a trap and most of his men are shot and killed on the beach about two miles north of where we now are. The Capone story has the bird going missing in Mexico from an old-line family that had it from the Aztecs. You can find that story on line, written by a Mexican professor. She recently wrote that a family member went missing about eighty years ago and took the booby with him."

"Al Capone," Belle responded, deflecting away from herself, "was in the twenties and thirties. That's about eighty years ago."

"Granted. But the real *Golden Booby* wasn't in Mexico at that point, it was in Peru. The woman who wrote it, name's Anna, set that story up as a diversion — I think she was covering for Grandpa. But I don't know why."

This was getting too close for comfort. This guy knew too much. Belle had to be careful. "You know that because…"

"It's not important how I know it. The important thing to know is that most, if not all, of the *Golden Booby* stories are red herrings. And I am coming to believe they were planted by…our grandfather."

"You think you're right on that?"

"Most certainly. From what I've pieced together, he found — or stole — the bird from a cave in the mountains of Peru on one of his expeditions. Even he, the world's expert on such things, didn't immediately realize what he had. But, for now, the important thing is that the booby does not belong to either the Peruvian or the Mexican governments."

"Why is that?"

"It was crafted on the island of Aurora, now called Maewo, in what is now known as the Republic of Vanuatu. From what I gather, the Vanuatu were adventuresome and sailed east, eventually landing and exploring coastal Peru. Apparently, the explorers found fish by following the boobies. Once back home they crafted the *Golden Booby* in tribute to their good fortune, using gold and jewels they found in Peru. How the Booby got back to Peru is anybody's guess, but most likely it was stolen from them by pirates operating in the South Pacific."

"And you found this on-line?"

"If you know what to look for."

"How about helping me."

"Get your computer and I'll help."

"It's in the den. I'll get it."

A moment later Belle yelled something Oscar couldn't make out. He ran toward the sound and found Belle kneeling on the floor surrounded by what appeared to be hundreds, possibly thousands, of pictures.

"Those bastards took my laptop!" Belle exclaimed.

"You certain it's gone?"

"It's gone! Trust me, it's gone!" She waved her hand across the floor. "At least they didn't take the originals."

~ CHAPTER ~
7

Oscar was rummaging through cabinets in the kitchen when Belle emerged from her bedroom.

"I was planning to make you coffee," he cheerfully announced despite having less than two hours of sleep, "but couldn't find any. I couldn't find eggs either. In fact, there's nothing much in the fridge."

"I don't cook much. Never eat breakfast, at least not here. I go over to *Ted's* when I feel the need, or grab a bagel at *BadaBing*. How late did you stay up?"

"Not long after you went to bed," Oscar replied, turning his head so Belle wouldn't detect the lie. In fact, he had been so engrossed in seeing his grandfather come alive that he had gone through all of the old photos. Some of the pictures even predated Belle, having been taken shortly after his grandfather moved to Brownsville and married Clare Laskin. Oscar had grown up thinking his grandfather was dead until the day he showed up and introduced himself. Oscar confronted his father who then confessed that his father had fallen prey to a woman out in Texas. That's all he would say and Oscar never could determine if his father knew more or not. "I would have slept another hour or so, but your cell woke me." Belle didn't immediately reply, so Oscar, said, "It must be important so early in the morning."

In fact, Belle did receive a call. A disturbing call from Professor Demont at Pitt informing her that his plane was running late and that he would miss the funeral, but he was coming anyway because he had to talk with her. The disturbing part came when she told him about Oscar Hugo.

"Be careful around that guy!" Demont's voice changed from softly modulated to highly agitated. "I've been looking for him. He's not...let's just say he's not a friend. Be careful." Belle had pressed for more information but all Demont would say was, "Just be careful what you tell him. I'll explain when I see you later today." Facing Oscar, Belle answered, "Funeral home. Just confirming the time for today." She was surprised at how easy the lie came out of her mouth.

Oscar's eyebrows raised, but he dropped the subject. Instead, he asked, "Where do you suppose the artwork went?"

"I have no idea. It all disappeared, as you can see from the photos, within about eighteen months."

"That coincides with when he set up the funds at Texas and Pittsburgh. Did he sell it all? If so, there's a lot of money missing. I believe you said Texas has ten million."

The call from Demont was still playing in her head. "I never said how much the Texas fund received. So where did you get that information?"

Without hesitation, Oscar replied, "Research into my grandfather."

"On the Internet — or where? I didn't know that kind of information is made public."

"What is this, twenty questions? If you must know, Pitt publishes their quarterly numbers."

"But that doesn't explain Texas. I think we better —"

"The funds are linked. You can check that out."

Calling his bluff, Belle said, "Okay, give me a name to call."

"I don't have..." Seeing Belle's frown, Oscar continued, "...you can call the faculty person in charge of the Pitt fund."

"Name please," Belle demanded, sensing Oscar's discomfort.

"A professor by the name of Demont, Winston Demont III."

"Do you know Professor Demont?"

"What's got in to you this morning? Last night we were...getting along fine. Now you're acting as if I'm someone...well to be frank, trying to take advantage of you."

"I have a lot to do today. I'll drive you over to your car. Or if you prefer, you can walk. *The Blue Marlin* is not that far. "

"Can we can get breakfast on the way? I'd like to discuss the art pieces with you."

"I've too much to do this morning. And besides, I'm not very hungry."

"The funeral isn't until late this afternoon. The funeral home does all the work. I can't imag —"

"Walk or ride," Belle said, her tone leaving no room for negotiation. "Choice is yours. I'm leaving — and so are you."

Oscar wisely stopped resisting. Following Belle's lead, he said, "I'm ready when you are." Then added, as if to regain a sense of team effort, "Have you had any luck figuring out the inscription on your egg?"

"No." What Belle didn't say was that even if she had figured it out she was not about to impart any more information to him — at least not until after speaking with Professor Demont. And most likely not even then.

Oscar, continuing his quest to build a relationship, said, "You seem...well, frankly, upset that I'm here. I'm sorry you feel that way. I'm excited to be finally learning about Grandpa and I only wish it had come sooner."

"It's all so sudden. His death. You showing up, claiming...being...his grandson. All of it. I need time to assimilate all this."

"I understand. I'll take you up on that ride if the offer's still open."

They drove back to *The Blue Marlin* in silence. "Thanks for the ride," Oscar said, stepping out of the car. He motioned for Belle to roll down the window. Leaning down, he called across the front seat, "I'll see you at the funeral home. Be careful."

The last remark rang in Belle's ears. From what danger was she supposed to be careful? Her house had already been broken into. Whoever it was got what they had come for. Or maybe they hadn't? They had left behind the bird, so at least that held no value to them. But what if they didn't know about the removable egg? Those scratch marks Oscar claims he didn't make. Maybe they made them. But then why leave the bird behind?

On impulse she made a U-turn on the mostly deserted street and headed back south to pay a visit to the town historian and her good friend, Steve Hathcock. He was always examining old books so she hoped he would have a magnifying glass strong enough to make out the missing letters on her egg. Belle turned the corner to Steve's house just as his car backed out of the driveway. She waved and he stopped along side her. "I have a favor to ask of you," Belle began, fighting back her anxiety. "It should only take a few minutes."

"Anything for you, Belle dear. Park here and I'll be back in a few minutes."

Steve lived above his locksmith shop, which doubled as a library of island history books. She walked up onto his small porch and sat in a rocking chair, the movement serving to calm her racing mind. The main question she wrestled with was how much to tell Oscar and how much to withhold. She knew she couldn't find the *Golden Booby* without him, but sharing it had not been her plan. I've come too far, sacrificed too much to allow the prize to get away from me now. Cousin or not, it's not his. Not even partially his. He hasn't earned it as I have.

Ten minutes hadn't passed when, true to his word, Hathcock rolled into his driveway, parking his car beside Belle's. Climbing the two steps up to the porch he called, "And just what is this favor? Hey, you look serious. Something going on? Something wrong?"

"My grandfather died. Actually several days ago, but I just found out. He's being buried later today."

"And you have a safe that needs to be opened?"

"Actually, I wish I did. It's a long story and not for now. But I do have this." She held open her hand, revealing the tiny gold nugget. "It has writing on it. Letters anyway. Some are scratched out. I'm hoping you can read all the letters."

Steve placed his hand under hers and motioned for her to turn her hand over. The object appeared even smaller nestled in Hathcock's large hand. "We'll see what we can do. I'll need to break out the microscope for something this small."

"It's an egg taken from a large bird my grandfather gave me. It unscrewed. I can see — using a reading glass — engraved letters. But one or two letters were…scratched when we tried to unscrew it."

"Here we go," Hathcock said when he worked his way across the crowded workshop. "You hold this, while I dig out the instrument we'll need." He returned the egg to Belle who breathed a sigh of relief to have it back in her palm. She squeezed it tightly to make certain she wouldn't drop it if she tripped on something.

Steve dug through several boxes before he exclaimed, "Here's the little bugger. Thought for a moment I'd misplaced it. Valuable instrument, but not required all that often." He carried a wooden case the size of a sewing machine over to a table, opened it, extracted a plug, and inserted the plug in a power socket. "Now, if the lamp isn't burnt out then we…oh, we're in luck, it's on." He busied himself adjusting several lenses. He then instructed Belle to place the egg in a small disk-like holder. "When the egg was settled in place, he bent forward, his right eye in contact with what appeared to be a lens. He adjusted a knob on the side. Then he twisted a second knob. "Okay, here goes. I see the scratches all right. And I suppose you were able to read the letters W-I-N-D-S and R? And possibly also H-T?"

"I got those," Belle replied, "but the others were too scratched."

"There are only two others. An O before the R and an S after the T. WINDSOR HTS. No other letters are missing, but those two are sure scratched to hell. A jeweler should be able to polish this for you."

"Are you certain you have all the letters?"

"Plain as day. But one thing is clear. That writing was added long after the egg was made. I'd say, no more than fifteen years ago, but that's only my guess. There are instruments that could tell you almost to the year when the egg was made and when the engraving was added. That's far beyond my pay grade."

"Do you have any idea what WINDSOR HTS means? I mean, is it a jewelry term or something?"

"That, my dear, is the sixty-four-thousand-dollar question."

~ CHAPTER ~
8

When the funeral service began, albeit thirty minutes late, Belle had no better answers to any of her questions than she had when she left Hathcock's shop. In fact, she was even more confused because her newfound cousin Oscar hadn't yet arrived, despite the delayed start. Apparently the plane bringing Professor Demont from Pittsburgh made up considerable time because he — or a professorial type sent from central casting — walked through the door and stood, arms folded over his chest, at the back of the small chapel. Demont was no taller than five-seven, but he carried his razor thin frame as a tall man would, back straight, head high, eyes unflinching. He commanded the room just as her grandfather always had.

Grandfather. So much had happened since she had gone into the Port Isabel police station looking for him that she hadn't had time to think about him being gone. It wasn't so much that he had died — she had been expecting that — but rather the way he had died. That, coupled with the fact that they hadn't exchanged proper goodbyes, made it feel as though she had unfinished business. It was as if he was off on one of his explorations, only this time there would be no excited return. No hugs, no pictures of exotic places, no crates to unpack, no straw to dig through, no hidden treasure.

The only mourners, beside herself and Demont, were four men, none younger than seventy, sitting together a few rows behind her. She recognized one of the men from years earlier when he had come to the house for lunch. She remembered him because he had spent so much time looking — examining would be more accurate — the art pieces. If her memory served her, his name was Samson, or Simpson, or possibly Stinson. Grandfather had introduced him as a professor working in his department.

No one got up to speak and Belle had told the funeral director earlier in the day that she would have nothing to say. The service was brief. The few mourners paraded past the closed casket whispering their last words to their fallen comrade.

Belle went last. "Grandfather," she began when the others were far enough away for privacy, "what have you done? All your life you were a mystery and now you leave this earth in a mystery. I should be upset with you, but I can't be. You have always treated me as an adult, taught me well. Thank you for giving me your love for fine art. Most importantly, you have taught me to see the world with open eyes. I will never forget you. May you rest forever in peace. Go with Godspeed. I love you."

She turned to join the others and realized Demont was standing directly behind her.

"Forgive me for eavesdropping, my dear. I'm Professor Demont. I like what you said about your grandfather. He was indeed a man of mystery. But he also was a wonderful teacher. He gathered around him great minds — giants in their fields. I noted Professor Emeritus Robert Stevenson was here. As you most certainly know, he's the world's expert on Pre-Inca culture, actually the Wari empire, that settled in the highlands of the Andean range. The Incas who lived there after them are much more well known, but the Wari produced important art, even though there are only a relatively few Wari art pieces in existence. The fact is, your grandfather possessed several of them." Demont glanced over his shoulder. "Perhaps we should find a place a bit more private than this to discuss what I have come for."

"There's a *Jason's Deli* about a mile up the road on the right. Back toward the airport. I'll meet you there in, say, fifteen minutes. I want to see if Oscar called. I can't imagine why he's not here."

At the mention of her cousin, Demont's eyes narrowed. He again glanced over his shoulder. Moving even closer, he said, "That man is not what he seems. His real name is Oscar Lowell. He changed it to Hugo just about the time —"

"Oh, hello there Dr. Demont." The man Demont had identified as the Wari expert said as he walked toward them. "I thought I noticed you come in. One supposes Sim's…August's…passing is sufficient to bring you down off that hill of yours in Pittsburgh. He indeed was most generous to your institution. Most generous I would say."

"I came to pay my respects, if you please. No different than you. Civility in the presence of…of our mutual friend is most appropriate."

Stevenson, without missing a beat, turned to face Belle. "I'm Professor Stevenson. I was a colleague of your grandfather at Brownsville until his retirement. You and I met several years back. You were just a young girl then. You're all grown up now I see."

"I most certainly do recall you coming for lunch," Belle replied, extending her hand in greeting, despite her discomfort. "Thank you for coming to Grandfather's funeral."

"Tragic how it ended for him. Very tragic. He was good people. May he rest in peace."

"Thank you, Professor," Belle replied. "He would be happy to know you were here."

"Least I could do. Well, I'll be going. Don't wish to miss my ride home." Stevenson turned on his heel and went back outside to where a car was waiting for him under the portico. One of the men he had been sitting with was driving and the other two were in the back seat. Something to do on a nice sunny day in the Valley, Belle thought as the car drove away. Just four old men reliving their past.

Funeral director de Cordoba had taken Demont's place when Belle came out of her thoughts. "Oh," she said, "You're just the person I was looking for. Did Oscar Hugo call or anything? He wasn't here."

"You said he would join us, but I've heard nothing. I'm terribly sorry, but we waited for him as long as we could."

"You did the right thing, Mr. de Cordoba. The service was appropriate. Do you require anything further from me?"

"Nothing. We will take care of the rest. It'll be about two weeks and we'll have his remains ready for you. You can pick an urn at that time if you wish. We will call when he's ready for pick up."

~ Chapter ~
9

Demont sat in a booth in the far back corner. The table was bare except for a glass of water sitting untouched in front of him. "Thanks for coming," he said, standing to usher Belle into the seat opposite him.

Instead of sitting, she said, "I suspect you're hungry. I certainly am. Ever been to a *Jason's* before?"

"Can't say as I have. I don't believe there are any in Pittsburgh. At least I haven't seen one."

"It's self-order, so we go over there to order. My favorite is the muffaletta — with ham. They are big. I can't eat more than a quarter."

When they were back at the table, Belle said, "If you ask me, you and Professor Stevenson aren't exactly best friends."

"Professional rivalry. Nothing more."

Belle didn't comment on his answer, but his tenor was slightly off. There was more to this than Demont wanted to talk about. For now, at least, Belle had other matters on her mind. "You came all this way. Why?"

"You certainly are of your grandfather's stock. Blunt and to the point. Okay, I'll pull no punches. I think you know your grandfather's name, the name he was born with, is Simpson Hugo. He attended Pitt on a partial football scholarship. He then went on to earn his PhD in natural sciences. He specialized in Peruvian art and particularly in works from the coastal Incas. That's where his association with Stevenson began. In the early days, it was a rich man's game. Grant money was not readily available as it is today, so it was necessary to find a benefactor. Often that led to a parent or grandparent. In my case, it was my grandmother. In Stevenson's case, it was his father. Oil money from Houston. Beaumont to be exact. He can't spend it as fast as it comes in — or came in. The money may have dried up now, I don't know."

"And my grandfather? Simpson. It's hard for me to even say that name without shuddering. Where did he get the money?"

"That's just it. He didn't. Well, not on his own he didn't. He teamed up with Stevenson and came out here."

"I thought he hired Stevenson, not the other way around."

"Neat little arrangement they had. Stevenson lives to explore in Peru. And I use explore loosely." Demont, as he was prone to do, checked his surroundings. Not seeing anything that disturbed him, he continued, "He's never been caught, but I have every reason to believe he's been illegally removing antiquities from Peru for more than a quarter century."

"I thought countries had stringent controls in place to prevent looting," Belle replied, concealing the fact that she knew full well the laws of Mexico and Peru—as well as how to circumvent those laws.

"They do. But there are ways around any control. Money mostly. A hundred thousand here, a hundred thousand there and pretty soon you have the locals carrying the contraband out for you.

Not to mention other so-called experts planting misleading information."

"So, where does Simpson fit into this?" Belle asked, as if she didn't already know the answer. "And what about Oscar? You keep saying he's to be watched."

"Let's begin with Oscar Lowell — Hugo." Demont spread a document on the table between them. "This is a name change order signed by a Pittsburgh

Common Pleas Court Judge. You can see that your cousin had his name changed from Oscar Lowell to Oscar Hugo. That fact is beyond question."

"But he...Oscar...looks exactly like my grandfather. Same eyes. Same smile."

"The mind sees what the mind wishes to see. He was born Oscar Lowell."

"I suppose I can't argue with a court order. Now for my grandfather."

"Being blunt I'm afraid he's smack in the middle. I believe Simpson Hugo changed his name simply to facilitate the smuggling."

Belle sat upright. The last thing she had expected was to be told her grandfather was a criminal. He, with her help, had worked hard to cover his tracks. "But didn't you say it was Stevenson who was the expert and who stole the art?"

"He masterminded it. Your grandfather carried it out. Listen, I know this is a lot for you to take in. If you would prefer, we can continue in the morning after a good night's sleep."

"You really think I can sleep knowing what I now know. Please continue."

Again Demont glanced around the restaurant before saying, "We at Pitt feel abused, victimized is a better term for it. We had no idea Hugo changed his name. We know him only as Simpson Hugo. We sponsored his trips with money we now know came from a fund controlled by Stevenson. So Hugo goes to Peru under Pitt sponsorship and crates of stuff come back to Professor Villanova at UT Brownsville. Part of the control process is for artifacts to be validated by an independent person. So Villanova values the artifacts as essentially worthless. Then the world expert, Stevenson, who is paid by the Peru government to oversee pre-Inca artifacts, signs off. Often another expert is consulted. As of late they have been using a Mexico City professor."

"So why are you here, Professor Demont?" Belle asked, anxious to end the conversation. "You already have the answers."

"Not all the answers. Not all the answers by any means. But the puzzle is coming together. My concern is that when this breaks open, and it will at some point, we in Pittsburgh will be left holding the bag. We are the ones who sponsored Hugo. We are the ones they will come after. It won't be pretty."

"And, let me guess, you are the ones who now have in your possession Pre-Inca artifacts that, in fact, are very much authentic, but which have been declared to be copies. Possession of stolen property in other words."

"I wouldn't go so far as to characterize the items as stolen. Let's just say they were improperly characterized."

"So characterize them properly."

"Easier said than done, I'm afraid. Besides the great embarrassment that will cause, the best person to perform such a recharacterization is, of course, Dr Stevenson. We've approached him and as you may imagine, he won't do it. Also, if he would, or if someone would, the items would have to go back to Peru. It's a mess no matter how you handle it."

"Pardon me, Professor. Call me a skeptic if you will, but you didn't come all this way to tell me your troubles. You want something. What is it?"

This time Demont studied every patron in the restaurant before answering. "if this comes out — I should say, when this comes out — my reputation will be ruined. It's too late to salvage that at this point."

"So why—"

Demont held his hand up. "I'm getting there. On one of the explorations we sponsored, your Hugo — your grandfather — uncovered the *Golden Booby*, a piece that was hand carved in the South Pacific. To those in the know, the *Golden Booby* is the Holy Grail of art. The current value of that artifact is well over two-hundred million and it belongs to...us."

"So where do you believe the booby is now?" Belle asked, holding no illusion that if Demont ever found the *Golden Booby* he would turn it over to his beloved institution. Money talks and right now she heard it screaming.

"Perhaps the only thing Dr. Stevenson and I agree on is that the bird was last seen in the possession of your grandfather."

"If your question is — do I know where that bird is? The answer is — I don't."

"But, my dear, you actually do know. You just don't know that you know. It appears that the *Golden Booby* was mounted on a base and two guardian birds, of far lesser value, were added to, shall we say, oversee the Booby. Each of the other birds is perched atop a nest of eggs. Two of those eggs, I suppose one egg from each of the guardian birds, is removable. Does any of this make sense to you?"

"Go on," Belle said, refusing to give up what she knew about the guardian birds and their eggs.

"It is my belief that the key to finding the *Golden Booby* is somehow contained in those eggs."

"I really would have no idea, Professor Demont. Grandfather certainly never told me any of this."

"Am I to believe you don't have the guardian birds? Or know where they are?"

"You can believe what you will." Belle stood to leave. "I'm sorry you came all this way to find a dead end. Have a good night."

"Before you go, I believe you will want to read this." Demont reached inside his sport coat and produced a section of a neatly folded newspaper article. He carefully unfolded the newsprint and held it out to Belle.

ICE returns stolen and looted art and antiquities to Peru

WASHINGTON — Today, U.S. Immigration and Customs Enforcement (ICE) returned 14 stolen and looted cultural paintings and artifacts to the government of Peru at a repatriation ceremony at the Embassy of Peru in Washington, D.C. The items were recovered in five separate investigations by special agents of ICE Homeland Security Investigations (HSI) in New York; West Virginia; Wilmington, Delaware; and Austin and Houston, Texas.

Returned to the Peruvian people were nine religious paintings, a monstrance and four archaeological items that date back more than 2,000 years. The return of this cultural property is the culmination of a long, hard fight by HSI, INTERPOL and the U.S. Attorney's Offices from the District of Delaware, the Southern District of New York, and the Southern District of Texas. Participating in today's repatriation were ICE Director John Morton, Peruvian Ambassador to the United States Harold Forsyth and U.S. Department of Justice Deputy Attorney General James Cole. Also in attendance were INTERPOL Washington Director Timothy A. Williams and representatives from the Southern District of New York and District of Delaware U.S. Attorney's Offices; U.S. Department of State Cultural Heritage Center; Smithsonian Institution; and HSI special agents from the respective investigative offices.

The article went on to list the archaeological items that were returned, but Belle stopped reading halfway through the list. She slumped back into her seat, her head down, trying to digest what it all meant.

"My goal," Demont said after a while, "was not to come down here to upset you. But I did hope to gain your confidence so that we could work together. There is a great deal of money involved here. And it is my experience that when a lot of money is on the table piles of it always seem to go missing. Hey, don't get me wrong. Those piles go missing in fees and retainers, things of that nature."

"You certainly have a strange way to gain one's confidence. I'll say that much."

"I also came down here to warn you of the danger you are in. And possibly to help."

Belle didn't immediately respond. When she did, her voice was composed, resigned to deal with what she was about to learn. "So I suppose you are saying my grandfather did not die a natural death."

"That's my thought, for what it's worth. I have reason to believe your grandfather tipped off Interpol. I assume you recognized at least some of the items recovered."

"Not the artwork, but the others. I have...pictures of those items. Then grandfather removed them from the house."

"He sold them, donated all the money by setting up funds at Pitt and at UT and I don't know where else. I believe he and Stevenson had a falling out. I also assume that most, if not all, of the artifacts they collected — I suppose I should be politically incorrect and say stole — belonged in some manner to Stevenson."

"Professor, pardon me for asking, but is that pure supposition, or do you have a basis for your conclusions?"

"Mostly supposition, I admit. But Peru, as well as many other countries have become increasing more assertive about their culture. It's become big money to them in terms of the tourist trade to house their own antiquities in their own museums. Interpol and Homeland Security have interviewed me extensively about the origin of many of the pieces we house. Many of them came from Hugo. They couldn't locate him, but it was only a matter of time until they connected all the dots."

Belle, wishing to get everything she could from Demont, volunteered, "I now do recall an article in the paper about Peru trying to stop a sale of antiquities, I think it was in France. Sothby's went ahead with the sale claiming they had verified all the lots as legally being able to sale. I'm sorry, I didn't mean to interrupt."

"Indeed, that was the Barbier-Mueller collection. And our friend Stevenson was the one who certified that the lots were good to go. In the end, they had a very poor bidder turnout and the lots were sold for a steal. Stevenson's involvement with Sothby's ticked off the Peruvian government because of his being their advisor as well. It was their pressure that put Stevenson on Interpol's short list. The fact that he had signed off on so many of the items originally and now was certifying those same items as being authentic and removed from the country legally raised red flags. He might have tipped the FBI to Villanova to get them off his back. We do know that about that same time your grandfather suddenly disposed of all the artwork. We also know he sold his house and moved to a trailer. Went into hiding, of a sort. One last fact. The FBI stopped pestering me to produce Hugo around the time of the tip to Interpol about the pre-Columbian items. That's why I believe he was cooperating with the authorities."

"You believe I am in danger. Why?"

"Much of the money made in stolen antiquities over the years went to fund the drug trade. Now, unfortunately, it is funding terrorism. So whereas years ago the surnames we heard were mostly Spanish in nature, now they have a Middle-Eastern flavor. And money is the name of the game."

"And they think I have the *Golden Booby*?"

"What you actually have, or what you actually know, is not the issue. They're working on the theory that if you don't have it you darn well know where it is. Your grandfather, may he rest in peace, would not have simply buried it with no possible method of finding it."

"But that's exactly what he did. I don't know where it is and I have no way to find it."

"Pardon me, Ms. Neuva, but if I am not buying that story, neither are the bad guys."

"I don't even have any idea where to begin looking, even assuming I wanted to find it."

~ CHAPTER ~
10

Driving back to the island, Belle took the two-lane road she called the back way. The few houses along the way were set back from the road making it appear deserted — and dark. The industrial zones were closed for the night and the fruit stands closed. Orchards, their trees laden with citrus, bordered the road for miles. Laguna Vista was still several miles ahead, as was the sign warning motorists not to pick up hitchhikers because of the Immigrant Detention Center located not far from the town.

The headlights from a car about a quarter of a mile back had her attention. She tried going fast, then slow, but the lights maintained the same spacing regardless of her speed. There was nowhere to go and nowhere to hide, so she stepped up her speed, hoping to rouse a patrol officer. Often, constables with nothing else going on parked their cruisers in driveways off to the side of the road in hopes of generating income for their jurisdictions.

The miles slid by, the headlights didn't move, and no sheriff materialized.

Finally, the far reaches of her headlights found the no hitchhiker sign. In seconds it disappeared behind her. She knew that Laguna Vista town center was just ahead. She also knew that there was a police station in town. She glanced once more in her rearview mirror to make certain her stalker was not closing the gap. If anything, a larger gap now existed. The car behind her had slowed slightly.

Belle allowed the car to slow just enough so that she could pull into the police lot without her brake lights coming on until the very last moment. Three, two, one. Go! Belle swung the wheel to the right and simultaneously pounded her foot onto the brake. The tires screeched and the car teetered, barely inches from overturning. For several long seconds Belle was convinced she would either flip the car or crash into the front of the building.

Then the car mercifully settled back, stopping barely inches from the brick structure. In the maneuver, Belle lost track of her pursuer. She flung her door open and raced for the front door of the police station. Out of the corner of her eye she caught the image of a man jumping out of his car and running toward her.

"Belle!" a voice rang out just as she passed through the door and into the safety of the police station. The voice had the cadence of her grandfather. She translated the identity to that of her cousin Oscar, but she had no way to be certain and this wasn't the time to sort it all out.

The lobby was empty. Several doors bordered the open lobby area. She ran toward the only door showing light.

"Belle! It's me, Oscar," the voice behind her called. "You have nothing to —"

Ignoring her pursuer, she ran into the room with the light. That room was also empty, but a table was positioned directly across from her with what looked to be an old-fashioned telephone operator's control panel in the center.

Behind her the footsteps were closing fast and still no one appeared. "Help!" she shouted, her voice cracking. "I need help! I'm being chased." At any minute she expected a hand to come over her shoulder and clamp itself around her mouth — or worse.

"Did I hear someone…Oh, what have we here?" an oversized officer said, coming into the room from a far corner. Immediately sizing up the situation, his hand moved toward his gun holster. "You, stop!' he commanded to the man behind her. "Don't take another step toward the lady! Lady, come stand over here." He motioned to a position behind him.

Belle gladly complied with the officer's instructions. It wasn't until she turned to face the person chasing her that she knew for certain that it was, indeed, Oscar Hugo, formerly Oscar Lowell.

"Now tell me, miss, what's going on here."

"This man," Belle began, her voice tentative, "is following me. He followed me from Harlingen. I didn't know until just now that I met him yesterday."

"Tell the officer, Belle. Tell him that we share the same grandfather."

"This man," Belle responded, "claims to be my...cousin. But...but his name was Oscar Lowell. Now it's Hugo. Oscar Hugo. He changed it. I don't —"

"Hold it!" the officer said. "All I want to know is whether or not this man is putting you in stress. Yes or no?"

"Well...yes. I don't know —"

"Yes or no?"

"Yes. Yes he is."

"You," the officer said to Oscar, "step over there with your hands over your head." He waited for Oscar to comply, then asked, "Do you have any weapons on you? Gun, knife, anything?"

"Gun," came the reply, "but please —"

The officer's gun came out. For his size he was surprisingly fast. "Hands over your head!" he ordered. "Don't move. Not a muscle." He keyed the mike pinned to his shirt. "I have an armed suspect. Need support. Now!"

Almost immediately two even larger officers came through the hall door, guns drawn. A third one appeared from the far corner. The original officer pointed his gun at Oscar and said, "He's armed. Band him and remove his weapon."

One of the backup officers produced a pair of yellow zip cuffs and moved toward Oscar. The three other officers had their guns trained directly on him. It seemed to Belle that they were itching to pull their triggers and she hoped Oscar would be smart enough not to resist. There was time enough later to get to the bottom of this — assuming they didn't shoot.

Oscar, his hands still over his head, his voice surprisingly calm, said, "Before this gets further out of control let me identify myself. I'm a Marshal. I am employed by the United States Marshal Service. My credentials are inside my jacket in the right side pocket."

"Keep your hands where they are," demanded the first officer, his tone softened. "Sanchez, get his identification. Oscar Hugo, or what the hell your real name is, don't you move a muscle. Marshal or not, I'll shoot you if you try anything while we're getting to the bottom of this mess."

The officer holding the zip cuffs continued toward Oscar being careful to keep his gun out of Oscar's reach. A moment later he handed the credential case to the officer in charge. After examining the contents and the badge and matching the picture against the person standing across from him, he said "Excuse me a moment. Don't anyone move. Oscar Hugo, please keep your hands where they are. Sanchez, until we verify this, treat him as a suspect." He then disappeared through the side door.

The minute lengthened into ten minutes during which time Belle struggled to understand the consequences if Oscar was, in fact, a U.S. Marshal. In that case, Demont was either lying, or badly misinformed. Perhaps Demont was actually working for the folks, the bad guys as he had put it, who wanted the *Golden Booby*. In any event, life just became more complicated.

"Put your weapons away," the officer in charge said when he finally returned. "Credentials check out. Hugo, you can put your hands down. He's a Federal Marshal assigned to Pittsburgh. He doesn't present a threat to the lady here, unless, of course he plans to arrest her." Turning to Belle, he said, "I believe we have a case of mistaken identity. I'll leave it at that. You're certainly not in any danger of being…molested or anything. But before you go we'll have to get your name and identification for our incident report. Shouldn't take but five minutes and you'll be on your way."

"Belle," Oscar said, "I'm sorry, but I couldn't tell you earlier. We can talk when they're finished. I'll wait here."

"I'm not sure I have anything further to say to you," Belle responded, "Federal Marshal or not."

Ignoring her comment, he said, "I'll be here when you're finished with them. We have to talk."

Belle was back in less than two minutes. The officer had simply photocopied her driver's license, handed the original back to her, and told her she was free to leave. What she wanted to ask, but didn't, was whether she could go out the back way as the hero always did in the movies. But she didn't think of herself as the hero. She felt more like the goat. A deceived goat at that.

'That didn't take long," Oscar greeted her when she appeared. "I was thinking, we could go to your place and talk or, if you wish, we can use a room here at the station. Your choice."

Keeping Oscar at arm's length felt better than having him follow her home. But on the other hand using a room at the police station would feel like an interrogation. Stalling for time, Belle said, "I didn't see your papers. For all I know, you and them—"

Before she finished her sentence his leather credential case was open in front of her displaying a round gold outer ring with a central star. The badge was set against a blue background with the words UNITED STATES MARSHALL prominently embossed on the gold ring. His picture on a Department of Justice ID was positioned on a flap hanging above the badge. There was little doubt who employed her cousin — assuming he really was her cousin.

"Okay, I concede." Oscar had spent last night on her sofa and if he was going to do anything to her he would have done it then. "It feels better to talk at my place. You know where I live. I'll see you there."

"That sounds fine, but please go straight to your home. No detours."

Oscar sounded serious. There was no smile to lessen the order; no wink to let Belle know he was only joking.

Her suspicion that events had become even more stressful was borne out the moment she stepped out of her car in her driveway. Oscar was immediately beside her. "Before you go in," he began, wearing the same official expression he had shown outside of the police station, "let me warn you that a search warrant has been executed on your property."

"What the hell does that mean?" Belle demanded.

"Federal Marshals have searched your house. We were looking for —"

"What the hell's going on?" Before he could respond, she added, "Is that why you weren't at the funeral? You missed your grandfather's funeral to search my house!"

"Look, calm down a moment here. First off, I didn't really know him, other than the one time he bought me lunch and gave me the bird. Second, we're in the middle of a murder investigation and we don't want anyone one else...hurt."

"Is that directed at me? I'm in danger?"

"Possibly, yes. Let's go inside and talk. We've swept for bug plants and you're now clean."

"You mean I wasn't before? A bug in my home! How...how in the hell could —"

"Whoever broke in before planted it. It's gone now."

Once inside, Belle said, "As you know, I don't have any coffee so I can't make you any."

"Water will be fine." She started for the kitchen, then shrieked, "The pictures are gone! All of them! Gone!"

"We have them. They're safe. That's what I started to tell you outside and got sidetracked. The FBI lab will digitize them, front and back, and return the originals as well as the digital images. They'll have it done in less than a day. This is a priority matter."

"I suppose you think I should say thank you!"

"I don't want you to say anything. Just sit for a few minutes and I'll do my best to bring you up to speed."

"I'm all ears," Belle said, collapsing onto the sofa with the hope of finding a measure of comfort in her favorite corner. "This better be good."

"I suppose Demont told you about my name change. I took the name Hugo after I found out Simpson was my grandfather. The truth is, he never married my grandmother. Her name was Katherine O'Connell. My father was adopted at birth by a family named Lowell and given the name Harold Lowell. So my original birth certificate name was Oscar Lowell. Nod if you're following me."

"Actually, I am. Go on."

"I grew up an average kid, doing average things. Went to a community college and joined the Marshal Service when I was twenty-two. That was eighteen years ago. About two-three years back Interpol was looking to speak with Simpson Hugo concerning art illegally removed from Peru. At that time no one had any inkling that Hugo and Villanova were one and the same. Interpol just wanted Hugo to verify the authenticity of certain pieces. The trouble was that Pitt informed Interpol that Hugo was out of the country. Interpol's investigation, however, did not show Hugo ever leaving the country. Pitt insisted that he went on many trips at their expense. This raised questions and the Service was called in to sort it out. At first the Hugo matter wasn't assigned to me. I heard the guys talking about this shadow guy by the name of Simpson Hugo. I went to my boss and told him that a guy by the name of Simpson Hugo had come to me not long before claiming to be my grandfather. Normally, they would never allow a family member to get involved in an investigation, but because everyone was coming up cold and because of the tenuous relationship between him and me, they agreed to put me on the Hugo team. I couldn't find him either. He truly was a shadow. One of the guys joked that I should change my name, perhaps draw him out that way. Justice worked a deal with a judge to issue the name change papers knowing it was a ruse."

"So is Hugo your real name now or not?"

"For now it is. The idea is to change it back once this is finished."

"Why not just keep it. Marshal Hugo fits you better than Marshal Lowell."

"Anyway, let's talk about your new best friend, Winston Demont III. He died a week ago. Just before Villanova. The same chemical was found in his blood stream as was in Villanova's."

"I just had dinner with —"

"An imposter. Most likely Demont's killer."

Belle jerked upright as if she had been hit by a bolt of lightning. "I ate with a killer! If he killed Demont then he could've killed my grandfather as well!"

"Probably not. That was most likely a guy by the name of Stevenson. Dr. Robert Stevenson."

"He was at the funeral as well. I met him years ago."

"I was told he was there. Him and three friends. They're known as the Four Thieves. Those folks have been draining Peru dry of valuable artifacts since the fifties."

"So what's changed? Why are they now killing their own?"

"I can't speak for what Demont did wrong in their eyes, but I'm pretty certain I know what sealed Grandfather's fate."

"And that was?"

"He tipped off the FBI to a major art transaction. Perhaps Demont was a collaborator as to the authenticity of the works being sold. Anyway, the art was confiscated and our government just returned that art to Peru. Several men were arrested. They had Middle East connections."

"How much art are we talking about?"

"Roughly eighty-five million."

"And if I follow what you just said, then Demont and Stevenson are in this together."

"Them and several others. We have them under surveillance."

"I take it you guys, and I mean the Feds, are after the *Golden Booby* as well as the other missing art," Belle said, getting into the hunt. "Are you thinking they are both in the same place?"

"At first we did. Now we're going on the assumption they're separate."

"What changed your mind?"

"The words on your egg and mine are the key to one location. They'll prove relatively easy to decode unless I miss my guess. I also think they'll lead us to the Booby."

"So you already know what the words mean?"

"Not exactly, but the DC gurus believe it's some form of a mail zip code cipher. Only a matter of time until we have it worked out."

"A zip code is a large area. A town or part of a big city. Grandfather would have been more precise."

"I'm willing to bet that once we have the codes broken, the actual location will become apparent."

"If you say there are two different locations there must be—"

"Other eggs with markings on them. That's what the subpoena was about. That, and making sure the art wasn't around. Sorry, but we had to eliminate all possibilities. Actually, lab's been working on it and we should have a first read vey soon."

"You assume they'll be able to decode what they find."

"The lab is expert on breaking ciphers. In fact, it's most likely the old guy counted on us breaking it. Unless…" Oscar fell silent. The intensity on his face suggesting deep thought.

"Penny for your thoughts," Belle finally said when Oscar showed no sign of returning his attention on her.

"Oh, sorry. Worth a lot more than a penny! Listen. There are numbers on your eggs, but not on mine. That means he wanted you to have something. You and you alone. But we both had words on the removable eggs. That means…he wanted us to cooperate in some manner with those words."

"Or that both words are required to decipher the code," Belle added, not sure where this was going. She also had no intention of sharing the *Golden Booby* with the Feds—or even with her cousin Oscar acting on his own.

Oscar's voice broke into her thoughts. "…he say anything when he gave you yours?"

"Like…"

"Like an instruction. Or anything?"

"As I think of it, he said something out of character. He said not to forget he loved apples."

"Apples?"

"That's what he said. He loved apples. Red Delicious. I remember because they've always been my favorites as well."

That's it!" Oscar exclaimed.

"That's what?"

"He told me he loved mangos. He also told me to strip the mango before I used it. What else did he tell you?"

Belle thought for a moment before answering. "I don't recall anything else."

"You said it was strange what he said. It made no sense. He must have said more. But truth be told, stripping mangos makes no sense."

Belle studied her small yard below the window, making a mental note to trim the bushes. Turning back to Oscar, she said, "I'm trying to recall his exact words. I dismissed them at the time so I don't think I can — wait! I remember. He said you have to watch those apples because they subtract from other fruit. That's what made no sense. Actually, that's why I remember it. It was the only time I ever thought Grandfather was...was losing it."

"Grandpa was not losing it, I can assure you of that. He set this up for us so we must assume everything he did and said had importance. He wanted us to follow his clues."

Oscar carefully wrote down exactly what his grandfather had said to him and then had Belle repeat exactly what she had been told. The two of them spent the next two hours dissecting what they had found. At the end of that time they were no closer to an answer than when they started.

"Can we pick this up in the morning?" Belle finally asked. "I'm beyond exhausted. You can use the sofa again. You know your way around. Don't wake me."

"I have a room over at the La Quinta. I understand the pecan pancakes at *Ted's* are worth the calories. I know you're not a breakfast eater but will you join me at ten?"

"Ten works for me."

"See you there. All that fruit talk woke up my appetite. Mind if I raid the fridge? Something to keep me occupied on the ride over to the hotel."

"Be my guest, but all you'll find are apples I'm afraid. Red Delicious to be exact."

Consulting his notes, Oscar mused, "I wonder if your apples will subtract from other fruit?"

"When you find out, let me know," Belle said already halfway to her bedroom. She was too tired to even tell him to let himself out.

~ CHAPTER ~
11

"Sorry, couldn't wait any longer," Oscar said, glancing at his mostly empty pancake plate. "I don't know what they do to the pecans, but these puppies are sure good."

"I'm glad you started without me," Belle said. "I walked. Needed something to get my motor going." Turning to the waitress, she said, "Olivia, a large orange juice, please. That'll do it." Turning back to Oscar, she said, "You look chipper this morning. Have a good night's sleep?"

"Matter of fact, I haven't been to bed. I —"

"Something else come up?"

"We'll know in a few minutes. The Federal Attorney is in chambers right now presenting evidence for a search warrant. Marshals are standing by to execute the order the moment it's issued. Should happen any moment."

"Based on what we discussed last night?"

"Mostly, but I had some lab help."

"Are you going to tell me, or must I solve it myself?

"The apple you gave me was the key. I ate it on the way to the motel. You know those stickers they have on fruit? Well, the one on the apple got in my mouth in the dark. I spit it on the floor of the car. But then I got to thinking about how stupid it was to put those things on food in the first place. Then I thought about why they were there at all."

"They have numbers that identify the fruit. All fruit —"

"Bingo!"

Mangos and apples. Not just any apple, but Red Delicious apples. I got on line and found 4961 for mangos and 3284 for Red Delicious."

"Grandfather said that apples subtract from other fruit. So —"

"You're good! So you get 1677."

"Now I'm lost," Belle confessed. "What's that mean?"

"Remember, he told me to strip the mango. There's an area in Pittsburgh called the Strip District."

"So you think 1677 is an address in this Strip area? But what street?"

"If necessary, we'd go to every 1677 and snoop around. Then we'd go get the warrant."

"But you said they're getting the warrant now. How do you know where?"

"Grandpa saved us all the trouble of figuring out the exact street by putting the letters PENN on some of your eggs. Penn Avenue is the main road through the Strip. Lots of warehouses and some abandoned buildings. 1677 is almost directly across from the old Pennsylvania railroad station which, I might add, makes it convenient for moving freight in and out. In the Strip District trucks move around all day and night so no one would ever pay any attention to activity at a warehouse down there."

"Is 1677 a warehouse?"

"A Store and Drop. Rent it by the year. Rent was paid for five years. Owner won't let us in. That's what the warrant's for. We don't need legal problems at this stage."

"Will a judge grant a search warrant on what you have? It's all guesswork."

"Investigation is always guesswork. It all fits. It's reasonable and it's a warehouse. Maybe if it was a home the warrant would be harder to obtain. But a warehouse should be —." Oscar looked down at his cell. "Got it! Let's get out of here." Oscar stood, dropped a twenty on the table and said, "They'll be inside in a few minutes. We'll watch live in the car. I've been working years to get to this point and I don't want to miss the finale."

"What do you suppose they'll find?"

"Most, if not all, of the artwork that went missing from his house. All the stuff you have pictures of."

"The *Golden Booby*?"

"No. It is my understanding that the Booby was his and his alone. The stuff in Pittsburgh, I think we will find, came from Peru. That's what Stevenson and his crew are looking for. The *Golden Booby* is from the South Pacific. I checked it out. There's nothing illegal about that bird being here. It may have been found in Peru, but it's not theirs anymore than it was Grandpa's. That's why I said before the code for the Booby is separate — and I assume easier — than for the other stuff. Hey, you — and I — now own the *Golden Booby*! Free and clear I might add."

"If we can find it, that is," Belle managed to say, still not certain where this was all leading. Demont and whomever he was working with, would not go away easily. Another killing would mean nothing to them.

"We'll find it," Oscar said, his eyes now animated. "Grandpa wanted us to have it, so we'll find it. But first things first." A beep sounded and Oscar set his cell phone on the dash. The picture was wobbly, as if the camera was being worn on someone's head. Three uniformed men and a woman came into view.

"That's Jackie's crew," Oscar said. "She's wearing the camera. I think she does that so her picture is never made public. She says that's her full employment protection. I doubt they'll have any problems. Grandpa was not the type to have set traps. They'll show the warrant to the manager and he'll allow them to cut the lock."

As Oscar was talking, that is exactly how it played out. Like a rehearsed scene, the man behind the counter looked at the badges, glanced quickly at the cell phone screen displaying the signed search warrant, and then motioned them to go back into the warehouse. "It's the entire fifth floor," the counterman called after them. "You can use the freight elevator if you wish. On your right. Elevator code's 5500. You clean up any mess you make."

The man had enough sense to remain in the office so he could later claim he didn't know what they saw or what they took. He wasn't being paid enough to get involved. And if bullets started to fly he wanted to be as far away as possible.

A minute later the door to the fifth floor flew open revealing exactly what Oscar had predicted. The art pieces that had been so carefully displayed in the Professor's house were now haphazardly heaped together, nothing protecting them from being scratched or broken. It appeared as if the storage floor was simply discarded trash. A female voice said, "Okay, this is what we came for. First, I want it all photographed in place as we found it. Then carefully lift the pieces out, beginning at the top. Albert, call for movers blankets, lots of them. I want this all preserved. We inventory and photograph it as it comes out. Nothing leaves this floor without being logged. Oscar, you nailed it!"

"Thanks Jackie," Oscar responded. "Set a perimeter and post some folks. We don't know all the players and we don't need surprises."

"Understood. Perimeter was secured and I'll get extra hands to watch over the nest. This is one hell of a treasure trove. Can't say as I've see this much art in one place in my whole career."

"Take care. Bye."

"Jackie's smart. I assume she appreciates what I just told her," Oscar said when the line went dead. "Grandpa didn't amass that much art work without some very powerful people pulling strings. They'll all want their cut — one way or another."

"Are you thinking the Marshals are compromised?"

"Could be any number of the agencies involved; from FBI to Border Patrol and beyond. Politicians have been known to —"

"I can't believe he pulled this off without political cover," Belle said. "I think that's why Grandfather went to such extremes. Only you turned out to be part of the law. If not, then… then we'd be —"

"Rich. We'd have it to ourselves. Sorry. But remember the *Golden Booby* is worth at least a hundred million to us. I'll bet we can each manage on that for awhile."

"Assuming we can find it."

Without hesitation, Oscar said, "We'll find it. I have an idea. But we'll need a computer. Let's go to your place. This could take a while."

"We'll use mine. I think I know where to find yours."

Belle's anger flared. "You should have told me up front who you worked for!"

"I wasn't at liberty at that point. I didn't know if Stevenson had gotten to you. Hell, for all we knew, you could have been working for him. Perhaps you even could have been involved in moving the artwork. Perhaps you knew where it was all along."

Belle started to respond but thought better of it. How easy it would be for Oscar to set her up with criminal charges. He could then make off with the *Golden Booby* while she was fighting the law. How very convenient. Greed, she knew full well, could do that. One would think that someone worth fifty million — as Oscar would be with half the *Golden Booby* — would be satisfied. But Stevenson, who was heir to an oil fortune, would never be satisfied.

"Judging from your expression," Oscar said, "that came out the wrong way. Let me assure you we have no reason to suspect you of any wrongdoing. Feel better?"

"Isn't this where I announce I want a lawyer before I say another word?"

"Only if you have something to hide."

"Spoken like a true lawman."

They drove in silence the few blocks to Belle's house. When the car stopped, Belle said, "Don't bother getting out. Cooperation is finished."

Despite her statement, Oscar slid out of his car and started for the front steps.

"I said no! Unless you have another warrant, which I haven't seen, you'll be trespassing. Federal Marshal or not, you can be arrested for breaking and entering." Belle held her cell phone in front of her. "One more step and I dial 911. Locals love puttin' it to the Feds."

Oscar hesitated, looked across the car at Belle, then climbed back inside. "You're making a huge mistake, young lady. A huge mistake!" The car's wheels skidded as he accelerated down the street as if to emphasize the magnitude of Belle's mistake.

Belle stood watching as Oscar's car turned onto Padre Boulevard without slowing. How long do I have before he cracks the code? It was now a race. Taking the steps two at a time, she raced to her bedroom and retrieved her iPad.

Now what?

Portland and Windsor Hts. Two cities in the U. S.

Belle entered Portland into the browser and up popped a goggle map with a little red A bubble. She scanned the facts about Portland, but nothing jumped out at her. She recalled that Oscar had said he spent a month up there and turned up nothing. So dredging up facts about Portland was a time-wasting rat hole. No sense going that route.

She reviewed how Oscar had solved the puzzle using the fruit codes. What is unique to a city name?.

A zip code.

She found a zip code database and the numbers 97208 popped up for Portland. She entered the name Windsor Heights in her browser and found that it was in Iowa. The zip code number came up as 50324.

Think, Belle. Think. The words played over and over in her mind. She wrote the numbers down forward and backward. She added them and subtracted them. Nothing came of it. She paced the floor, looking first in the pantry and then in the refrigerator, as if by eating the answer would appear. But nothing worked. She fled the house and headed for the comfort of the beach, hoping sand beneath her feet would somehow lubricate her brain.

Peering out into the water, the wind whipping across her face, she envisioned a sailboat, the one her grandfather had hired, many years earlier. It was her thirteenth birthday present. A weeklong cruise. Just the two of them and a captain. They sailed from Port Isabel out through the Brazos Santiago ship channel and up to Port Aransas. Then they came home by way of the inland waterway, mostly under motor. It was her job to check off the waypoints one by one as they came back south. "They're numbered," the captain had told her. But on this device," he pointed to a computer-like screen, "the points show up as dots with latitude and longitude numbers next to each dot." He then went on to explain, "Longitude is a function of how far west we are from London. Since we are motoring essentially due south we are not moving further west from London so the longitude numbers won't change much at all. But latitude tells us how far north we are from the equator. See here, the latitude numbers are always on top and read first. The top numbers will change, get smaller, as we go south. You match those numbers against the waypoints and you'll see them getting smaller. That's how sailors get home."

How thrilled she had been, almost afraid to take her eyes from the screen until her grandfather told her she was missing the scenery, the birds. Even then she had kept one eye on the latitude numbers all the way south. They had indeed changed by the hour, going from twenty-seven point eight something down to twenty-six point something. The longitude always hovered around minus ninety-seven something.

Ninety-seven something! One of the zip codes had been ninety-seven something! She turned and raced home, sand flying as she went.

There it was. Portland, Oregon, 97208. But Windsor Heights, Iowa was 50324. A far cry from twenty-six something. She found a table on the Internet and dutifully plugged in 50324 for Lat and -97.208 for Lon. Up popped Gunton, Canada.

Gunton, Canada? Why would grandfather hide the *Golden Booby* in Gunton, Canada? But she wrote it down anyway. If nothing else came up, she would fly up there to investigate even though it made no sense.

Again she paced, this time replaying her conversation with Oscar about Portland. He had mentioned that there was only one Portland as far as he knew.

She ran back to the computer and found a site that listed all US towns in alphabetical order. There it was. Windsor Heights, WV.

Hurriedly, she pulled up the zip code database. 26075 was next to Windsor Hts. WV.

Now she tried 26.075 for Lat and -97.208 for Lon. Before she could blink, the town of Port Isabel, Texas appeared on her screen, the red A bubble sitting squarely in the center of the small town.

"Institutions," Oscar had said. "Schools, museums, that's where it will be," he had said. Then it came to her, the old railroad he had loved. *Pelican Station.* The train was long gone, but a museum was there, opposite to where the tracks had been.

That's exactly where it is, she told herself, trying to remain calm and failing miserably. She started for her car and then thought better of it. Oscar could be watching. Better to take it cautiously. Instead of driving over the bridge she took herself back down to the beach. A long walk would do her good.

Tomorrow would be time enough to go and claim the *Golden Booby* for her very own.

MURDER

CAN BE

GOLDEN

Pat McGrath Avery

~ Chapter ~
1

Since Belle Neuva found the priceless *Golden Booby* and loaned it to the *Treasures of the Gulf Museum* in Port Isabel, life had been crazy. Held in a place of honor and carefully encased under unbreakable glass, the statue's opening exhibition was expected to draw thousands of visitors.

I'm Hap Lynch, a Port Isabel resident and a spectator of historical artifacts.

"Come on, Hap. Quit daydreaming. We're going to be late for the opening," Peg said, not for the first time.

"I'm coming. I've just been thinking about the stories that statue could tell if it could talk."

"It's unbelievable, isn't it? It dates back to the 1500s. It's been stolen and hoarded, people have died getting it here and we are going to see it today," Peg's enthusiasm amused me. Life was never dull with my wife around.

As it turned out, the predictions were too conservative. All weekend, lines stretched around the block and the small museum couldn't manage the crowds. Many left to return another day.

Although the museum extended the exhibit the entire months of February and March to accommodate the visitors, April was halfway over before the crowds thinned out.

Did I tell you about the *Golden Booby*? I'm not an artist but the statue is breathtaking. The gleaming gold almost blinds the eye but it's the spectacular blue sapphires that really jump out at you. The eyes and feet are sapphire stones and the body is solid gold. The statue was created to honor the Blue-footed Booby, a bird that lives off the western coast of Central and South America. Supposedly the Boobies led the explorers to the fish.

As Peg says, "Booby's a perfect name for the males who strut around the females showing off their blue feet."

I have to admit she's probably right. All of us males strut around the females. It may not be blue feet we're proud of, but it's definitely our manhood.

On March 15, we attended a gala to honor Marne Law, an area artist who created a beautiful watercolor of the *Golden Booby*. The gala ended by auctioning off the painting. It now hangs in *Paragraphs* Bookstore on the island.

Once the museum returned to semi-normal, we visited the statue again. This time, the former cop in me came out. I spent the time checking out the security system.

Guarding a valuable artifact in such a small museum is a nightmare. Although six state-of-the-art cameras focused on the statue and alarms would go off if anyone touched the base or the glass case, there was no way to keep the exhibit far enough away from an exit door. I had a terrible feeling that a thief could be out the door before police could answer an alarm call. New doors had cameras inside and out. It helped that the front opened onto the busy Queen Isabella Boulevard that leads to the island causeway.

Nevertheless, it concerned me. The back exit led to a quiet parking lot. During the day, the museum's size turned out to be advantageous. A staff member would always be close if the alarm sounded. That gave me a little consolation but not enough to relax. I knew that anything this valuable tempted thieves who were smart enough to figure out a way, and dumb enough to try it.

As April came and attention turned to the real birds migrating through the Rio Grande Valley, life quieted down at the museum. The Convention Center on the island drew hundreds of birders and photographers. Every day Peg showed me beautiful pictures people had posted on Facebook.

I felt relieved that the *Golden Booby* still rested safely in the museum. Belle had found the statue buried in a box in the back room of the old *Port Isabel Historical Museum*. After she certified its authenticity and polished it, she loaned it to the *Treasures of the Gulf Museum*. Oscar, her cousin, filed a suit to reverse the loan. The judge quickly decided that the statue could remain at the museum until the legal issues were settled. Belle's lawyer said they could easily drag it out a year. The citizens and visitors to the area rejoiced because the legal gods smiled on them.

Peg had a meeting with local historian Steve Hathcock. Luke and I decided to tag along. Steve's always good for interesting tidbits of history about the island and besides, I love the burgers at the *Palm Street Pier*.

"Can you believe how popular the *Golden Booby* has been?" Peg's excitement level still ran high.

"It's quite a find and certainly verifies another element of our coastal history," Steve stroked his beard. "I'm fascinated by the possible Al Capone connection and I've been researching some more information…"

We spent the next few minutes soaking up Steve's findings. With his background as a locksmith, he understood my worry about the security of the museum. When we finished our burgers, Steve and Peg turned to their book business. He is the author of several books about South Padre Island history and treasure hunting.

After a delicious lunch and good company, we stopped by *Paragraphs*. Peg had to drop off some more copies of her dog books. Griff, the owner's husband, was talking to a big, burly kind of guy with long graying hair.

"Hey, let me introduce you to one of our local authors and the writer dog," Griff told the guy as we walked in.

Peg walked over and reached out her hand. "Hi, I'm Peg Lynch and this is Luke." Luke growled, Griff laughed and DL ignored them both.

"Pleased to meet you. I'm DL Casa."

"Shhh, Luke. Sorry he's acting up. Are you visiting the island?"

"Yes. I'm a songwriter and I have a couple of children's books that I was just showing to Griff."

He looked somewhat familiar and I wondered where I'd seen him before.

After a few more pleasantries I took Luke and wandered off so Peg, DL, and Griff could talk. Griff welcomed all new visitors to the store and people felt at home within minutes.

I watched several other people perusing the bookshelves. I'd seen one guy around town but really didn't know him. An overweight older woman kept rubbing her neck. I thought maybe she had a headache. As I watched, I remembered that I'd seen her at the museum the other day.

A woman with two young kids headed over to the children's section. I sat down, picked up a magazine and leafed through it until Peg was ready to leave. I vaguely heard the two kids begging their mom for books.

Peg and I enjoyed a quiet evening watching a couple of episodes of *The Good Wife*. We were halfway through Season Two and we loved it.

That night was the last good sleep I would get for quite a while.

"Have you had your coffee yet?" Rachel Vasquez, a detective on the Port Isabel Police Department and my neighbor, said as I answered my phone.

"It's not even 7:30. I still have to find the coffee pot," I grumbled.

"My, aren't we testy this morning. I hope Peg is out of harm's way." She laid it on thick.

"She's walking Luke, and yes, I'm awake now and need my coffee."

"Coming up, sir. Hope you're decent to answer your door."

The doorbell rang before I hung up the phone. I pasted a smile on my face and opened the door to an altogether-too-happy police officer holding out a mug of hot coffee.

"Come in," my pasted smile turned real at the sight of her. Rachel is a single mother to a cute little boy who inherited her energy.

"I need your help again," she began. I had helped her with her first murder investigation a couple of years ago.

"Not another…"

"Yes, and we have a mess on our hands."

"What do you mean?" I wasn't awake enough to keep up with the conversation.

"The statue…"

"Not the *Golden Booby* statue." I couldn't keep from interrupting her.

"Yes and no."

"What's that mean?" I stopped to take a sip of coffee but I needed to chug-a-lug the whole mug full.

"The thief was able to get to the statue…"

"No way. But yes, I worried about that," I interrupted again.

"Hap, let me get a word in edgewise, okay?"

"Sorry, the caffeine hasn't reached my brain yet. What happened? Did he escape?" That worry had niggled at me since the opening of the exhibit.

"Yes, but there's more. He killed Carol."

"Carol Flores, the curator?"

"Yes, he hit her over the head with the statue. Bashed her really hard."

"When did this happen? Was the museum still open?"

"It happened around 7:00 pm yesterday. The museum had closed but apparently Carol stayed late. The coroner thinks she died instantly."

"Sit down, Rachel. I need to think. Are you on the investigation team?"

"I'm leading it. Rudy Vega is at the museum now. I told him I'd be there in a few minutes."

"Who turned it in?"

"Betty Ryan discovered Carol's body. She went in early to do some bookwork before the museum opened." I tried to picture Betty. "Is she the tall lady with auburn hair?"

"Yes, she's the assistant curator. There's something else I haven't told you. The statue…"

"It's gone, isn't it?"

"No, well yes. It's puzzling."

"Why?"

"It broke into a million pieces. Betty said gold chards are everywhere."

"That's impossible. Gold is too hard… Oh, my God, that means the statue is a fake. It can't be. Oh, my God." I couldn't quite wrap my mind around the implications of this news.

"I have to go meet Rudy. I wanted you to hear it from me," Rachel kept talking but I wasn't listening.

"A fake. How long have we been displaying a fake? It was authenticated. Someone already stole it."

"Hap, I have to go. I'll get in touch with you later." Rachel left me sitting there with my mind in a whirl. I was wide awake.

~ Chapter ~

2

Ineeded to do something. Anything. I knew I'd be a nervous wreck until I heard from Rachel again. Since I'm retired, I have no authority but I guessed that Rachel might involve me. I helped her a couple of years ago when a book editor was murdered in his Port Isabel home. During that investigation I discovered that Rachel is sharp, detail-oriented, and patient — all good qualities for a detective.

I hated spoiling Peg's happy mood when she and Luke returned but I had to tell her. Shock immediately cast its quiet pall. Her lack of response — of any kind of movement — frightened me.

"Are you okay?" I grabbed her arms and looked in her eyes.

Only a slight nod acknowledged my question. I waited and worried.

"Oh Hap," she dissolved into my arms as tears began to roll down her cheeks.

"I'm sorry I had to tell you," I began.

"Don't be silly. It's not your fault. I don't know what to say first. I liked Carol. I didn't know her well but I liked her. Everyone did. She did a great job at the museum and, oh my God, what about her family?" By now the tears had soaked my shirt and Peg couldn't continue. She slumped against me. I think she would have slid to the floor if I hadn't been holding her.

"I can't think...the statue...it was a fake? How could that be? Belle had it authenticated."

"Someone had to replace it after it was in the museum," I said. "That's unimaginable but that's the only thing that could have happened."

"Poor Betty. She found her? Can you imagine what she must be going through?"

That's a difference between men and women. Here I was all worried about how the statue could be replaced but Peg focused on the really important things — Betty and Carol's family. That brought me back to earth. Carol could never be replaced.

"Maybe we should call Betty," I offered.

"Not now, Hap. If the police are there, she's probably a nervous wreck."

I had picked up my phone and noticed that I had a text message from Elena.

Hap, guess what! I may be coming to South Padre Island next week.

Good. My messages are short and to the point because I'm a hunt-and-peck kind of guy.

Dad has a consulting gig with the Coast Guard and he's trying to talk Mom into letting me go with him. It will be all week.

Call me. I didn't want to mess with this texting stuff.

When I answered the phone, I laughed out loud at her exuberance. I'd almost forgotten how much I enjoyed this thirteen-going-on-twenty whiz kid. I pictured her with iPad in hand as she talked a mile a minute.

I met Elena in Jefferson City when I toured the Missouri State Penitentiary. She's a bright, naturally curious girl who did some online research for me during a murder investigation.

"Dad has to do some consulting with the Coast Guard. If I come down there with him, can I see you? I miss you and Peg. Luke too."

"We'd love to see you. When would you come and where would you stay?"

"Next week if Mom agrees. Pray she does, Hap. I want to come in the worst way. I think I've talked Dad into staying in a historic hotel in Port Isabel. It's right on the bay and it may have ghosts. Wouldn't that be great — to see another real ghost?"

"I think you mean the *Queen Isabella Inn*. That would be great. Lots of history right around there. You'd love it."

"Doesn't it sound exciting? I can't wait."

"When will you know if you're coming?"

"Dad's going to talk to Mom again tonight. I think she's okay with it but she hasn't said yes yet. I've already talked to my teachers and they will give me homework to do while I'm there."

"Good deal. Let me know."

Elena still insisted that she had seen the ghost of a murdered woman, Senator Sandra Harrold, at the prison. She'd been researching ghosts since then.

I turned my mind back to the business at hand.

"I've got to do something," I looked at Peg. "I can't just sit here."

"You need to stay calm. You know Rachel will let you know. But please tell her that you won't be involved in this one."

"She'll handle it by herself." I hoped that she'd ask for my help but I wasn't about to admit that to Peg.

"I can't absorb this," she patted a tissue to her eyes and blew her nose.

"I know. I've got to go."

"Why don't you go to the post office for me? That will give you something to do. I don't feel like going anywhere."

I readily agreed because the post office is just a couple of blocks from the museum. At least I had half a reason to drive by — good enough for me.

The Port Isabel Police Department had blocked off the sidewalk in front of the building. Police cars from Port Isabel and the island were everywhere. Two officers were directing traffic to move the rubberneckers along. I noticed a couple of TV trucks. An ambulance waited in front of the building. I didn't see any sign of Rachel.

I had only met her new partner, Rudy Vega, a couple of times. Rachel said they were still developing a working relationship. This case would most likely put it to the test.

I drove around the block, noticing that an officer guarded the back door. A sheriff's car pulled up and parked in front of the door. He was struggling to get his overweight body out of the car by the time I passed by. As much as I wanted to drive by again, I turned my car toward home.

By late afternoon when Rachel called, I'd played about a thousand computer games, read and re-read Facebook, snacked on a couple of cookies (okay, maybe more like four or five) and walked Luke a couple of times.

"Hap, need a job?" She went right to the point and I loved it.

"Well, I'm awfully busy," I began.

"Meet me at *Will and Jack's* in thirty minutes, okay?"

"Yep."

If I danced, I'd be doing a jig. I didn't stop to analyze whether I wanted to be part of another murder investigation or if it was the missing *Golden Booby* that intrigued me.

Will and Jack's is a small burger joint and beer garden on the lighthouse square. Peg loves the big hibiscus tree that stands in the middle of the courtyard. I love the food.

"Good to see you, Hap," Jackie, the owner, greeted me when I walked in.

"Thanks. I just realized I haven't been here for a while."

"Glad you're here now," she answered. Jackie stacked an order in both hands and headed toward the door. I rushed to open it for her.

Rachel and Rudy were already in the courtyard, drinking their iced teas. Rudy was digging into a huge plate of loaded nachos.

"Hap, I asked Rudy to join us," Rachel began. "He knows you helped with the last investigation. He investigated the murder of the professor who had the *Golden Booby*. I want your help because this one already has us baffled."

"What do you mean?"

"The cameras were off. We have no pictures."

"Those cameras are never turned off," Rudy said. "The guy had to know that Carol had access to them. He had to get her to turn them off before he entered the building or a camera would have caught him. By the way, have some nachos."

"Thanks. I believe I will. You've reviewed all of the videos?" Stupid question, I knew the answer.

"Yes, there's no activity after the museum closed at 6:00."

"None," Rachel added. "We have no idea why she turned them off."

"Did they go off exactly at 6:00?"

"No, they went off at 5:48 to be exact."

"Do you think the killer made her do it?"

"That makes sense but we don't know how he did it — if he did."

"One thing we do know," Rudy said. "Carol suffered a terrible blow to the head. Whoever hit her packed some power."

"We're assuming it was a man," Rachel frowned. "I guess it could have been a woman, but Carol was hit by a tall person. She was 5'10" and the blow came from above her."

"Putting the height and strength together, I'd say you're probably right," I knew you could never say anything for certain.

I stacked some tomato and jalapenos on a nacho chip, hoping my mind would stop whirling. I noticed that Rudy couldn't keep his eyes off Rachel. I filed that away to think about later.

"Did Betty have any idea why Carol would have turned off the cameras and alarms?"

"No," Rachel stared into her tea as she swirled her straw. People read tea leaves but not a leaf was in sight. "She said they left the alarm on all the time and they had the cameras connected to the same switch. She seemed like she had something on her mind but that's all she said."

"Rachel, I'd like to look through the videos of the last few days, if that's okay with you." I didn't want to overstep my bounds.

"That would be great, Hap. I'll get them for you. You want to start with the last three days?"

"Fine. I'm not sure I'll find anything but we have to start somewhere."

"I'll drop them by your house. We need them as soon as possible. Okay?"

"Not a problem."

As soon as Rachel brought the flash drive, I started going through it. I started with yesterday's video. In the first few minutes, I realized this would be a tedious job. Although the museum was never crowded, a steady stream of visitors came through the doors. Most walked through the front entrance, stopped at the *Golden Booby* exhibit and then meandered through the rest of the building. I guessed the average person spent the better part of an hour reading all the display signs.

I saw a couple of locals I recognized. Debbi, the Cookie Lady, came in with a young girl about Elena's age. The two kept up a running conversation as they studied the statue. Sally Scaman, Peg's friend from the bookstore, spent about ten minutes taking pictures with her phone before she moved away from the statue. She rushed over to Carol to show her a good shot. I wondered how many photos Carol had looked at since the *Golden Booby* came to town. I hated knowing she died because of that bird.

About noon, Steve Hathcock stopped by and spent quite a bit of time studying the statue. I pictured his mind going back to the long-ago day when the statue first came to North America.

I didn't see anyone else I recognized until it was nearly closing time. That big guy we met at the bookstore yesterday entered the back door to the museum. He knew his way around so I assumed it wasn't his first visit. I couldn't remember his name.

"Peg, what was the name of that storyteller guy we met at *Paragraphs* yesterday?"

"DL Casa. Why?" Peg walked into the room.

"Nothing. I just saw him on a surveillance video and couldn't remember his name."

A middle-aged Hispanic man spent a long time studying the statue from every angle. He took out a small notebook and made some notes.

By the time I finished yesterday's video, I was ready for a break. I poured myself a glass of iced tea and headed to the porch. For some reason, the weather pattern had caused a record number of migrating birds to land on the island and around the area. These poor little guys were tired and hungry after their long flight across the Gulf. We'd had visitors in our back yard that I'd never seen before. Today I saw a couple I didn't recognize but I knew the Yellow-bellied Sapsucker hanging out in a palm tree.

I watched him for a while and let my mind replay what little I knew about the murder and the missing statue.

I had many questions and no answers. Why was Carol killed? Why did she turn the alarm off? Where did the fake statue come from and how long had it been there?

I wondered if we ever saw the real statue. Was it still in Mexico or somewhere else? I knew the loss of human life was more important than a missing statue, but curiosity ran rampant in my mind.

I tackled the next video but found little of interest. I saw a few more familiar faces including Lola and Jasmine from *Le Sandwich Boutique*. They ran a great little lunch place just about a block away from the museum. I looked at the time: 3:45. They must have come straight from work.

The middle-aged guy from yesterday's video studied the statue, again taking notes, or maybe creating a sketch.

Around 4:00, a familiar-looking older woman entered the museum, spent a few minutes looking at the statue, glanced around rather furtively, and then wandered off to other exhibits. She didn't seem interested in the exhibits. As she checked her watch for the umpteenth time, I realized she could be the same woman I saw at *Paragraphs* yesterday.

A young couple came in about 4:30, checked out the *Golden Booby*, kissed a couple of times and left. An antique artifact didn't hold their interest for long.

Four women spent close to twenty minutes drooling over the *Golden Booby*'s gold and sapphires. The statue entranced all of them, but one taller lady couldn't take her eyes off it.

At 5:45, Carol gave a fifteen-minute warning to the last few visitors. By 5:55, the last group left and Carol locked the door behind them.

I turned the video off.

"I'm ready to go to dinner whenever you are," I told Peg.

"Super, How about *La Hacienda*?"

When we drove across the causeway, we watched the dolphin boats, the pirate ship, and a couple of fishing boats enjoying the last rays of light before the sunset.

La Hacienda is on the bayside of the island and offers a great view of the sunset. Peg urged me to hurry so we didn't miss it.

We made it in time to enjoy our margaritas while the water reflected striking red-orange clouds and the sun slipped over the horizon.

"That's why people choose to live here," Peg said.

I agreed.

"It took your mind off those videos for at least a few minutes, didn't it?" Peg read me like a well-loved book.

"It did. After we order, I'd like to talk about the *Golden Booby* though. I'm trying to remember the details about how it came to the museum."

"Don't you remember? That professor who lived here willed it to his grandchildren."

The waiter brought our drinks and took our order.

"Yeah, but didn't it originally come from the South Pacific or was it Peru? What I really remember is the generosity of the grandchildren to loan it to our museum free of charge for a year."

"Grandchild. Remember, the grandson is fighting the loan. Hap, think about what a fake means. Did the granddaughter loan a fake or did the museum replace the original?"

"Or did someone steal the original? It could be any of those. What about those guys who tried to steal it from the grandchildren? Did they ever put them behind bars?"

"Not yet. Poor Carol. I think her death will get lost amid the questions about a fake antiquity."

~ Chapter ~
3

I spent the next morning reviewing the third recording Rachel had given me. Once again, I recognized a few locals. The crowd had been heavier that day. Several harried adults worked to corral a group of kids from a Brownsville elementary school. I don't remember ever taking a field trip when I was in school but I hoped these kids would remember this spectacular statue.

A skinny young woman took pictures. I realized it was a local blogger who covered the area's happenings. I'd met her before but couldn't remember her name. I did recall that it was the same as some famous criminal. After she took loads of pictures of the *Golden Booby*, she tried to interview a couple of the kids. I realized that if that was Peg with her camera, she'd probably focus on the faces of the kids looking at the statue.

Gloria Bates flitted in and out of camera range several times. Peg and I had attended several of her plays. One of Gloria's paintings hung above Peg's desk.

A middle-aged man helped steady an older man as they studied the statue. Both men wore beards. From their similar stances and looks, I guessed that it was a father and his son.

I noticed a woman observing the statue from the corner of the room. She was tall, slender, and a bundle of nerves. I thought I read fear on her face and in her constant glances at the people around her. She stood glued to the same spot for at least twenty minutes.

I looked for the man I'd noticed on the first two videos but there was no sign of him today.

Nothing else on this video. As 5:30 came and went, the visitors dwindled to one or two. They left by 5:45.

I turned off the computer, wishing I'd found something of interest. I'd poured an iced tea and headed for a snack when I noticed my phone blinking with a text message from Elena. *Arriving at Harlingen airport Sunday 3pm. Staying at Queen Isabella Inn.*

After I answered Elena's text, I called Rachel and let her know that the videos produced little of interest. I didn't bother to give her the details.

"We've been canvassing the neighborhood. Found a couple of people who saw a car in the back parking lot about the time of the murder," she said.

"Any descriptions?"

"Both people reported the car to be an older model. One said brown and the other said it was definitely blue. Neither saw anybody in or near it."

"Any reason they remember it?" I wondered why a parked car would get anybody's attention.

"The "brown car" guy said when the police showed up, he remembered seeing a car. The "definitely blue car" lady said she always notices blue cars because that's the color of her car. Not a lot of help, huh?"

"I suppose neither looked at a license plate or noticed any stickers?"

"No. It's all too vague to be helpful."

"Any word back from the M.E.?"

"Preliminary of the wound suggests a tall man but we can't rule out a strong woman."

"Or a short man on a ladder?"

My attempt at humor fell on deaf ears. I could already feel Rachel's frustration and it was early in the investigation.

"Hap, I'd like you to talk to Betty. She seems so uncomfortable."

"Not a problem. I'll give her a call. What do you mean by uncomfortable?"

"I'm not sure. She's grieving but there's something else. I just want to know what you think."

I hung up the phone and thought what it must be like to be in Betty's shoes right now. She worked with Carol and had helped with the exhibition of the statue. Emotional stress would be understandable and expected.

I punched Betty's number into my phone and waited.

"Hello."

"Betty, it's Hap Lynch."

"Hap, thank you for calling. It's all so horrible and I'm so upset. Poor Carol…"

"Are you all right?"

"Yes, and no. I feel so lost."

"Betty, Detective Vasquez asked me to give you a call."

"I told her everything I know."

"I understand but I'd like to buy you a cup of coffee. Are you free this afternoon?"

"Yes, the museum's closed. Do you have any idea how long? I forgot to ask the detectives."

"I'm not sure but they will let you know. Would you like to meet me at *Yummies* in about thirty minutes?"

"That sounds good. I'll be there. It shouldn't be too busy this time of day."

I arrived before Betty and found a comfortable table in front. I figured that she might relax a little in the outside air and sunshine.

Luckily we were alone when Betty sat down. She didn't try to hide the heartbreak in her eyes.

"It's hard, isn't it? Let's just relax a few minutes before we talk about it," I tried to put her at ease. The warm, salty breeze certainly had a relaxing effect on me. Made me want to take a nap.

By the time our server brought our coffee and rolls, Betty seemed a little calmer.

"Hap, I was with Carol most of that day. We'd talked and laughed. She enjoyed all the people." Betty twisted a strand of her salt-and-pepper hair. I briefly wondered how long it would take the mostly auburn to become mostly gray. Carol's death would probably help it along.

"I know she did. I didn't know her very well, but I liked her."

"She was a good person and great for the museum. She'll be missed. I will miss her." Betty's eyes filled with tears.

"Betty, I need your help," I tried to steer her away from the emotion.

"What can I do? I wasn't even there. If I'd stayed longer, she'd still be here."

"There's no way you can know that. Did she usually let you go home first?"

"Yes, well lately. She'd tell me I could leave when it slowed down in the late afternoons. I usually got there first in the mornings which suited me fine. Carol would get there just before we opened the doors. Then at night, she did most of the closing."

"You said 'lately.' What did you mean? Had your schedule changed?"

"Not really. I don't know why I said that." She twisted her napkin into a knot.

"Is something troubling you?"

"No, of course not. I just miss Carol. I can't believe I'll never see her again. I don't know if I can ever go back to work. They will open the museum again, won't they?"

"Yes, I'm sure the city will open it again. You need time, Betty. I'm sorry to ask you so many questions but the police need information."

"I know but…I can't talk about it anymore. Do you mind?"

No, I understand." I did mind and I'm not sure I understood but Betty was an emotional wreck. We might find out more in a few days but she still seemed in a state of shock.

"The coffee and roll are on me. Why don't you go home and rest? We'll talk later."

Betty nodded, stood — and hesitated as she turned to walk away.

"There is something, maybe," she said as she turned back to me.

I waited.

"It's probably nothing. Oh, never mind. I'm just upset."

"About Carol?"

"Yes. I think she had a new friend."

"Do you mean boyfriend?"

"Yes, I think so. That's all I know. I don't know if that helps. Goodbye, Hap."

I sat staring after her. Did Betty know more or did the information mean anything at all?

I wanted to call her back but I knew I needed to give her more time.

~ Chapter ~
4

*C*arol *met a man at* **Louie's Back Yard**. *They joked and laughed their way through a couple of drinks. The man brushed the back of his finger down her cheek before he reached up and tucked a strand of hair behind her ear. She smiled and touched his hand.*

He took her face between his hands, slowly sliding them down to her neck. Suddenly and violently, he squeezed her breath away. She opened her mouth but no sound escaped.

Turn around, my mind screamed as I awoke with a start. I sat up in bed and tried to calm my racing heart.

"Are you okay?" Peg reached for me

"Just a nightmare but it seemed so real."

"Want to tell me about it?"

"It was silly. Carol Flores was with a man at *Louie's.* They had a couple of drinks, started to get romantic… and then he choked her. I couldn't see his face. He wouldn't turn around."

"That's what you were mumbling, something about turning around. Can't you leave this case alone? You get too involved," Peg waited for my response.

"No, you can't," she answered for me.

I knew the dream came from my unsubstantiated thoughts about Carol's new 'friend.' I needed facts, not my imagination.

When I told Rachel about my conversation with Betty, she suggested I follow up on it. I needed to know more about Carol — who were her friends, where did she like to eat, where did she shop, and what did she do for entertainment.

Peg and I knew her only through the museum. We had appreciated her friendliness and her managerial ability. The museum was a vibrant part of the community and events were well-attended.

I hated to call Betty again, but I knew she had the information I needed. Today she held her emotions under control and gave me a list of names. Carol loved to eat breakfast at *Manuel's*. For luncheon meetings, she usually chose *Pelican Station* or picked up something at *Le Sandwich Boutique*. She and Jasmine were good friends. At night, she headed to the island for entertainment. She didn't shop much but she liked *Becky's Place* and *Renee's* on the island.

She loved the boardwalk at the Convention Center and she took sandcastle-building lessons with *Sandy Feet*. On her days off she liked to drive the beach and end the day at *Clayton's Beach Bar*. She frequently ate at *Cafe Kranzler* or *Grapevine*.

I finished my second cup of coffee and told Peg that breakfast at *Manuel's* was a good place to start.

"Life is hard, huh? I'm sure Rachel will appreciate the effort." Peg teased.

I gave her my sexiest grin and told her to grab her phone and purse.

Manuel's was crowded and we had to wait for a table. After we sat down, Frank took our order. When I asked, he told me Carol frequently ate breakfast there but almost always alone. Sometimes she ordered to go because she was running late.

"Do you know anything about her personal life?"

"Like what?" Frank asked.

"Did she have a new boyfriend?"

Jay, Frank's brother, stopped by our table. "You're asking about Carol. Have you found out who killed her?"

"The police are working on it. Did Carol ever mention a new boyfriend?"

"No, not really. She said she had a new friend she wanted me to meet. I was always teasing her about her love life so I assumed it was a boyfriend." Jay put his arm around Peg. "You know, I'm always interested in love life."

"In YOUR love life," Peg retorted.

"That's enough to fill a book," Jay grinned.

"A long, boring one," Frank added.

"Back to business. Is that all Carol said?" I tried to steer the conversation back on topic.

"I don't remember anything else."

"If you do, will you get back with me or Detective Vasquez?"

"Forget you. Rachel is a whole lot cuter."

Frank shook his head as Jay turned his attention to the woman at the next table.

Before we left, Frank said he'd keep his ears open and let me know if he heard anything.

I wanted to talk to Jasmine but *Le Sandwich Boutique* wouldn't open for another hour.

"Hap, you know if she went to the Convention Center a lot, she probably knew Scarlet Colley. Why don't we stop at the *Sea Life Center* and see if she's there? If not, I'll give her a call." Peg pulled out her phone.

Scarlet was giving a birding tour on her boat so Peg said she'd call her later. We drove over to *Grapevine* but had no luck at all. Our next stop was *Cafe Kranzler.* Shirley, the co-owner, had a couple minutes to talk.

"I knew Carol well. It's so awful because she was a beautiful person. She cared deeply about this area and its history,"

"She will be missed," I agreed. "Did she usually come here alone?"

"Not really. She often met a couple of other women. I heard them talking. I think they'd been friends for years. One of them is Susan O'Malley. I can't remember the other one's name right now."

"Does Susan live on the island?"

"Yes, she volunteers at *Sea Turtle Inc* and *Whiskers*, I think."

"I'll check. Did Carol come here with a man recently?"

"Once, but I was busy and didn't get a chance to meet him."

"Can you describe him?"

"He had dark, longish hair. That's all I remember. Probably about Carol's age."

"Anything else you can remember about him?" Long, dark hair described a lot of men you see here.

"No, we were really busy. One thing though, it was within the last week. In fact, I think it might have been last Saturday evening."

After a couple more questions and little new information, I left. I checked out *Whiskers* and found out that Susan worked at *Sea Turtle Inc* today.

When we arrived, Susan was ready for a break so we walked outside to talk.

I asked her about Carol's new friend.

"Boy, was she ever keeping him under wraps. She'd had some what she called 'bad luck' with men, so she wanted to take it easy this time. She wanted to be sure she could introduce him with pride," Susan said.

"What did she mean?"

"I always thought Carol was attracted to the wrong kind of men, or maybe she attracted them. Anyway, she'd dated a couple of guys who mistreated her."

"In what way?"

"One physically abused her. You know she was married once, to a guy who beat her up one too many times. Anyway, she met this guy who she really liked until he slapped her around a couple of times. Thank God she saw the light on that one. Then another guy, I think his name was Dave, abused her emotionally. I couldn't believe the way he belittled her in front of her friends. I was afraid she'd stick with him so I was proud of her when she stopped that relationship. None of the men took it well so Carol was really gun-shy."

"Do you know how this new guy treated her?"

"Carol didn't want to talk about him. She told me if it worked out, she'd introduce me. I couldn't get anything else out of her."

"How long had she been seeing him?"

"Not long at all. I guess she had bad luck all the way around. I can't believe she's gone."

I didn't learn any more from Susan but I realized that Carol's friendly smile had covered up a lot of stress and heartache. I've never understood how competent women can get messed up with guys that mistreat them.

Harder yet for me to understand how guys can mistreat women. I never wanted to turn into one of those old guys who blame everything on 'today's society,' but I did frequently ponder what caused one person to abuse or harm another.

~ Chapter ~
5

We stopped at *Le Sandwich Boutique* but it was closed. It's Saturday and I'd forgotten they're only open on weekdays.

I called Rachel and we agreed to meet in a couple of hours. She had an appointment with the captain and a meeting with forensics first.

I dropped Peg off at the house, spent some time playing with Luke, and tried to organize my thoughts for Rachel.

We met at *Whataburger*. Rachel was alone because Rudy had an appointment with the security people.

"I'm afraid we have a problem, Hap," Rachel said after she took a drink of Coke. "Rudy's checking it out now, but the security company has been checking the museum's history. The alarm system was shut off two other evenings last week."

"At the same time?"

"Within a couple of minutes. It stayed off for about twenty minutes the first time and about an hour the second time."

"Somebody practicing, you think?"

"Sounds like it, doesn't it?

"Rachel, have you asked Betty about it? She leaves early most nights but she may know."

"No, I haven't wanted to bother her any more than we already have. Besides, like you said, she leaves early."

"Why didn't the security company report it?"

"They said they talked to Carol the day she was murdered. She said she knew nothing about it but would check into it."

I thought about it. Something didn't make sense. Did Carol lie to the security company?

"Could it have been a glitch in the system? Did they say?"

"I don't know. Hopefully, Rudy will find out more." Rachel sat back in the booth. "I don't like where my mind is going with this, Hap."

"What is it?"

"Do you think we could be looking for more than one person? Should we be looking for thieves instead of one thief?"

"It's possible." I hadn't given that much thought. "Carol could have died simply because she was in the way. I'd been thinking more in terms of a boyfriend who wanted the statue."

"You mean someone who used her to get to the statue?"

"Yes, maybe he talked her into turning off the alarm. He grabbed the statue and then got rid of her because he couldn't trust her."

"What makes you think that? What have you discovered?"

I filled Rachel in on the conversations with Shirley and Susan. I had narrowed my focus to finding Carol's new boyfriend. Maybe I was wrong but we had nothing to support more than one thief.

"You're probably right," Rachel said. "We need to find this boyfriend. Any ideas? What if this guy talked Carol into helping him?"

"Let's wait to see what Rudy finds out. I still want to talk with Jasmine at *Le Sandwich Boutique* and Scarlet Colley. I think we have the motive."

"The statue. Greed. I'm sorry Mr. Villanova's family ever loaned the statue to the museum. It changed our town," Rachel was losing her detachment. It's easy to do when scandal or crime hits your world.

"Rachel, cheer up. Greed can be anywhere. We agree on the motive. For Carol's sake, we need to find out if she was a victim or a participant. We can't let her down."

"I know. We owe her that. She had a positive influence on the museum and Port Isabel. I can't believe she was involved in the theft."

"It wouldn't be the first time that a good person has given into temptation."

Peg called Scarlet who backed up Susan's comments. Carol had a new friend but didn't talk about him.

If nothing broke before Monday, hopefully Jasmine could shed some light on this mystery man.

I re-watched the videos on Sunday but found nothing new. Rachel called to tell me that Rudy verified that the alarms had been shut off. There had never been a problem until a few days before the theft.

Elena called when she and her dad landed in Harlingen. She said she'd text as soon as they settled in the hotel. I knew that she would forget about me when she saw the bay and the old hotel.

"You'll find several cats that have made the hotel their home. Find out their names when you register," I told her, "and don't call me until you explore."

"Hap, Dad said he'd like to have dinner together. He starts work in the morning."

"Sounds good. We'll wait for your call." I looked forward to meeting her dad and spending time with her.

We met at *Pelican Station* at 7:00. I suggested the shrimp and she couldn't believe anybody served shrimp that big. Both Peg and I were impressed with John Reyes. He was friendly, well-informed, and interested in the area. We had a pleasant dinner and we promised to show Elena the island on Monday.

"Okay, but tell me about the murder investigation."

"How do you know about that?"

"The Internet," Elena said. "You're helping, aren't you?"

"Did you read that on the Internet too?"

"No, I read about Detective Vasquez and I remembered you helped a lady detective a couple of years ago. I put two and two together."

"And you drew the correct conclusion. I am helping Detectives Vasquez and Vega."

"Do you need me? Can I help?"

"I don't right now but if I need any research, you'll be the first person I call. However, there's no ghost involved here."

"No, but I read there have been ghost sightings in the hotel and in Port Isabel. Will you go on a ghost tour with me next weekend? Please."

Peg laughed. "You bet we will."

~ Chapter ~
6

I awoke Monday morning to sunshine and a light breeze. I sent a quick prayer of thanksgiving for a perfect day. I knew Elena would fall in love with our little corner of Paradise. Weather like this added a little extra sparkle.

I planned to take her to breakfast at *Ted's* on the island. Neither *Manuel's* nor *The Chef House* was open on Mondays. After that I planned the *SPI Birding Center* and *Sea Turtle Inc.* I planned to come back across the causeway for lunch at *Le Sandwich Boutique*. I wanted to talk to Jasmine.

All great plans go awry. Elena, in all her thirteen-year-old wisdom, wanted to start the day at *McDonald's*. After I ate an Egg McMuffin while dreaming about pecan pancakes, I suggested the birding center. Of course, she'd researched the island and had her own agenda. We spent the morning on the beach. We looked for shells and sea beans, walked in the dunes, watched Luke cavort in the sand, and drove several miles north of town. Elena's awestruck expressions made the change in plans all right.

She took hundreds of pictures with her iPad. I watched her laughing with Peg and had a sudden vision of Peg at Elena's age. I'm sure she had the same love of life.

Elena wanted to go on a dolphin cruise so Peg called Scarlet. We grabbed a quick hamburger at *Whataburger* and headed back across the causeway. Engrossed in Elena's enthusiasm, I forgot about talking to Jasmine. We spent the next couple hours out on the bay with the dolphins. Scarlet and her dog, Rozzi, attract the dolphins almost as much as they attract people. Several times, I feared that Elena's iPad would land in the water.

By the time we finished playing with the dolphins and communing with nature, Peg and I were exhausted. We took Elena back to the hotel and agreed to meet her and her dad for dinner again.

Luke attracts sand like a magnet so the first order of business when we got home was his bath.

By the time I remembered Jasmine, it was late afternoon. I'd have to wait until tomorrow. I took a drink out on the porch and called Rachel. She and Rudy had spent the day talking to other city employees. They ended it with no new clues to the identity of Carol's new friend.

We decided to take Elena and her dad to *La Hacienda* for dinner. We planned the time to be there for the sunset. I looked around at the crowd and noticed the songwriter guy from *Paragraphs* with a pretty young woman. Looked like he was enjoying his island time.

I always look for Griff Mangan or Steve Hathcock because they both love the place. We didn't see them but Charles and Mary Russell Muchmore were enjoying the bay view from their table by the window.

I introduced them to Elena and her dad.

"I'm so happy to meet you, Elena," Mary Russell smiled. "You'll love it here. We spend the winters here and find it fascinating. So many good people."

"I already love it and I've taken gobs of pictures."

"I noticed your iPad. Do you use it for your photos?"

"Yes. I also love to do research."

"Then you have to meet Steve Hathcock while you're here."

"Great idea, Mary Russell," Peg chimed in. "I'll make that happen."

"Who is he?" Elena stopped looking at her photos.

"A friend and our local historian. You'll enjoy him," Peg assured her.

"Super."

"He's also a treasure hunter. Why don't you two join us at a bigger table?" Peg invited Mary Russell and Charles.

"We'd love to," Mary Russell answered. Charles never said a word. He just smiled.

The minute John started telling us about his first day with the Coast Guard, Charles' ears perked up. I remembered Peg saying he had an engineering background but I couldn't remember what specific field. They were soon conversing like a couple of long-time colleagues.

When her dad finished, Elena talked non-stop, telling him how much she loved the island and the Gulf. I noticed other patrons smiling at her enthusiastic comments.

A man stopped by our table to welcome Elena to the island. It took me a minute to place him as one of the guys in the museum videos. He was the one who took notes while he studied the *Golden Booby.*

I didn't hear Elena's answer to his comment.

"I'm Hap Lynch," I reached my hand out toward him. "Elena is visiting us from Missouri."

"A pleasure. I'm impressed by her love of my favorite place on earth."

"I do love it." Elena's smile lit her face. "We're only here for a week but I already know I want to come back. I may move here after I finish school. Hap lives down here and we'd have fun."

I caught Peg's grin out of the corner of my eye but the man had captured my attention.

"I'm sorry. I didn't catch your name," I told him.

"I am Roberto Rodriquez-Garcia — Bert to my friends. I too live here. Are you on the island?"

"No, Port Isabel."

"Aw, the historical side of our little paradise."

"Speaking of history, I believe I saw you at the museum one day," I said before I thought.

Roberto looked confused. "I don't remember seeing you, but yes, I was there recently."

"To see the *Golden Booby*?"

"Yes."

His curt answer surprised me.

"You live here on the island?" Elena asked. "Do you spend a lot of time on the beach or on the water? I would."

"Yes, I do when I have time."

He seemed different and I knew something about my mention of the museum changed the tone of the conversation.

He nodded, excused himself and headed for the door.

"Boy, what happened to him?"

"I guess he needed to go," John told her.

"So you're from Missouri?" Mary Russell's question dispersed the tension that had tightened the air.

"Yes…"

"We're practically neighbors. We live in Illinois. Where do you live?"

"Dad lives in Kansas City. I live with my mom in Jefferson City but I love to spend time with Dad," Elena's eyes radiated hurt.

"Well, I'll send happy thoughts to all of you every time we're in or near Missouri," Mary Russell's smile spoke of honest affection.

After I paid the check, we said our goodbyes to the Muchmores.

When we stepped outside, I heard Luke growling in the car. "Be quiet, Luke," I admonished when I opened the door. In a matter of seconds, he was wagging his tail and climbing all over Elena.

"He has rapid mood changes, doesn't he?" John laughed.

"But Dad, you've never seen a dog this cute, have you?" Elena scratched both of Luke's ears.

"He's cute all right, and about the friendliest fella I've ever seen. At least most of the time."

As we pulled up at the Queen Isabella, I told Elena I had to work in the morning but we could take her to one of our favorite little restaurants for lunch.

"Awesome. I want to try all the places you told me about," she answered.

On the way home, I told Peg I wanted to watch those videos again. I had questions about Roberto Rodriquez-Garcia.

"Okay. Did you notice DL Casa was in the restaurant tonight?"

"Yes, I was going to point him out but got sidetracked. He's getting to know the town."

"And obviously some of the residents," she said.

~ Chapter ~
7

I watched the tapes one more time on Tuesday morning. Several people bothered me but it was only a gut instinct. Roberto Rodriquez-Garcia was at the top of my list. I admitted to myself that he hadn't concerned me until he seemed anxious to meet Elena last night but left so abruptly after I mentioned the museum.

The songwriter guy, whose name I could never remember, seemed too familiar with the museum for a stranger in town.

The woman standing in the corner. What made her so nervous? Did she have something to hide? Then there was the tall woman in that group. She couldn't take her eyes off the statue. Did I see greed or did I imagine it?

I realized that the videos no longer helped me. I was imagining everyone guilty of something. I checked the local newspapers until about 10:00. I wanted to talk to Jasmine before *Le Sandwich Boutique* opened at 11:00, and the lunch crowd soon followed.

After I talked with her, I'd pick up Elena and we'd go back for lunch. Peg decided to stay home and work.

I stopped by the post office for Peg. As I waited in line to mail a package, one of the women I saw on the museum videos came in. She wasn't the one who stared at the statue so intensely. She ignored my friendly greeting, at least I thought it was friendly.

When I arrived at the restaurant, Jasmine had finished prepping for the day. She had a few minutes so I asked about her friendship with Carol.

"We were friends forever. We went to grade school together. I can't imagine life without her."

"Did she share her personal life with you?"

"Like what?"

"I heard she had a new boyfriend. Is that true and if it is, do you know who he is?"

"She did have a new friend. She was secretive about him because she's been hurt too many times. She was one of those women who couldn't seem to pick good men."

"Did she tell you his name?"

Yes, why? You don't suspect he killed her, do you?"

"I don't know," I told her. "Right now, I just want to talk with him. Rachel Vasquez asked for my help."

"I don't know if Carol would want me to tell you, Hap."

"You'll be doing it for Carol. You're the first person who's been able to give us any answer at all. We need to talk to everyone involved with Carol. I know you want her killer brought to justice."

"I do, but let me think a minute. What will you do when I tell you his name?"

"I'll ask what you know about him and then I'll relay that information to the police. Most likely Rachel will talk with him but if she asks me to do so, I will. Okay?"

"Since it's you, okay. He lives on the island. His name is Roberto Rodriquez."

"Not Roberto Rodriquez-Garcia!"

"Yes, that's him. Why?"

"I've met him, that's all. In fact, I met him at *La Hacienda* last night."

"Did you talk to him?"

"Briefly," I answered. I thanked Jasmine and told her I was bringing a friend back for lunch.

I needed a few minutes before I picked up Elena. I called Rachel and gave her Roberto's name. I expressed Jasmine's concern. She assured me she would handle it personally.

When I picked up Elena, I smiled. She wore a big floppy hat, shorts, a tank top and flip-flops. Today she was an islander. Her iPad was her only accessory.

I introduced her to Jasmine and Lola. We grabbed the empty table in the corner. Elena ordered Cream of Asparagus soup. I ordered the French Dip sandwich. Elena had made plans for the afternoon. *Sea Turtle Inc* was the first stop on her list. She had read about Allison and a couple of the other turtles. It was too early in the year for any hatchling releases. I hoped she'd get to see one someday.

Jasmine stopped by our table to tell me that Lola would like to talk with me. When we finished, a group was waiting for our table. I walked around to the kitchen door to see Lola.

"I'm swamped right now. Can you come back or call me at home tonight?"

"Sure." After writing down her number, we left for turtle land. Elena loved the turtles and once again took loads of photos. She spent a couple of hours watching the turtles and asking questions.

"I bookmarked their website and liked their Facebook page. When I get older, I want to intern there," Elena said. I knew she'd find dozens of interests between now and then but wherever she landed, she'd make the world a better place.

"Sounds good. What's next on our list?"

"How 'bout the birding center?"

"See that yellow building," I pointed to the building on the bay. "You'll love this. Peg loves to take pictures from the boardwalk."

We spent a couple hours watching the birds and critters. Elena took photos, especially when we saw an alligator enjoying the afternoon sun.

I told her about the whale wall and more boardwalks at the convention center.

"The SPI Historical Commission has some interesting displays inside. Would you like to check them out while we're here?"

As I suspected, she became enthralled with all of the old pictures.

"Yuck! Look at those bathing suits. I'd never wear anything like that," she said.

"There were really fashionable at the time. Look at the pictures of the women's clothes. Kind of makes you glad you live today, huh?"

We looked at the artifacts. Several were new including a wood-grained bird statue and three old bottles. The Civil War uniform buttons intrigued me. Steve Hathcock said hundreds had been found around Port Isabel and at some local battle sites.

We spent the rest of the afternoon taking photos of South Padre Island landmarks. When I dropped Elena at her hotel, she planned to research Padre Balli and the shrimpers memorialized in the Christ of the Fishermen statue.

I called Rachel. She had spent much of the day tracking down Roberto Rodriquez-Garcia. He'd been in Brownsville. She and Rudy were just pulling up in front of his condo. She said she'd call back as soon as they finished the interview.

As I waited, I focused on why Roberto bothered me. I had to admit I'm sometimes quick to judge people, particularly other men. Arrogance and superiority bothered me almost as much as belligerence. Roberto exuded both. I always have to face my own prejudices when I deal with people like that. Funny thing is, arrogance in women doesn't bother me but belligerence does. I suppose psychologists would tell me I'm sexist or I have an issue with my masculinity.

Aside from all that, Roberto's intense interest in the statue bothered me. I remembered watching the videos of him studying the statue and taking notes. Was he planning the theft or did he know it was a fake? If the alarm had been off before, was it possible he had stolen the real statue and replaced it with the fake?

Was he Carol's new love interest? I hoped she hadn't been in cahoots with him.

I answered the phone on the first ring and was relieved to hear Rachel's voice. I needed something to take my thoughts in a different direction.

"He's the boyfriend, Hap," Rachel began. "He admitted it. He and Carol had been seeing each other for a couple of weeks. He met her when he first visited the museum."

"Did he admit to anything?"

"Only the relationship. He swears he cared for Carol and felt they were moving forward. He denies everything about the theft and murder."

"Did he give you any reason for his interest in the statue?"

"Only that he collects art and appreciates beautiful work when he sees it. That's why he went to the museum in the first place."

Obviously Rachel and Rudy hadn't unearthed anything new.

"What's your gut feeling about him, Rachel?"

"I don't like him but that doesn't make him guilty of anything. I get the feeling that everything in a relationship would have to be his way. By the way, he's twice divorced. Not a good candidate."

"Yeah, that's how he strikes me, too."

"Do you want to have a go at him?"

"I think so. Can you set something up for tomorrow morning?"

"Sure. I'll get back to you."

I took Luke for his evening walk. Elena had texted me while I was gone. I decided to wait until morning to get back with her.

As I got in bed, I remembered that I was supposed to call Lola.

~ Chapter ~
8

I awoke with the feeling that if I came face to face with a clue, I wouldn't recognize it. One of those nightmares that didn't quite happen flitted around the edges creating restlessness.

Even Luke's morning excitement couldn't shake the fog in my head. It took three cups of coffee before I admitted to myself that caffeine wasn't going to do the trick today.

I hate the stage in an investigation when you know you're missing something important.

Rachel called. "Meet me in the *Whataburger* parking lot at 9:30. We'll drive over together for your interview with Mr. Rodriquez-Garcia."

"I'll be there."

We talked about the case on the way. Rachel shared my frustration. Rudy was spending the morning doing some paperwork. We'd meet up with him after our interview.

Roberto answered after the first knock. Today he wore a light blue open-necked shirt with purple-colored flowers. A gold cross hung on a chain around his neck. He smiled at Rachel and ignored me. Obviously I wasn't the one he wanted to impress.

Rachel returned his smile. For a moment I wondered why I was there.

"Roberto, Hap is a former police officer and he often assists me in investigations," she said. Glad she didn't admit I'd only helped her on one other case. "I'd like for you to answer his questions."

"But, Detective, I've already answered all of yours. I will try but it is still so hard to talk about my dear Carol."

Boy, did he lay it on thick. I took out my notebook to look official.

"I understand." Rachel gave him a look filled with sympathy and charm. "Go ahead, Hap."

"I have some questions about the security system." I dove right in. "Did you ever see Carol turn it off at night?"

"Why, no. I wasn't there at night. I usually met her for dinner."

"We know that she had company after she closed the museum," I bluffed.

"Well, it wasn't me. I wish I would have been there for her."

"You spent a lot of time at the museum. I've watched the surveillance videos. What fascination did the *Golden Booby* have?"

"It's a piece of art. I don't know what you mean."

"I mean you were the only person on the videos who spent so much time studying the statue and taking notes. Why?"

"It's beautiful art. I was trying to sketch it. Its lines were so perfect."

"May I see your sketches?"

No, you may not." Roberto lost his interest in keeping it friendly. "I don't have to show you anything unless you have a warrant."

"I can get one."

"Go ahead. It won't do you any good. I threw the sketches away. They weren't good."

"Did Carol turn the alarm off before you picked her up?"

"I… What are you trying to do? I told you I didn't pick her up."

"Never?"

"No, if you must know, she wanted to keep our relationship a secret. We usually drove to Brownsville for dinner so no one she knew would see us. I never picked her up at her condo."

"That must be tough. Dating a woman who's ashamed to be seen with you," I pushed. "Why did you hang around the museum so much?"

"We never let on that we knew each other."

"Then why were you there?"

"The statue. I was looking at the statue."

"Come on. It's just a bird, an artifact. It can't hold that much interest."

"You're a fool."

"From where I'm standing, I'd say it looks the other way around," I answered.

"You're all fools," Roberto flicked his hand over his shirt collar. "Don't you realize there's a curse on that statue? When it's gone, death follows. You think it's just about Carol? What about the rest of you?"

"Whoa, who's skin are you interested in? I thought you were grieving for Carol but you're just worried about your own hide," I wanted to deck this pompous idiot.

"If you knew any history, you'd be worried too. The *Golden Booby* is said to have come from an ancient Indian culture. They placed a curse on it. Follow its history, man. It's killed too many people. I don't intend to be one of them."

I realized that it was fear I saw in Roberto, not arrogance and attitude. Well, maybe those too, but mostly fear.

"I don't understand. If you're afraid of it, why keep going back to it?"

"Because it has the power to affect all of us. I knew that Carol could die because of it and she did."

"She died because of a thief who bashed her over the head."

"You don't understand curses, man." Roberto deflated right before my eyes. "If Carol died, I could be next. You're involved in this investigation. The curse could spread to you, too."

"As we now know, it wasn't the real statue so the curse shouldn't apply."

"The real statue was there at some time and it's still around. If we don't find it, the curse will work."

I wasn't getting anywhere. I glanced at Rachel and saw that she knew it too.

"Roberto, that's all I have for now. If you hear anything about the real statue, will you let Detective Vasquez know?"

"I don't think he's the killer," I told Rachel as we drove away.

"I agree. He's a little strange, but I think he may have really cared for Carol."

"Or for the statue. It still doesn't make sense to hang around something that scares you that much."

"I think he has a fascination with the idea of a curse. Then it became too real when Carol died."

"I suppose you're right. He made me wonder if the idea of a curse played into motive. Strange."

We dropped by the station and talked with Rudy. He had finished his reports and was watching an earlier surveillance video.

"Finding anything?" Rachel watched the screen.

"Nothing except that I keep seeing the same people. Why would anyone keep going back to the museum?"

"Going a couple of times is understandable," I said. "The statue is impressive. I imagine people see it and then go home and Google it."

"I'd agree with that." Rudy took off his plaid sport jacket and hung it over the back of his chair. "But I've watched three videos and the same woman is in all three. Roberto was in one of them and I know you saw him in the ones you watched."

"Who's the woman?" Rachel asked.

"Hang on a minute. I'll find them."

As soon as a woman came into view, I recognized her. It was the older woman from the bookstore. I'd seen her in one of the videos too. Rudy continued scrolling through until he found another woman standing back in the corner. I might not have recognized her face but I'd seen that tall, slender bundle of nerves.

"We have the guest book here. I've gone through it for those days. Hap, could you see if any names correlate with the same women on the videos you have?" Rachel handed me the book. "Bring it back this afternoon, okay?"

"Sure. I have to pick up Elena for lunch. I'll have her help me. She'll love that."

Elena was thrilled to be involved. After lunch, we checked the guest book against the videos and came up with two names.

"Adele Something — I can't read her handwriting — and Michaela Flanagan. Those should match," Elena said. "How do we find them?"

"That's the not-so-fun side of police work. We start checking out hotels and condos. We'll check the phone book first but I doubt if they are locals. I'll call Griff at the bookstore and see if he remembers the one woman."

"I can check those names on my iPad and see if either are area residents," Elena suggested.

"Okay. Let's get busy."

I called Griff and described the woman I'd seen in the store. He didn't recall her until I mentioned she was there the same day as the songwriter guy, Casa.

"Yes, I remember now. Adele. She's staying at the *KOA Campground*. Said she rented a trailer for the month, I believe. I can't think of her last name but it was J-something."

"Adele isn't that common. Maybe we can find her with just the J."

Elena googled the *KOA Campground* as I took notes. She gave me the number and I called. I told the attendant that I was supposed to meet a woman named Adele in the office but I was going to be late and I couldn't reach her on her cell phone.

"She was in here for change a few minutes ago," he said.

I thanked him for his helpfulness. I called Rachel. She said she'd call the South Padre Police and head over there. Hopefully she'd find Adele in her trailer.

Elena found out that Michaela Flanagan wasn't listed in the current phone book either. She did find someone by that name on Facebook but no updates had been made in almost two years. If she were the same person, she lived in Lexington, KY.

"Hap, there are a lot of entries when I Google her. There's someone by her name in Loveland, Colorado. She apparently witnessed a shooting there last year. Shall I keep looking?"

"She may be visiting here. I'll tell Rachel. She will probably start canvassing the hotels on the island."

When Rachel arrived at the *KOA Campground*, Officer Duron was waiting. They talked to Adele. When Rachel called, she said that Adele admitted to an interest in the statue but knew nothing about the crime.

"She seemed appalled that the statue was a fake," Rachel said. "I get the funny feeling that too many people wanted to get their hands on it."

"We have to deal with the fact that one of them did."

"She came here just to see the statue. The legend captivated her. She always loved ancient cultures. She said she's been to the island before and wanted to look for treasure but never took the time. Said she's horrified by the murder — that was almost an afterthought for her."

"She sounds dramatic."

"She is, but I don't believe she has any knowledge of the murder. Officer Duron agreed. Did you and Elena have any luck tracking down the other woman?"

"Michaela? No. Elena found references to women — or a woman — by the same name in Kentucky and Colorado. She's not in the local phone book. Do you want to check with the hotels or do you want me to do that?"

"Let me see what Rudy has come up with. I'll get back with you."

After Rachel's call, I told Elena we had nothing more to do until we heard back from her. "Would you like to go to the bookstore?"

"I'd love that."

I introduced her to Griff and told him we'd talked with Adele. Elena lost herself in rows of books. I knew she could spend hours here. She loved seeing Peg's books in the front of the store. Griff took a break and our conversation soon turned to the murder. When customers came through the door, Griff's "Welcome to *Paragraphs*..." spiel put him in bookseller mode.

"We're looking for a woman who showed up at the museum several times before the murder. Her name is Michaela Flanagan," I did my best to describe her. "She was tall and slender. I don't remember the color of her hair, but it was dark and fairly long. The thing I remember is the fear in her face. She was really nervous."

"I don't think she's been in here. I'd notice that kind of nervousness. Let me ask Joni."

While he went in search of Joni, I picked up a magazine from the coffee table in front of my chair. It featured Rio Grande Valley culture. As I flipped through, my eyes caught sight of a woman with long, dark hair. I found the page and there she was — Michaela Flanagan, a nature artist new to the Valley.

"Griff… Griff," I called out.

"What is it?"

"It's her." I held up the magazine. "This is Michaela Flanagan, right here in this magazine. Give me a minute."

I skimmed the article. I'm a slow reader but I couldn't take the time now. "Looks like she moved to the island. I need to call Rachel."

I handed Griff the magazine while I made the call. She asked the name of the magazine and said she could take it from there.

"I can't believe it. Police work is never that easy," I told him.

"Your lucky break. Reminds me of the old guy who came in here talking about the booby. Remember me telling you about him?"

"Yeah, what was his name. Buck or something like that?"

"Buster. He had some story about being responsible for the statue being found. Said he knew its history. Some story about Al Capone. I didn't pay much attention."

"Is he still around?"

"Haven't seen him. I'm surprised he hasn't come back to tell me he knew the statue was a fake."

"This investigation is a tough one," I said. Griff knew I was working with Rachel.

"I keep wondering how the killer got around the alarm," Griff said.

I was surprised he hadn't heard the alarm was off. If the police had kept it quiet, I wasn't going to be the one to spill the beans.

"I even talked to Steve Hathcock about it," Griff continued. "Since he's a locksmith, I thought he might know something about security systems."

"Did he?"

"He said he didn't know how it was done unless the alarm was off."

"Hap, I found some books I want to buy," Elena interrupted our conversation. I'd forgotten all about her but her timing was perfect.

"Well, I can make that happen," Griff ambled over the to counter.

Rachel called the magazine publisher for Michaela's contact info. She then called Michaela, explained who she was and what she wanted. She agreed to talk to us and Rachel told her we could be there in fifteen minutes.

Elena asked if she could wait in the bookstore.

When Michaela opened her door, you could almost smell the fear oozing out of her. I wondered if this could be the same Michaela Flanagan who had witnessed a shooting in Colorado. Even then, her fear seemed extreme.

Her walls were covered with paintings. As Rachel began to tell Michaela why we wanted to talk to her, I wandered over to a scene of a bay sunset.

"Do you like landscapes?" She focused on me.

"Yes, I do. My wife loves to take photos and it's made me more aware of my surroundings. Did you paint this?"

"Yes, most of these paintings are my work. I hang them on my walls to help me choose selections for exhibits."

"I like them," I said as Rachel began to study them.

"You're very good," she told Michaela. "Is your work displayed locally?"

"It is displayed at the *Laguna Madre Art Gallery* and I'm working with a gallery in McAllen."

"You need to meet Marne Law."

"Oh, I've met her and I love her work. I saw the painting she did of the *Golden Booby*."

"We're here because we noticed you visited the museum several times. We'd like to know what drew you back repeatedly," Rachel got back to the business at hand.

"I love art. To see a classic piece of ancient art is such a rare privilege. I could study it for months. I was crushed to learn it was a fake."

"We all were," I agreed.

"Have you caught the murderer? What about the real statue? Is there one or has the whole thing been a ruse? That's the kind of scandal that can turn the art world upside down.

"I spent hours studying its lines and the placement of the jewels. It seemed so perfect."

Rachel caught my eye. We both knew that Michaela had nothing to do with either the murder or the robbery.

"No, we haven't caught the murderer and at this stage, we have no idea about the statue," Rachel said. "Michaela, I'm sorry we bothered you. Unless you noticed something that we need to be aware of, we'll let you get on with your day."

"She never relaxed," Rachel said as we settled in the car. "Did you notice that?"

"Yes. She's a talented, but deeply troubled person."

~ Chapter ~
9

I woke up trying to remember something I should have done yesterday. I had dropped Elena off at her hotel after we left the bookstore. She and her dad had reservations for the *Black Dragon Pirate Cruise*. Peg and I spent a quiet evening.

I hadn't heard back from Rachel so I needed to call her after I had my coffee. Peg had already walked Luke and was checking something on her computer. I made my coffee — thank God for the Keurig — and picked up my iPad to read the news.

Neither area paper reported anything new on the investigation. I suspected it wouldn't be long before the police department started drawing fire if they didn't find the killer.

The Brownsville Herald carried an update on an old guy who'd been beaten up a couple of weeks ago and was still in a coma. An officer reportedly said they still may be looking at murder rather than assault. Robert Stevenson. I thought I'd heard the name before but I dismissed it. I couldn't deal with another question rolling around in my brain.

The weather reported rain across the middle states but unfortunately not in Texas. Looked like we were headed for another year of drought.

"Let's call Elena and take her to *Manuel's* this morning," Peg broke into my thoughts.

"Sounds great. What made you think of that?"

"Just looking at *Le Sandwich Boutique's* special today and I realized we…"

"That's it. That's what I forgot," I interrupted.

"What are you talking about?"

"Lola wants to talk to me. Let's stop by there after we finish breakfast. Okay?"

We introduced Elena to Frank and Jay.

"We've been waiting for you." Frank said.

"What..how did you know…? Elena's shocked expression was priceless.

"We know everything that goes on," Jay bragged.

"How could you know?" Elena asked.

"Don't pay any attention to Jay," Frank said. "Mary Russell Muchmore was here earlier. She told us you were visiting Hap and Peg." He took our order and Elena chattered away, thrilled that she was part of the community.

Frank stopped by again and by the time he brought our food, he'd learned all about Elena's background, why she was here, how she knew me, and that she liked to play chess. We laughed as Jay's flirtatious manner brought several blushes to her cheeks.

"I loved the food and Frank and Jay, too," Elena said when we walked outside. "I want to bring Dad back here. Can you believe Mary Russell remembered me? That is awesome."

"I'm sure your dad will love it too. Mary Russell is a sharp lady and she'll do what she told you the other night. She'll think about you when she travels through Missouri."

We still had time to stop by *Le Sandwich Boutique* before they opened for lunch.

"I'm glad you're here," Lola said. "I'm not sure this is important but I wanted you to know."

"Any information can help."

"You know Betty, Carol's assistant?"

"Yes, I've talked with her."

"Did she tell you about her friends?"

"No, who are they?"

"She has two new friends. I've known Betty for a long time. She's pretty much a loner but she often comes here for lunch. She mentioned a new friend who came to see the *Golden Booby*. She said this lady started hanging out at the museum a lot and they got to know each other."

"What's her name?"

"Adele. Betty said she likes her but there's something about her that makes her nervous."

"Oh, boy. We've talked with her too. I'll have to talk to Rachel about her. Anything else?"

"Yes, a man. She made a big deal about Carol being secretive but she's nearly as bad. I know he's a writer and a singer too. She said she'd tell me about him when we had more time."

"Do you know his name?"

"It's initials but it was kinda strange — D and I'm not sure what the second initial is."

"DL?"

"Hmmm..."

DL Casa?"

"Yes, that's it."

Did you ever meet him?"

"No, she kept him under wraps. She said they met at the museum in the evenings. He was fascinated with the statue."

"Think, Lola. Anything else? Did she ever mention anything else about the museum?"

"Just to not let Carol know that she met him there. That's why I thought you should know."

"Thanks. I've got to call Rachel. I'll talk to you later."

My heart raced as I thought what this could mean. Could Betty be part of this? I called Rachel from the car and she asked me to meet her at the station. Peg dropped me off. I hated to think I may have been looking in the wrong place.

"It makes sense but if Betty lets him in the museum after hours, where was she the night Carol was killed?" Rachel seemed upset too. "Rudy, will you ask Betty to meet us here? We have to find out where DL Casa is staying but I want to talk to Betty first. Hap, will you help me?"

Rudy couldn't reach Betty by phone. He said he'd check at her home. She was not at home and a neighbor said she left town for a couple of days because the museum was closed.

Rachel and I spent the afternoon tracking down DL Casa. We checked all the area hotels and found he was registered at the *Hilton Garden Inn*. He wasn't at home but we figured a singer would be hanging out at a local joint.

Rachel told Rudy to check *Kelly's, Parrot Eyes,* and *Padre Sunset*. She and I would check *Louie's Backyard* and *The Quarterdeck*. If we didn't find him, we'd try the beach bars.

We spotted him as soon as we walked into *Louie's*. He was singing along, practically drowning out vocalist Leslie Blasing.

Rachel called Officer Duron. We took a seat in the back so we could enjoy Leslie's performance until Duron arrived. Too bad we had to listen to Casa too.

Officer Duron arrived within a few minutes.

"Thanks for coming, Daniel" Rachel told him. "I wanted you to be part of this." Both knew the importance of working together and sharing information.

The three of us walked over to Casa. Duron showed his badge. "DL Casa, I'd like to have a word with you."

With a few drinks under his belt, DL seemed agreeable to anything.

"Sure. Sit down."

"We'd like you to step outside with us, please."

"And miss Leslie's next song?"

Leslie heard his comment. "I'll save it until you come back, big guy."

Casa's complaints reached everyone as we walked him through the restaurant and out the door. Liquor may have loosened him up but he sobered quickly when Rachel hit him with her first question.

"DL, are you in a relationship with Betty Ryan?"

"What are you talking about?"

"We know that you are seeing her and that you have spent evenings with her in the museum."

"Wait a minute. What are you accusing me of?"

"We're asking the questions. Are you in a relationship with Betty Ryan?"

"No, I'm not."

"Do you admit you know her?"

"Yes."

Do you admit you've met her in the museum several evenings?"

"Where did you hear that? Did Betty say I did?" Casa stroked his beard. I saw his eyes harden.

"I'm asking the questions, remember. Do you admit you've met her in the museum several evenings?"

"No, I'm not admitting anything. Do I need a lawyer?"

"I don't know. Do you?"

DL had transformed from Mr. Friendly to Mr. Belligerent. I watched his futile effort to intimidate Rachel.

"I want a lawyer now."

"Since you need a lawyer, let's take a ride over to Port Isabel to the police station. You can contact your attorney from there."

"You can't take me in. I've done nothing. You have no right."

"You're the one who asked for a lawyer. We need to hold you for questioning until your attorney shows up. We'll do that at the station."

"Wait a minute, Detective. I didn't mean I wouldn't cooperate but I'm having a good time listening to Leslie. Can't we do this tomorrow?"

I laughed as he tried to sweet talk Rachel. He definitely underrated her. I felt pride watching that girl grow into a top-notch detective.

"Now or later, it's your choice," Rachel stood firm.

"Okay, what do you want to know?"

"Did you meet Betty Ryan in the museum several evenings?"

"I need to talk to Betty."

"You can do that later. Where is she? She's not at home."

"She went to Brownsville to visit a relative. She should be home tomorrow."

"Thank you, but you still have not answered my question."

"Look," DL started. "I know Betty. Okay. I don't want to get her in trouble so I don't want to say anything until I talk to her."

"No go. You answer our questions now or you come to the station with us."

"Let's go. I've got nothing to hide."

Officer Duron did the honors of escorting Casa to our vehicle.

"He's all yours," he told Rachel.

"Thanks," Rachel grinned.

I hoped for a quiet ride to the station but Casa's fingers drummed a constant rhythm on the back-seat door. By the time we crossed the causeway, I wanted to toss him into the bay.

When we arrived, DL refused to talk until he saw Betty. We didn't think a night in jail would hurt him. He felt otherwise.

It was the next afternoon when Betty came home. Rudy had spent the day checking on her. Rachel suggested I talk to her first because we had already talked about Carol's death.

Her appearance startled me. I thought she'd had time to recover from the shock of Carol's death, but she answered her door with watery eyes and a red splotchy face.

"Are you all right?" My first impulse was to comfort her.

"Not really. What can I do for you?"

"Betty, we'd like to talk to you for a few minutes. Do you have time now?" Rachel's calm voice seemed to soothe her.

"Yes, come in." We followed her into her living room where she waved her hand toward two wicker chairs.

"Sit down, please." Betty sat on a love seat, smoothed her skirt and folded her hands in her lap. Except for a tight grip on a kleenex, she appeared calm.

"We heard you were in Brownsville visiting a relative," Rachel began.

"Yes." Betty twisted the Kleenex.

"Did you have a good time?"

"No. I mean, okay. Oh, I might as well tell you. Do you know Robert Stevenson? He was a professor at the university. He is my uncle. I visited him in the hospital."

"Is he doing well?"

"No, not at all. He'd been the picture of health for a man his age. Then he was attacked and badly beaten. He's recovering from broken ribs and severe internal injuries, especially to his kidneys. The doctors are keeping him in a medically-induced coma. He may never recover. I spent the night with him. I hoped that family memories would stir an awareness in him."

"I'm sorry," Rachel paused to let Betty compose herself. "When did this happen?"

"A few weeks ago."

I realized this was the guy I'd read about this morning in the *Brownsville Herald*. Was this another piece in the puzzle or was it just coincidence?

"Who did it?" Rachel asked.

"We don't know. He attacked Uncle Robert from the back. Hit him on the head first and knocked him down. Apparently the attacker beat him with a blunt object and kicked him repeatedly."

"I hope he'll recover."

"Me too. I know he'll want to go home if and when he wakes up."

"Betty, we need to ask you some questions about Carol's murder. I'm sorry you have so much on your plate right now but we need your help."

"I'll try."

"Do you know a DL Casa?"

Betty's eyes widened and her mouth dropped open but she quickly recovered. She didn't answer.

"He says you know each other."

"Y-yes, I know him." She twisted the tissue and I wondered what kept it in one piece.

"What is your relationship with him?"

"I… I know him."

"We know that you've been meeting him at the museum after hours," Rachel's patience dwindled.

"I… How do you know that?"

"Why did you meet him there?"

"I… Who told you?"

"Betty, we need answers. We know that the alarm was turned off several evenings and we know that you met DL Casa at the museum. Carol was murdered after hours and the alarm was off. We need your help."

"I… I…," Betty sputtered and broke into tears. She buried her face in her hands and sobbed.

Rachel relented. She reached over and put her hand on Betty's shoulder.

We waited quietly while Betty brought her emotions under control.

"I knew…" she dabbed her eyes with her now-shredded Kleenex. I saw a box on a table, pulled a fresh one out, and handed it to her.

"T-thanks," she whispered.

"You knew what?" Rachel prompted.

"I knew someone would find out we met there. I told him it wasn't safe but he insisted."

"Why don't you start at the beginning? Are you dating him? How did you meet him?"

"Heavens no!"

We waited.

"It's not like that. I told him…"

Another pause. My impatience grew. At this rate, we'd be here until next week, but I held my tongue.

"I've known him for several years. He's…he's my half-brother from back east. My mother went away when I was three. She came back when I was a teenager. I didn't find out until she died that I had a brother. She left him when she came back."

"I understand, Betty, but why did you meet him at the museum?"

"I let him talk me into it. I didn't see any harm in it."

"Why turn off the alarm?" I asked.

"Because the cameras are tied to the alarm. He said Carol would know we were meeting there if it was on the videos."

"That doesn't make sense. Why didn't you meet for dinner or here at your house?"

"I don't know. My God, I let him talk me into it. You think… do you think he killed Carol? Is that what this is about?"

"It's possible," Rachel kept her voice low and even. I wanted to shout.

"He'll kill me for telling you this," Betty stood and paced the floor as she realized the full implication of her honesty. She'd let DL use her and now she'd admitted it out loud.

~ Chapter ~
10

Rachel called Rudy and by the time we arrived at the station, DL Casa sat alone in the interrogation room.

"Good morning, DL," Rachel laid a pen and notepad in front of her as she took the seat opposite him.

I leaned against the wall. Over the years I learned that I picked up more nonverbal response when I'm standing. Maybe I just paid closer attention.

DL responded with a slight nod.

"We've found Betty," Rachel picked up her pen.

"I want to see her."

"Later."

"I need to see her."

"I'm sure you do but not now. I need you to tell us how you met her."

"I don't remember."

"She does."

"What did she say?"

"I'm not playing that game," Rachel leaned forward, swapping the professional look for one of strength. "I ask the questions and you give the answers. Got it?"

DL locked eyes with Rachel but he broke away first.

"Now let's start over," Rachel straightened in her chair. "Where and when did you meet Betty?"

"It's a long story and has nothing to do with anything."

"I have all the time in the world."

"Okay, she's kinda family. Her old lady and mine are the same person. Dear Old Ma left her first old man and Betty, came to the Carolinas, met my dad, and here I am."

"That tells me who you are but not how you met your half-sister."

"When our old lady died. I didn't even know Betty existed 'til then. She's a wimpy old gal and a bore, I might add."

"Wow, what a jewel of a brother you turned out to be."

"Whatever…"

I wanted to grab this guy and knock his hard head against the wall. I smiled at the thought of that hard head cracking. DL caught it out of the corner of his eye.

"What's he got to smile about?" He asked Rachel.

"Probably the pleasure he'd take in hitting you up the side of the head, or some such thing." The girl learned fast. Time for me to make my presence known.

"Detective Vasquez is too nice," I straightened, walked over to DL and stood looking down at him. "I don't have that problem. Here's what we know. You are Betty's half-brother. You cajoled her into meeting you at the museum. You made her turn off the alarm several nights while you were there so you could learn how it operated. You came here to steal the *Golden Booby*. How am I doing so far?"

"I... I want a lawyer."

"Let him make his call but first I want to finish the story." I never took my eyes off of our suspect.

"I'm listening. I hope you are, DL," Rachel sat back in her chair.

"Here's how we see it. You used Betty to learn about the museum, the display, and the alarm system. Then one evening when you couldn't wait any longer, you got to the museum right at closing time. While Carol completed her closing duties, you kept her talking and distracted. Somehow you managed to turn off the alarm system. Then either when she discovered it or when you were ready, you broke into the display case, grabbed the statue and hit her over the head. I would have loved to see your face when it shattered into a thousand pieces. The things we don't know are how you found out about the *Golden Booby* and how long you planned the theft."

"If I did all that, how did I break into the display case? I thought it was unbreakable. Did you find a weapon at the museum?"

"Funny how he doesn't deny anything but he brings up the one piece of evidence we're missing." Rachel smiled and leaned forward.

"It's likely at the bottom of the bay. Let Mr. Casa call his attorney."

"Wait. Can't we talk?

Rachel and I left the room. She grinned, turned around and opened the door again. "About what?"

Darn, that girl was good.

"It's Friday and I have a chance to sing with Leslie tonight," DL now tried begging.

"Sorry. That duet will have to wait. I'm sure Leslie can manage on her own," Rachel refused to cut him any slack.

"Is Betty's uncle your uncle too?" I tossed the question at him.

"Wh-what? I'm talking to Detective Vasquez. What did you say?"

"You heard me. Yes or no."

"How did you break the display case?" Rachel tossed in another question.

"Wait. What are you doing?" Mixed emotions slid across his face. "Where's my lawyer?"

"Okay. Call your lawyer. Then we'll have an officer take you back to your cell until your attorney is here."

This time we walked out of the room with no intention of turning around.

At least we left DL on edge.

~ Chapter ~
11

I received a text from Elena during my phone call with Rachel on Saturday morning.

Remember, we are going on the ghost tour tonight, Elena's text read. Peg was spending the day with her.

Rachel's call wasn't social. DL's attorney would meet us at 10:30. While I drank my coffee and ate a bowl of Cheerios, I tried to prepare questions that the attorney would allow. I'd been bluffing with DL yesterday but I wouldn't get away with it today. On the other hand, Rachel didn't need me. I doubted she knew how good she was. She had a gift for knowing when and where to slash her victim with razor-sharp questions.

We had agreed that I would be backup only. Rachel and Rudy would conduct the interrogation. Rachel would introduce me to the attorney as a consultant.

I might have guessed that DL's attorney would be a classy young woman. If she had stepped out of Fortune Magazine, she wouldn't be any more perfect.

"I'm Mary Anne Bonnaire, with Stuttgart, Bissette and Bonnaire in Harlingen." She took the chair next to her client.

Rachel once again sat opposite DL. Rudy and I stood against the wall.

"State your name and place of residence, please." Rachel's matter-of-fact question set the tone.

"DL Casa. Jacksonville, Florida."

Is DL your full name?"

"Yes, I'm named after both of my grandfathers — Donovan and Leonard."

"Your occupation?"

"Singer, writer. You know all this."

Ms Bonnaire gave him a quick nod.

"Did you come here to steal the *Golden Booby*?" Rudy stepped forward.

"No." DL's voice rose.

"Is this your first visit to the Rio Grande Valley?" Rachel asked.

"No. I've visited before."

"Is it true that Betty Ryan is your half-sister?"

"Yes."

"You share the same mother?"

"Yes."

"Is Robert Stevenson your uncle?" Rudy threw DL off his rhythm again.

"Who?"

"Robert Stevenson, Betty's uncle," Rachel's voice soothed. "Is he your uncle too?"

"I don't know. My dad raised me. I don't know my mother's relatives."

I almost laughed at the change in tone from yesterday. Ms Bonnaire must be good or sexy enough he wanted to impress her.

"What happened to the 'old lady' endearment you used yesterday?" I decided my laugh wouldn't hurt anyone. From the look on Ms Bonnaire's face, she disagreed.

"Did you and Betty meet several evenings in the museum?" Rachel was all business.

"Where is Betty?"

"Please answer the question."

"I want to talk to Betty."

"Answer Detective Vasquez's question, DL," Ms Bonnaire advised.

"Yes, we met there. Betty told you, didn't she?"

"Yes, she did. You asked her to turn off the alarm each time?"

"Yes, because I didn't want her to get in trouble for taking me in there at night."

"So sweet of you," Rudy said.

DL glared at him.

"How did you break the glass in the display case?"

"I — did Betty say I did?"

"I'm asking the questions. Please answer them."

"Forget me. You should be looking for whoever stole the real *Golden Booby*. I knew as soon as I lifted it…"

"I'd like a moment with my client," Ms Bonnaire interrupted.

We stepped out of the room. "He wants to tell us how he did it. He can't hold it in." We agreed with Rachel.

"Plus he's furious he did it all for a fake," I added.

When we walked back in the room, Ms Bonnaire looked composed and DL was staring at his hands.

"We'd like to make a deal," Ms Bonnaire began. "We want to plead manslaughter and attempted assault.

"We need to hear his story first," Rachel said.

"We want to make a deal first," Ms Bonnaire repeated.

"Okay, a deal is on the table, but we can't define the charge until we know the whole story."

"Go ahead and tell them."

"I went to a conference in DC. One night I met a guy in the hotel bar. We struck up a conversation and had a few drinks. He started talking about a bird that should have made him rich by now. Said he would have been but his cousin messed it up."

"What was his name?" I interrupted.

"Oscar. I don't remember his last name. He was from Pittsburgh. I remember that. Anyway, as the evening wore on, I got a convoluted story out of him. His grandfather had a statue of a bird — a booby — that was solid gold with jewels on it. He called it the *Golden Booby*. He and a cousin he never knew existed inherited it when the old guy was killed."

DL paused. We waited.

"Since them I've read everything about the *Golden Booby*. There are all kinds of legends about it. Some said it was Pre-Inca or Aztec. Others said it came from the South Pacific. But they all had one thing in common. It was worth millions. It took me months to trace it to south Texas. Thank God the old man was killed. There was enough coverage in the papers to track it down.

He paused, licking his lips as if they were the gold he coveted.

"I didn't plan to use Betty even though I knew she was down here. I found the name of Oscar's cousin. I planned to meet her, woo her, and go from there. Women always fall for sweet talk trash. I figured Belle Neuva was no different. When I got down here, I found out she was on an extended trip to South America. I heard she was trying to retrace the old man's steps.

"Then I remembered Betty. She's such an insecure, lonely old gal that I knew I could get her to help me. It worked. Give her a little attention and she's putty in your hands."

"Did she help you with the robbery?"

"Are you kidding? She's clueless. She was obsessed with the idea that we could be close, be family. She kept telling me I was her only family now, except for some old guy in Brownsville and he was gonna croak."

"Then Betty had nothing to do it with?" Rachel asked again.

"I told you. She doesn't have the smarts to be tempted. I used her and I'd do it again."

"Why did you kill Carol?"

"It was an accident. I hadn't meant to do it. I brought a high-grade glass cutter with me. I figured to weaken the glass by creating what they call a 'rip' in it. I read an article on the Internet about a thief that used that successfully. I knew where the camera's dead spots were. I came in before closing and hung around until I could get to the alarm. Once I turned it off, I started talking to Carol. She'd seen me around before and, of course, she thought the alarm was on. I flirted with her enough to find out she had a new man in her life. She went about her closing rituals and tried to ignore me. She kept suggesting I leave.

"I'd been able to sneak in some use of the glass cutter. But Carol caught me at it. I had no choice.

"I tried to tell her I'd split the money with her but she wouldn't listen. I had to stop her."

"DL Casa, you're under arrest for the murder of Carol Flores and the attempted theft of the *Golden Booby*."

"Read him his rights," Rachel said to Rudy as she picked up her paperwork, stood and motioned to me to leave with her.

~ Chapter ~
12

We picked up Elena and lost ourselves in her hopes of ghost sightings in Port Isabel. For me, the sight of DL Casa behind bars made my day.

The case involved a murder and he had strong legal representation. I didn't know what kind of deal the Prosecutor would accept, but I hoped they would go for first-degree murder. DL knew when he walked in the museum that he'd kill Carol if he needed to. However, that decision was out of my hands.

We had put a killer behind bars. I was ready for fun and relaxation. Right now, looking for ghosts seemed the thing to do.

We stopped at *Whataburger* for a hamburger before the tour. Elena plied me with questions. I filled her in on the basic facts.

"But how did he break the glass?"

"He used a glass cutter," I told her. "He read on the Internet about a thief who successfully broke unbreakable glass with it."

"Doesn't he know you can't believe everything you read on the Internet?"

"He does now."

PARAGRAPHS

Joyce Faulkner

~ Chapter ~
1

Paragraphs on South Padre Boulevard

Noon

"I think books smell like candy, don't you?"

"What kind?" The woman pulled her shopping bag closer to her feet and hugged her purse.

"Each genre is different." I smiled and sat down beside her. "For example, history has a musty old caramel scent — like the ones you leave in the pockets of your overcoat in March and don't find again until November? On the other hand, mysteries remind me of licorice."

Her eyebrows were coarse and at odds with her silvery-blonde bob. "Why licorice?"

I winked. "All those twisty plots."

"What about adventure?" There wasn't a hint of amusement in her eyes.

The door to the book store opened and Steve Hathcock came in. He nodded to the three authors sitting behind the table in front of the room and waved at me. Then, like everyone else who came in, he went over to admire Marne Law's painting of the infamous *Golden Booby* before taking his seat.

The door opened again and a slight, dark-haired girl came in. She went immediately to the Law painting and took several quick photos with an iPhone before settling into a chair in front of Steve.

The woman beside me glanced over her shoulder and then quickly faced forward, focusing on something deep within her cavernous Consuelo bag. She was a little hairy for my tastes — but I would have taken her to *Ted's* for Pecan Pancakes if she'd given me half a chance.

"Dark Chocolate?"

She turned back toward me — and frowned, "What?"

"Adventure? Dark Chocolate?" I thought I was charming. I didn't smell like musty caramels and I'd just had my teeth whitened — but she seemed to barely tolerate me.

"Welcome to *Paragraphs*." A large elf stood beside the authors' table.

The audience quieted.

"Don't you think Griff is adorable?" A tiny woman muttered under her breath. Her hoarse voice echoed in the sudden silence and everyone laughed — including the elf himself although his cheeks flushed.

"Thank you all for joining us this afternoon." Griff looked beyond the folks in the second row where his octogenarian admirer sat. "I'm impressed that you made it so close to the hour. However, we are on island time and we are still waiting for one of our authors. She should be here shortly. In the meantime, get acquainted — and talk among yourselves. That is all."

The dark haired girl sighed and lowered her phone.

"My name is Nigel," I said to the woman beside me. "I used to be in business, but my wife died last year and now I'm into adventure — and romance."

"I'm Merry Miller." She shook my hand. "I'm an actress."

"Nice to meet you, Merry." I wiggled my fingers to get the blood back into them. "Why are you here today?"

"Research."

I was about to ask her about that, but Griff caught my eye from across the room.

"Nigel, have you met Adele?" He stood beside a voluptuous blonde holding a copy of *Padre Puzzle*. I fancied that her eyes matched the sapphire blue booby feet in the picture behind her. Relieved that the unpleasant Ms. Miller wasn't the only possibility for the afternoon, I left Merry to her own devices and squeezed through the crowd. I wrinkled my nose. She must have left traces of her scent on my hand. Maybe I was imagining it, but I was sure there was anise in Merry's perfume.

"Nigel, this is Adele JPlus. She is a photographer. She's new to South Padre Island."

Adele smiled at me.

As if a giant hand had turned down the volume, Griff's voice and the background noise in *Paragraphs* dropped to a soft buzz. I didn't need violins, but they would have been nice. Adele's angelic face captured my heart. I took her hand and kissed it. "It's an honor to meet you, beautiful lady."

She squealed and jerked her hand back, dropping her book, and bumping the painting on the wall behind her — knocking it askew. "Who are you?"

"I ... I'm Nigel Rutherford." I bent over to pick up her book and slammed the crown of my head against the same bookcase. I wanted to howl in pain, but the store was filled with strangers and it wouldn't have been dignified. "I'm sorry. I'm a bit of a romantic. I didn't mean to offend."

She rubbed her elbow. "You didn't offend. You just surprised me. No one has kissed my hand in a long time. Ever, actually."

Griff grabbed her hand and pretended to kiss it as well. "Let's make it two in one day, fair damsel."

"Oh you guys are nuts!" Adele giggled and put both hands behind her lovely round rump.

"If you are going to start kissing hands, there are more ladies in this room!" The diminutive old lady who had her eye on Griff grumbled.

"Now Sylvie, play nice before you get me in trouble with my wife." Griff straightened the picture of the Booby and clapped his hands to get everyone's attention again. "Since this is getting rowdy, maybe we should we get started. I'll introduce Pat Avery when she gets here."

I waited until Adele sat down in one of the upholstered chairs in the back row, before squeezing in beside her. By chance, the seat I chose put me between my fantasy woman and Steve Hathcock.

Griff made his way to the front of the room. "Hello, everyone. Before we start, I'd like to introduce one of our local bloggers, Bonnie Parker. Stand up, Bonnie."

The dark-haired girl stood up, nodded, and sat down again.

"Bonnie will be taking pictures of our little event for her blog, *Who and What's on South Padre Island*. I'm sorry that Mrs. Avery isn't here but maybe she'll make it a little later. In the meantime, let me introduce this year's Mystery Week authors. First, we have Bob Doerr. Bob is the author of the Jim West mystery novels. This is Bob's third year with us and he is always informative and entertaining."

A tall man executed a two-finger salute.

Bonnie held up her iPhone and snapped a quick picture.

"Oh, he's adorable too," Sylvie croaked. "Look at that beautiful head of hair!"

Merry Miller turned around in her seat. "I'd appreciate if you kept it down, lady! I'd like to hear the program."

"What a witch," Adele said to me behind her hand. "Sylvie doesn't mean any harm. She's just a little dotty. How dare that woman be mean to her!"

Although I didn't care about the Merry Miller/Sylvie conflict, I was thrilled that Adele JPlus had confided in me of her own accord. I glanced at Steve on the other side of me and he grinned. Was I that obvious?

"I'd also like to introduce you to Joyce Faulkner." Griff ignored the audience altercation. "Joyce writes both historical fiction and mystery thrillers." The plump little woman with a red ponytail acknowledged the introduction.

"And finally, you all know David Harry — the author of a series of books set right here on South Padre Island."

"Hello, everyone." David greeted his fans with a friendly grin.

Bonnie took a quick photo of David too.

Bob Doerr stood up and began his presentation. "Some of you know me, but for those of you who I've not met before, I was an investigator in the OSI. That's the Air Force version of NCIS that you see on television — only the OSI is better."

He grinned and we all grinned back.

"I've always thought about writing. I used to make up stories for my kids when they were little. When I retired, I sat down and started my first novel about a fellow named Jim West who has just retired from the OSI."

"So do you write about your old cases?"

Merry's sigh was dramatic. I guess she didn't like Sylvie's question — or maybe she just didn't like Sylvie.

I wasn't sure if Bob's chuckle was because of the question or the feminine fracas he was causing. "I certainly have enough material from way back when, Sylvie — but my character, Jim West, is a reluctant hero — like Griff here."

Griff laughed and puffed up his chest.

"Jim tries to live an unassuming life," Bob continued, "but crime happens all around him and people call him to help."

"Does that happen to you in real life?" A pretty woman seated beside Sylvie asked.

"You know, Sally, it never has. In real life, cops do their jobs — without the help of retired OSI officers."

I hadn't noticed Sally before, but she was quite lovely. I wondered if she was married.

"So what's coming up next, Bob?" Steve Hathcock had Bob's latest novel, *No One Else Left to Kill*, in his lap. "Another Jim West mystery?"

Doerr glanced at Griff before answering. "Actually, my newest project is a little different — and it's based on something that happened when I was here on South Padre Island last year. After the signing, my wife and I spent some time at the Port Isabel Museum — and I became fascinated with the *Golden Booby* display."

Sylvie nudged Sally. "I still have nightmares about what happened to Carol Flores."

"I was excited when I learned about that statue," Sally said. "I thought we were fortunate to have it in our museum — but now, I don't know what to think."

"Refresh my memory, Bob," David Harry said. "Was that before or after the murder?"

Bonnie held up her phone and I guessed that she was recording whatever Bob might say.

"Which one? There have been several — other places and a few right here on the island in recent years."

"And a few probables that were never confirmed one way or another." David tapped the table in front of him with his index finger.

Beside me, Steve Hathcock leaned forward in his seat. The women in the front two rows fidgeted. In fact, the atmosphere in *Paragraphs* had changed. I shook away a sudden shiver.

"But I was talking about the one in the museum," David continued. "Most of us living here knew the lady who was killed, you know."

Doerr nodded. "Before. I got to see the Booby display — and I even mentioned some security concerns to Ms. Flores. "

David shook his head. "Sad business."

"I was already well into my research when I heard she'd been killed," Bob said. "And of course, I moved the book to the top of my priority list."

"What exactly are you researching?" Merry Miller made a simple question seem rude.

"The book is tentatively titled, *The Legend of the Golden Booby*."

A middle-aged couple came in and squeezed into the row in front of me. Doerr smiled and waved at them. I figured they were newlyweds just by the way the man touched the woman's arm as they took their seats.

"Are you going to share some of that research now?" Adele gave voice to my own question even though I could tell Doerr was irritated by the interruption — and her tone.

"Maybe a little. Apparently, that bird has brought luck — good and bad — from the time it was first created."

"How?"

Doerr turned to Sylvie. "Good fortune to the person who has it — very BAD luck if he or she ever tries to get rid of it."

"Oh." Sylvie's eyes widened as she digested what Doerr was telling us. "How bad?"

I could tell that Doerr was searching for the right word, but apparently he couldn't find a gentle one. "Death," he said.

Silence.

The man in the row in front of me took the woman's hand. It reminded me of my wife and my life — before.

No! I closed my eyes and took a deep breath. Back to the Booby.

I watched the little group as they digested this information.

"Wait," Sally said, "Let me see if I understand this. The *Golden Booby* is worth many millions of dollars just in its materials — let alone its value as a historical artifact or as a piece of art. How would you get anything out of it if you couldn't sell it — or even give it away?"

"That's absurd!" Merry Miller burst out. "Where do people come up with such silliness?"

Doerr laughed. "Hey, I didn't make this stuff up. That's the legend — you can take it or leave it."

Bonnie Parker lowered her iPhone.

Steve Hathcock chuckled and shrugged. I didn't believe Steve took the *Golden Booby* that lightly, but I smiled in spite of myself. He was a historian — and an adventurer too. There's nothing more exciting than a mystery for the likes of us. However, Steve loved Boobymania for what it was — a phenomenon that brought business to South Padre Island.

I turned to Adele. She frowned and whispered in my ear, "He's out to find that statue himself."

"Who?"

"Doerr, of course. He knows more than some silly legend."

"Maybe there's more information in his book."

"But it's not out yet." Adele folded her arms over her chest and gave Doerr what my wife Edie used to call the *evil eye*."

"This is garbage! I thought the four of you — the mystery week writers — made a pact last year. You were each going to take a part of the legend and write a book about it. That's why I came today. — but all I see here are your old novels." Merry shook a thick finger at Doerr. "Where are the books about the Booby?"

Doerr didn't flinch, I'll give him that. "Booby lore is extensive. It takes time — and money — to do research on the level that I think is required for this project. I'm not finished yet." He stared into Merry's eyes for a moment longer than necessary — and then glanced around the room. "Any other questions?"

No one had the nerve to challenge him.

"Thank you," he said and sat down.

I guessed Bob Doerr was tired of us.

The couple in front of me was too. They got up, nodded at Doerr — and left.

Since it was clear that Bob Doerr had nothing else to say, Griff nodded to David Harry.

David stood up. "I guess it's my turn."

"Is it true, David? Did the four of you make a pact last year?"

"Sounds like you are excited by that idea, Sylvie." David straightened the stacks of "Puzzle" novels in front of him.

"I'm like everyone here. I already read everything else you wrote, David. And Bob too — and I still can't sleep without the lights on after reading what missy over there wrote last year."

The woman author sitting beside Doerr smiled behind her hand. There was no sign of a new book on the table in front of her either.

"May I ask how you all got this information?" David grinned.

Even Doerr got over his annoyance and smirked. Authors seem to take great pleasure when their fans are salivating for a new book.

"It's all over the island, man." Steve Hathcock laughed.

"And how did that happen?"

"Well, I admit to telling Sylvie and Nigel here." He clapped me on the back.

"And who told you, Steve?"

"I heard it from Frank and Jay when I had breakfast at *Manuel's* the other day — and there was a whole table of Winter Texans talking about it over at *Grapevine's* a couple weeks ago — and Gloria Bates mentioned it to me way last fall."

David turned around to his fellow authors, rubbing the palms of his hands together. "So much for keeping secrets on South Padre Island."

Everyone laughed — and merriment replaced the tension Merry Miller had injected into the room.

"So you've read all of my books, eh?" David winked at Sylvie. "What about the rest of you?"

"All except *Padre Paranoia* — but Griff sold it to me last week. I'll get to it after I finish Pat Avery's new book, *Murder Takes No Prisoners*," Sally Scaman said. "It's really, really good, by the way — and I did buy *A Cold Winter's Kill*, Bob. I still have two more in your series after that. I read *Windshift*, Joyce, and I'm working up my nerve for *Username*."

David looked at me.

"Griff sells me one every time I come into *Paragraphs*." I felt as defensive as Sally sounded.

"Get on with it," Merry said when it was her turn. "I haven't got all day for this."

"You want to know about *The Professor*?" He was playing with us. Of course, we wanted to know about his new Booby book.

"Well, unlike Doerr who is still working on his — and unlike Pat Avery who isn't here — and unlike Joyce Faulkner ..." He glanced at her. "What's your reason for not having a Booby book yet?

"The story's not over." Her eyes sparkled with mischief — or amusement — or something.

"Can't write a book until you know how it ends, eh?" David laughed. "Well, unlike my colleagues here, I finished my book."

"So where is it? Adele demanded.

"I know this is going to sound like the cat ate my homework ..."

Merry Miller groaned.

David took a deep breath. "Did you hear about that UPS truck that was hijacked in Brownsville yesterday?"

Everyone groaned this time. Everyone but the three authors and Griff.

Adele's face contorted. I wasn't sure if she was astonished or furious. "Someone hijacked a UPS truck with your books in it?"

"That's about the size of it." David feigned helplessness but somewhere inside, I knew he was lying — about something.

"Griff, pardon my saying this, but why didn't you just cancel this shindig then?" Sylvie wasn't gushing anymore.

Griff wiped his forehead with the back of his hand. "We didn't realize you all were Boobyites — and each of these authors have many books for you to choose from — and we didn't hear that David's books had been hijacked until this morning."

"As I understand it, you three — and Pat Avery — are now Booby experts," Adele said. "I don't want inside scoop — well, I do, but right now I'd settle for what you put in your books — and I'd love to know why you have delayed publishing them."

Griff shuffled from one foot to the other. Why was he so nervous? I bet that there were four boxes of books hidden away somewhere — maybe in this very building — but why?

The redhead put the palms of her hands on the table in front of her and frowned. "Listen, folks — we don't have any inside information about the stolen Booby. We are novelists. Do you expect us to put real clues in our books that will lead you to the prize? Don't you think that if we knew where it was, we'd go after it ourselves?"

"I think you drew us here with false advertising!" Sylvie growled.

"Be fair, Sylvie," Griff said. "We didn't advertise a Booby event."

"Well, someone led us to believe the books would be here today." Merry Miller gathered her shopping bag and her purse and stood up. "But I can see now that it was a colossal waste of time."

"Look, I'm not from around here," Joyce said. "But someone you all liked and cared about was killed — not even a year ago — over that damned bird." She pointed at the Law painting. "Now we know that the Booby on display in that museum was a fake which means that someone has the real deal — and has either sold it or hidden it. Bird watching has taken on new meaning around here — and to make things worse, Carol Flores' alleged murderer has escaped from the Port Isabel jail. Seems to me that poking around looking for the real Booby might be dangerous right now."

She was right. I stared at my shoes.

"Maybe we are somewhere between taking the legend too seriously — and too lightly," Sally said finally. "I've been running around the island like a beach combing Sherlock Holmes — treating it like a game. I even bought one of those Booby Tee-shirts thinking there might be something in the artwork that would be a clue."

Sylvie stuffed her new books into a roller bag."You are right, missy — we all did like Carol. I'm ashamed I forgot about what happened to her. My only excuse is that I'm broke again."

"I know you all have your reasons — but why don't you let the authorities do their jobs." Joyce glanced at Doerr whose nod was almost imperceptible. "Why don't we talk about the books that we do have?" She picked up a copy of *Username*. "For example, you already know the secrets of this book — just from the title."

A loud screech.

Everyone turned to look out the front door. A red Chevy bounced on its shocks in the parking lot.

Griff hustled over to the door, pushed it open, and looked out. "It's Everett Avery!"

Joyce dropped her book and I turned back to look at her. "Something's wrong." I could barely hear her but both David and Bob reacted to her words.

"Are you all right, Everett?" Griff called out the door.

A tall man in a tropical print shirt got out of the car — and ran up the steps into *Paragraphs*. "Is Pat here? Did she come with Joyce?"

Everyone's eyes went to a tiny blue shoe in Everett's hand.

"No, she's not here," Griff said. "We waited as long as we could and then figured you two were held up — so we started without her."

Everett lurched backwards — as if someone had punched him. Steve reached out to steady him on one side and I jumped up to lend my support as well.

"What is it, Everett?" Griff turned the chair I'd been sitting in around and guided the shaking man into it. "Let me get you some water."

"I hoped she was here — that her phone was dead. She does that, you know — lets her phone battery go down."

I glanced around the room. The Parker woman was recording again. The three authors were all standing.

"I thought she was with you, Everett," Joyce said. "We were on our way here and she had a phone call. She said you were having car trouble and she needed to go get you. So she left me here to get things started."

Everett grabbed Griff's arm. "Someone's got her."

"Got her?" Griff's eyes grew wider.

"Kidnapped her." Everett's breathing grew faster and I was afraid that he might collapse.

"What makes you think that?" Joyce pushed me out of the way and knelt down beside Everett's chair.

"She texted me to copy her *Murder Can Be Golden* manuscript to a thumb drive and meet her at *La Hacienda's*. I knew right away that something was wrong."

"Why is that?" I whispered to Steve who shrugged and shook his head.

Joyce turned around and looked into my eyes. "Because we haven't used thumb drives in years. Since we moved to MAC, we use the cloud."

Merry Miller dropped her bag. It made a loud noise and everyone jumped. She was a big woman and when she reached down to pick up her things, she knocked over her chair.

"I'd help you, but I gotta bad knee," Sylvie croaked.

Fumbling for lipsticks and hairbrushes and an array of electronics, Merry growled without raising her head. Something long and round rolled across the floor. David bent down to pick it up, but Merry slapped his hand and pocketed it.

When David stood up, I could see that he was embarrassed — and annoyed. He saw me looking at him and shrugged.

All that for a fat tube of lipstick? The woman was both selfish and rude! How could I have been so taken with her only a few minutes before?

"So what happened when you got to *La Hacienda*?" Joyce's voice drew my attention back to the drama at the front of the store.

"Our Honda was in the parking lot, but there was no sign of her inside the restaurant. I talked to the waiter but he hadn't seen her. When I came back out, I saw her shoe setting on the hood." He held up a smart phone. "This was in it."

Joyce leaned back on her heels. "She left her phone?"

Griff shouted over his shoulder. "Joni, call the police."

I glanced over my shoulder. Bob Doerr stood behind the book table. He caught my eye and I realized he was examining everyone in the room — one at a time. I started to smile and wink but that didn't seem right, what with this lady author, Pat Avery, being missing and all. The man had been a detective. What if he thought I was involved? I blushed — and looked away. Why did I do that? He must think I'm stupid — or guilty — or stupid and guilty. I stole a quick look back at him and was relieved to see that he had directed his gaze on someone else. Then I snapped to what he had noticed.

Everyone in that room — save one — focused his or her attention toward Everett Avery.

Ignoring the drama in the back of the room, Merry Miller tapped at a smartphone.

I sighed and turned back to the little group gathered around Everett.

"Have you had any suspicious phone calls, emails, or texts lately?" David pushed aside a plastic chair and squeezed past an upholstered one.

"No, nothing like that — well, nothing that stood out. Pat has been writing this new book about the *Golden Booby* and she's been all over town talking to people about it. She took notes and pictures with that little iPad she carries around — and the other day, someone stole it out of her purse." Everett's voice was loud in the suddenly-silent store.

"What kind of pictures, do you remember?" David sat down beside Everett. I remembered Griff telling me that he was a criminal lawyer who had retired to South Padre Island to write. The rest of us fed on Everett's anxiety and our confusion and fear made it harder for the poor guy. David's approach was much better. The questions gave Everett a reason for staying calm — something to do that might help find his wife.

"I don't know — landscapes, birds, places around the island, I guess."

We heard murmuring from the back room of the little store. I heard Griff's pretty little wife say, "You are kidding?"

"They aren't coming, are they?" Everett said.

"Pat is a grown woman. There's no sign of violence, no indication that someone is holding her other than her own text, and she hasn't been gone an hour. Maybe she met someone and they went off to take pictures. Maybe her phone died as you said, Everett — and she left it behind." Steve Hathcock stood up and fished his car keys out of his pocket. "I'll take a quick cruise around the island and see if I can find her."

Steve and I were becoming good friends. Both of us had a particular interest in preserving history and in treasure hunting. We always had plenty to talk about — and I was sure he had a lot of background on these people. I considered going with him to search for the author lady, but I had my eye on the lovely Adele and I was sure Steve would understand my reluctance to leave right now. Besides, I figured the interesting part of this story was going down right in the middle of *Paragraphs* and I didn't want to miss anything.

Steve laid a comforting hand on Everett's shoulder. "Hang in there, buddy." And he was out the door and climbing into his jeep.

"The pictures were no longer on her iPad," Joyce said. "She'd already moved them to our Dropbox."

Merry Miller muttered something under her breath but by now, everyone just ignored her.

"What about the book? Her new book? Where is it?" David glanced back at Bob Doerr and I could swear that something passed between the two men. I figured they knew something that I didn't.

"I guess it's on her computer." Everett wrung his hands again. "I haven't had time to look."

"It's probably in our Dropbox too." Joyce stood up. "Let's take a look." She went back to the table where she had planned on signing her books and picked up a bag that sat beside the folding chair. She rummaged through the it and produced another iPad. "Do you have wifi in here, Griff?"

"Sure, no problem." Griff sounded distracted — like his thoughts weren't on wifi signals.

"There it is…got a password?"

"What?"

"A password?"

"GuestBooby. No space between."

Joyce tapped on the screen of her tablet. Everyone waited.

"It's not here," she announced. "I could have sworn she posted it here for me to edit."

"I'm out of here." Merry Miller elbowed her way out of the crowded room.

"Good riddance, if you ask me," Sylvie called after her.

The glass door caught Merry's heel and stripped off her sandal. She cursed as she hopped down the short flight of concrete steps to a yellow Corvette convertible.

Everyone chuckled. It wasn't so much delight in Merry's misfortune but in the release of tension her departure brought. Okay, so maybe some of us were amused just because she was so unlikeable.

Bonnie Parker slipped out after Merry along with Sally Scaman and other attendees.

"Maybe I'll go too," Adele said to me. "This hasn't turned out to be very useful."

I stood up. "Can I give you a ride?"

"Oh no, that's okay." I came with Sylvie. I'll see if she's ready now."

I wasn't ready to let her go. "Would you give me the pleasure of buying you dinner this evening?"

Adele pushed her big square glasses up her nose. "It's only 3 pm."

"We'll make it a late lunch then."

"What about Sylvie?"

"She is welcome to join us." I tried to hide my disappointment.

Adele made her way through the maze of chairs to where Sylvie sat. I crossed my fingers as the two women discussed their plans. My heart dropped to my shoes when Sylvie struggled to her feet. Leaning on her cane, she hobbled toward me while Adele wrangled the roller bag.

I tried to make my smile gracious.

"Nigel, this is my great aunt. Sylvie, this is the gentleman who has offered to buy our dinner." Adele picked up her purse and hooked it around the roller bag handle.

"I'm very glad to meet you, ma'am." I could feel the delicate bones in her hand when I took it. Something in her eyes made my reluctance to have her along on my "date" with Adele evaporate. "I'm so happy you will be joining us."

"You are gallant, Nigel — and I'd love to come along another time. But I must go back to Brownsville now. I need my oxygen machine and a nap. All this excitement has worn me out."

"Are you sure you feel up to driving?"

"I've driven every day of my life since I was twelve, young man. I think I can manage." She bopped my leg with her cane and cackled.

"Well, let me escort you to your car then, milady." I offered her my arm.

"This one's a doozy, Adele," the old lady said as I opened the door and led her out to a dented fifteen-year-old Corolla. "Enjoy your dinner."

"I'll take good care of her," I told Sylvie as I closed her car door.

"For goodness sake, I'm a grown woman — and it's not like I'm going off to college or anything." Adele put Sylvie's roller bag in the passenger seat. "Now, get out of here, go home!" She laughed and tapped the roof of the car.

Sylvie put the car in gear and pulled out into traffic on Padre Boulevard.

As I turned back to Adele, I realized that the parking lot was now nearly empty. Rather than ending, the non-Booby event had just petered out for lack of interest."Ready to go?"

"Oh no, I left my things inside. And I need to check out Griff's bathroon before we leave too."

I was less than enthusiastic but there wasn't much a man could do when the girl of his dreams needed to go potty. I shrugged and followed her back inside.

Five people were huddled around the book signing table. They turned to look at us as we came in — but no one met my eyes.

"What?" Adele sounded angry.

"We were … uh…just trying to figure out why anyone would want to uh … kidnap Pat." Griff stepped forward, blocking the table with his body.

"What is that?" Adele pushed him aside. "A manuscript?"

Griff sighed and rolled his eyes.

"They've seen what they've seen." David Harry turned back to the stack of papers on the table.

"It's an early version of Pat's manuscript," Griff said. "She came in here to show it to me several months ago. We were going to promote the Booby books — until that treasure hunter murdered Carol."

I leaned over to look at it. "Then, it just didn't seem important anymore?"

Griff nodded. "I told Pat that we should shelve it for a while — at least until after Casa's trial. I don't remember why she left it for me — maybe to read it at my leisure or something, but honestly, I just forgot I had it."

"You had it here?"

"It was …uh…in a notebook. I stuck it in a drawer and never got around to reading it."

He stepped aside and I saw paper scattered on the table. Joyce ignored me as she scanned page after page. Bob Doerr stood behind her and took each piece of paper as she finished.

"So have you found anything?" Adele elbowed Bob and leaned over to examine the pile of documents they had finished.

"Nothing to indicate what someone might want from Pat." David gathered the pages together into a single stack and handed them to Griff.

"Anything about the Booby?" Adele squeezed in between David and Joyce and reached for the binder itself which was open on the table.

Without looking up, Joyce casually placed her hand on the binder.

"Adele." I touched her shoulder. "Let's go now."

"No!" She pulled away from me. "I came here to find out about the Booby. I want to know about it."

Her determination surprised me — but I could see suspicion in Bob's eyes and disgust in David's. I wanted them to think well of my dream girl so I said, "Adele studies legends. She's working on her PhD." I had no idea if that was true or not.

"Pat wrote about the murder of Carol Flores. So far, there's nothing here about where the original statue might be now." Bob laid down another page.

"Why then? Why would someone take her?" Everett's voice broke my heart. In all the many years that Edie and I were married, I always knew exactly where she was. Even now, I know where she lies and think of her there — every day.

"It's not for what she knew, I'm afraid — but for what someone thinks she might know." Bob's voice was kind but his thought was pretty scary. If someone was holding Pat for information that she didn't have, would he ever let her go?

"Maybe she doesn't know that she knows where the Booby is?" Adele shifted from one foot to the other. I backed away lest she step on me. Her intensity was beginning to make me anxious too.

"If that's true, there's nothing in this manuscript to indicate what it might be — at least not so far," David said. "But of course, it's a novel. It's hard to determine what is fact and what is fiction."

"She talks about what the security cameras show at the museum." Joyce held up a page for Bob to read. "Apparently, the cops used this to determine who visited the Booby Exhibit from the time it opened until the murder."

"DL Casa?" Adele stood on tiptoe to read over Bob's shoulder, but he turned away from her — page in hand.

"Of course."

"My aunt and I were there a couple of times."

Bob looked at her over his glasses. "So I saw."

"So much for fiction." Adele scowled. "Whatever happened to privacy?"

"An illusion." Bob handed the page he had been reading to David.

"Any maps in there?"

"None so far."

~ Chapter ~
2

Enough was enough. It's not that I didn't care about the search for a golden statue, but I was comfortable. Money didn't motivate me. Adventure and responsibility pushed my buttons — and romance, of course.

"There's nothing more to be discovered here." I put my hand on Adele's back and guided her toward the door.

"But, but ..." Adele twisted her head for one last look at the authors rummaging through their colleague's manuscript. "What if they find something?"

I leaned down and put my mouth near her ear. "Do you think they would share it if they did?"

She sighed. "I guess not."

"Let's go have dinner and talk, okay?"

She nodded. I led her out of *Paragraphs* and to my rented Focus. After helping her with the seatbelt and closing her door, I hurried around to the driver's side. My heart pounded. It had been a long time since I'd had a date with anyone but Edie — and it felt odd now that I'd accomplished it.

"Where are you taking me?" Adele tried to cross her legs but there wasn't room in the footwell.

I smiled inside my head. Edie had been tall too — and then I sighed. She might still be alive if she had been shorter. "If you want to slide the seat back, there's a button on the side."

Adele felt around and then her seat moved backwards. There was a crackling sound. "What's that?" She released the button and her seat stopped.

"Oh, it's something that belonged to my wife. I'll put it in the trunk." I jumped out and ran around the car to retrieve the package.

"So," I said as I got back behind the driver's seat. "Where are you staying?"

"In a rented camper in the *KOA Campground.*"

"Wonderful!" I started the car and pulled out onto Padre Boulevard. "I'm staying there too — in one of the little blue-roofed cabins overlooking the bay."

Adele squirmed and I realized that she may have misinterpreted by intentions.

"Since we are both in the same park, why don't we go to *Sea Ranch* for dinner?" I hurried to clarify. "It's near the *KOA* and I hear it's wonderful."

Her head popped up. "Oh but it's so expensive." Her protest was weak but her smile was glorious.

"Have you already dined there?"

"Oh no — but I'd love to."

"Great, I'll make a reservation." I patted my pockets.

She looked concerned. "What's wrong?"

I opened the door and got out. "Can't find my phone."

"Try your back pocket?"

I checked them all, front and back. "I had it right before I got here. It must have fallen out of my pocket inside. I'll be right back." Feeling foolish, I ran back into *Paragraphs.*

"Well if it isn't Mr. Romance," Griff chuckled as I came back in. "Did she dump you already?"

"Ha, Ha! No, but I'm definitely out of practice. She must think I'm a dolt. I keep saying and doing stupid things."

David Harry grinned. "It's a male compulsion, Nigel. Even Jimmy Redstone does it."

"You are back at least twenty minutes sooner than I figured," Griff chuckled.

"It's here?"

"Just found it on the chair over there." Griff pointed to the front row. "Not only did you strike out with Merry Miller, it's pretty hard to call for help without a phone."

"I don't need help from the likes of you guys." I pretended to heft up my pants and rubbed my nose with the back of my hand. "You'd lead me astray just to see me fumble."

"You got that right," David chuckled. "Nothing funnier than watching Barney Fife hit on Sofia Loren."

Griff handed me my phone. "Or Porky Pig go after The Little Mermaid."

"Cruel, cruel," I howled and stuffed my phone in my back pocket.

"Good luck, Nigel." Joyce smiled at me.

"And have fun," Bob said as they all turned back to Pat Avery's manuscript.

"Did you find it?" Adele smiled as I got back into the Focus.

"Left it on a chair. Griff had already rescued it for me."

"Great. I'm paranoid about losing my phone."

"They *are* expensive." I started the car and pulled out of the parking lot.

"Expensive — and someone could steal your identity."

"Ah, you've read too many of Joyce Faulkner's books." I grinned at her and pulled around a slow-moving pedal car filled with tourists.

"Thank you, Nigel. I know we are going to have a nice time."

This softer side of Adele warmed my heart. "So why does Griff call you Adele JPlus?"

She covered her laugh with her knuckles. "My name is Adele Jones-Hashimoto-Riverez-Steinmetz-Cleaver. I've been married a lot."

I chuckled. "I'll never remember that."

"JPlus is okay — Jones was my maiden name. I never want to lose that one."

"What happened to all of those guys?"

She didn't answer right away.

"I'm sorry — I didn't mean to pry." Inexperience was no excuse for rudeness and I was mortified.

"No, no — it's not that. I was trying to figure out how to explain four missing husbands — where to start?"

I kept my eyes on the road and waited. Marriage was complicated — like life itself. Edie was an angel but I wasn't. Still she met me half way — a long time ago — and saved me from my own stupidity. Not everyone falls in love with an angel though.

"I married Kenichi in college," Adele began. "He spoke thermodynamics, I didn't. A week after we got married he told me that my approach to life was 'entropic' and left."

"Where is he now?" I tried to sound understanding.

"MIT, I think."

"So who was next?"

"Benito. He was gorgeous. A sexual god." She sighed and stared out the window.

A yellow Corvette screeched out of a parking lot. I hit my brakes and threw out an arm to protect Adele.

"Seat belt, Nigel! I have a seat belt on." She pushed my arm away.

"Oh, I'm sorry. Habit, I guess." Would I ever stop making social mistakes?

"It's okay." Her square-framed glasses had slipped down on her nose.

The driver of the Corvette over corrected — first left, then right — and then roared off ahead of us. I followed at a cautious distance.

"So where is he now?"

"Who?"

"Benito?"

"In a Peruvian monastery."

"Ah."

"Pretty hard to compete with God."

"Yes, I'm sure."

"Abe Steinmetz was next — he was older than me, but I loved him madly."

"What happened to him?"

"Dead — two days into our honeymoon."

"And Cleaver?"

"Prison. Danny told me he was a body guard — and I believed him. He had the look of a pit bull and his nick name was 'Meat.' No one messed with him."

"I guess not."

"He got hired by a group of professors in Pittsburgh. They were into South American antiquities. Anyway, one of them — a Dr. Demont — ended up dead under the stone footbridge in Schenley Park. The cops were waiting for us at Pittsburgh International when we got off the plane after our honeymoon."

I swallowed and licked my lips. "Do you think Danny did it?"

"I don't know." She took my hand. "They say the professor was poisoned. I hardly think Meat Cleaver would use poison. I need to find this bird. I just know it had something to do with Demont's death."

I was tickled that she touched me of her own accord — but what she was telling me broke through my euphoria. "This is dangerous stuff, Adele. Do you love Danny enough to risk your life to get him out of prison?"

She laughed. "Oh no. I don't care if Danny's in prison. It's a good place for him. I think these professors were after the *Golden Booby* and it got more than one of them killed."

I couldn't decide if her bluntness was charming or scary. "So why did you and Sylvie come to South Padre Island?"

"After Danny was convicted, I took what was left in his account — $3720.43 — and flew to Brownsville where Sylvie lives. She moved down here from Pittsburgh when her husband died about fifteen years ago."

"Why did she come here in particular?"

"She had a beau back in the day who had a beautiful home in Brownsville. She described it to me as a mansion — but she exaggerated everything about Simpson Hugo. If you believed her, he was part Einstein and part Brando. Anyway, she wanted to be near him. I guess it was a way of reclaiming a youthful romance. He's gone now too."

As we approached the causeway, the yellow Corvette merged right and headed toward Port Isabel at top speed. Everything about Merry Miller was overly dramatic. I couldn't figure her out.

"Do you want to go to your trailer first?" I turned to Adele who was focused on the disappearing Corvette as well.

"No, that's okay." She seemed embarrassed.

Why did I say that? She probably thought I was a lech. "I ...uh ... meant that maybe you might want to freshen up?"

"No. I'm fine."

Great. Now she thinks I think she's unfresh. I'd forgotten how difficult courting could be. I longed for the comfortable relationship I had with Edie.

"It's okay, Nigel." Adele squeezed my hand. "I'm just hungry."

Relieved that I hadn't messed up too much, I drove past the *KOA*. "So why are you chasing the *Golden Booby* if not to get Meat Cleaver out of prison?"

"Because Sylvie's high school lover was one of the Pitt professors doing research on it. Her grandson Oscar was also Hugo's in a weird way."

"What do you mean weird?"

"She was already married to my grandmother's brother when Hugo showed up one night and asked them to take a baby boy. I presume that baby was his."

"Wait, I'm confused. Sylvie and her husband raised Simpson Hugo's son?"

"His name was Harold — Harold Lowell. And Harold's son Oscar is a Federal Marshal. We all think Hugo intended to leave Oscar the *Golden Booby*."

"Ah."

"But then it turns out that Hugo had another name and another family — and another heir. Some woman named Belle and rather than share the fortune, she gave it to the Port Isabel museum — and now it's missing."

"And you and Sylvie are broke …"

She nodded. "Sylvie has outlived her husband's pension and she's about to lose her house. And a series of medical issues have kept me from working for almost five years — and drained my bank account."

"What about your aunt's grandson — what's his name — can't he help her?"

"Oscar says he would have if he'd been able to sell the Booby — it's worth many millions of dollars."

I slowed and pulled into the *Sea Ranch* parking lot. "That's too bad," I said and shut off the engine. I got out of the car, went around to open Adele's door, and I held out my hand to her.

"Sorry" she said as she struggled to get out of the low car. "I just had my knee replaced last year — and when I get some dough, the other one is due soon."

"Happens to the best of us." I couldn't believe I said that. She probably thought I was implying that she's old.

"Happens to me a lot." She smoothed the wrinkles out of her blouse and patted her hair. "Okay, I'm ready."

We walked up the steps to the restaurant. I pushed on the door but it didn't open. "What the … ?"

Adele pointed to a small sign. "Oh no, it's only 4:10. The bar doesn't open until 4:30, the restaurant not until 5."

"How about we take a walk?"

"Okay, but not too far. I'm not as nimble as I used to be."

I held out my arm. "Lean on me, milady."

She giggled, but she took my arm and we started across the parking lot heading toward the marina.

"Have you ever done that?" She gestured toward a building with 'Dolphin Watch' painted on the slanted roof.

"Edie loved wild life. She and I had a routine whenever we came down. First we checked in with Scarlet and the dolphins, then the turtles, then we'd go horseback riding on the beach — and then we'd spend an evening or two at the Nature Center taking pictures of birds. Perhaps you and I can do some of those things together one day." I knew I was pushing my luck, but you have to swing to get a hit.

"Oh, look! The light's on at *Kingfisher*. Sandy Margret is still working. Want to go take a look?"

I had no idea who Sandy Margret was, but I was game even if my dream girl wanted to go visit Ann Margaret. "Okay, let's do it."

We walked across the parking lot and up a short set of cement steps.

"Down here." Adele tugged at my arm. "You will love her work."

I let her pull me along a few steps until we came to the *Kingfisher Gallery.*

"Adele!" A slim young woman called from the back of the room as we opened the door. "I'd come give you a hug but I'm doing a fish. Come watch me."

The studio was filled with beautiful things — large models of sea life, paintings — and driftwood sculptures. We walked past many beautiful and obviously expensive items. Sandy was at the back table, wrestling with an enormous gray fish.

"What are you doing exactly?"

"Gyotaku," Sandy grunted as she stretched to lay a piece of cloth over the behemoth on her table. "It's an ancient Japanese art."

"I … uh…I don't get it. What's the point?"

"Back before there were cameras, Japanese fisherman had no way to verify their fish tales."

"I guess no one would believe a drawing?" I laughed.

"That's it. They were very competitive and proud of their catches — but they had to sell the fish to make a living — so they developed this technique for show and tell." She patted the fish through the cloth.

"So let me get this straight, you ink up a fish and then lay it on cloth to get an impression? Like a stamp?"

"I hope the results are more artistic than that, but that captures the spirit of the process." She peeked under the cloth near the dorsal fin — and then replaced it and patted again.

"Sandy does traditional taxidermy too — but I'm intrigued with Gyotaku," Adele said. "Aren't they beautiful?"

I shrugged. "Haven't seen the final product yet."

Both women giggled — and once again, I felt my cheeks burn.

"There." Adele pointed to a blue and yellow sword fish picture hanging on the wall behind me. "And there — and there."

I spun around. There were dozens of Sandy's fish rubbings — and they were exquisite

"My goodness, I had no idea that's how you did these."

"Yes, I do skin mounts and replicas too," Sandy said.

"What are they?"

"Well, a skin mount is the traditional approach to fish taxidermy. Your trophy is your catch. Folks who want to fish but don't want to kill and keep it usually ask for a replica. They take a picture and measure it. Then I build them a trophy from the photo."

"One of these days, I'm going to buy one of her treasures," Adele said behind her hand. "But they are too dear for my wallet."

"Do you do replicas of other animals, Sandy? Like mammals — or birds?"

Sandy's hands paused over the fish — and then continued with her ministrations. "Yes, of course." She didn't meet my eyes.

I glanced at Adele but she was staring at a large gold fish mounted on a piece of wood.

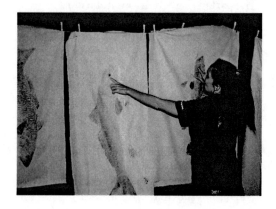

I helped Adele up on the bar stool.

"Can I help you," a young man asked.

"Can we have a cloth napkin and a glass of ice to start out?"

He nodded and turned to fetch the required items.

"I'm so embarrassed," Adele said. "I can't even walk down a little ramp without falling off of it."

I examined her knee. It was swollen and there was a slight discoloration on her shin. "We should go to a clinic or a doctor or something."

"I told you no, Nigel." Adele winced. "I'm not going anywhere. Just put some ice on it and I'll be fine."

The bartender set a glass of ice on the bar and handed me a large white napkin. I dumped half of the ice into the cloth, folded it, and tied it on Adele's leg.

"Oh!" She gasped.

"I'm sorry, but if we aren't going to the doctor, we need to do what we can so it doesn't hurt so much."

She frowned at me. "I'm fine, I'm fine — just buy me a drink."

"Here," a man sitting next to us at the bar said. "Let me buy you both a Cucumber Martini."

Adele sighed. "I'd love one. It's been a long day."

"How about you?" He turned to me.

I could see my date going down in flames, but I nodded. "I never heard of a Cucumber Martini."

"It's a *Sea Ranch* specialty." The man signaled to the waiter who jumped to make our drinks. "My name is Sam Wiesel — and this is my wife Stella. We saw you at *Paragraphs* this afternoon."

I flashed to the couple who had obviously come to hear Bob Doerr speak — and who had left as soon as he was finished. "Nice to meet you," I said as I shook his hand. "I'm Nigel Rutherford and this is…" I froze trying to remember Adele's long list of last names.

She frowned at me and then turned to Sam and Stella. "I'm Adele Jones-Hashimoto-Riverez-Steinmetz-Cleaver."

Seeking safety from Adele's wrath, I turned to Sam. "Do you live here?"

"Oh no, Stella and I live in Dallas. We came down to renew our vows at *Casa Mariposa* tomorrow night."

Adele perked up. "Oh my, that's wonderful." It was nice to see her interested in something other than a gold bird. "Why did you choose South Padre Island?"

Sam took Stella's hand. "The island represents a turning point in our story. I used to come down here alone — but something happened during my last visit that made me change how I saw myself — and us. When I went home, I had the courage to do something I'd never been able to do before."

The bartender set our martinis on the bar in front of us.

Adele took a sip of her drink. "What was that?"

"Appreciate my life — and my wife."

"It took us two years, but we have learned to love again." Stella beamed.

I envied Sam and Stella their second chance. I stared at my martini — my excitement about meeting Adele melting away like ice in the napkin on her knee.

Adele sighed and took a bigger swallow of her drink. "So how did you learn to do that — a statue spoke to you or something?"

"Something like that." Sam winked at Stella. "I heard a murder, caught a big fish, picked up a bit of Booby lore — and got kidnapped."

"And that fixed your marriage?" Adele spilled a few drops of her drink down the front of her blouse.

"Oh no," Stella said. "It made him *want* to fix it."

"Uh huh."

I could tell that Adele didn't really understand what Stella was saying.

She rubbed at her blouse with her thumb. "So what did you learn about the *Golden Booby*?"

"We can seat you now." A woman holding menus beckoned from the doorway.

"Would you like to join us?" Sam lifted Stella off her bar stool and set her on her feet.

"Sure." Adele hopped down on her own before I could help. "That would be great, wouldn't it, Nigel?"

I didn't think it was that great.

"Don't pout, Nigel," she whispered into my ear as she hobbled past me. "Maybe we'll get some clues out of him over dinner."

Right. Clues. Just what I had in mind.

"Look at that." Adele pointed upwards.

Sam and Stella and the hostess looked up too.

"What?" I said because no one else would admit to not knowing what Adele wanted us to see.

"The fan."

"What about it?"

Adele snorted. "The paddles are shaped like palm leaves."

No one spoke for a moment — including the hostess.

"Looks just like the leaves in Marne Law's painting of the *Golden Booby*."

"Ah," Sam said.

For a moment, I was afraid he was going to withdraw his invitation and leave me alone with Adele and her fan paddle clue.

"I'm hungry. How about you all?" Sam clapped his hands together.

"Starving." I picked up Adele's half empty glass and my untouched one and followed the other three up a wooden stairway to a dining room.

Our hostess seated us at a table near the window overlooking the bay. Boats came and went in the marina below us — and beyond that, the sun was setting over Port Isabel.

Adele focused on Sam and Stella who were sitting across from us. I wondered why I had been so enchanted with her only a couple of hours before. Now she seemed obsessed and pushy — and maybe a little desperate. Now that I thought about it, she wasn't at all like …I closed my eyes for a moment. When the ache passed, I realized that I had lost track of the conversation.

"Maybe it was magic, young lady," Sam said. "Maybe that legend is potent enough to touch someone as peripheral as I am. All I know is that the sadness I'd carried all my life lifted — if I were a religious man, I might say I'd been saved."

"But you never actually saw it?" Adele leaned forward and licked the rim of her glass.

"No, never laid eyes on it."

"Oh my goodness, look who is here, Sam." Stella waved at a foursome who were being seated at the table beside us.

"Sam, is that you?" A handsome fellow with a Superman physique squinted and shaded his eyes against the sinking sun.

"Clint Smith — I was going to call you tomorrow. We just got into town a few hours ago. How are you, man?" Sam jumped to his feet and pumped Clint's hand. "Is that Jim West over there too?"

"I'm here, Sam." Another tall man stood up and allowed Sam to give him a bear hug.

The famed detective wasn't as physically impressive as Clint — and he hid his celebrity with an almost shy smile. I liked him right away — although

I had read so many of Bob Doerr's books that Jim West seemed like an old friend.

"Can I give this beautiful lady a kiss, Sam?" West didn't wait for an answer and leaned down to graze Stella's cheek with his lips.

"It's so good to see you, Jim. It means the world to us that you decided to come for our special day," she said.

Clint collected his kiss too and turned to the rest of us. "Let me introduce you to Port Isabel's finest — Detectives Rudy Vega and Rachel Vasquez. A trip to South Texas is not the same without spending some time with these two. If anything is going down anywhere in the area, they know about it."

I choked back my excitement. Rudy Vega had played an important role in David Harry's work about the island — and Pat Avery had introduced Rachel Vasquez to the literary world several years ago. It was one thing to meet authors like Doerr, Harry, and Avery — it was quite another to have dinner in the same restaurant with their characters.

Sam turned to Adele, "This is Adele — I'm sorry, my dear — I can't remember your extraordinary array of last names."

Adele took a final swallow of her Cucumber Martini. "Shorten it to JPlus — that's what Griff does."

"And this is Nigel Rutherford."

I shook each of their hands — amused at my childish excitement at being in their presence.

"Stella and I were just getting to know Adele and Nigel," Sam told everyone.

"Peg!" Rachel Vasquez squealed and ran toward a couple being seated just behind us. "I'm so glad to see you and Hap. I just heard about Pat."

"What do you mean?" The petite woman's eyebrows rose into her thick bangs. "Pat Avery?"

"Is something wrong?" The man with her turned toward us.

I recoiled with shock. It was Hap Lynch. I swear. In the flesh. I reached for my drink, but realized that Adele had polished it off after she drank her own.

"Pat McGrath Avery? The author?" Stella twisted in her seat to view the growing crowd in the dining room.

"Yes," Rachel said. "I just heard from Griff that she never showed up for this afternoon's book signing — and her husband doesn't know where she is."

Stella turned back to Adele and me. "You never told us that Pat Avery was missing."

Adele stuck out her lower lip. "We haven't had a chance — now have we?"

She was feeling the Cucumber Martinis, I'm sure — but I was once again embarrassed by her tone.

"Would you all like to be seated together?" The hostess had to raise her squeaky voice to be heard in the hubbub. "We can turn the tables around long ways if you want."

"Yes, yes — please," Sam said. "We have a lot to talk about."

"How many do we have here?"

He counted. "Ten, I think. And put all of this on my bill."

I realized that most of the main characters of the authors at this afternoon's signing were gathered for dinner. Except for Joyce Faulkner's serial killer Rod — and Miriam, her identity thief. I shivered and glanced around the room — wondering if I would recognize either of them if I saw them — and then relaxing when I remembered the closing scenes of *Username*.

The employees at *Sea Ranch* are efficient. It didn't take them long to set up a suitable table arrangement for our party. We had no sooner taken our seats when two waiters brought us more drinks — and plates of Escargot, Peel and Eat Shrimp, Frog Legs, and Ahi Tuna. Adele filled her appetizer plate and started eating right away. I moved my new Cucumber Martini away from her and concentrated on the general conversation.

"So no word from Griff on what the authors are doing?" Peg Lynch wrinkled her nose and passed the Frog Legs to Hap.

"Nothing in the last hour." Rachel had a long relationship with the Lynches. A lot longer than the one she had with Rudy Vega, her new partner. I watched them — wondering if they knew they were in love yet.

"I don't know about the rest of you, but the very idea of losing an author makes me feel queazy," Rudy said. "I wouldn't even have this job without David Harry."

"We might never even have heard of the *Golden Booby* without Doerr." Clint filled his plate with Ahi Tuna. "And Jim here owes his career to the man."

"There's not much of a future for Hap and me without Pat." Peg wrinkled her nose again and passed Hap the escargot. "I can't imagine that she would just take off without a by your leave. I'm scared someone has her."

"Now, Peg," Hap said. "The woman hasn't been gone that long — maybe she just went to interview someone and they went out on the dunes or something. Give her a few hours — she'll call when she gets to where she can."

"I get revved up about things some times," Peg said to the rest of us. "Hap keeps me balanced."

I remembered Hap's orderly way of dealing with a problem — and the straightforward way his mind worked. If anyone could find Pat — if she was really in trouble — it would be Hap.

"Did Pat ever tell you anything about her search for the *Golden Booby*?" Adele bit into a piece of shrimp.

Hap turned his gaze on Adele. "We don't usually know the outcome of a case until Pat publishes a book."

"What about the murder of Carol Flores?"

Hap didn't answer but he continued to evaluate Adele. I took a second look myself — she had gone from angel to needy to rude — all in the course of one afternoon. Or of course, maybe she had always been rude and demanding and I put the halo on her myself. I took my first sip of Cucumber Martini — and remembered why I was a Negra Modelo man.

"We were involved in the capture of DL Casa," Rudy said. "Carol was a part of this community. She was so excited when Belle Neuva donated that bird to the museum. I remember asking her if she was confident of the security system. She insisted that no one could get it out of its protective case and out of the museum before the cops could get there."

Rachel sighed. "I would have given ten *Golden Boobies* if Carol had never met Casa."

"Hap didn't like him right off the bat," Peg said.

"Wasn't me." Hap squeezed her hand. "It was that crazy little dog of yours. Luke has a nose for crime. He growled every time Casa was around. Acted like he was going to eat him alive."

"Bad guys must stink," Stella said and everyone laughed.

"They sure do, sugar." Sam slapped the table, shaking the plates and silverware. "Those guys that Clint and Jim saved me from the last time I was here smelled like candy."

"Candy?" Adele finished off her drink.

I shrugged and handed her my martini.

"I think there's still a lot that we don't know about the mysterious Mr. Casa," Jim said. "Rudy is right

"And his escape?"

"Now that's a mystery," Rachel said. "He was in his cell at dinner time — and gone at bed check. Either he is a magician or someone smuggled him a key."

Hap narrowed his eyes. "The first option isn't likely — the second is possible I guess. Then again, maybe one of his jailers let him out."

The room was silent as everyone digested this possibility. Rachel whispered something into Rudy's ear. I presumed they had already investigated this possibility and wondered where it had led them.

"From what I understand, Casa hadn't been on the island for long before his attack on Carol Flores in the Port Isabel museum," Clint Smith said. "Did he have time to find associates? It would take a good friend to take a chance like that."

"Or someone who wanted the treasure for himself and thought Casa would lead him to it," Hap said. "The number of Booby seekers in the area are legion."

"He's been gone six weeks now," Jim West said. "He's either long gone or in hiding."

"Depends on whether he has the Booby." I was surprised to hear my own voice. I hadn't planned on doing anything but listen. After all, these guys were the experts.

Jim nodded. "And if he doesn't have the Booby — and he thinks it's still in this area, then he's still here."

"Why does he want it?" Rudy countered. "Assuming you are right and he's here, knowing what he's after could make it easier to find him."

"Ha!" Adele set her martini glass down hard on the table. "That's easy! Money!"

"It's not exactly easy to convert into cash," Jim observed. "It's about the most recognizable piece of artwork since the Mona Lisa — especially in this part of the country — and in Pennsylvania."

"And it's heavy. You can't just tuck it under your arm and mosey down the street with it," Rudy said. "I remember back when we first started hearing about that thing — back when August Villonova was killed. His granddaughter called us down to the museum to explain why she was putting it on display. She believed that the Professor intended to leave the Booby to her and her alone — but she knew that Oscar Hugo might have a legal claim to it as well. She thought that keeping it in her home made her a target. Her grandfather had been murdered because of that statue — and she was aware of the various Booby legends. It all sounded like trouble — and she wanted to be able to live her life in peace."

I felt Adele straighten in her seat at the mention of Sylvie's foster son, Oscar Hugo or Lowell or whatever he was currently calling himself. I imagined how frustrated she and her relatives must have been with Belle Nueva's decision. If Casa hadn't murdered Carol Flores and stolen the Booby first, they would have probably sued to regain rights to the bird.

"What if Casa doesn't have the Booby? Wouldn't that put whoever does have it in danger?"

Jim sighed. "He seems to be relentless in his pursuit of that bird, so I think you are right, Stella."

"How can Pat Avery's disappearance not be related?" She reached across the table to put a comforting hand on Peg Lynch's arm.

"*If* she's missing," Vega said.

"You don't understand," Peg insisted. "Pat Avery would no more go somewhere without telling her husband than I would. They are close — as close as two people can be. She wouldn't disappear on her own."

"We don't have to wait until some arbitrary time has elapsed to start looking for her." Clint popped a shrimp into his mouth and chewed slowly. "I'm not associated with any police department — and I'm not afraid of much."

The man was as big as a mountain — and as agile as a mountain goat. No wonder nothing thing scared him.

"So how do we go about looking for her?" Sam nodded to the waiter who produced the stack of menus and distributed them around our table. "We don't have a whole lot of information to go on — and Stella and I never heard of the lady before today."

"I go back to my first premise for any investigation," Rudy said. "Why? Why is she missing if she is missing?"

"She knows where the Booby is." Adele slurred her words but she was still intent on her purpose. "Or Casa thinks she knows. That's what they were guessing back at *Paragraphs*."

"So you think Casa has taken her?" Peg choked on that idea and coughed convulsively, covering her mouth with both hands.

"Or killed her," Adele muttered under her breath.

I was aghast — not so much that Adele said it but that I thinking the same thing.

Jim West waited for Peg to take a sip of water from the glass that Hap handed her and then tapped the table to get our attention. "Casa murders for a purpose. He's ruthless when he thinks it will get him what he wants. If for some reason, he has zeroed in on Pat Avery, he must think she has information that will lead him to the Booby."

"Aren't we jumping to conclusions here?" Clint accepted a menu from the waiter. "Casa's not the only bad guy in town, I'm sure."

"What can we do then?" I remembered Everett Avery's desperation.

"Clint and I will take a look into things after dinner," Jim said. "Maybe Hap will work with us."

Rudy's cheeks flushed. I didn't know if he was angry or embarrassed. No one likes implied criticism, I guess.

"Stella and I will help look. Just tell us what to do," Sam said.

Rudy shook his head. "This is getting out of hand, folks. Rachel and I will start looking for Mrs. Avery tonight after dinner. It will be preliminary since we have no reason to think she's in danger yet — but we will look, I promise. The best way for you to help is to go about your business tomorrow — but if you see anything unusual — anything that you think might help find her — call the police."

"Rudy's right," Rachel said. "If Pat is in trouble, don't make our jobs harder by getting in trouble too."

I glanced around the table. I figured the Lynches would be looking for the lady author — no matter what the detectives said. Jim West and Clint Smith were formidable. They would do what they wanted although I'm sure they would work with the police. The Wiesels cared that Pat was missing — but they didn't want trouble. They were on South Padre Island for romance, not adventure. Then there was Adele — she'd look for Pat only if she thought the missing woman had the Booby. Me — I was done with it all. I didn't know whether Pat was missing or not — but I wouldn't recognize her if I saw her. A lot of other people were going to be looking for her anyway — people far more qualified for that job than me. After an expensive dinner, I'd take Adele home to sleep off her Cucumber Martinis — and go back to my rented bungalow on the bay — and try to get on with the task that brought me here.

~ Chapter ~
3

Back at my cabin, I splashed cold water on my face — and changed into shorts and sneakers. I'd asked Steve Hathcock to stock my kitchen before I arrived from Pittsburgh. Big mistake. Several boxes of Cracker Jacks were stacked on the counter and the fridge held a case of Canada Dry — no trace of Negra Modelo. Just as well, I guessed. I grabbed a bottle and held it to my forehead.

Out on my porch, I leaned back in a wooden chair and propped my feet up on the porch railing. The bay gleamed only a few yards away. I took a swig of ginger ale and sighed.

A car pulled into the graveled parking area. The lights stayed on a few seconds after the driver turned off the engine and got out.

"What do you think?" Steve Hathcock said as he stepped up onto the porch. "Was I right?"

"You are always right." I jerked a thumb toward the screen door behind me. "Get yourself a beer — or whatever."

"Don't mind if I do." He went inside and emerged a few minutes later with a bottle of Canada Dry and a box of Cracker Jacks. "Mighty lean pickin's in there, Nigel."

"Yep."

Steve sat down beside me and tore open the Cracker Jacks. "Want some?"

"It's all yours, buddy. I just got back from *Sea Ranch* and I'm still digesting. What's the word on the lady author?"

Steve took a drink and wiped his upper lip with the back of his hand. "I don't know what to think. I drove around the island, talked with a ton of people — no one's seen her. I called Everett about a half hour ago. She's still not home."

"Do you know her well?"

"Well enough to know this is something to worry about."

"Is she after the Booby?"

"Pat?" He thought it over. "No, but she is after the story."

"How much does she know?"

"Nothing."

"It's spun completely out of control."

"You've done nothing wrong, Nigel."

"I let Demont fill my head with misinformation."

"If being stupid was a crime, would be lots of people in prison right now." Steve took off his hat and stretched out his chair. "Including me."

"We just wanted to get it right."

Steve crunched on a mouth full of Cracker Jacks. "That's still what we want, right?"

The cool breeze off the water felt wonderful. I lingered on the porch another hour after Steve left — enjoying the soft silence of the night. Edie loved it here. The thought of her brought both a pang of anguish and a smile. I couldn't get used to life without her. Everyday, I thought maybe I'd find another woman like her — but so far, I'd only met the likes of Adele Jplus and Merry Miller. I chuckled. They probably found me equally unattractive.

I stood up, stretched — and checked my phone. Nine-thirty. I wasn't sleepy so I decided to take a walk. I patted my pockets feeling for my key and wallet. Then I locked the front door and headed across the parking lot. Just past the boat launch piers, I turned right and headed up the service road toward the campground entrance. The tensions of the day had made my muscles stiff but as I warmed up, I increased my pace. Tourists sitting in beach chairs outside their campers barely noticed me as I trotted past. The tiny trailer where I'd left Adele was dark — she must have gone to bed early after our long evening of food and drink. I ran past, choking on my own bitter aftertaste about her.

At Padre Boulevard, I turned left and headed towards the Queen Isabella Causeway. It wasn't far to the Padre Balli monument, but by the time I got there I was winded. I sank down on the step below the statue and panted, reflecting on the effects of age and a heavy meal on my body.

In an exercise-induced fugue, I leaned against the base of the monument and closed my eyes.

I was driving. We approached the Fort Pitt Tunnels, headed toward downtown Pittsburgh. Edie slid a Joan Osborne CD into the player and guitar music filled the car.

"I love this song," she said. "One of these days I'm going to learn to play guitar so I can sing this song for you."

I reached across the console and squeezed her hand. "You need to have a guitar first."

"Oh yeah," she smiled and tapped my hand in time with the music. "One more item for my bucket list. BUY guitar and then learn to play it."

"So why don't you just sing?"

"Lumina — come and wrap around me. Lumina, take me through the snow." Her voice was pretty but she had a tin ear.

"What does that mean, do you think?"

"What? Lumina?"

"The whole song."

"Eve took a train, Eve took a train — went to see her man. Melting inside, melting away like butter in a pan." Osborne's lyrics filled my head with interesting images.

"Light or knowledge — or love?" Edie's voice softened like it did whenever she was thinking.

"Maybe all three," I said.

"Maybe those are things we have to die to know completely." She was staring out the front window.

I turned my attention back to the road.

She made a sound — a soft intake of breath.

"What's wrong?"

A red car emerged from the tunnel in the outside lane. It struck something lying on the highway. Wood? The object flew up and an eighteen wheeler passing the car in the inside lane hit it again — hard — and it went airborne, bouncing off the divider twenty yards in front of us.

"Eve took the fruit, Eve bit the fruit — juice ran down her chin," Osborne sang.

In slow motion, the wood spun end over end. I could see it clearly now. It was a thick branch. I didn't know whether to speed up or slow down. I stole one more look at Edie. She was frozen, her eyes on the object hurtling toward us. I slammed on the brakes.

For a moment, I thought it would hit the road right in front of us — but then there was the screech of tires and a Volkswagen bumped us from behind ever so slightly — pushing us forward.

The branch pierced our windshield like a spear.

I opened my eyes.

Cars were coming across the causeway and the lights were blinding. I threw up an arm against the glare and struggled to my feet. As my vision cleared, I glimpsed the yellow Corvette speeding past. It was Merry Miller's car — but she wasn't driving it. I wondered where she was before realizing that I didn't much care.

Undecided as to what to do next, I looked around the maze of streets circling the Padre monument. A young couple made out on a bench across the street behind me. I didn't want to interrupt them so I turned back toward the causeway just as a black limousine accelerated through the turn a few seconds behind the Corvette.

I took a few steps and another dark car followed the first two. I started running. I didn't know what was happening but it had to be about the missing Booby — and that was trouble. I wasn't sure what a man my age and physical condition could do about it. I'd come to South Texas to do Edie a final favor — not to do battle with Booby bandits.

My legs burned and I struggled to breathe by the time I reached the *KOA* entrance. I don't know what I expected — a hubbub of some sort, I guess. But the campgrounds were quiet. I stopped and bent over, fighting a cramp and breathing into my inhaler. I dug into the back pocket of my shorts and found my phone. Steve didn't answer. Neither did Griff. I didn't know who else to call — 911 seemed like overkill since there was no sign of the Corvette or the two black cars.

I was limping by the time I passed Adele's trailer. The lights were on this time — but nothing seemed wrong. No shadowy figures lurking around or anything like that.

I was relieved. I don't know why the causeway traffic had seemed so ominous. I sighed and chalked it up to the excitement at *Paragraphs* — and the intense Adele Jplus — and the characters at *Sea Ranch*. It was a long day of drama and I was ready for bed.

The parking lot near my bungalow was dark. The gravel crunched under my Nikes. I rummaged for the key in my pocket as I stepped up on the porch. I needn't have bothered — my front door was wide open.

"Good evening, Mr. Rutherford."

It was dark inside the bungalow and I couldn't make out the speaker in the gloom — but the raspy voice filled me with dread.

I turned to run, but a tough-looking fellow I'd never seen before stood on the porch behind me.

"Oh for goodness sake," the voice inside my cabin said. "Are we really going to do this, Nigel?"

The man blocking my path smiled at me.

I stomped on his instep with all my considerable weight. He screamed and lurched backwards. I leapt over the left porch railing and ran through the yard towards the swimming pool.

"Go get him, please, Mr. Lowell." I heard the man inside say as I sprinted into the darkness.

"He about broke my foot," Lowell complained as he lumbered after me.

"Run," I said to myself, pumping my arms. "Run, run, run, run."

It wasn't much of a race. Lowell was at least 30 years younger than me — and 60 pounds lighter. He ran me down and grabbed the back of my shirt. I spun, trying to rip the fabric — anything to get away. "Help! Help! Help!"

"What is your problem, man?" He manhandled me and covered my mouth with my hand. "Is this the way to treat guests?"

"Who are you?" I tried to bluster through his fingers but my voice quivered.

"An interested party, okay?" Lowell expertly twisted my arm behind my back and nudged me forward. "Why did you flip out?"

Was he kidding?

"What's going on back there," a woman called from one of the trailers.

"Dog stole my dinner," Lowell yelled back, keeping a firm hold on my face and my arm.

"Dogs are supposed to be on leash around here," she said and the trailer door slammed shut.

My heart pounded as he pushed me back toward my bungalow. Was I being kidnapped? Was this what happened to the lady author? I lifted my feet trying use my body weight to throw him off balance, but that put intense pressure on my arm and I quickly put my feet back on the ground.

"I thought you were supposed to be smart," Lowell snorted and jerked my arm up higher behind my back. "Why do you think we do this?"

I winced in pain — and for the briefest moment, thought about biting at the hand over my face. Then, I lost my breath and the fight went out of me. Feeling foolish, I let Lowell march me back to the cabin.

"Ah, Nigel. There's no need for all of this drama. I'm not here to hurt you." An older gentleman — older than me — sat on my couch. A folded aluminum walker leaned against my fridge.

Lowell shoved me into a kitchen chair and closed the door behind him.

I frowned and rubbed my arm. "I don't know that, Robert. I've heard all kinds of things about you since I came down here."

"I won't deny working with August to wrest control of historical artifacts from the University of Pittsburgh — but I'm not — and never have been — a violent man."

Lowell picked up a second kitchen chair and set it in front of the door. He sat down and took off his shoe. The top of his foot was red and starting to swell.

Feeling that my manhood was vindicated, I smirked.

"Look, I didn't hit you — even though I was tempted." He limped over to the fridge, grabbed a bag of ice, and took out a cube. "But you started all of this, Rutherford." He sat back down and rubbed the ice over his foot.

"Who are you, Lowell?"

"Oscar Hugo Lowell — adopted grandson of Sylvie Lowell, grandson of Simpson Hugo — cousin of Belle Nueva. I think I have as big a stake in all of this Booby business as anyone else. On top of that, I'm a U.S. Marshal — assigned to look after Dr. Stevenson here. Someone tried to kill him before the attack in the Museum."

"And that someone did a pretty good job," Robert said. "I'm lucky to be lucid now they tell me."

"Do you know who it was?"

"I don't think it was any of my associates since they have been dying with alarming frequency in the last year. And I trust Mr. Lowell here and the cops. I've been working with them to find the murderer of August Villanova and Winnie Demont."

"Everyone thought you were behind those crimes."

"What?" The old man put his hand to his ear like that would make him hear better.

I lifted my chin and stared him straight in the eyes — well sort of. The left lens of his spectacles was black — and the right was so thick that his eye looked milky. "We thought you killed Winnie Demont."

"What made you think such a ridiculous thing, young man? Winston Demont was a friend of mine — and even if he wasn't, none of the Texas contingent of our little group knew where August put that bird. Winnie was our only hope of finding it — our golden goose, so to speak."

"He was my friend too, Robert. My wife was his graduate assistant back in the day — and then his colleague. I knew him when both of us had hair — and he was in love with Edie. He was best man at our wedding — almost 45 years ago." My outrage spent, I lowered my head and mumbled. "I lost my wife and my best friend the same month."

"Yes, yes — I know the two of you were close. And I'm sorry about your wife. Such a bizarre accident! Edie was cute and smart — an irresistible combination for men like us."

I frowned. Edie was the only innocent person in this whole mess and the one who everyone loved in some way.

"I guess you know that my grandfather was a careful man, Nigel." Oscar wiped his foot with his sock.

"I still can't get used to hearing people refer to Sim as August," I said. "Everything is mixed up. Nothing is what I believed it to be for most of my life."

"You were a fool then, Nigel." Robert's good eye was cruel.

"Grandpa must have realized how dangerous that bird was early on," Lowell said. "Wherever he put it, he didn't intend it to be easily found. He left clues that required the recipients to work together. He gave the guardian birds to my cousin Belle and me — so naturally, we thought — we each thought we'd figure out the puzzle and go after the treasure on our own. The spectacle in the museum was the result of that — Belle unwittingly donated another fake and that poor woman was murdered as a result."

"And what did you do with the information you had, Lowell? I imagine you thought the museum bird was the real Booby like everyone else."

"Actually, Grandpa had a strange sense of humor — I was winging my way to the South Pacific when Belle found and donated her fake to the museum — and I was digging through a warehouse full of lesser Boobies in Pittsburgh when Ms. Flores died. It seems that there is at least one if not two or more clues yet to be found before the information on Belle's golden egg and my golden egg will make sense."

"What's all of this got to do with me?"

"Don't play with us!" Robert Stevenson gave up all pretense of being friendly.

"Grandpa trusted Winnie Demont, Nigel — and Winnie Demont's closest colleague was your wife, Dr. Edie Rutherford."

"They were friends and colleagues — nothing else." I could barely contain my outrage. "Edie never would have ..."

Lowell rolled his eyes. "I never said she did — or would. I'm just saying, who would Demont entrust with one of Grandpa's clues?"

"Why would he entrust it to anyone?" I countered.

"If he was threatened, maybe? Or if he was trying to protect the Booby at all costs?"

"They shared an office, Nigel." Robert raised a bushy eye brow. "Edie had a key to every cabinet in there."

"When Winnie was murdered, the cops impounded their office. Edie died before they would let her back in."

"Exactly." Robert's sanctimonious tone irritated me.

"I checked," Lowell said. "The Pittsburgh cops released the contents of that office — all of them — to you."

The idea of Lowell researching Edie's relationship with Winnie was a burr under my skin. The idea of him trying to get her possessions infuriated me further and I clammed up.

Lowell realized I was't going to respond and tried again. "Did you go through her things?"

I seethed in silence.

"Help us find this artifact!"

"Maybe that bird shouldn't be found — seems that looking for it causes more heartache than joy." I folded my arms over my chest and stuck out my chin.

"I'm sure you know best, Nigel." Robert's good eye glowed. "But tell that to an island full of Booby seekers. The desperate and the devious are mixing together as we speak — that's a dangerous cocktail. Are you going to let things blow up just because you are a moral man?"

"There's nothing I can do about any of this, Robert." I never did like him — ogling Edie the way he did — the way they all did.

Robert hit the side of my fridge with his fist.

I tried to remain stoic but I flinched in spite of myself.

"What if you are wrong, Nigel? What if there's any number of things that you can do to fix this little problem?"

Silence was my only weapon.

Lowell sighed and stood up. "Seems to me that if people knew where it was — without doubt — and it was some where safe — where no one could ever use it to get an advantage over anyone else — it would calm these folks down." He flexed his foot before putting weight on it.

"Think about it, Nigel," Robert said. "This young man here is trained in dealing with situations like this."

I shook my head. "I don't have any power to make that happen — and if I did, I don't think it would help matters."

"You Pittsburghers are a stubborn lot." Robert held out a hand for Lowell to help him stand.

"You forget that the man you knew as August Villanova was also my friend and colleague — only I knew him as Sim Hugo — another stubborn Pittsburgher. Another of my wife's many suiters back in the day. I've lost them all now. My life is in splinters because of a stupid historical artifact that no one cared about until Sim figured out where Capone hid it in the *Queen Isabella Inn*. So now it's gone again — protected by a flock of pretender birds — and maybe that's just as well. Even if I knew where that statue is — or which one it is — why would I tell the two of you?"

"Because whoever killed Winnie and August — and tried to kill me — probably killed that woman in the museum." Leaning heavily on Lowell, Robert Stevenson did look bad — one side of his face sagged under the black lens and he had lost a lot of weight since I'd last seen him.

"Everyone involved in your little Pittsburgh/Brownsville rivalry is in danger until we find that monster — and the only way he will show himself is if he thinks he has a chance of scoring the Booby." Lowell unfolded Robert's walker and set it in front of him.

Now that they were leaving, I felt more talkative. "They tell me that Hap Lynch and the Port Isabel detectives identified Carol Flores' murderer. He wasn't the brightest of criminals. They caught him on the security cameras scoping out the Booby display."

"He was bright enough to find a way to escape." The old man leaned on the walker and headed for the door. "That's why I keep a U.S. Marshal close by." He winked at me — and I remembered him flirting with Edie at a conference in Paris about thirty years ago.

"DL Casa is a chameleon," Oscar Lowell said. "Don't underestimate him."

"I never heard of him before dinner tonight."

"That you know of ..."

"Are you trying to scare me, Lowell?"

"It's time to be scared when there are sharks in the water." He opened the door and helped Robert out on the porch.

They were almost to the parking lot, when I called out. "Would he kidnap a woman if he thought she had information about the Booby?"

They both turned to me — alarm etched in Lowell's face, something else playing across Robert's.

"What are you talking about?" Lowell kept a grip on Robert's upper arm. "There's not been any report of a missing woman."

For a moment, I wondered if Oscar Lowell was protecting Robert from the world or if he was protecting the world from Robert. A weak snake is still a snake after all.

"I … uh … don't know if they've reported it yet."

"Reported what?" Lowell's intensity revived my own nerves from earlier.

"Pat Avery — one of the authors who was supposed to be at the signing at *Paragraphs* this afternoon — didn't show up."

"What makes you think she was kidnapped?"

"Her husband was very upset — and everyone who knows them said she wouldn't go off without telling him. Griff was worried about her — and the other three authors were too. They were going through one of her manuscripts when I left."

A slow smile spread across Robert's face and I knew I'd said too much.

"Do you think she's okay? Do you think Casa has her?" Now I couldn't stop talking. "I had dinner with Jim West and Clint Smith and Hap and Peg Lynch and a few others tonight. Even a couple of Port Isabel detectives were there. They were going to look for her tonight."

"Ha!" Robert Stevenson's laugh was ugly. Winnie had once told me that Robert was a selfish narcissist — and over the years, I'd come to realize Edie despised the man, too.

Lowell frowned. "I think there are a bunch of amateurs on the prowl — and someone's going to get hurt.

I locked the door behind them — feeling tired and discouraged. I grabbed another Canada Dry and set it with my phone and keys on the nightstand by the bed — and went into the bathroom.

I had stripped down to my shorts and was about to get into the shower when the Psycho movie murder shrieks went off. Eeek! Eeek! Eeek! Spooked, I turned off the water and peeked out the bathroom door — first left and then right. I shuddered — and then laughed at myself. What did I think was going to happen? Some lunatic in a wig was going to break into the cabin and stab me to death in the tub? Even though I acknowledged to myself that was a remote possibility and I had probably imagined that sound, I couldn't make myself take a shower.

I went back to the bedroom, opened the Canada Dry — and took a long drink. I stared at myself in the mirror over the dresser. I wasn't really up to the task at hand — but maybe I would get lucky and it would work out. I took one more drink and crawled between the sheets. I turned off the lights, but as tired as I was — I couldn't stop watching the doors and windows.

I'd just drifted off into an uneasy slumber when the Psycho music began again — this time close to me.

I sat up and grabbed my phone.

I had several texts. The first four said the same thing, over and over, "Don't trust Stevenson." I didn't recognize the number. And I didn't remember having put the Psycho sounds on my phone.

Who would send me these? My breaths came faster and faster until I thought my chest would burst. Someone must have seen my visitors! I couldn't stop panting. What if someone was watching me now? I imagined an evil presence outside my window listening to me gasp for air. My inhaler was still in my pants pocket, lying on the bathroom floor. I was already feeling faint — I didn't want to get up. No! I wouldn't allow it. I wouldn't freak out and leave before I finished what I came to South Padre Island to do. I willed myself to stop this crazy panting and within a few minutes, my anxiety attack reached its peak and a shaky logic returned.

I took another drink of ginger ale. Was the person spying on me a friend or a dangerous villain? Was he — or she — watching me first and just happened to see Dr. Stevenson and Oscar Lowell break into my cabin? Or did he follow them to me?

I forced a long, slow deep breath and checked my other texts.

Griff had sent me, "Got your voicemail. No sign of Pat. Marne is fine."

I hoped Mrs. Avery was okay, but was even more relieved that no one had figured out the message in Marne Law's painting of the Booby.

Steve Hathcock's text said, "The game's in play."

I sighed and held the phone to my chest. "Edie, I hope this is what you wanted. I wish you were here. I could use some light now."

~ Chapter ~

4

People walking their dogs, fisherman rattling their gear as they tromped down the pier — and the screech of hungry gulls — woke me. I lay in bed thinking about the things I had to do before the sun rising over the Gulf set on the other side of Laguna Madre Bay.

I wondered about my partners — the people who would help me accomplish the plan. Would they do what they said they would? The only person I really trusted was Edie. My co-conspirators were her friends before they were mine. For forty-three years, that's how I turned acquaintances into friends — trusting Edie's judgment. Now I had to figure these things out for myself — and I hated it.

I was trimming my beard when Adele knocked on the door.

"Oh, hi!" I was glad to see her — and nervous at the same time. Who would she be this morning? My fantasy angel? Or the pushy drunk who wouldn't talk about anything but the Booby?

"I wanted to thank you for dinner last night," she said as I let her in. "And to apologize. I don't drink often — and I'm afraid I can't handle it anymore. I have a nasty hangover this morning."

She did look more subdued than when I'd delivered her to her trailer the night before. "I'd offer you coffee to help with that, but all I have is Canada Dry and Cracker Jacks."

The couch squeaked as she sat on it. "What is that?" She leaned sideways and fished around under the cushion.

"What is what?"

"This?" She held up a three-inch long blue metal container.

"I never saw it before." That was true, but I'd seen something very similar to it somewhere — but where?

She examined it. "Looks like a fancy lip gloss — or a battery charger of some kind."

I reached for it. "I had company last night, one of them must have left it. I'll return it to them."

She frowned but handed the shiny tube over to me. "I've seen them on QVC. You can charge everything from a cell phone to a flashlight with it."

I pocketed the tube and tried to be charming. "Let me get myself together and let's go have breakfast."

"Okay," she said almost too quickly. "Where?"

"How about *Manuel's*?" I called from the bedroom as I put on my sneakers. "I hit town right before the event at Paragraphs yesterday, and haven't been over to see Frank and Jay yet."

"That sounds good." Her voice was muffled.

I stuck my head around the doorframe. She was opening cabinet doors, peering behind the fridge — and under the table. Did she really think I would hide a solid gold statue under the kitchen sink?

I coughed and kicked a trash can to warn her that I was returning to the living area. She scurried back to the couch. For a woman with a bad knee and a sprained ankle, she was fast on her feet.

I clapped my hands and said, "Ready to go?"

She stood up. "I didn't expect an invitation. Can we stop at my trailer so I can get my purse?"

"Of course, milady." I offered my arm — and she took it without embarrassment this time. I opened the door and she stepped out on the porch. It was the first time I could actually see her eyes. They were disappointingly gray.

It seemed useless to lock the cabin but I did it anyway. If nothing else, it would annoy any Booby hunters eager to sort through my duffle bag.

We got into my rented Focus and drove the 300 feet to her trailer.

"I'll be right back," she said and before I could get out of the car to open her door, she was unlocking her trailer.

Several windows were open to take advantage of the sea breezes, I presume. I could see Adele inside talking on a cell phone. She saw me watching her and turned her back.

Two could play that game. I pulled the metal tube out of my pants pocket.

A couple with a white poodle on a leash walked by — followed by a young man on a bicycle.

I kept the blue object in my lap. I felt guilty — like when I used to steal snickerdoodles out of Edie's pig-shaped cookie jar. It made a loud oinking noise whenever I lifted the lid and she always caught me in the act of gluttony. She got a big kick out of scolding me and I got a big kick out of her snickerdoodles.

I waited until the walkers had disappeared into the dog run — and then stole a quick glance at Adele's trailer. She was pacing back and forth with the cell phone pressed against her ear.

Annoyed that she was keeping me waiting, I twisted the top of the tube, trying to open it. Nothing. The surface of the metal was scored with tiny etchings — like starbursts. A strange decorative scheme for a lowly battery charger. I tried pulling on the left end and it popped open. The lid section flipped against the dash and rolled under the passenger seat. I looked around again. No one was close by. I took my chance and looked into the bottom section of the tube.

Something glowed inside — something shaped like a tiny egg.

I didn't want to get caught with my hand in this particular cookie jar. I rummaged under the seat for the lid.

The door opened and Adele got in. "What did you find?"

I replaced the lid and put the tube back in my pocket. "Uh — nothing. Just a battery charger like you said. Doesn't look like it still works. The tenant before me must have left it in the couch. There are no wires or anything." Shut up, Nigel. I told myself. But like most bad liars, I couldn't. "I thought maybe I could use it, but I guess I'll have to go into Brownsville and see if I can get those — what do you call them? The thing that techie star invented on that commercial? UBZ? You know to link your phone to a computer?"

"USB cables?"

"Yes, USB — things."

"You aren't very good at electronics, are you?" Adele set her purse beside her leg in the footwell and snapped on her seatbelt.

I took a deep breath and put the car in gear. "No, I'm a Luddite actually. The only reason I have a phone is because my wife bought it for me and insisted that I carry it."

"I hear she was quite a lady."

"She was." I rolled down the window as we sped across the causeway towards Port Isabel, enjoying the cool breeze.

"I never even knew anyone who knew anyone who won a Pulitzer."

"One of her many accomplishments."

"Did she really climb Everest?"

I smiled at the memory. "She most definitely did."

"Where were you?"

"Base camp."

"Not much of a climber?"

"Insurance risk. The board of my company didn't like me going that far." And besides that, I had altitude sickness — but Adele didn't need to know that.

"Being worth something is as much a bother as not being worth anything, I guess."

I thought about Edie's constant search for knowledge and the joy she took in it. I wasn't in her league when it came to smarts. Oh sure, I know a great deal about a lot of things but I wouldn't have sought them out if it hadn't been for Edie — and certainly I wouldn't be in on this venture if not for her.

We turned right just past the lighthouse and then left on Maxan. Cars lined the street, but I saw a parking spot in the small lot beside *Manuel's* and zipped in. "I get a kick out of these guys whenever I come to town," I said as we got out of the car. "Everything is super sized — tortillas the size of hubcaps stuffed with huge chunks of chicken or meat with cheese — oh my!"

I took her hand and led her into the tiny restaurant. Jay was busy seating someone else so we stood in front of a small podium.

"Look!" Adele pointed. "There's one of Pat Avery's books."

"She must be a *Manuel's* fan too," I said. "I wonder if they have heard from her."

"Heard from who, Pappi?" Jay wore a knit cap even though it was 80 degrees outside — and 75 inside. He grinned at Adele. "Who is this beauty, Mr. Rutherford?"

"Jay, let me introduce you to a new friend of mine — Adele ... uh...Adele Juh...."

"Jones," she said and giggled when Jay kissed her hand. "I like this custom."

"What custom is that?" Jay's eyes sparkled.

"All these hand kisses." She wiggled her fingers. "I go my whole life without any and then I come to the island — but I love it."

"If you want a table of your own, you will have to wait a bit — but if you'd like to sit with your friend over there, I can seat you right now."

"My friend?" I looked around. All the tables but two were filled with families or groups.

Jay put an arm around Adele and guided her to a table near a bookshelf at the front of the restaurant. "Here you go, Mr. Rutherford."

Griff turned around. "I didn't think you'd ever get here, Nigel."

I laughed. "Did we have a date?"

"Do we need one?" Griff stood up and shook my hand. "How long have you and Edie been coming to South Padre Island?"

"Years."

"And where do you eat the morning after you arrive?"

"I am so predictable." I sat down between Adele and Griff. "But it seems odd this time — lonelier."

"Edie left a big footprint, no doubt about that." Griff had already ordered coffee and it arrived just as Adele and I were examining the menu.

"The portions here are big if you prefer to share something," I whispered to Adele.

She blushed. "I'd rather have my own and take home what I can't eat — if you don't mind."

"Of course." I had embarrassed her and myself once again.

Jay took our drink orders and left after giving Adele another big smack on the cheek. She grinned and looked around — then she gasped.

I leaned over, "Are you okay?"

"Yes," she whispered back, keeping her eyes on the table in front of her.

"Are you sure?"

"Of course, I'm sure."

I felt like I was dealing with Dr. Jekyll and Ms. Hyde. I never knew who was going to bite my head off next.

"So, what's on the agenda today?" I turned to Griff. "Did you hear from Mrs. Avery yet?"

"Nothing. The cops came by this morning and asked Joni and me a few questions — but we don't know anything. I couldn't sleep last night for worrying about that poor woman — and I can't imagine what Everett is going through."

Adele pushed back her chair and stood up. "Excuse me, I'm not feeling well."

"Is there anything I can do?" I stood up with her.

"I just need to go to the bathroom, okay?"

I nodded and sat back down, defeated.

She marched off towards the back of the restaurant.

A stylish woman sitting alone with her back to us waited until Adele went past, before standing up and following her to the restroom.

Griff and I watched them disappear into the back of the restaurant before turning back to our coffees.

"Two pm at the *First National Bank* on the Island okay with you?" I kept my voice low.

"Can we make it two thirty? We won't be finished at the Convention Center until one."

"That's fine. How many do we have now?"

"Four, for sure. I keep thinking Pat has found another but until we find her, we can't count on it."

"I think I have another one."

Griff choked on his coffee. "How? Where?"

"I had a visitor last night — and before he left, he either hid it in the cushions of the couch in my cabin — or it fell out and he'll be coming back for it soon."

Out of the corner of my eye, I saw Adele returning to our table. She'd been crying.

"Who?" Griff whispered.

"Stevenson," I mouthed before turning my attention to Adele.

I stood up and pulled back her chair. "What's wrong?"

"Nothing." She dabbed under her glasses with a tiny shred of toilet paper as she sat down.

The tall woman who had followed her to the bathroom elbowed her way through the brunch crowd. It was then that I recognized Merry Miller. She'd changed her hair color overnight. She glared at Adele before bumping Jay out of her way as she exited the restaurant.

"Whoa." Jay spun around in exaggerated good humor, but I could tell that he was annoyed.

"Who was that?" Griff glanced first at Adele and then at Jay.

"Never saw her before." Jay came over to our table, picked up a chair, turned it around backwards, and straddled it. "But she is in a big hurry, I'll say that much about her."

"Don't you remember," I said to Griff. "She was at the book signing yesterday — the one with the big bag sitting up front?"

"Aha." Griff frowned. "That's who she is. She looked familiar, but I couldn't place her."

"That's one tough lady." Jay folded his arms on top of the back of his chair and grinned. "She's got five o'clock shadow at 11 in the morning."

Griff and I laughed at Jay's antics but Adele remained quiet and teary-eyed. Remembering the nasty exchanges between Merry and Sylvie, I had a feeling that she knew this woman but I respected her silence. Maybe she would tell me what was going on later.

"It's been the strangest week," Jay said. "Everyone who comes in here has been asking to see the Booby."

"There's a Booby in here?" Adele perked up.

"More than one," Jay chuckled.

Griff laughed out loud.

"Is Jay telling that Booby joke again?" Frank, Jay's brother and fellow waiter, set a plate of Chicken Fajita Con Todo with Enchilada Wrap in front of Griff.

"Be still," Griff commanded as he stared at his food.

Adele dropped her wadded up tissue. "What's wrong?"

"I'm having a spiritual moment."

"Oh, you!" Her giggle was soft and feminine and natural — for a change.

Griff held up his fork. "Would you like a bite?"

"It smells good, but I want to see that Booby first."

"It's too good not to share." Jay winked at Adele.

"We'll each have one of our own," I said and Frank nodded and scribbled down our order on a tiny pad of paper.

"So where is it?" Adele's voice was almost a whisper.

"What? You want to see our Booby?"

She nodded.

"Look behind you." Frank pointed.

She spun around — but after a moment, her shoulders slumped. "A picture of some guy in a football outfit?"

"You are kidding, right?" The woman was from Pittsburgh, for crying out loud.

She frowned. "What's a football guy got to do with the Golden Booby?"

The door to the cafe opened and two customers came in. "She's not much of a fan, is she?" Jay turned away to greet the newcomers.

How could she not recognize Joe Montana? "He's a native son, Adele," I said.

"He's an Indian?"

Griff choked on his fajita. "He's a TV star — sells shoes."

"Oh." She pressed her face against the cabinet. "So where's the Booby?"

"One track mind," I mouthed and Griff grinned.

"Oh, oh — there it is." Adele pushed at the glass. "Behind the football guy."

"The football guy," Griff mouthed back at me.

The cabinet door opened suddenly and pinched Adle's plump fingers. "Ow!"

"Do you want me to get it for you?"

She nodded and sucked on her bruised pinkie.

The statue looked like a cookie jar. The shiny yellow glaze was chipped and one of the blue feet was missing a toe.

"Oh it's beautiful," Adele cooed. "Look at it, Nigel."

"It's handsome," I agreed although I thought this particular Booby had seen better days.

"Do you think there's a clue on it somewhere?"

"Doesn't look authentic." I fought to keep my amusement in check. "What kind of clue are you looking for?"

I handed it to her and she held it close to her face and squinted. I half expected her to pull out a jeweler's loupe.

"No codes or anything?" Griff egged her on.

"I don't see any." She turned it upside down. There was a stoppered hole on the bottom of the ceramic bird. "Maybe there's something inside." She tried to pull out the rubber seal. "Ow," she squealed. "I broke a fingernail."

It was dangerous just sitting next to this woman.

"There's definitely something inside it," she insisted.

"Here." I took the statue from her and tried to run my thumb under the edge of the rubber stopper. When that proved fruitless, I poked at it with my butter knife.

"Can I help?" Frank took the figurine from me and pulled the stopper out with a pair of pliers that he retrieved from a back pocket.

"Oh, oh, oh!" Adele squealed and clapped her hands.

Frank handed it to her and she shook it until a small card fell out onto the table.

"What is it?" Griff asked between bites although I figured he knew exactly what it was already.

I reached for the small piece of paper but Adele knocked my hand away and grabbed it.

"It's yours." I held my hands up palms outward. "I'm not trying to steal it."

She ignored me and examined both sides of the card. "I don't know what it is."

Jay reappeared to set our food on the table. "A coupon, silly."

Adele looked like she might cry again. "Not a clue?"

"Not that I know of. Just a coupon for happy hour at Will and Jack's. There used to be a bunch of them in that bird — until all the Boobyites came to town and started raiding it all the time."

"Sounds like fun to me," Griff reached for the little card. "It's Port Isabel's little salute to sunset — like they do at Malory Square in Key West — except we have fewer drunks and more Booby seekers these days."

Adele was crushed — and I felt bad for her. "Maybe you will find a real clue at Will and Jack's tonight."

She tucked the little card into her bag and sat down to eat. She took bite after bite before chewing, another tear trickling down her left cheek.

Griff laid his fork beside his plate. I chose not to meet his eyes. Neither of us knew what to do so we did nothing. I didn't owe Adele anything — not even a good time. As soon as we were finished with our meal, I'd take her back to her little trailer at the KOA — and I never had to see her again.

We ate quietly in the noisy restaurant. The dish was excellent — as promised, but it was far more than I could finish.

"Any word about Mrs. Avery," Frank asked the next time he came by our table.

"Nothing from her directly," Griff said. "Rachel called me this morning and said they were looking for her."

"She's a nice lady."

"Yes she is."

"She put me and Jay in a couple of her books."

"I saw."

"Is there anything I can do to help find her?"

"Nothing but keep an eye out for her." Griff wiped his mouth with his napkin.

"Can I have a box to take all of this home with me?" Adele pointed to her half-finished plate. "And can I have the rest of his too?"

I was startled that she assumed I'd give her the rest of my food — but I nodded.

"She left her battery charger here the other day." Frank laid our bill on the table.

"Who?" Griff dug into his pocket and threw some cash on the table.

Frank picked up Griff's empty plate. "Mrs. Avery."

I glanced at Adele. She pushed her glasses up on her nose and held the card she found inside the Booby close to her nose.

"Would you like me to take it to her husband?" Griff tried to be casual but he too was excited.

"It would probably be the best thing to do." Frank said over his shoulder as he headed back toward the kitchen.

"Probably," Griff said softly.

Adele focused on the card, her lips moving as she read the tiny type.

Frank returned with two takeout boxes and a shiny red tube that looked very much like the blue one I'd found in my couch.

Adele tucked her clue card into her purse and busied herself with filling the boxes. She was quiet and distant.

Frank handed the charger to Griff who quickly pocketed it.

"I need to get back to Paragraphs or Joni will have my head." He stood up.

I pushed Griff's cash back across the table. "I'll get this, but you are going to owe me big time very soon."

"Thanks, Nigel. I'll talk to you later."

After Griff left, I took the bill and headed toward the register.

"Jay and I will help look for Mrs. Avery. All you need to do is call us here at the restaurant." Frank whispered as we passed each other.

I paid and returned to escort Adele, her arms full of leftovers, back to the car.

I arrived at the *First National Bank* a few minutes early. There were several other cars in the lot so I parked in the only slot available directly in front of the door. I rolled down my window to enjoy the island breeze while I waited for the others.

It didn't seem real that I was doing this. Edie would approve. Even though her estate provided me with more resources than I had ever realized, I was a wealthy man in my own right. A golden statue wasn't going to add anything to my life — and if the legends were true, it belonged here on the island anyway. However, this whole Booby adventure was fun … and I was enjoying myself for the first time since that branch broke through our windshield.

An SUV in the space next to me started up. The woman driving it scolded several noisy kids bouncing in their seats as she backed out. Afraid that she was more focused on her rambunctious offspring than on being careful not to scratch my car, I watched her in the rear view mirror — and then straightened up in my seat.

There was a yellow Corvette parked behind me.

How many of them could be on this tiny island? Was Merry Miller following me? It wasn't a pleasant thought — the woman was downright creepy. I couldn't imagine what had compelled me to approach her at Paragraphs. It was a stupid thing to do. Maybe she was an identity thief like in that lady author's book with the scary green eye. Maybe Ms. Miller was a stalker!

The more practical side of me challenged this thought. I couldn't imagine a woman being that interested in me — unless she knew about my money. My mouth went dry. Was I in danger? Maybe that wasn't so ridiculous after all. Mrs. Avery was still missing — and Carol Flores and Sim Hugo and Winnie Demont were all dead. No, not just dead — murdered.

I couldn't get a breath. I patted my pockets for my inhaler and grabbed the battery charger/egg case instead. Wretched thing! I threw it against the passenger side door. It bounced off the seat and rolled around in the footwell. I forced myself to calm down and my hand finally found the puffer. I met my own eyes in the mirror as I breathed in the medication — and then stole another glance at the Corvette.

It was empty.

As air reached my oxygen-starved brain, I realized that this was a public place. Just about everyone had business at a bank. Maybe Merry Miller just needed to cash a check.

A man with spiky black hair came out of the building, spit on the pavement, and came toward me, holding a bag to his chest. I was sure that he saw me — and that he recognized me, but he hurried past my car without acknowledging my presence. Something was wrong with his hair — it was darker than his cheeks which were swarthy dark. In fact, his scalp looked dirty dark. What was it that Jay said about the rude woman at Manuel's this morning? She had five o'clock shadow? And Griff — he thought Merry Miller was familiar...

I hit the automatic lock button and all four doors of my car clicked.

The man startled and increased his pace. His sandals slapped against his heels and I flashed on Merry Miller losing her sandal as she left Paragraphs — hopping down the steps.

For a moment, I thought the man might get into the Corvette — but he trotted right past it, across a grassy slope, and out onto the road.

Who was he afraid of? Me?

I checked my phone — it was two twenty-eight. I tapped out a number I knew by heart.

"Steve, Merry Miller's here at the bank but she's really a man."

"Whoa!" Steve's laugh made me realize how bizarre this sounded.

"Merry Miller just came out of the bank but she's dressed as a man — and I think she really is one."

"You think this is more than a sexual picadillo, don't you?"

I appreciated Steve's quick mind once again. "I think whoever this is must be someone that you all would recognize — and so he has disguised himself."

"I'm only a couple of blocks away," Steve said. "Where is he now?"

"He started to get into that yellow Corvette but when he saw me watching him, he took off running."

"Which way?"

"Hm..he turned right once he got to State Park Road — heading toward the causeway."

"What's he look like?"

"Think Merry Miller without a dress."

"Aw, man. I don't even want to go there."

My anxiety lifted enough for me to get a good laugh at myself. "No, I don't mean that — just think same size. She — er — he is wearing a purple flowered shirt and tan shorts. No hat. And his hair is strange — too dark, if you know what I mean."

"I don't have a clue what you mean."

"I don't know — maybe he dyed it or something. In general, think tourist."

"That narrows it down."

I ignored the sarcasm. "And Steve — he's carrying some kind of bag."

"Okay, I'm coming from the *Kingfisher Gallery*, but I left late and there's traffic. Griff will probably get to the bank before me. Tell him what's going on and call Rachel and Rudy and give them a description."

I was shaking but coherent when Griff pulled into the parking lot two minutes later.

"Get in the car," I shouted to him as he pulled into the slot beside me.

"I am in the car."

"Very funny."

"Yes, but you aren't laughing." Griff got out and reached into the backseat to retrieve his briefcase.

"Hurry," I hissed as I started the Focus.

"Aren't we meeting Steve here?"

I gunned the engine. "No, we are going to chase Merry Miller. Get in the car!" I unlocked my doors and pointed toward the front passenger seat.

"Oh good — a chase." He jerked open the door and started to get in. "Did you get extra insurance with this thing?"

"I don't remember."

"Why don't we take that?" He jerked a thumb toward the yellow Corvette.

"I have the keys for this one."

"Even better." He got in and pulled the seatbelt around him. It snapped into the lock with a loud click.

"Are you ready?" I hope I didn't sound as frustrated as I felt.

"Almost." He kicked something in the wheel well with his toe. "What the heck is that?"

I revved the engine. "The egg container I found in my sofa this morning."

"Complete with eggs?"

"Little gold ones." I put the car in reverse and backed slowly out of the parking space.

"All show and no go?"

"Very funny." I braked, put the car in gear, and pulled around the curving driveway and stopped at the intersection with the road — looking both ways. There was no sign of anyone running on the berm.

"I get it," Griff laughed. "This must be one of those slow O.J. chases."

I pulled onto State Park Road and fell into position behind a bus — keeping at least two car lengths back. "The suspect is on foot. This isn't like *Bullitt*."

"Suspect?" Griff sat primly with his briefcase on his lap. "Are you going to tell me what's going on now?"

"It's Merry Miller."

"Okay — why are we chasing that mean-spirited hag?"

"She's a he."

"Say what?"

"I finally figured it out — Merry Miller is a man disguised as a woman so that no one will recognize her — him."

"And who would do that?" Griff peered at me over his glasses.

"Someone you know?" I pulled out into the left lane to get around the bus. "Someone who wants to move around without anyone questioning him."

"Who?"

"I don't know — you tell me." I bit my lip as I accelerated up to 25 mph.

"Can't you drive any faster?" Griff held his briefcase like a shield over his chest.

"How fast can this guy run?"

"As fast as he needs to, I guess."

"Oh yeah," I pulled over onto the side of the road. "Steve said we should call Rachel or Rudy and tell them what's going on." I pulled out my phone and tapped the keys. "I don't see him now."

"I'm approaching Gabriella's," Steve said. "Why don't the two of you meet me in the parking lot there and we'll figure out what to do next."

"Okay."

"Did you call Rudy Vega?"

"Was about to and then decided to call you instead."

"I'll do it. Come on around and meet me."

I hung up and put my cell back in my pocket. Sighing, I looked out the window. A long line of cars were coming. In no mood for a wait, I gunned it.

"What *is* going on?"

"I think Merry Miller is really that Casa guy."

"That's it!" Griff put both hands to his face. "I knew that woman looked familiar."

"So what's Casa look like?"

"About your height — grey ponytail, raspy voice, carries a banjo — writes songs for kids."

"Hmm. Hard to tell — Merry Miller the guy dyes his hair black — and it's short. No ponytail."

"You are thinking that the Casa persona was a disguise too?"

"No, but now that you mention it, it fits."

"How did you figure it out?"

"The egg cases — the one Pat Avery left at *Manuel's* looks just like the one someone left at my cabin last night — and they both look like something I saw Merry drop out of her purse yesterday at the book store."

"I was going to tell you and Steve at the bank." Griff ducked as I drove over a curb.

"What?" I steered back onto the road. "We're fine."

Griff sighed. "Not that — it's the egg case that Frank gave me."

"What about it?"

Griff flinched but honestly, I don't know what was scaring him. Sure I was driving right down the middle of the road but no one was anywhere near me.

"It's empty. No eggs."

No eggs meant someone had already stolen them — it could be Jay or Frank — after all, they might have an interest in the Booby too. Still I doubted they would steal it — and obviously Pat Avery trusted them too — at least enough to leave the egg case with them.

"We don't need to find them all," I said.

"I know."

"Just enough to keep Booby seekers from figuring out the code."

"Or put enough of them back into circulation with misleading messages."

Griff was devious — I'll give him that.

Up ahead on the left, I saw Steve turn into Gabriella's. I followed quickly and Griff gasped like he thought that green car speeding our way had a chance of hitting us.

"I've got it," I said soothingly before I slammed on the brakes to avoid hitting a Mexican nun.

Griff's glasses slid down his nose and fell into his lap. "Nigel, you are no Steve McQueen."

"Ouch, that hurt." I unhooked my seatbelt and jumped out of the car.

"What in the world is going on?" I could hear Griff shouting at me as I ran toward Steve's jeep.

"You didn't find him?"

Steve rolled down the driver's side window and held up one finger. I didn't know what he was trying to tell me at first, and then I realized that he was talking to someone on his cell.

"You didn't see him?"

He shook his head.

"How could you miss an old man with dyed hair running down the street?" I threw my hands in the air and turned back to get into my own car.

"NIGEL!"

I turned back toward him. "What?"

He held up that finger again, still talking on the phone.

Standing still — waiting for Steve to finish his conversation when a murderer was getting away was almost impossible to bear. I ran across the parking lot and stood in the traffic divider, squinting back down Padre Boulevard looking for Casa.

The Focus door slammed and Griff came after me. "I called Jim West. He and Clint were out on the water today but they said they would find a way to get here fast." He put a hand on my shoulder.

"This guy might have Mrs. Avery, did you ever think of that?"

"I've thought of that." Griff kept his voice low.

I realized that I'd been yelling. "I'm sorry." I stared at my toes. "I'm … anxious."

"After what you went through, anyone would be."

"It's all so confusing. Edie funding these guys all these years and they are all turning up dead or …"

"Not who you thought?"

Several cars whizzed past us. "I … I hate to judge people, Griff."

"You have to … evaluate … them sometimes." He winked at me. "Not everyone is a good guy … or gal. You have to protect yourself."

"You are sounding like Edie."

"She was a smart lady."

Traffic was beginning to back up on the causeway. A brown Honda slowed to a stop four lanes away. Sally Scaman was driving. Hands tight around the steering wheel, she glanced my way. I waved. She quickly turned her gaze back to the car in front of her.

"What's wrong with Sally?" Griff frowned.

"I don't know her very well … maybe she thought I was a bad guy or something."

"She knows me. She comes into Paragraphs at least once a week."

Sally leaned back in her seat and I realized that she had a passenger.

"Who is that?" I nudged Griff with my elbow.

"Someone with dark hair." Griff started across the busy highway, holding up his hands to stop traffic.

A pickup truck slid sideways. A man in a delivery van behind it, beeped his horn and maneuvered to miss Griff and the pickup.

Sally looked out her car window again. Her eyes were wide.

"CASA!" Griff reached for the door handle.

I turned to look at Steve who was still in Gabriella's parking lot. I waved my arms and he put down the phone and drove up to me.

"It's Casa," I told him. "He's got Sally. Griff's gone to rescue her."

I pointed to Griff and Sally standing beside her Honda. Casa had bolted out of the passenger door and was running again.

"Rudy?" Steve raised his cell to his mouth again. "Forget Plan A. Casa just carjacked Sally Scaman. No, Sally's okay. Griff has her — but when he saw

Griff, he abandoned the car and took off on foot again. No. I can see him. He's still heading toward the causeway. Okay, I'll try to keep him in sight."

"Where is Rudy?" I kept my eyes on the figure running past the line of stopped cars.

"He's on the causeway headed this way. It's backed up on that side too."

Griff helped Sally back to her car and held up a hand to discourage traffic trying to squeeze past it. She made a wide U turn and headed back up the island, beeping and waving at us as she accelerated.

"Should we call King Bob?" Steve called as Griff made his way back to the parking lot.

"Who's King Bob," I asked Steve.

"Sally's husband."

"His name is King?"

"Long story," he said under his breath.

"No, she's okay," Griff said as he joined us in the parking lot. "Shook up and still a little scared. King Bob is waiting for her back at *Cafe Kranzler*. He doesn't know what just happened — probably just thinks she's late for their date. She wants to keep it that way until she can tell him in person. I told her that Nigel and I would take her back but she wasn't having any of it."

"Just as well," Steve said. "No need to scare him too much."

"The idea of a known murderer roaming around our island is frightening." Griff shook his head. "We have to do something."

"Assuming Port Isabel is where Casa is headed, Rudy will have the cops grab him when he gets over there." Steve was trying to soothe our anxieties.

"How did we miss him running along South Padre Boulevard?" I wrung my hands.

"He probably hid somewhere along the way, Nigel. I bet he wanted to get back to that Corvette so maybe he doubled back to the bank."

Steve was right. Maybe there was something important in that fancy car. "What should we do now?"

"I'm going to nose my way into that mess out there and follow him."

"He could be dangerous, Steve," Griff said. "Don't get too close."

"I won't try to take him by myself, if that's what you mean. I'll just make sure we don't lose sight of him." Steve waved and accelerated into traffic, making a wide left turn.

Griff and I went back to the Focus.

"What should we do?" I stuck the key into the ignition and looked at Griff.

He shrugged. "Slow chase Casa across the causeway?"

"Traffic is obnoxious right now. He's not going to get very far on foot — and if he tries to carjack someone else, he'll just be sitting in traffic in a stolen car."

"You have a better idea?"

"Let's go take a look at that Corvette back at the bank."

Griff grinned. "What if it's locked?"

"The tops down." I grinned back and gunned the engine.

"You are quite the gumshoe, aren't you?"

I pulled out onto Padre Boulevard and headed back toward the bank. "Just curious," I said as I accelerated back up to 20 miles an hour.

~ Chapter ~
5

The Corvette gleamed in the sunshine. I backed into the spot beside it and sat with the motor running in air-conditioned silence.

Griff stared out the front window. "So what are we going to do?"

"Have you ever broken into a car?"

"Not yet."

"Me either."

"What exactly are we looking for?"

"Something that belongs to Mrs. Avery?"

"How will we know if it belongs to her or Merry Miller?"

We both burst out laughing.

"Okay, Nigel. Let's do the dirty deed." Griff took a deep breath and got out of the car. He walked around to the Corvette and reached for the door handle.

My nerves got the best of me. "Should we ... you know, put on gloves before we touch it?"

Griff jerked his hand back like the Vette had burned him.

I laughed. "Some car theives we are."

"I signed up to toss it, not steal it." Griff leaned over and peered into the convertible. "There's that bag Merry Miller was toting at the signing yesterday. And that fool just threw his wallet into the passenger seat."

"Can you reach it?"

"Not without falling in head first."

"Now that I think about it, it's probably got an obnoxious alarm that would raise the dead if we actually touch it."

"We? You are just sitting there watching me get in trouble."

"Maybe it's not even locked."

He touched the leather seat with the tip of his finger.

I closed my eyes and held my breath — but nothing happened."Maybe we should call the cops before someone else calls them on us."

"Oh don't be a ninny." Griff rubbed his hands together. "Let's get on with it." With one long arm, he grabbed the bag."

"Get the wallet too," I hissed.

He lunged for it, ran back around the Focus, and got in. "Floor it, Nigel." Sweat trickled down the side of his face.

"Where are we going now?" I looked both ways and pulled out of the bank parking lot.

He looked over his shoulder.

"Anyone following us?"

"Just an old lady on a walker and she's gaining on us."

"Ha ha."

"Really, Nigel. Let's get on down the road. I know the bank manager and it would be humiliating to have him testify against me at my trial."

"Back to *Paragraphs*? Or go help Steve?"

"Let's head over to Port Isabel. They might need some muscle."

We giggled like guilty eleven-year-olds.

"What's in the bag?"

Griff's hands shook as he opened Merry Miller's huge purse. "It's almost empty. There's a hotel key card." He took it out and laid it on the console between us. "And here's a little print of Marne Law's Booby painting that he bought from me yesterday — and another egg case."

"Empty?"

Griff pulled off the lid and peered inside. "Booby eggs. Two."

"You think he found them or stole them?"

"Could be either, but my money's on steal." He pawed through the objects in the bag. "Wait. Look at this!" He held up a thin gray case.

"What is it?" I braked as we approached the car-clogged causeway.

"It looks like Pat Avery's iPad."

My heart pounded. "Are you sure?"

"No." Griff's hands shook as he opened the case and fired up the little tablet. He tapped on the mail icon. "Yes, here's her email."

"It's not speculation anymore," I said. "Casa has Pat Avery."

"I don't like this." He continued tapping on the iPad.

Flashing lights from behind caused me to hit my brakes and merge as far to the right as possible even though we weren't quite on the bridge yet. A cop car squeezed past us.

Griff gasped. "Listen." Soft voices came from the iPad. I strained to make out what they were saying. It sounded like someone was crying.

"What is that?"

"We need to call Rudy Vega and Rachel Vasquez right now," he said.

"Rachel passed us a minute ago." I strained to see the screen in his lap.

"And Steve."

"Tell me!"

Griff held up the iPad. It was a video of a small woman tied up in a dark room. She was crying and struggling against her bonds.

"Who is that?"

"That's Pat Avery!"

A South Padre Island cop car sped past with lights flashing.

"Oh no! Is she hurt?"

Griff held the iPad to his chest for a moment, his eyes wide. "She doesn't look hurt, but she is terrified. She must have been there all night."

"Can you tell where she's being kept?" The cars ahead of me moved forward a few yards. I glanced into my rearview mirror before doing the same.

Griff played the video again. "Too dark to see much. Looks like she's lying on a blanket or sleeping bag or something. Someone is talking to her. Sounds like a man's voice."

"Is it Casa?"

"Maybe — but what do I know? After all, I'd heard Casa do his kids' songs and I never realized that Merry Miller was him and he was Merry."

Traffic was at a complete standstill again — but there was movement or some kind of ruckus up ahead. I rolled down the window and stuck my out my head. Without the air conditioning, we could hear yelling and cursing.

"Now what?" Griff turned off the iPad and slipped it back into Merry Miller's bag.

"I don't know. Looks like a fight or something."

"Maybe it's road rage. Sitting for twenty minutes can get to some people." He rolled down his window too. "Someone's running this way."

"There's Steve." I squinted into the sun. "He's coming this way too!"

"On foot?"

"He's chasing someone."

A dark-haired man in a purple shirt ran toward us on the right hand side of the road.

"That's Casa!"

Griff opened his door. Casa ran right into it and felt back on his butt.

"Good move, Griff!" Steve clambered over the hood of the Focus and made a grab for Casa. Growling, Casa threw a sloppy punch that missed Steve and landed on the window frame of the open car door. He screamed and danced in a little circle, rubbing one hand with the other.

Steve reached for him again, but Casa spun out of his grasp and started running back the other way toward Port Isabel.

"Give it up, Casa!" Rachel Vasquez stood in his path, holding her service revolver with both hands. Rudy Vega wasn't far behind her.

Casa stopped. He looked behind him. Steve and Griff blocked his way. He turned to his left. Two South Padre Island uniformed cops advanced on him with their guns out. The wall was on his right and beyond that, the bay.

"There's no where to go," Rachel yelled. "Put up your hands. Now!"

Snarling something unintelligible from where I sat, Casa climbed up on the wall — and jumped seconds before a multitude of hands reached for him.

I ran around to the passenger side of the car and looked over the wall. It took a moment before Casa surfaced.

"I can't believe he did that," Rachel said as she peered over the wall at the small figure treading water below us.

"He's crazy!" Steve shook his head. "Plain crazy."

Horns and curses from impatient motorists trapped on the causeway made it hard to hear him.

"We can't let him get away — or drown," Griff said. "He has Pat Avery tied up somewhere."

"Are you sure?" Steve said without taking his eyes off of Casa who swam in a circle as if disoriented.

Griff reached into the Focus for Mrs. Avery's iPad and played the video for Rachel, Rudy, and Steve. "He's the only one who knows where she is."

Rachel turned away, speaking to someone on her cell. Rudy ran down the entrance of the bridge to confront Casa if he returned to the island. The two South Padre Island uniformed police officers holstered their weapons and followed him

Steve looked at Rachel — and then back at Griff and me. Then he took off his hat and handed it to me.

"Oh no, Steve. You could kill yourself!" I tried to hand it back to him but he was already taking off his shoes.

Griff's eyes were huge. "Are you really going to do this?"

"Someone has to," Steve grunted as he pulled off his socks.

"Far out!" Someone said behind me.

I turned around to see Bonnie Parker holding up her cell phone to take pictures as Steve emptied his pockets of keys, money, and cellphone into Griff's hands.

"Where did she come from?" I whispered to Griff who glanced over my shoulder at the woman and shrugged.

I peeked over the wall again. A couple of teenagers on a jet ski slowed as they approached Casa. Clearly, they wanted to help him.

"Hurry up, Steve, you are drawing a crowd." Griff took Steve's shirt and folded it over his arm.

"What are you going to do if you catch him?" I couldn't imagine tackling a man in the water.

"I'll figure that out when I get there." And with that, Steve held his nose and jumped into the bay.

Before either Griff or I could comment, Rachel ran back to where we were standing. "Now what happened?"

"Steve Hathcock jumped into the bay!" Griff pointed to the water below us.

Rachel climbed up on the wall, her phone in her hand. "Two in the water now, the bad guy and Steve Hathcock. No, not yet — oh, there he is now. No, Detective Vega is on the beach with Officers Morris and Duron. Hathcock is swimming toward Casa."

"Are they going to shoot him?" Bonnie Parker squeezed past us to take more pictures of the action in the water below.

"Casa just pushed a kid off his jet ski!" Rachel said into her phone.

"Look!" Bonnie pointed at a boat pulling two guys with parasails racing toward the ruckus. "Think they will bomb him?"

Griff raised one eyebrow. "Bomb him?" He mouthed.

I choked back a snort. I felt bad about Mrs. Avery and that poor lady at the museum, but this was somewhere between scary and fun — and at the moment, Griff and I were having fun.

"Hathcock pulled Casa off the jet ski. No, the kids are okay. They let Casa have the ski and swam for shore. What? No. Hathcock and Casa are trying to drown one another. They are rolling around in the water."

"Steve's winning!" Griff double punched the air.

I squinted at the splashes below me. "How can you tell?"

"Got Casa right in the snoot."

The two figures disappeared under the surface of the water. I leaned forward, imagining the worst. Moments passed. I gritted my teeth.

"Steve is tough."

Who was he kidding? Griff was as anxious as I was.

The two combatants rose out of the water together like a hooked fish fighting the line.

"Get Rudy over there," Rachel said into her phone. "Looks like Casa's got a knife."

Alarm smothered fun and I fumbled for my puffer.

"Back off, Steve. Let the cops do it," Griff yelled.

I doubt that Steve heard him, but he reacted to the blade under his nose and gave up the fight, backstroking away from Casa.

"He's okay, Nigel." Griff patted me on the back as I leaned on the Focus and gasped for air.

Rachel's voice was faint — like she was inside a bottle. "Casa's back up on the jetski. No, I don't see them — oh, there they are. I can see Rudy and Officer Morris. They are out in the water, but they are at least a fifty yards away. Casa's got it started now."

"How does she stay so calm," I said between pants.

"She's young." Griff kept his eyes on the drama below us.

"Bad guy's headed across the bay now," Rachel said. "I don't know where he'll go but get someone out on the Pirates' Landing fishing dock. Maybe he'll go there. No, Hathcock's okay. Officer Morris is helping him wade to shore now."

I forced myself to calm down, putting my head back for one long, slow inhalation. Something moved in the sky. "Look." I pointed. "There's someone waving to us up there."

The crowd on the causeway cheered.

"Wait, that's Clint Smith and Jim West up in the parasails. Yeah, I know. They seem to know when someone needs help." Rachel pointed toward the jetski with her gun.

"Look who's driving the boat," Griff said.

I straightened my glasses and peered through them. "That's what's his name — the author the women swooned over at *Paragraphs* yesterday."

"Bob Doerr."

"Yes, that's him!" He waved at them but they were focused on Steve, Rachel, and Rudy who had almost made it back to the beach.

Rachel gestured toward Casa racing across the bay. Doerr nodded and sped after the jetski with Clint and Jim flying behind him.

Bonnie Parker took one last photo and whirled to follow the action across the bridge. Within seconds, I couldn't see her anymore. "That woman sure has a nose for news," I said.

"I guess this is more exciting than the things she usually writes about." Griff chuckled.

"Bob Doerr, Clint Smith, and Jim West followed them," Rachel said into her phone.

A larger boat arrived and circled below us. A tall man with a phone was behind the wheel.

"Now what's going on?" My eyes were beginning to water in the bright sun.

"That's Noe, the captain of *Fish Tales* over by *Pelican Station*," Griff explained. "It's been drydocked to install some new equipment for the last month, so he's been taking tourists out on fishing trips in this rental."

In all the years, Edie and I visited South Padre Island we had never gone fishing on *Fish Tales*. It was one of those things on our mutual bucket list that would never happen now. "So Rachel is talking to Noe?"

"I imagine she's talking to the police dispatcher and they are relaying her messages to Noe."

"Tell him to pick up Rudy and Steve and meet me at the marina on the other side." Rachel jumped down off the wall and ran back to her vehicle which was ahead of us somewhere in the traffic jam between our car and Port Isabel.

We watched as Noe made a big circle and headed toward the beach where Rudy Vega and Steve Hathcock waited.

Officers Morris and Duron were talking with a couple of their colleagues at the entrance to the bridge.

Griff sighed. "I guess they don't need us."

I relaxed. "They'll catch that — that ..." I couldn't think of anything bad enough to call Casa.

"Murderer and kidnapper?" Griff nudged me.

"A cross-dressing murderer, kidnapper, thief, and extortionist," I said as we got back into the car.

"And he's ugly too."

I started the Focus — and waited. "I really want to know what's happening on the other side of this bridge."

"The worst thing Casa could do is try to make a run for it through Port Isabel. He should go up or down the coast a little bit where there's not so many people looking for him," Griff opined.

A few minutes ticked by in silence. In the air-conditioned comfort of the car, I pondered what might be happening. I imagined Casa looking for a way to get away from his pursuers. "What will they do?"

"Who?"

"Jim West and Clint Smith."

"They'll get him."

"How?" I visualized good guys in bathing trunks dropping from the sky to hogtie a bad guy on the jet ski. I swallowed my amusement until I glanced at Griff who started humming the theme from *The Magnificent Seven*. We were still laughing when Steve's phone buzzed.

"Who is it?" I whispered.

Griff stared at the tiny screen. "Kay."

It stopped buzzing and we both took a deep breath.

"Whew. I didn't want to get old Steve in trouble," Griff said.

The phone vibrated again.

"You'll get him in more trouble by *not* answering."

"So I answer and tell her that he jumped off the bridge while chasing a bad guy and attacked the ruffian in the bay and then the guy came after him with a knife — but that he got away and he's with the police now in a boat and we don't know where they went and that he left us his phone for safekeeping?"

"You're right," I said. "Turn it off."

He turned the cantankerous device up side down looking for the 'off' button.

"Or just pull the battery."

"No, there it is." The buzzing stopped abruptly and we both sighed.

"I'll buy her lunch the next time I see her," he said.

"Good idea. An expensive one."

Five minutes. No one moved forward an inch. I rolled down the windows and turned off the engine.

Griff picked up Merry Miller's bag and opened it again.

"That smell! It's familiar."

Griff lifted it to his nose. "Licorice?"

"Or anise," I said. "I smelled it on Merry at *Paragraphs* yesterday — and somewhere else too. I just can't think where."

"Is licorice a clue?" Griff looked at me over his glasses.

"Maybe. If it was on Merry Miller/DL Casa — and if he's the one that has Pat Avery, maybe where he's keeping her has that smell. Where do you find it around here?"

"Well, candy at Walmart. Can't imagine he's keeping her in the candy aisle though."

"Indian food restaurants sometimes have aniseeds in a dish that you can use to clear your palate after a big meal."

"Does Casa strike you as the kind of guy who worries about clearing his palate?"

I shrugged "I never actually met Casa. I hit on Merry Miller for ninety seconds yesterday afternoon. We aren't particuarly close."

"I thought he was your basic everyday troubador until he murdered Carol Flores."

"You know what else smells like that? Absinthe. Think Casa is a connoisseur?"

"I don't know, maybe. It's expensive, isn't it?"

"It might be." I drummed my fingers on the steering wheel. "What do you think is happening on the other side?"

"Whatever it is, it's more exciting than sitting here." Griff swiped a finger over Pat Avery's iPad screen.

I stuck out my head out the window. "What's going on now?"

"Huh?" Griff was absorbed in the video of Pat in that dark scary room.

"People are getting out of their cars again." I opened my door and shaded my eyes with my arm. "Think they are reacting to the cops nailing Casa on the fishing boardwalk?"

Griff put the iPad away and joined me by the front fender of the Focus. "They can't see much from here."

"This bridge is how long? Two miles?"

"Two and a half."

We stared at each other for a moment.

"Get the bag," I said and started walking down the middle of the two lanes of the causeway.

We trudged up the sloping bridge about ten minutes before we saw what was holding up traffic. A black limosene was stopped in the middle of the highway and all four doors were open. A small crowd had gathered around it. Others were pointing toward Port Isabel and someone else was running.

"Nigel!" The voice was high and shakey. "Griff!"

I spun around in response to the cry.

"Who *is* that?" Sweat dripped off Griff's nose .

At first, I didn't see anyone familiar — then I saw Adele, waving from inside the limosene.

"There!"

Griff and I jogged the last fifty yards. Adele crawled out of the big black car and limped toward us, crying. She threw her arms around my neck and the force of her body forced me to step back onto Griff's foot.

"What's wrong?" Not knowing what else to do, I patted her back until she finally let go.

"Do you have a phone?"

"Sure," I pulled it out of my pocket and handed it to her. "Where's yours?"

"In the bay." She tapped a number into my phone and held it to her ear.

People filled both sides of the causeway but none of the vehicles seemed to be moving.

"There's Rachel's car," Griff whispered in my ear.

Sure enough, the cruiser was parked criss-cross in front of the limo, but Rachel was no where to be seen.

"Sylvie, are you okay?" Adele's voice was overly loud. "You need to listen to me. Be quiet, okay? I know, I don't mean to be rude — but you need to get out of that house now. I don't mean to scare you. Yes. Go to a neighbor or to the church or something. Don't let anyone know where you go though — not even me. I know. Go now, Sylvie. I mean it. What? Uh huh. Okay. Take it with you." She clicked off and handed the phone back to me.

"Are you going to tell us what's up now?"

"I'm in trouble, Nigel — and so is Sylvie. I know I've sounded like a greedy Boobyite the last couple of days, but I haven't been honest with you. Certain people think Sylvie and I have that bird and they are threatening us."

"It sounds like you need to call the cops," Griff said. "We have some mighty fine folks around here. There's no need for anyone to be living in fear."

"We've been counting on Oscar to work things out but someone shot him last night."

"Shot? " Griff's voice broke. "Who?"

"Oscar Lowell. Sylvie's grandson."

"Is he — you know — dead?" I sounded like the fool that I was.

"No but he's on the way to the hospital in Brownsville. They have to cut a bullet out of his thigh and another one out of his bicep."

Griff leaned into the limo and pocketed something shiny. "Does Sylvie know?"

"I haven't told her yet." She bit her lower lip. "I...was afraid that she'd want to rush to the hospital to ...well, you know."

I lifted her chin so that she had to look at me. "I don't know, Adele. Tell us what is going on here. Who shot Oscar Lowell?"

"I..I have no idea." She lowered her eyes. "He was guarding Professor Stevenson at the *Hilton Garden Inn* this morning — dozing in a chair by the door while the doctor slept. Someone with a key got the door open and either they knew Oscar was there and flat out tried to murder him or he surprised them. Neither of his wounds would normally be that serious but he lay there for hours and he lost a lot of blood. He's still unconscious and can't answer any questions."

I thought about the *Hilton* key card Griff found in Casa's bag. "What happened to Stevenson?"

"I don't know, Nigel. He's gone."

"Surely someone in the Hotel knows where he went," Griff said. "There's security cameras all over the place these days."

"He just disappeared. So far, the cops haven't found anything that helps explain it."

I thought about the Corvette followed by long black cars heading toward the *KOA* last night — and the visit Stevenson and Lowell paid me. "So how did you get the limo?"

She stepped back, a faint trace of red on her cheeks and neck. "I...uh...I had a key."

Loud voices and screams interrupted us.

Alarmed, Griff squeezed between cars and ran to the wall again.

I grabbed Adele's wrist and dragged her after me. "What is it?"

"Someone is shooting," Griff called back.

"Casa!" I gritted my teeth.

"Casa?" Adele pulled her hand away from me. "Are they shooting him?"

I turned to her in surprise. "It's more likely he's shooting at the cops and Jim West and Clint Smith. They were chasing him across the bay."

"Jim West?" A familar voice interrupted us. I spun around to see Sam and Stella Wiesel. They wore straw hats and sunglasses.

"Yes, he and Clint Smith and Bob Doerr went after Casa after I recognized him. The cops are chasing him too — and Steve Hathcock."

"Oh my word!" Stella covered her lips with freshly manicured fingers. Today was supposed to be her big day, I realized.

"Isn't Casa that escaped murderer?" Sam pushed his way through the crowd to see what was happening.

"They say he killed that lady at the Port Isabel museum," I said to Sam but I kept my eyes on Adele. I couldn't figure out if she was scared or angry. In fact, I couldn't figure her out at all. What was she doing in the middle of the causeway in an empty limosene?

"We abandoned our rental a ways back. I hated to add to this problem but we have an appointment at *Tesori's* in twenty minutes." Sam put his arm around Stella who was standing on tip-toe to see over the wall.

A small explosion shook the pavement below our feet.

Stella screamed and staggered sideways out of Sam's grip.

Cries from the people on the bridge grew louder and everyone ran — pushing and shoving to get off the causeway.

"It's a boat! A boat hit the bridge!" Someone screamed.

The panicked crowd pushed Griff away from us like a duck being swept off a porch with a broom.

Stella fell to one knee and her sunglasses skittered across the decking. She reached for them, but people rushing to get off the causeway kicked them out of her reach and knocked her flat, trampling her outstretched arm.

Sam fought his way through the onslaught of terrified bodies, but they pushed him backward twice.

Without thinking, I let go of Adele and threw myself in front of Stella, blocking the stampede with my body.

~ Chapter ~
6

The first body that crashed into me was the last, thank goodness. Realizing that the bridge wasn't in danger of falling into the bay, the people who were running had already begun to slow down. Without the pressure from behind, those in front relaxed — and the surge ended.

Another man and I lay in a tangle of arms and legs a few feet in front of Stella Wiesel who was moaning in pain. By the time, I disentangled myself, Sam had worked his way back to his wife.

"Oh baby," he sat down on the pavement and lifted her into his lap.

I stood up, moving my arms and legs — testing for injury. As best I could tell, I was okay except for a jammed finger on my left hand. I knelt down by the man lying on the road. "Are you okay?"

"I think so." His left eye twitched as I helped him to his feet. "A bit wobbly, but I think that's it."

We turned to Sam and Stella. Sam cradled his wife in his arms and she whimpered. Her right arm dangled and there was a clear footprint on her hand. I shuddered and ugly memories of Edie's broken body swept over me.

"We need to get someone out here to take care of her." This time his nose twitched. "Do you have a phone?"

I called 911 and explained the situation while the man took off his golf shirt and cut it to pieces with a Swiss Army knife. He knelt in front of Stella and while Sam held her arm, gently moved the bones into place and wrapped the strips of cloth around it.

"You really need a splint but I don't have anything like that right now," he said to her. "Try to be as still as possible until help gets here."

When he stood up, I stuck out my hand. "I'm Nigel Rutherford."

"Roberto Rodriquez-Garcia." He shook my hand. "I'm so sorry about what happened here."

"No apologies, really. It was my fault. I just ... well, you know this lady was down and was already hurt and I..." I gave up trying to explain why I blocked him. I could see that he knew.

"It was bad luck," Roberto said. "I knew it would happen."

"You knew a boat would hit the bridge?"

"It's about a curse. *The* curse."

"You mean the Booby?" He was an interesting character, I'll give him that.

"Yes, of course. I knew there would be trouble when I first heard that that professor in Brownsville had it."

Rachel Vasquez pushed her way through the crowd and knelt down in front of Stella and Sam. "The paramedics are on their way, Stella. Hang in there."

Stella's smile was stiff but it was a smile.

"How about you, Sam? Are you okay?"

"Not until we get her to the hospital."

"I hear ya, buddy." She squeezed his shoulder and stood up. "Anyone else here hurt?"

"Cuts and bruises," someone yelled.

"Could have been worse," I said to her. "Given that a boat hit the bridge."

She looked at me with her mouth open. "A what?"

"A boat."

"No it didn't."

"That's what started all of this. There was an explosion and the causeway shook and well, people started running to get off of it before it fell into the bay like back in 2001."

She muttered something in Spanish under her breath.

"What?"

"Well there were certainly plenty of boats out there zooming around chasing that lunatic, but no boat hit the bridge. It was the jet ski. Casa aimed it at the piling closest to Port Isabel and then jumped off at the last minute. It made a big boom, but it hurt the jet ski a lot more than the causeway."

The paramedics arrived, got Stella onto a gurney — and hustled her off the bridge with Sam trotting along beside her. Her arm looked bad but they assured the Wiesels that while it might hurt now, they could fix her up fine at the hospital.

Roberto and I waited while Rachel took another phone call.

"Did you catch Casa?" I said when she clicked off.

"Not yet — and not the other guy either."

"What other guy?"

"Some scumbag by the name of Cleaver. We had a BOLO on him this morning and someone saw him and a woman trying to leave the island in a big black limo. I got a bead on him after our close encounter with Casa, but he saw me and abandoned ship so to speak. I was chasing him when they contacted me that there were casualties back here."

"They just let him go?" I was shocked.

She laughed. "I can't be in two places at the same time, Nigel — but Rudy and I aren't the only cops in Port Isabel. They have someone else waiting to nab Cleaver when he comes off the causeway."

Roberto fidgited.

I was usually the resident worry-wort, but this guy made me seem as serene as Buddha. I tried not to look at him or think about Booby curses, so I turned back to Rachel. "Why?"

"Why do we want to catch him? He skipped out on his parole officer in Pennsylvania a couple days ago. They think he came down here to find his wife. But he also fits the description of a person of interest in a shooting at the *Hilton* last night."

My mouth went dry and I glanced over my shoulder. "Do you know his wife's name?"

She pulled out her phone and tapped the screen a couple of times. "Mary Cleaver."

Good. Some Cleaver other than Meat. It was a coincidence. That's all. But that big of a coincidence? "Rachel, would you check to see if the wife has any aliases?"

She chuckled. "You turning into a detective now?" She tapped on her phone again. No aliases that I can see."

"What about a middle name?"

"No middle name but we do have an initial. Mary A. Cleaver. Does that help?"

"A as in Adele?"

The amusement faded from her face. "Adele as in the lady you were escorting at dinner last night?"

"Adele Jplus. That's what Griff calls her because she's been married so many times. I can't remember any of her last names but Jones and Cleaver. Her last husband was a bad guy in prison in Pennsylvania."

"What's his first name?"

What *was* his name? "I can't remember his real name but everyone called him 'Meat.'"

"Of course they did." She chuckled. "What makes you think this Adele is the same woman as Mary A. Cleaver?"

"Gut instinct?" It sounded silly even as I said it. "No, no — all kinds of reasons. Now that I think of it, her behavior has been strange since I met her yesterday afternoon at *Paragraphs*. One minute she's charming, the next she's rude — then she's crying and then she's almost desperate. She and Sylvie were very interested in the booby. Apparently, they think they have a stake in it."

Rachel tapped into her phone. "What kind of stake?"

"Oscar Hugo is actually Oscar Lowell — Sylvie's grandson. And you know about that big to-do between Oscar Hugo and Belle Nueva over that museum donation."

"August Villanova's grandson is also Sylvie Lowell's grandson?"

"It's a long story, but trust me on it for now."

She put her hands on her hips. "Okay, so anything else?"

"Food. She always orders big and takes most of it home with her."

"You think she's feeding someone?"

"Exactly."

"Not a slam dunk but possible. What else?"

"She is afraid of Casa."

"What's that got to do with Cleaver?"

"I don't know but we saw Casa dressed as Merry Miller this morning. He followed her to the bathroom and she was crying when she came back to the table. Both Griff and I tried to cheer her up but she was laser focused on Jay's *Golden Booby* cookie jar. Like it was a matter of life and death."

"Okay, we'll look into Adele Jplus." Rachel pocketed her phone and started to walk away.

"Wait!" I reached for her arm. "One more thing!"

To her credit, Rachel seemed to respect my dramatics. "What?"

"Sylvie Lowell. Griff and I saw Adele in that limo back there before people panicked. She ran to me and asked for my phone. She called Sylvie and told her to get out of the house right away."

Rachel frowned.

I touched the inhaler in my pocket, but it was too soon to use it again. "And now, she's gone."

"I'll take care of it, Nigel."

After Rachel left, I realized that Roberto and I were alone on a bridge filled with empty cars. There were flashing lights on the Port Isabel side of the causeway. I presumed the South Padre Island cops were clearing the vehicles from the other side too. I thought about the rental and the package in the trunk. They would tow the Focus to an impound lot, but maybe that was just as well.

"I don't know about you, Roberto, but I could use a drink."

Roberto grinned. "How about a Negra Modelo?"

Maybe it was my imagination, but all of a sudden Roberto's twitches didn't seem so annoying. "On me, my man." I clapped him on the back and we started hiking toward Port Isabel.

It was almost 5 by the time we got off the causeway and merged with a crowd of people who had obviously been on the bridge all afternoon too.

"These folks are tired and hungry and sunburned," I said to Roberto. "I'm sure *Pirate's Landing* and *Pelican Station* will be packed. Why don't we try for *Will and Jack's*?"

"Okay by me." Roberto sounded cheerful but he resembled a sad-faced hound dog. "I'd feel a lot more comfortable there anyway."

As we passed the lighthouse, Bonnie Parker jumped out at us. "Can I take your picture?

Roberto startled and covered his face with his hands. "No, no pictures!"

"Why do you want pictures of us?"

"Because I'm writing about the Causeway Riot," she said. "And I saw you when Steve Hathcock jumped into the bay."

"Ah!" She was a pretty girl but something about her put me on guard. "So why don't you go take Steve Hathcock's picture?"

"I would if I could find him, but you were there. You can give me a quote and I'll put it under your picture."

I'm not interested in being in the paper."

"It's not really a paper you know. It's on the internet — a blog." She trotted along beside us.

"No blog either."

As we walked away, I could hear her phone whirring as she photographed our backs.

"Who is she?" I asked Roberto.

"Bonnie Parker? She's a freelancer around here. Always sticking her nose in where it shouldn't be. Remember those murders back a couple of years ago? She's the one that labeled them the Booby murders on her blog."

"Rousing the rabble, eh?"

"That's her."

I took off my hat and walked through the small front building into the cool courtyard out back. "Jackie!" Roberto nodded at a tall woman who was cleaning off a table under a Hibiscus tree.

"How ya doing, Bert? Where's your shirt?"

"Long day. Did you hear about the mess out on the causeway?"

"Been hearing about it all day long. Bet you need a Negra Modelo."

He nodded and sat down at the table. "You know me well."

"How about your friend here?"

"Make it two and put it on my check." I lowered myself into the chair and leaned back, looking at the sky through the lacy branches of the tree above me.

"On the way. You want a menu too?"

"Sure."

After Jackie went inside, Roberto sighed deeply.

I kept my eyes on the sky. "Is it Roberto or Bert?"

"Bert works."

"Why do you seem familiar to me, Bert?"

"Because I am just like you right now."

"How so?"

"Maybe because we both lost an irreplaceable woman in the last year."

I startled. "How do you ..."

"Everyone knows what happened to Dr. Rutherford, Nigel."

"A fluke — if we'd been going slower...if only I'd been going slower..."

"It made no difference how fast you were going."

"Or faster...if I'd only been going ..."

"Makes no difference. Dr. Rutherford was touched by the Booby — however tangential. Like my Carol — she was the innocent party."

"You knew Carol Flores?"

He took a linen handkerchief out of his pocket and wiped his eyes. "She was a shy, delicate woman — interesting to be around. She was still unsure of me, but I knew that there would be more. Other than being the curator of the museum, she wasn't the least bit interested in that statue — yet she was the one who paid the price demanded by the Booby's curse."

"I'm sorry for your loss, Bert ..."

"Your wife — Dr. Rutherford — the curse took her too."

At first I thought he was kidding, but then I realized that this man was frightened. In fact, he was scaring me too.

Jackie brought us our beers. "How ... did you know about us? How did you know I was in town?"

Bert's eyes blinked several times. "I have a confession, Nigel. I've been following you — now don't get scared, I'm the most benign of stalkers — but that's the essence of it. Of course, if I'd been good at it, I wouldn't have run into you out on that bridge. You'd have never known I was there."

"I can't say that I'm comfortable with this information." My heart pounded. "Why are you..uh...stalking me?"

"It's an unfortunate word." He ran a finger around the rim of his glass. "It started when Carol died and I realized that the various Booby legends might be true — and that I might be in danger."

"And that led you to me?"

"To August Villanova and Simpson Hugo first."

"And Winston Demont," I sighed.

"Yes. Then Edie and Nigel Rutherford."

"Research is one thing, Bert. You went beyond research."

"I know."

We sat quietly for a minute, our glasses chilling our palms.

"So why are you telling me this now? I've been here two days and never noticed a thing. Surely you weren't going to just ..."

"Run over you?" For a man sitting in his undershirt in an outdoor restaurant drinking Negra Modelo, he seemed dignified. "No, but I knew eventually we would need to talk."

"About the Booby?"

"About the *curse*!" It was a hiss.

I sensed no danger from him, but I dreaded what he might tell me. "Okay." It was a whisper. "Tell me."

"We are next."

The hair raised on my arms. "How?"

"I don't know."

"Why?"

"We both loved and lost women who were involved with *The Golden Booby* in some way."

"But Bert, neither of them were buying or selling it — or trying to destroy it in any way."

"I can't explain why — I just know it's true."

"My God, man, you are giving me the heeby jeebies." I forced a laugh and tossed back another swallow.

Bodies burst through *Will and Jack's* screen door out onto the patio. I could make out the fishing boat captain Noe, Griff, and Steve Hathcock — and someone else — before the flailing fists and kicking feet knocked over our table.

Bert fell backwards against the Hibiscus tree knocking blossoms into my lap.

A strange thick-necked hulk with thin white hair disengaged himself from the melee and rolled to his feet. He pointed a silver gun at the men sprawled on the patio in front of him. "I want those eggs! NOW!"

Griff grasped the tree trunk and pulled himself to a standing position, the bag he'd liberated from Casa's Corvette strapped across his chest. "What makes you think we have eggs?"

"Don't play me for a fool." The big man pointed his weapon at Steve Hathcock's head. "You all have been collecting eggs since Lowell and Nuevo first discovered they were clues."

Noe regained his footing easily and faced the gunman, his fists clenched at his sides.

Bert pulled his phone out of his back pocket and tapped on it.

Steve sat up. "What if we worked a deal, Cleaver?"

I strangled on my own cough. This terrifying ogre was Adele JPlus' husband, Meat Cleaver?

He grunted. "What kind of deal?"

"How about an exchange? We give you some eggs and you tell us where you are keeping Pat Avery." Steve was cool as a man could be who had been chasing bad guys all afternoon.

"Who?" Cleaver scratched his nose with the barrel of his gun.

"The lady author who disappeared yesterday," Steve said. "You know, the one who wrote about the murder at the museum?"

"Get over to *Will and Jack's* quick," Bert whispered into his phone.

"Hang up that phone," Cleaver growled.

Bert turned his back and continued his phone conversation. "Big fight."

"What about it, Cleaver?" Steve shouted.

Meat startled and refocused on Steve. "I don't know anything about murders or missing authors. I only got into town late last night. I'm looking for a big golden bird that someone stole from my wife."

"Surely you don't think you can get away with an artifact like that," Steve said. "It's big and heavy and ugly."

Griff moved away from the tree trunk. "And everyone wants it. You'll never have a moment of peace with it."

"I'm not looking to date it," Cleaver snorted. "All I want is to please the missus and her aunt."

"No," Bert said into his phone. "This is someone *else*."

"This is robbery, Meat — and kidnapping." I found my voice. "With a firearm. They'll put you back in prison. How would that help Adele?"

"I don't know how it would help. I just know she wants it — and that some guy is leaning on her to get it for him."

Jackie came out of the front building with a bottle of beer in her hand.

Griff winked at me.

I frowned. What in the world was that? A sign? A secret message? Feeling like the world's worst side kick, I mouthed, "What?"

Meat seemed to understand what was going on better than me. "Don't try it!" He shook the gun under Griff's nose.

The barrel wiggled — I swear — and of course, the jig was up.

Like an angry bear, Griff batted the toy away and it bounced off Steve's forehead.

"Rubber?" Griff roared. "You were holding us up with a rubber gun?"

Meat stuck out his lower lip.

"That's enough!" Jackie stepped between Griff and Cleaver.

"*You* are going to stop me?"

"Watch me."

Meat squatted like a linebacker a heartbeat before handoff. I thought sure he was going to slam into Jackie. Steve must have thought so too because he jumped to his feet. As it turns out, Jackie didn't need any of us. As Cleaver lunged forward, she bopped him on top of the head with the bottle, knocking him to his knees.

The other customers on the patio cheered — including Griff and Noe.

The big man covered his head with both hands. "There was no call to do that," he whined. "I wasn't about to hurt anyone."

"So sit down and be a good boy." She drew back her arm to bean him again.

"All right, all right! I give up."

Griff nudged the gun with his toe and laughed. "Are you kidding? A rubber gun?"

Meat shrugged. "I'm a felon. I'm not supposed to be carrying."

A distant siren.

"So where is Mrs. Avery?" Steve leaned forward so that he was nose to nose with the Meat Cleaver.

"I wasn't lying. I have no idea."

Griff held up the tiny iPad and tapped the "Play" button.

At the sound of Pat Avery crying, Meat leaned forward and watched the video intently. "Is she okay?"

"You tell us," Steve was still barefoot and damp from his leap into the bay earlier in the afternoon. I'd never thought of Steve as a hero before — yet he risked his life for Pat Avery without a second thought. I'd have never even considered jumping like that and I felt ashamed.

Noe stiffened. "Let me see that," he reached for the iPad. "How do you make it play again?"

"Here." Griff touched the screen.

Noe held the iPad close to his face and squinted. "That's my boat. That's the hold in *Fish Tales*."

Griff leaned forward to watch the video one more time. "Are you sure?"

"I ought to know my own boat."

Griff pulled out his cell. "Rachel, Noe thinks the video of Pat Avery is on *Fish Tales*. Yes, I understand. No, we aren't staying here. Pat's a friend. We'll see you there." He headed for the door with Noe and Steve on his heels.

The sirens grew louder.

Jackie dropped the beer bottle and followed them.

Meat's eyes darted around the patio dining area. Seeing his chance, he bolted out the back way. I thought about chasing him, but I didn't have Steve's nerve.

Bert sank back down in his seat by the Hibiscus tree, the corners of his mouth curling upwards. Something in his twitching eye seemed satisfied — and angry.

Spooked, I dug into my pocket, tossed money on the table, and took off after Noe too. As I stepped out of the bar, a Port Isabel police car stopped in front of *Will and Jack's* and officers jumped out. Jackie ran up to them and pointed back inside the building where she'd last seen Meat Cleaver and then toward the small group of determined men heading toward Noe's boat.

Tourists and local business owners peered out of stores and restaurants with wide eyes. Noe, Steve, and Griff stormed across East Maxan Street and over the grass under the Port Isabel Lighthouse. Bonnie Parker was sitting in a parked car across from *Will and Jack's*. She snapped a photo of me as I struggled to catch up with the larger group. Rachel Vasquez and Rudy Vega pulled into the marina parking lot as we crossed the highway at South Garcia Avenue and headed toward *Dolphin Docks* where *Fish Tales* sat below the causeway.

We filed around a small building. Although the boat was supposed to be under repairs, there was no activity around it. Rachel and Rudy pulled out their service revolvers, ran down the wooden dock, and checked the boat — inside and out — before they would allow anyone near it.

Griff refused to stay away and we all followed him as he tromped down the boardwalk. We were close enough that I could hear the detectives footsteps as they moved around the boat. Then there was a noise — wood against wood.

"Noe, can you come here?" It was Rudy's voice.

Noe climbed down into the boat and disappeared into the small cabin. I could hear their voices but couldn't make out what they were saying. Then another noise and a grunt.

Rachel came out on the deck, waved, and smiled. "She's here!"

Griff stepped forward and peered into the vessel. "Is she okay?"

"Hungry and mad. Other than that, she's fine." Rachel pulled out her cell and called to her superiors, I presumed.

"Thank God." Griff's legs seemed to give out from under him and he collapsed onto the boardwalk.

Rachel put her hand over the speaker of her phone. "Get your sea legs, Griff. We are going to need you to help with Pat. She's eager to get out of that hold and the paramedics are about fifteen minutes away. It's been a busy day for them."

Griff pulled himself together. "How can I help?"

She pointed to the cabin of the boat.

"I'm here too," Steve stepped forward.

Rachel nodded and spoke into the phone again.

Both of them jumped into the boat and disappeared into the cabin.

"No, we are okay for the moment. What? No, no. That's fine.Pat says that Casa planned to grab Sylvie Lowell tonight since he finally accepted that Pat dosen't know where the statue is. I'm sure he's on his way to Brownsville. Yes. Better get someone out there now. Adele? Oh, I see. Okay. I'll tell him. He'll need transportation. Oh? Okay, we'll find a way." She clicked off and pocketed her phone.

The other men on the boardwalk were restless. They kept their voices low as they speculated about Mrs. Avery, DL Casa, and the whole Booby problem. We could hear Noe and Steve grunting as they worked with Rudy to lift Pat out of her prison.

I shifted from foot to foot, wringing my hands.

A moment later, Griff emerged from the cabin carrying a small woman. The sun was setting and a chilly breeze lifted her hair. Mrs. Avery was pale and shivering. Other than that, she seemed to be uninjured. The others followed and supported Griff as he climbed out onto the boardwalk. "Does anyone have a jacket or a blanket?"

We all wore light clothes — tee shirts, shorts, sandals. I had a beach blanket in the trunk of the Focus, but who knew where it was now? Suddenly, everyone was stripping off their shirts to wrap around the shivering lady author.

Rachel tossed Steve her keys. "You and Griff get her to my car and turn on the heater. The paramedics will have blankets."

Steve walked ahead, pushing curiosity seekers aside to make way for Griff and Pat Avery.

As they passed me, she reached out and grabbed my hand. "Wait!"

I could barely hear Pat's voice what with the wind and all the voices. Her fingers were cold and strong.

I put my hand over hers. "What is it, Mrs. Avery?"

"He...he knows!"

"Who?"

"Casa. He figured out the secret in Marne Law's painting."

"What should I do?"

She coughed. "Change the plan."

~ Chapter ~
7

I backed away from the crowd as Griff and Steve focused on Pat Avery. So many people had been hurt by their obsessions with that statue and unless something changed, others were in danger. Adele, my former dream girl, and her husband Meat, her aunt Sylvie, Oscar Lowell, Dr. Stevenson — the good people of South Padre Island and Port Isabel — the *Golden Booby* had thrown a cloud over them all. Casa was only the current bad guy. There would be others.

I sat down on a bench beside a little yellow building. Paramedics nosed their van into the parking lot and rushed to check out Pat Avery who was lying in a police car a few feet from me, surrounded by her friends. As they worked on her, I realized that Edie's original plan was the right one and that my only choice was to do what I had done most of my life — depend on her insight and judgment.

I stood up and made my way through the crowd. As I left the parking lot, a red Chevrolet raced past me and skidded to a stop a few feet in front of the yellow building. Everett Avery jumped out of the car and ran to his wife who raised up to embrace him. A happy ending. I wiped my eyes with the back of my hand. If only Edie was still with me, this would be so much easier.

Who could I trust? Who? Certainly Griff and Steve. Edie had vouched for them long ago. The authors? They were and would always be in charge. It would be a mistake to challenge that dynamic. Instinctively, I knew that Jim West and Clint Smith had reach and power — and that I could count on them to find Casa and deal with him appropriately. I'd have to rely on the cops to rescue Sylvie Lowell and protect Oscar. Adele? My introduction to Meat Cleaver was strange to be sure. I didn't like him, but he obviously loved her and was willing to do whatever he could to take care of her.

That left the cursed Booby.

The Queen Isabella Causeway was still a mess but the police had managed to clear a lane in each direction. Without my rental car, I started walking up the ramp. I hadn't gotten very far before a Port Isabel cop stopped me.

"What are you doing, Mister?"

"I need to get back to the island."

"It's getting dark and traffic has started to flow again. It's a bad time for pedestrians. Hitch a ride with someone — or call a taxi." Like everyone else after this long, long day, he looked tired.

"Okay, officer." I turned around and headed back toward the Port Isabel Lighthouse.

Bright lights blinded me. I heard a car and a light hum as electric windows were lowered.

"Nigel?"

I shaded my eyes and tried to make out who or what was in front of me. "Yes?"

"It's Bert. Do you want a ride?"

I sighed in relief. "So glad to see you, Bert. I need to get back to the *KOA* cabins."

Horns behind Bert's SUV blared.

"Get in."

The locks released and I hurried around the truck. Crawling into the seat, I fussed with the seat belt. "This side always feels strange to me," I said as the buckle slid home.

"You are a creature of habit," Bert said as he accelerated forward, throwing me back into my seat. "Eating at the same time and place every day, watching the same television shows, listening to the same songs."

My relief at finding a ride evaporated. "Two days of vacation doesn't make for a pattern." I hoped I sounded annoyed.

"Same in Pittsburgh — *Papa Gallo's* every day for breakfast, *Starbucks* for lunch, Triscuits and cream cheese in the evening in front of the big screen in your bedroom."

"How would you know that?" I patted my pocket for my puffer.

He laughed and pressed down on the gas pedal. "You *know* how I know, Nigel."

"What do you want?"

"Yessss, so now we come to it. Just you and me, no interruptions like this afternoon."

I reached for the door handle and focused on my breathing. "Is it the Booby?"

"Of course, it's the Booby." He slammed the heel of his hand against the steering wheel. "I've spent a fortune looking for it. I've had to deal with all kinds of vile characters in my pursuit of it — the good, the bad, and the stupid. The Lowells and Cleavers think Casa has it. Belle Nuevo still thinks that someone stole the *real* bird when Carol Flores was murdered. Casa is still willing to kill for it, so he doesn't have it. Bonnie Parker still thinks he will share it with her when he does find it. Stevenson's gone. It's come down to you, Nigel. It had to have been in the office that your wife shared with Winston Demont. There's no other possibility — and that means *you* have it."

"Even if I did have it, what makes you think I'd give it to you?" It would have been a brave and defiant statement if my voice hadn't cracked.

"Give?" His twitches seemed normal now. "That word doesn't quite represent the spirit of what I want from you."

"What then?"

"I want you to 'disappear' it — like they did people during the Cold War."

"Why?"

"I've already told you."

"The curse?"

"The curse. You can't outrun it, Nigel."

I sighed. "I don't want that bird. It's ugly. Doesn't suit any decor— and it's not what people think it is."

"It's worth millions."

"I have millions."

"Then give it up."

"To you?"

Up ahead, the South Padre Island Welcome sign materialized.

"God no — not me." He spun the steering wheel to the right and took the curve at full speed. "It's too late for me anyway."

"Eeek! Eeek! Eeek! Eeek!"

I jumped and fumbled for my phone. "Who *is* this?"

The voice was commanding. "Don't give it to him, Nigel."

"You don't sound like yourself, Casa." I longed for the good old days when one could end a call by slamming the receiver down on the hook. Clicking off lacked emphasis.

Bert's lights caught a big black limo parked crossways in the entrance to the *KOA*. Two people stood in front of it. I blinked and looked again. DL Casa and Bonnie Parker were armed with long rifles of some sort.

"We can't get around them, Bert."

"I know." He pressed a button and familiar guitar music filled the SUV.

Eve took the fruit, Eve bit the fruit...

"Bert!"

"Eeek! Eeek! Eeek! Eeek!"

Acceleration pushed me back into my seat.

"BERT!"

I didn't feel the crash, but suddenly I was floating above myself, above the steaming chunk of merged metal, above South Padre Island. Lightning flickered and still I flew higher.

"Edie?"

~ Chapter ~
8

Nigel,

I hope you are enjoying your new accomodations. We are all doing well down here. We do miss you, of course — but we understand your situation. At least I do. Your old side kick Griff is a different story. Joni says that not a day goes by that he doesn't mention you and Edie. He says to say hello and to reassure you that he's taken care of *Paragraphs: Mysteries of the Golden Booby*. The authors have agreed to protect you from an onslaught of Booby hunters by a few literary sleights of hand and some flat out lies. Don't get too much of a kick out of that. They lie for a living, you know.

Oscar Lowell is healing nicely. As per your instructions through Edie's contacts, he's been promoted and moved to Washington DC. I don't think he's given up on finding the Booby he believes is his rightful inheritance, but he's busy doing other things for the time being.

Belle Nueva continues to believe that someone stole the real Booby. We let her.

Pat and Everett Avery are fine given this terrible experience. Casa didn't actually hurt her, but he caused her to hurt herself by struggling against the restraints for hours. A few scars, but you can't keep that woman down. She had the two eggs from the case she'd left with Frank and Jay hidden in her bra the whole time.

Jim West and Clint Smith continue to work with Bob Doerr. That they chased Casa across the bay and through Port Isabel probably saved Sylvie Lowell's life. After he shot Oscar Lowell Hugo, Casa figured Sylvie had to have Oscar's eggs — and maybe one or two of her own. It never once occurred to him that they might be fakes. Anyway, he was planning on going after Sylvie when you saw him at the bank and you know the rest of that story.

The Brownsville cops found Sylvie and got her to a safe house in case Casa had an accomplice. It's a good thing they did because Bonnie Parker showed up a few hours later and tossed her house. The sad thing about Bonnie is that I knew her and her family. We all did. She was a fixture on the island but no one expected this.

Speaking of Bonnie, the cops are pretty sure she and Casa hustled Dr. Stevenson out of the *Hilton* that morning — and it's like he disappeared off the face of the earth. Of course, Casa and Bonnie are gone too so there's no one left to ask about the old man. We all look for him in every face that comes to the island, but I'm beginning to lose hope we'll ever see that old rascal again.

You were right, by the way. Casa had at least one other identity. He owned a store in Brownsville that specialized in all things licorice — from candy to candles to teas. He even sold medical supplements made out of the stuff. You have the nose of a bloodhound.

That's all of the old news

I believe that we have followed your instructions to a T. Griff and I went to the bank the day after your accident and removed the eggs we'd been collecting and storing in the safety deposit box. We found most of Casa's stash in his condo, some that he had with him in the limo, and the ones we found in the Corvette. Altogether we found eleven plus the ones Stevenson left at your cabin and the ones Pat Avery found. We melted them down and poured the gold into a flat mold. Most folks can't tell that it's solid from more than a foot away.

It took us awhile to convince the cops to let us have access to the Focus in the impound lot. Griff had to promise to introduce one of them to David Harry. She was all aflutter until we told her that David is married. We found the package in the trunk just like you said. I took Edie's "paperweight" out of the wrappings and I must say, you were right. The real thing looks nothing like those fabulous fakes Villanova gave to his grandkids. As you suggested, I had Sandy Margret create a large hollow turtle as a disguise, but in the end, Griff and I decided to put the humble little bird in the case at the Convention Center just as it is — with a plaque made from the golden eggs. It says, "Donated by Nigel and Dr. Edie Rutherford." Griff thought of that one. The Wiesels attended the dedication and Sally and King Bob. Mary Russell and her husband were there too and of course Pat and Everett and the Faulkners and Doerrs and Harrys. The only one missing was you. Since the dedication, thousands of people have enjoyed the exhibit and no one has guessed the truth. It's a secret that Griff and I will take to our graves.

I took care of Sylvie's house as you asked. All she knows is that a "friend" bought the mortgage and signed it over to her. She was thrilled — not only by your kindness, but by the mystery of it all. She'd say thank you directly to you if she could.

Adele Jplus is fine. Disappointed that no one can find the infamous *Golden Booby* but happy to have the five thousand dollar a month stipend you asked me to set up for her. She bought a nice trailer and is living in Port Isabel permanently now. She has the Sandy Margret gyotaku fish rubbing you had me buy for her hanging over the couch. Meat is back in prison for jumping parole, but I think they might make a go of it after he gets out. He's a crazy mixed up kid, but not really a bad guy.

Finally, Griff and I have enjoyed the attention from our community. Being called heroes is heady stuff sometimes. But what you and Edie did for us, for the island, and for so many others is beyond heroics. Thank you.

Steve Hathcock

P.S. The secret of Marne Law's painting is safe.

CPSIA information can be obtained at www.ICGtesting.com
Printed in the USA
LVOW12s1701071213

364314LV00005B/10/P

9 781937 958541